THE
DEVIL'S
SHADOW

Forge Books by Hugh Holton

Chicago Blues
The Devil's Shadow
The Left Hand of God
Presumed Dead
Red Lightning
Time of the Assassins
Violent Crimes
Windy City

HUGH HOLTON

THE DEVIL'S SHADOW

A TOM DOHERTY ASSOCIATES BOOK

NEW YORK

THE DEVIL'S SHADOW

This book is printed on acid-free paper.

A Forge Book
Published by Tom Doherty Associates, LLC
175 Fifth Avenue
New York, NY 10010

www.tor.com

Forge® is a registered trademark of Tom Doherty Associates, LLC.

Library of Congress Cataloging-in-Publication Data

Holton, Hugh.
    The devil's shadow / Hugh Holton.—1st ed.
        p. cm.
    "A Tom Doherty Associates book."
    ISBN 0-312-87784-6 (alk. paper)
    1. Cole, Larry (Fictitious character)—Fiction. 2. Police—Illinois—
Chicago—Fiction. 3. Female offenders—Fiction. 4. Bank robberies—
Fiction. 5. Caribbean Area—Fiction. 6. Chicago (Ill.)—Fiction. I. Title.

PS3558.O4373 D48 2001
813'.54—dc21

2001018785

First Edition: May 2001

Printed in the United States of America

0 9 8 7 6 5 4 3 2 1

The Devil's Shadow is dedicated to
Ms. Victoria Adele Hatch,
born on March 5, 2000,

and

To the men of Mount Carmel High School—
past, present, and future—
whose commitment to excellence
has left a fine tradition in the history of
academics and sports in the State of Illinois.

Cast of Characters

THE COPS

LARRY COLE—Chief of Detectives
BLACKIE SILVESTRI—A lieutenant assigned to Cole's staff
JUDY DANIELS—A sergeant assigned to Cole's staff
MANNY SHERLOCK—A sergeant assigned to Cole's staff

THE DEVIL'S SHADOW AND ASSOCIATES

JULIANNA SAINT
CHRISTOPHE LA CROIX
HUBERT METAYER
IAN FITZWALTER JELLICOE

THE MOB

JACOB "BIG JAKE" ROMANO

THE MYSTERY WRITERS

JAMAL GARTH
GREG ENNIS
BARBARA ZORIN

SIGNIFICANT OTHERS

LAUREN SHERLOCK—Manny Sherlock's wife
BUTCH COLE—Larry Cole's son
VIVIAN MATTIOLI—Mafia Princess
ALICIA ROMANO—Jake Romano's wife
ANGELA DUBOIS—Jamal Garth's companion
DOCTOR SILVERNAIL SMITH—Historian

ACKNOWLEDGMENTS

I would like to again acknowledge some of the people who have been instrumental in advancing my writing career. To the members of my fiction readers' group—Barbara D'Amato and Mark Richard Zubro, who always catch the missing hyphens, commas, and misspellings; thank you for many enjoyable Friday nights over pizza, beer, and manuscripts in progress. To Randy Albers, Chair of the Fiction Writing Department; and John Schultz and Betty Schiflett, Professors Emeriti of Columbia College, who gave me very valuable fiction writing training. To Commander Marienne Perry and Police Officer Tarita Preston, whose knowledge of the French language helped me with the French language references in *The Devil's Shadow*. To Sergeant Eugene Warling, who helped me plot the fictional bank and train robbery sequences. And to John W. Richardson, the Chicago Police Department Chief of the Patrol Division, who has always been supportive of both my fiction writing and police careers.

Hugh Holton
December 2000

PROLOGUE

The Metropolitan Bank of Chicago was located on Michigan Avenue between Washington and Madison streets. It was a commercial financial institution that offered a wide range of services to its patrons. Among these services were safety-deposit boxes secured in an impregnable steel vault on the lower level. During the bank's hours of operation there was always a pair of armed security guards on duty at the vault entrance. When the bank was closed, the vault was on a time lock. It was considered as secure as was humanly possible. That made the challenge all the more intriguing.

Julianna Saint was an exceptionally beautiful woman. She had flawless ebony skin, thick, black, shoulder-length hair, long lashes, and exotic dark brown eyes that many believed to be hypnotic. She had a thin nose above full, sensuous lips and a stunning figure. By nationality she was French, as she had been born on Saint Martin in the Leeward Islands east of the British Virgin Islands. Besides being beautiful, she was intelligent and well educated, having earned advanced degrees in mathematics from the Sorbonne. She was also a thief.

Actually, applying such a crude criminal term to Julianna was an understatement. In fact, she did steal things that belonged to others, but only very special things. Now she was in Chicago to steal something from the impregnable vault of the Metropolitan Bank.

The black Mercedes was driven north on Michigan Avenue and cruised slowly past the bank. Julianna was seated in the backseat.

Her assistants, Christophe La Croix and Hubert (pronounced Hu-BER) Metayer, were in the front seat. Christophe—a tall, muscular, handsome man of thirty—was driving. Hubert, who was as tall and broad as Christophe, was fifty, of mixed African/French ancestry, and exuded an aura of menace. He had dark features and had once been a member of an organized criminal faction in France. He had been a bank robber, a pickpocket, a cat burglar, and a safecracker. During his criminal career he had killed seven men.

Christophe and Hubert were above-average criminals and could have made a decent living on their own. But they realized that they were not in the same league professionally as the woman seated behind them. In her particular criminal specialty, she had no peer anywhere in the world. She was known as the Devil's Shadow, or *L'Ombre du Diable* in French, because she seemed to be capable of moving with such stealth as to be invisible, and there was nothing in the world that she couldn't steal, no matter how well it was guarded.

The Mercedes was driven around the block to arrive a few minutes later on Washington between Michigan and Wabash. Julianna and Hubert exited the car and walked around the corner to the Metropolitan Bank Building. Christophe backed the car into a loading zone in front of the Pittsfield Building and settled in to wait. If a police car showed up and displayed any interest in him, he was prepared to provide a halfway plausible lie to explain his presence. If the lie wasn't sufficient to satisfy the officers, then the Frenchman was prepared to take more drastic measures, although he had never killed anyone before in his life and he didn't plan to start now. After all, he was a thief and a lover, and not necessarily in that order.

Julianna Saint and Hubert Metayer walked side by side toward the Metropolitan Bank. She was dressed in a black wool turtleneck sweater, tight black slacks, a waist-length black leather jacket, and black soft-soled shoes. She carried a large carryall canvas bag draped over her shoulder. Her male companion was dressed in similar dark garb, and he also carried a black canvas bag.

There was an alley beside the bank building. Despite this early hour of the morning and cold, dry air hovering just above the freezing mark, there was some sparse traffic on the avenue. Most of it was vehicular, but there were a couple of people on foot within sight of the pair in black. Julianna and Hubert were aware of their presence and scrutinized them carefully.

One of them was a well-dressed man whose back was to the thieves as he walked rapidly toward the entrance to the Grant Park underground garage. In a moment he had vanished down the steps. The other pedestrian was a homeless person, who was carrying a pair of shopping bags and approached with a slow shuffle from the far end of the block. He didn't appear to notice Julianna and Hubert.

They kept walking at the same pace. At the mouth of the alley, without breaking stride, they stepped into the darkness.

Julianna went to a door set in the north wall of the bank building. There was a garbage Dumpster beside this door. Hubert walked a short distance past her to a utility pole. With the canvas bag slung over his shoulder, displaying formidable athletic prowess, he climbed the pole. Julianna paid more attention to the mouth of the alley than to her accomplice's progress.

At the transformer atop the pole, Hubert went to work. He had practiced what he was about to do so many times he could literally do it with his eyes closed or . . . in the dark. With the box open, the thief located the main lead, which he did not touch as direct contact with it would instantly kill him and send such a high amperage through his corpse that it would become a blazing bonfire within seconds. But he was extremely careful and managed to attach the black box in the right place. Then he flipped a switch on the face of the box. Nothing occurred, or at least nothing of a noticeable nature; however, something was indeed taking place.

The black box was bleeding off electrical power being supplied by Commonwealth Edison to the Metropolitan Bank of Chicago. A power drain that had succeeded in temporarily incapacitating the burglar alarm system serving the bank. His task completed, Hubert turned and motioned silently to the woman on the ground.

Julianna Saint began moving very quickly. With the alarm disabled, she used an electronic lockpick to gain access to the bank through the alley entrance. This led her into a maintenance room. The area was in pitch blackness, which was quickly rectified by a pair of night goggles she retrieved from the canvas bag. Then Hubert was there beside her, wearing a pair of goggles identical to hers. She looked back to make sure that he had closed the door behind him. Once in Monte Carlo, during the burglary of a casino, he had failed to do this, which had nearly led to their capture. Satisfied that the integrity of the mission was being maintained, she started forward with him following.

The bank was equipped with every state-of-the-art antitheft device available, from motion detectors to infrared light beams, which were randomly operated by computer. There were also two guards on the premises, who were in contact by radio with a mobile unit outside the bank. The guards also possessed a direct hookup to the City of Chicago's Office of Emergency Communications, which if activated would result in a squadron of police cars being dispatched to surround the building within seconds. But Julianna Saint understood antitheft alarm systems, computers, and police communication networks like few people alive in this world. In fact, she could have taught the security experts a thing or two about the sophisticated systems they were so proud of. Particularly how to defeat those systems.

As they made their way toward the vault, defeating obstacle after obstacle, they failed to encounter any guards, although they noticed three surveillance cameras. Surveillance cameras whose lenses they managed to avoid by hugging the darkness, becoming the embodiment of the Devil's Shadow. Finally they reached the vault.

Standing in the blackness outside the massive steel door, Julianna studied it through her night goggles. This huge safe was a tribute to mankind's ingenuity in constructing a theft-proof, virtually impregnable fortress in which to store material wealth. But long before they arrived at this place, Julianna had come up with the means of getting inside.

She removed two items from her bag. One was a vial of acid, the other a timed, minimal-charge, plastic explosive. As she went to work on the vault door, Hubert Metayer went in search of the guards. A frown of annoyance crossed his hard features. He was under strict orders not to kill the guards, but to merely incapacitate them. This was a requirement that was not explained to him. However, Hubert had been an associate of Julianna Saint long enough to realize that all he had to do was what she told him.

Out on Washington Street, Christophe looked up in the rearview mirror of the Mercedes and saw a marked police car cruising slowly across Wabash toward him. The Frenchman willed himself to relax and be prepared for questioning. The police car slowed as it pulled up beside him.

The guards were in the security complex on the second floor of the building. This was the hub of all the security functions for the Metropolitan Bank of Chicago. It resembled a Pentagon war room and was just as sophisticated. The male and female on duty tonight had had no law enforcement experience prior to being hired by the Stewart Private Detective and Security Agency. They had received forty hours of classroom training and spent ten hours on the pistol range before their first assignment. Their uniforms and weapons were issued by the agency. They made $7.25 an hour and worked a minimum of twenty, but no more than forty, hours a week. This gave them an income below minimal subsistence level, so they had day jobs. The man was a city garbage collector, and the woman was a public schoolteacher. As it was three weeks before Christmas and they had families with small children, both guards were trying to get in all of the overtime that they could. A security agency supervisor had obliged and the guards were working ten-hour shifts through the New Year. Although they were looking forward to substantial paychecks, they were both currently exhausted.

The male guard, who was sixtyish, overweight, and diabetic, had begun dozing an hour after his ten-o'clock arrival at the bank. This left the teacher to do all the work, which she did without protest. She was a meticulous, thorough person by nature, so she tried to do the best job possible. She had made her hourly rounds on time, monitored the closed-circuit screens for a while, and had even become mildly alarmed when she detected a slight power surge, which caused the lights to briefly dim to candle power before brightening back to normal. She started to wake her partner, but he had been exhausted when he walked in, and she didn't think there was really any problem with the power failure. After all, this was a bank located in downtown Chicago.

She poured herself a cup of coffee from a Thermos jug, took a sip, and grimaced at the bitter taste. Her eyes strayed to one of the monitors, which revealed a portion of the lower level of the bank. For a moment she thought she saw something moving down there, but when she blinked there was nothing on the screen. She figured that the night shift was making her jumpy.

She was taking another sip of coffee when she became suddenly light-headed. She managed to place the cup down on the closed-circuit monitor console before she lost consciousness and slumped back in her chair. The small, broken plastic vial of knockout gas that Hubert Metayer had tossed onto the floor of the bank's security center had done its job well. With a filter mask over his face, the assistant of *L'Ombre du Diable* stepped from the exterior corridor into the security center. After retrieving the empty plastic vial from the floor, he examined the unconscious guards. Beneath the filter mask, he smiled. They would be asleep for an hour and awake with a slight headache that would pass before dawn. They would never admit to their employer that they had been asleep during the burglary. It wouldn't save their jobs, but at least their personal integrity would remain intact.

Hubert Metayer left the security center and returned to the vault.

*   *   *

Out on Washington Street the police car drove past Christophe La Croix. Neither of the two cops inside even glanced in his direction. Breathing a sigh of relief, he continued to wait.

Julianna Saint pulled open the heavy door and entered the vault. She realized that there was a fortune in cash, jewelry, and other valuables here, but she had only taken this hazardous assignment to remove the contents of one safety-deposit box from the vault. That box number was 8697.

Through her night goggles, she was able to locate it quickly. Using her lockpick device, she opened the box and peered inside. There was a six-inch-barrel .44-caliber magnum Smith & Wesson revolver in a sealed plastic envelope along with a videocassette tape. This was what the Devil's Shadow had come to steal.

Removing the gun and the cassette from the box, she placed them in her canvas bag before returning the container to its rightful place inside the vault. At that moment Hubert arrived and they began retracing their steps to leave the bank.

Less than a minute later they were about to exit the alley onto Michigan Avenue when the homeless man they had seen earlier stepped from the side of the bank building to confront them.

"You folks got any spare change?"

Before she could stop him, Hubert stepped forward, grabbed the man, spun him around, and, utilizing his formidable strength, broke his neck.

"You fool," she said, angrily. "I told you, no violence!"

"But he saw us, Julianna," the big man argued. "What else could I do?"

She realized that this was not the time to debate the issue. "Place his body down there beside the garbage Dumpster," she said, pointing back down the alley. "And hurry."

Quickly he did as she instructed. By the time he returned to the mouth of the alley, Christophe was there with the Mercedes. They sped away from the scene of the crime.

PART

I

"When you're dealing with the Mafia, if you don't have insurance you'll end up dead just like that writer."
Julianna Saint

1

Jacob "Big Jake" Romano sat at his private table in the Pump Room of the Ambassador East Hotel. His bodyguards were seated at a table a short distance away. In order to get to Romano, anyone approaching his table would have to go through them. The bodyguards were licensed by the State of Illinois as private detectives, which authorized them to carry firearms. They were big, brutal-featured men with broad shoulders and heavy fists. Their presence made the maître d' nervous, because they frightened the other diners. However, there was no way that he could ever refuse service to them or the man they were protecting. He was certain that if he did, his life would be in danger. The maître d' at the Pump Room was absolutely right in this regard.

Big Jake Romano was a physically imposing man standing six feet five inches tall and weighing 240 well-fed pounds. He had curly black hair and thick eyebrows, which, before he had them plucked, had extended in a heavy line from temple to temple. At the age of forty, he could be considered marginally handsome. He dressed in tailor-made suits and had his hair styled once a week by a North Michigan Avenue barber. He was well read and had earned a bachelor's degree in business administration from the Illinois Institute of Technology. Romano spoke with a soft, cultured voice, used very little slang, no profanity, and could have passed for a successful businessman, which in fact he was. However, Jake Romano's business was organized crime, and he was one of the most vicious criminals in the Mafia hierarchy of the United States.

A burgundy-jacketed waiter carrying a tray approached the table, which was set off from the others in a far corner of the dining area. Dutifully the waiter stopped so that the bodyguards could examine the chicken salad sandwich on whole wheat toast and the glass of iced tea the mobster had ordered. The guards had frisked the waiter for weapons before he was allowed to take the order.

Romano was reading the novel *Evil Places,* by Barbara Schurla Zorin. He didn't even look up as the waiter set the sandwich and glass down in front of him. The mobster was an avid reader and consumed four to five books a week. Now he was three-quarters of the way through the novel and enjoying it so much that he ignored his lunch. The guards continued to maintain their diligence and Jake Romano continued to read.

The tall Englishman was escorted to the bodyguards' table by the maître d'. The new arrival was dressed in a gray, single-breasted suit, gray silk tie, and white cotton shirt. Aware of the drill, he submitted to a frisk under the curious stares of a number of midday Pump Room diners. Finally, his pale cheeks coloring at the indignity he had been subjected to, he was allowed to sit at Jake Romano's table.

"I think . . . ," the Englishmen began, but the mobster stopped him with an upraised palm.

"I'm almost at the end of the chapter. Just give me a minute." Romano never took his eyes out of the book.

Silently seething, the Englishman crossed his legs and settled in to wait.

His name was Ian Fitzwalter Jellicoe. He had been born into a family of civil servants who had served the British Empire dating back to the Victorian era. Jellicoes had been diplomats and ministers in every generation up to and including that of Ian's father, Sir Charles Jellicoe. It was expected that the Oxford-educated Ian would follow in the family tradition. However, this member of the Jellicoe family had other plans. From a very early age, he realized that he was not going to spend his life as a government employee.

In addition to that, he had the temperament and appetites of a rich man. A very rich man. So he decided to use his family contacts to further his ambition. This had led him into the world of crime.

Jake Romano placed a bookmark on the page to mark his place and closed the novel. He laid it down on the table beside his plate, unfolded a linen napkin on his lap, and picked up a segment of his sandwich. Before taking a bite, he said, "What have you got for me, Mr. Jellicoe?"

The Englishman, who had blond hair, pinched features, and gray eyes of such a pale shade as to appear opaque, replied, "Exactly what you asked for, Mr. Romano."

The big man returned the sandwich to his plate and dabbed his lips with the napkin. He took a sip of tea and carefully replaced the glass on the white tablecloth. Romano was making a fairly gallant effort to hide a growing excitement.

Jellicoe could tell that his client was pleased. For the money Romano would be paying for the service, only complete satisfaction could be tolerated.

"When can I accept delivery of the merchandise?" the mobster asked.

Ian Jellicoe's icy front did not thaw one degree as he responded. "Whenever you pay the balance of my fee."

2

DECEMBER 4, 2004
2:15 P.M.

Chief of Detectives Larry Cole, a tall, handsome black man, returned to police headquarters after attending the funeral of former First Deputy Superintendent Terrence Jonathan Kennedy. Terry, as he was called, had been in poor health since his retirement from the department and had suffered from a number of lingering ailments complicated by a brain tumor and a stroke. Finally he had succumbed to a heart attack in his sleep.

Cole was accompanied by Lieutenant Blackie Silvestri and Sergeants Judy Daniels and Manny Sherlock, all in uniform. When he had put the blue suit on this morning, Cole smiled because it fit the same as it had when he had purchased it sixteen years before. That was right after his promotion to the rank of commander. Now he wore the silver stars of a division chief on his shoulder epaulets.

Blackie, a heavyset man cut in the mold of macho actors Sean Connery and Anthony Quinn, had been a plainclothes officer for most of his police career and hated uniforms. This was obvious from the scowl on his face and the way he kept tugging at the bill of his cap, which never seemed to fit properly on his head. Judy and Manny also looked odd to Cole simply because he was not used to seeing them like this. Especially Judy, who, as the Mistress of Disguise/High Priestess of Mayhem, appeared in a different guise just about every day.

Inside his private office at the police headquarters complex on Thirty-fifth Street, Cole removed his navy blue overcoat and cap with the gold "scrambled eggs" ornamentation on the bill. Going behind his desk, he scanned the telephone message slips that had been left for him by the Detective Division headquarters desk officer. One in particular caught his eye.

"Chief Cole, please call Jamal Garth at 555-8256. Urgent!"

Jamal was a mystery writer, who had helped Cole apprehend diabolical serial killer Margo DeWitt. Cole hadn't seen him or his fellow author Barbara Zorin since that past summer when they had almost been killed in a plane bombing. Now the chief wondered what could be so urgent. He picked up the telephone.

Half an hour later, Cole and Blackie, still in uniform, knocked on the door to Jamal Garth's penthouse condominium in the Presidential Towers complex just west of the Loop. The author answered the door.

"Thanks for coming so quickly, Larry," said Garth, a distinguished-looking black man with white hair. "Good to see you again, Blackie."

After the greetings they took seats in the living room. Garth's companion, Angela DuBois, a stunning black woman who appeared ageless, came in from the kitchen to say hello and offer the policemen refreshments. She left to get them coffee.

Garth appeared worried, and it took him a moment to compose his thoughts. "The reason I asked to see you was actually to get some advice on a matter that I didn't wish to discuss over the telephone."

"No problem, Jamal," Cole said. "We'll do anything that we can to help."

Angela returned with a silver coffee service on a matching tray, which she set down on the cocktail table before leaving them alone.

"Are you in some kind of trouble, Jamal?" Blackie asked.

"It's not me, Blackie," Garth responded. "Have you ever heard of an author named Greg Ennis?"

"Yeah," Blackie said. "He writes about the Chicago Mob. Some pretty good stuff if you ask me."

Cole smiled. "Coming from someone who was raised around Mob types, that's quite a compliment."

"Greg is very thorough with the research he does for his books," Garth said. "Maybe too thorough."

"How so?" Cole asked.

"He takes a lot of risks, Larry. He frequents Mob hangouts and cultivates gangland types as sources for his fiction. He's even started talking and acting like a Mob guy."

"So he's a Mob groupie," Blackie said. "There are always a few guys and gals like that hanging around outfit types. The dentist who got whacked in the St. Valentine's Day Massacre was a Bugs Moran Gang groupie and it cost him his life."

"Did the Mob types ever have any objections to what Ennis writes about?" Cole asked.

"No," Garth said. "He usually associates with fringe players, who probably exaggerated their importance and really couldn't tell Greg anything that would be threatening to the outfit. In fact, he told me a couple of times that some of the soldiers he hung out with were actually flattered when they recognized themselves in his books. That is, until recently."

The cops waited.

"Yesterday Greg received an anonymous death threat on the telephone. He believes that it came from someone in the Mob."

"Why?" Cole asked.

"He didn't say and he wouldn't tell me the substance of the threat. I don't think that it had anything to do with his writing, but I'll tell you one thing, he's scared to death. He has an office in the Metropolitan Bank Building on Michigan Avenue, where he writes and operates something called Ennis Enterprises. I went down there this morning to try and talk to him, but he's locked himself in and refuses to see anybody."

"You want us to talk to him?" Cole asked.

"Would you please?"

"What do you think is going on with this Greg Ennis, boss?" Blackie asked as they drove down Congress Parkway heading for the Metropolitan Bank Building on Michigan Avenue.

"Beats me, but Jamal isn't the type to go sounding the alarm unless there is something very wrong. All we can do at this point is ask Mr. Ennis himself and see if we can find out."

They were on Michigan Avenue traveling north less than a block from the bank building when it happened. Both Cole and Blackie saw it at the same time. Initially they thought it was a bird. However, it was too big and was not flying, but falling. As the two cops looked on in amazement, the body of mystery writer Greg Ennis smashed into the sidewalk in front of the Metropolitan Bank.

3

The Metropolitan Bank Building stood thirty-two stories tall. Greg Ennis's office was on the twenty-first floor. He had either jumped or been pushed from one of the windows of that office. Now his body, or what was left of it, was splattered all over the sidewalk of North Michigan Avenue.

Cole and Blackie were the first police officers on the scene and were forced to keep the crowd of curious spectators from stomping all over the dead mystery writer. On impact Ennis was completely pulverized. One of his legs had been dislocated and was stretched across his body, with the left foot next to his right ear. His eyes had exploded from his head and were lying at separate locations some distance from the body. One of his arm bones had been ejected from the body to smash into the back door of a Yellow Cab, which was waiting for a fare in front of the bank. A dent was visible in the door. Then there were the pedestrians who had gathered.

The original handful of bystanders grew into a throng standing at least four deep surrounding the corpse and straining forward to catch a glimpse of something to haunt their nightmares. Against this onslaught, Cole and Blackie battled to keep the crowd back. Two women fainted and were nearly trampled by those surging forward. A young student, carrying a Roosevelt University book bag, became violently ill and barely made it to the curb before he vomited. And still the crowd continued fighting to see the body. Finally reinforcements from the First Police District arrived to help Cole and Blackie.

A rubber sheet was thrown over the body; however, an ever-expanding pool of blood covered a substantial part of the sidewalk surrounding the point of impact. When enough policemen had been put in place, Cole and Blackie, accompanied by a uniformed sergeant, moved over to the entrance to the Metropolitan Bank Building, which was next to the bank.

"I know your people are stretched a bit thin, Sarge," Cole said, "but I want this building sealed off until we can take a look upstairs and try to find out what happened."

"Sure thing, Chief," the short, rotund sergeant said. "You think that this guy met with foul play?"

Cole shrugged. "You never can tell."

Leaving the sergeant on the street, they entered the lobby to find it deserted, because everyone was outside. An elevator whisked them to the twenty-first floor, where they followed a directory to the office of Ennis Enterprises in suite 2132. The business name was stenciled on the frosted glass pane in the upper door panel. The door itself was unlocked.

Ennis Enterprises consisted of three rooms: a small reception area; a private inner office equipped with a computer, fax machine, file cabinets, a laser printer, and a desk with matching chair; and a bathroom equipped with a shower. There was also an army cot and a hot plate, indicating that Greg Ennis had lived in this place before his death. The window overlooking Michigan Avenue was open and the office had been ransacked.

"We'd better get the crime lab up here, Blackie," Cole said. "This is starting to look like a homicide."

Without a word, the lieutenant pulled a compact radio from his uniform coat pocket and made the call. The investigation of the murder of mystery writer Greg Ennis had begun.

The two broad-shouldered men got off the elevator and crossed the lobby toward the Michigan Avenue exit. They walked rapidly until they spotted the pair of uniformed police officers blocking the doors. A few people attempting to leave the building had also been stopped by the cops. The building had been sealed. The two men slowed their pace and looked around for an alternate route to escape the building. The only place they could go was into the bank, but they would still be trapped, as there was another pair of cops blocking that exit as well.

Briefly they considered using force, but there were too many cops around, both inside and outside of the building. So they would just have to wait and hope.

The crime lab technicians arrived at suite 2132 of the Metropolitan Bank Building within minutes of Blackie's call. As they moved in to begin processing the scene, Cole and Blackie returned to the elevator.

As they descended, Blackie said, "This was a hit, boss. Whoever Ennis was afraid of caught up with him and tossed him out that window."

"It's obvious that they were looking for something in his office," Cole said. "There's also the possibility that they didn't find it."

They stepped out into the lobby.

"So you've got to figure that this was a Mob execution, right?" Blackie said.

"I would agree with that."

"Then we need to talk to those two gentlemen standing over there."

Cole followed Blackie's gaze to the people at the lobby exit, where the policemen stood guard. The two men, who looked like pro football middle linebackers, were very noticeable. However, Cole didn't recognize them.

Blackie filled him in. "That's Joey Randall and Pete Debenedetto. They're enforcers for Jake Romano. Have a reputation for killing people in exotic ways like hangings, burnings, and . . ."

Cole completed the statement for him. "And tossing them out of skyscraper windows."

4

Jake Romano lived with his wife, Alicia, in a North Lake Shore Drive brownstone with an estimated value of three million dollars. The Romanos were childless and very active socially. The former Alicia Holland was a North suburban socialite, who had inherited a fortune in her own right before she married Jake. When she had met him, she knew of his alleged Mafia connections, which she found wickedly intriguing. Surprisingly, she had found her future husband to be intelligent, soft-spoken, and an interesting conversationalist. He also let her have her way in just about every area of their personal lives, and she never interfered with his business dealings. And although her husband had never threatened or abused her in any way, she could sense that he was a very dangerous man.

On this winter afternoon they were both in the brownstone. She was in the music room practicing classical works on a grand piano. Jake was in his study next to the music room. When he had entered the study, he had securely locked the door behind him. The grounds consisted of the main house, a greenhouse containing plants and flowers that both he and Alicia cultivated, and a coach house, which had been converted into living quarters. There was a staff of six servants, two of them full-time, and there were always at least two bodyguards around. Too many prying eyes, which necessitated the locked door.

Jake went to a wall safe concealed behind a painting of the Chicago skyline. After working the combination, he removed the videocassette that he had purchased from Ian Jellicoe. The .44 magnum revolver was also in there. Romano had considered getting rid of both the tape and the gun, but something had made him keep them. Perhaps it was his vanity or a desire to live life on the razor's edge, because if that tape and the gun ever became public, Jake

Romano would be in a great deal of trouble. Trouble that would come not only from the police, but from the National Mafia Commission. The cops, he could deal with; the National Commission wouldn't hesitate to have him killed.

Romano had played the tape a number of times since he had acquired it. Now he put it in the video recorder in his study and settled in to watch it for the twelfth time.

The TV screen broadcast snow before going dark. Then a large conference room appeared. Eight men were seated around this table. A meeting was in progress. A meeting that was being chaired by Victor Mattioli, the former boss of the Chicago Mob.

Oak Brook, Illinois
AUGUST 16, 2002
2:17 P.M.

At the time the videotape was made in August 2002, Vic Mattioli had been seventy-eight years old. Six years before, he had succeeded Antonio "Tuxedo Tony" DeLisa as the head of the Chicago Mob. Mattioli, a widower, lived with his adult daughter, Vivian, in a modest ranch-style home in the western suburb of Chicago. The don was thin to the point of emaciation, had a bald, liver-spotted skull, and was rapidly going blind.

Mattioli's reputation was less than stellar within Mob circles. Prior to becoming the boss, he had been mostly a gofer for every Mob boss from Sam "Momo" Giancana to Tuxedo Tony DeLisa. Mattioli's area of illegal expertise was loan sharking, but he hadn't been a very good criminal, as he allowed too many juice loans to go uncollected. But when DeLisa's daughter Rachel bashed in his skull in a Loop hotel room, Mattioli had been named to replace the Tuxedo by the National Commission that oversaw all Mafia activities in the United States. Mattioli's appointment caused a great deal of dissension within the ranks of the Chicago Mob. But Mattioli had been named the boss and the local mobsters would just have to accept that. At least for the time being.

Vic Mattioli turned out to be just as much of a disaster as the top man of the Chicago Mob as he had been a Mob soldier. The only logical reason the underbosses could figure that the National Commission had named him to run Chicago was that he was the senior Mafioso in the area, and he was the exact opposite of his predecessor. Whereas DeLisa had been flamboyant, high profile, and insanely violent, Mattioli was low-key and withdrawn to the point of reticence. Mattioli was also indecisive.

Shortly after he took over as the boss, the Black Gangster Disciples street gang began moving in on Mafia enterprises in Chicago, such as prostitution, the protection racket, and loan sharking. Jake Romano and his fellow Mob underbosses wanted to make a move against the Disciples and wipe out all of the gang's leaders. But Mattioli wouldn't approve what he felt would turn into a highly publicized gang war, which would bring the local cops and maybe even the feds down on them, or more specifically, him. The underbosses were forced to fight a secret, limited war against the black street gang. A war that they were losing.

To address this problem, they had requested a "sit-down" with the boss. A meeting that no one in attendance knew that Vic Mattioli was secretly taping.

Chicago, Illinois
DECEMBER 4, 2004
4:30 P.M.

Jake Romano settled in to watch a replay of the video.

Underboss Carmine Giordano was talking. Giordano, a fleshy man with reptilian eyes and a gravelly voice, said, "Don Victor, we can't go on like this. Six years ago my soldiers could go anywhere in the Chicago area without being challenged by anyone. They were also able to operate any kind of racket they chose. We could move in on any business, put juice money out on the street, and charge a street head tax on any of the pimps operating whores out there. And everybody was afraid to do anything but pay up. Now not only are our people threatened, but they're told that the Disciples are running the streets." Giordano leaned closer to Mattioli to make his final point. Everyone present watched the Mob boss appear to recoil, as if he felt threatened by the larger man. "Mark my words, Don Victor, if we don't do something about these people soon, the lives of every man in this room will be threatened."

Having made his point, the underboss leaned back in his chair and lit a Cuban cigar. This was another subtle insult aimed at Victor Mattioli, as he usually prohibited smoking in his presence. Now, as Giordano puffed thick clouds of smoke into the air, the Mafia don remained silent.

There were a few more comments made by the others, but none as vociferous as those of Carmine Giordano. Jake Romano said nothing.

It came time for the don to speak. At his position at the head of the conference table, Mattioli stood. In a voice that trembled, he began.

"I have addressed this problem with you a number of times in the past. Now I must tell you for one last time that there will be no war between us and the black street gang. Currently most of our businesses are legitimate. Those criminal enterprises that you mentioned are only a small part of what we are involved in. As such, I don't want our entire operation jeopardized because of a few colored street punks."

Now underboss Jake Romano spoke up. "You heard your don, gentlemen," he said in a commanding tone. "Now I think we've taken up enough of his time."

The other underbosses didn't look in Romano's direction as they filed out of the conference room. Romano remained behind with Mattioli.

"I wonder if I could have a moment of your time, Don Victor."

Mattioli motioned for him to return to his seat. Now the don shuffled across the conference room to a cabinet from which he removed a can of aerosol air freshener. He began spraying the room to eliminate the odor of Carmine Giordano's cigar.

Romano waited until the boss returned to his seat at the conference table. The others were still in the house, but would not come in until after the deed was done. Mattioli's daughter was in Italy visiting relatives.

"I don't want to attempt to change your mind, Don Victor," Romano said in a semiwhisper, forcing Mattioli to lean toward him. "But I can possibly propose a remedy to this situation with the Disciples."

"What is it, Jake?"

"Perhaps we could enter into some type of truce. Possibly come to an agreement that will help us save face."

For a moment Mattioli silently considered what the underboss had just proposed. Then he said, "That would be an acceptable option, and I'm certain I can make a case for it with the other underbosses." The don patted the back of Romano's hand. "I want you to handle everything on my behalf in this matter, Jake. If you carry this off, it will definitely be quite a feather in your cap. Perhaps this will provide the impetus you need to become the next boss of the Chicago Organization after I retire." With that Mattioli got to his feet.

Jake Romano also stood and extended his hand to the don. Vic Mattioli took the hand.

"There's only one thing I want you to be aware of." Romano still held the old man's hand. "Making peace with the black street gang won't put me in line to be your successor, but this will."

With that Jake Romano removed a six-inch-barrel Smith & Wesson .44-caliber magnum from a holster beneath his suit jacket, stuck the barrel of the gun in Victor Mattioli's abdomen, and pulled the trigger six times. The explosive force of the steel-jacketed hollow-point bullets literally cut the don in two. When Jake Romano released the hand, Mattioli was quite dead.

The handle and the trigger of the magnum had been wrapped with a special tape, so Romano had left no fingerprints. The assassination completed, Romano dropped the gun on the floor next to the body. The crime would be classified as a Mob hit by the cops, who would have a lot of suspects, but no real concrete evidence to make a case. At least that was what Jake Romano thought at the time. But on that August afternoon the cops were not the assassin's primary concern.

Jake Romano had just carried out a hit on a National Commission–appointed Mafia don. This was not unprecedented, but was still frowned upon. Severely frowned upon. So the underbosses would have to stick together and Romano would have to carefully cover his tracks and, if necessary, call in a few favors. Actually, he didn't feel that he had anything to worry about at the time. He was wrong.

Romano watched himself on the videotape, walking out of the conference room, leaving the body of Mafia don Victor Mattioli behind. For three months following the assassination there had been a great deal of heat from the cops and a lot of questions from the National Commission. Jake Romano had been interrogated by none other than Chief of Detectives Larry Cole and Lieutenant Blackie Silvestri. But no one was talking. Romano knew that all Cole and Silvestri had was a dead body. The gun had mysteriously disappeared, which did not initially alarm Romano, because there were no fingerprints on it. The Black Gangster Disciples street gang became the primary suspects in Mattioli's assassination, and to some extent Romano and his fellow underbosses were reasonably certain that they were in the clear. Romano had been named to succeed Mattioli as the Chicago Mob boss. Everything was going well until early November of that year when the new boss received a call from mystery writer Greg Ennis. Then things had started to go seriously wrong.

But as was the case with Victor Mattioli before and Greg Ennis now, Romano had taken care of everything. He had the videotape and the gun, and by now the rest should have been taken care of.

Romano rewound the tape and again replayed the assassination. At that instant he made the decision to keep the incriminating video. Yes, it would be dangerous, but Jake Romano was in fact a very dangerous man.

There came a knock on his locked study door. "Jake, it's me," his wife, Alicia, called.

"Just a minute." He removed the tape from the recorder and returned it to the safe. When it was secured, he crossed the study and opened the door.

He instantly noticed the shocked look on her face.

"I just saw it on the news. Joey Randall and Pete Debenedetto have been arrested by those policemen who questioned you two years ago."

Romano's jaw muscles rippled, but he otherwise maintained his outward cool. "Are you talking about Larry Cole and Blackie Silvestri?"

She nodded.

Although he knew the answer to the question, he asked, "What were Joey and Pete arrested for, dear?"

"They are suspected of murdering mystery writer Greg Ennis by tossing him out of a window of the Metropolitan Bank Building downtown."

"Really?" Romano said.

5

DECEMBER 4, 2004
5:37 P.M.

The death of Greg Ennis caused a flood of media coverage. Reporters from local TV stations and the print media were staked out in the lobby of police headquarters waiting for a spokesman to make some kind of statement about the dead writer. So far the media types knew that Chief Larry Cole and Lieutenant Blackie Silvestri, who were two cops with a reputation for solving big headline cases, were the first officers on the scene after Ennis's plunge from a twenty-first-floor window of the Metropolitan Bank Building. And although the cops had been noncommittal about the cause of the mystery writer's death, a few of the dead author's colleagues, including fellow authors Jamal Garth and Barbara Zorin, had ruled out Ennis having committed suicide. Also, an enterprising WGN News cameraman had managed to capture reputed mobsters Joey Randall and Pete Debenedetto in handcuffs being ushered into a rear entrance of police headquarters.

Greg Ennis had been the author of seven published crime novels. Each one had the inner workings of organized crime as an integral part of the plot. The most recent book-jacket photograph of the author showed a stone-faced man glaring into the camera. A couple of television commentators covering the writer's death remarked that in this pose Ennis bore an uncanny resemblance to the actor James Caan in his role as Santino "Sonny" Corleone in the movie *The Godfather.*

There hadn't been a death investigation quite like this one in Chicago since the suicide of another mystery novelist named Guy Izzi. Izzi was found hanging from a fourteenth-floor window on North Michigan Avenue only a short distance from the Metropolitan Bank Building on December 6, 1996. Foul play was also suspected in Izzi's death, but the investigation had, in the absence of any evidence to the contrary, revealed that Izzi had killed himself. Greg Ennis had said on more than one occasion that Izzi had had a profound influence on him. Now Ennis had followed Izzi in having died mysteriously.

But this case would be a great deal different from the suicide of Guy Izzi. A great deal different indeed.

Joey Randall and Pete Debenedetto were locked in an interrogation room equipped with a one-way mirror. Both of the mobsters appeared relaxed to the point of boredom. They had refused to say anything when Cole and Silvestri attempted to question them in the lobby of the Metropolitan Bank Building. This had led to them being detained and brought into police headquarters. They had been allowed to make a call, which they did, to attorney Sol Engstrom, who represented certain businessmen with reputed ties to the Chicago Mob. Before Cole and Silvestri could say, "probable cause," Engstrom would have Randall and Debenedetto out of there.

Cole and Blackie were standing on the other side of the glass looking in at the pair of hoodlums. The policemen were aware that Sol Engstrom was on the way, and that meant that if they couldn't charge Randall and Debenedetto, they would be forced to let them go.

Judy entered the viewing area.

"What have you got for us?" Cole asked, hopefully.

"Well, there was a lot of stuff in Greg Ennis's office, Chief, but nothing to connect our two pinup boys in there to the scene. We did a canvass of the building, but couldn't find anyone who saw them either on the twenty-first floor or anyplace else. And they wouldn't tell us why they were in the building."

"Which is their right," Cole said, quietly. "But they made a mistake. We can place them at the scene. Now our job is to find out why they killed Greg Ennis. Once we establish motive, we'll have them and whoever ordered the murder." As Cole turned to leave the room, he said to Blackie, "Cut them loose."

Jamel Garth and Barbara Zorin, who was an attractive woman with silver hair, were seated in Cole's office when he returned. He had asked them to come to headquarters to give him a hand with this investigation. Despite the fact that they were writers, Cole had used them on cases in the past and had a great deal of respect for their investigative acumen and powers of deduction. They were also former professional colleagues of Greg Ennis.

"I've known Greg for about twelve years, Larry," Barbara said. "He was a successful securities investment and insurance salesman for a large firm. But the job bored him silly. I gave a mystery writing course at the Harold Washington Library and Greg signed up."

"Had he ever done any writing before he took your course?" Cole asked.

"He had never written any fiction, but he wrote a series of well-received articles for a financial publication. But once he started writing fiction, he was very good."

"Did everything he wrote have a Mob connection?"

She nodded. "Right from the start, even with his early short stories, his main topic was the Mafia. He was fascinated by the workings of organized crime. It came close to being an obsession with him."

"I think I can provide some insight into Greg's fascination with the Mob," Garth said.

Cole and Barbara turned to look at him.

"Greg Ennis spent three years in the Joliet State Penitentiary for grand larceny. His cell-mate for two of those years was Jake Romano."

6

DECEMBER 4, 2004
6:12 P.M.

The Admirals' Club was located in terminal three at O'Hare International Airport. Access to the upper-level luxury facility could only be gained via an elevator from the main terminal. Upon exiting the elevator, the visitor came face-to-face with a receptionist. Admirals' Club memberships were checked, and if all was in order, the guest was permitted entry into one of the most exclusive private travel clubs in the world.

There were Admirals' Clubs in all the major cities served by international airlines, and although memberships were expensive, it was considered the only way to travel for the frequent first-class traveler. Each club offered its members a place to relax, refresh themselves, have meetings, and even shower in a luxurious atmosphere in which solicitous attendants were available to cater to the traveler's every whim. That is, every whim within reason.

Ian Jellicoe was a member of the Admirals' Club. He had used club facilities to conduct business in London, Paris, New York, Denver, Los Angeles, Hong Kong, Cairo, Rome, and, of course, Chicago. Now he sat in the Admirals' Club at O'Hare International Airport waiting for Julianna Saint.

For this occasion the Englishman had reserved a small conference room that could seat eight. For a member of the Admirals' Club in good standing, complimentary refreshments consisting of cocktails, canapés, and desserts were available on the sideboard. Jellicoe was here to pay off the woman known as *L'Ombre du Diable,* who had stolen the tape and handgun that he had sold to Jake Romano. A sale that the Englishman was aware had resulted in the death of an American author named Greg Ennis. However, Jellicoe had no interest or concern about what had happened to Ennis or why.

There was a knock on the conference room door, followed by one of the attendants ushering in Julianna Saint, Christophe La Croix, and Hubert Metayer. The Devil's Shadow, as she was known within the ranks of the international underworld, was dressed to the nines in a blue knee-length Paris original dress, matching blue wide-brim hat, full-length mink coat, and a diamond necklace, which sparkled brilliantly in the overhead lights. Christophe and Hubert, whom Jellicoe thoroughly despised, were clad casually in pullover sweaters, rumpled sport jackets, and jeans. The five-o'clock shadows on both men's faces made them look like the cheap crooks Ian Jellicoe considered them to be.

By their demeanor, the two Frenchmen displayed that they had just as little regard for the Englishman as he had for them.

This was particularly evidenced as Christophe said with a sarcastic grin, *"Bonjour,* Lord Jellyfish."

"Monsieur Jellicoe," Hubert added, helping himself to a canapé, popping it in his mouth and continuing to talk with his mouth full, "you ever wear anything other than those pinstripes? Makes you look like Alfred, Batman's frigging butler."

Julianna gave them a sternly disapproving look. "We are here to discuss business, gentlemen, so I want you to conduct yourselves accordingly."

Christophe's grin didn't alter and Hubert continued to cast a mocking glare at Jellicoe. But they both remained obediently silent.

"Christophe," Julianna ordered, "pour me a glass of champagne."

Without urgency, but with a fair degree of efficiency, the young man poured from a bottle in an ice bucket on the sideboard. He carefully set the glass down on a paper napkin on the table beside her and went back to lounging against the wall at Hubert's side.

Wishing to get these proceedings over with as quickly as possible so he could catch the 7:15 P.M. British Airways flight to London, Ian Jellicoe reached into the black leather portfolio he carried and removed a thick, baby blue envelope. He handed this envelope to Julianna Saint.

Without opening it she placed it on the surface of the conference table. "Is this the sum we agreed upon, Ian?"

"To the farthing," he replied.

Turning her head ever so slightly, she said to her companions, "Wait outside."

Christophe and Hubert displayed mild surprise at this order, but she didn't have to repeat the command. In a moment they were gone.

Julianna made a show of opening the expensive handbag she carried and removing a package of Kool filtered cigarettes and a gold lighter. After she got one of the cigarettes going she said, "The fee isn't enough."

Ian Jellicoe displayed glacial distress. "But it is the sum we agreed upon."

She shook her head. "It was the sum we agreed upon for me to enter the Metropolitan Bank and break into its vault at great risk to myself."

"For which you were well paid." He pointed to the envelope on the table in front of her.

Her eyes flared angrily at him. "But I was not appropriately compensated for the value of the items I removed from safety-deposit box number 8697."

A chill began settling over Jellicoe. Yes, Julianna Saint was known as the Devil's Shadow, but the Englishman was not without his own nefarious reputation and violent resources. "I'm not certain as to what you're getting at, Julianna."

"How much was the merchandise I obtained worth to you, Ian?"

"It was valued highly enough for me to pay you a very sub-stantial fee to steal it for me."

"How much was it worth to Jake Romano?"

A dangerous situation began developing between Ian Jellicoe and Julianna Saint.

"I don't understand what you are talking about, Julianna."

She puffed casually on her cigarette. "I am a film buff, Ian. Particularly true-crime documentaries. The videotape you had me remove from the vault of the Metropolitan Bank was just such a documentary. In fact, it was so interesting that I made a copy of it for myself. Didn't come out as good as the original, but it is still quite viewable."

Ian Jellicoe had gone pale. In a strangled whisper he managed to say, "You must be insane. This is the Mafia you're trifling with."

"No, Ian, I am not insane, and I don't believe that you possess any mental deficiencies either. That is why I'm quite certain that you also made a copy of the tape."

Ian Jellicoe's eyes gave him away. It was a momentary lapse in his vigilance, but Julianna Saint was an extremely observant per-son. The Englishman's eyes flicked to the leather portfolio on the conference table and then back to the thief. This transmitted to her that he had indeed made a copy of the incriminating Romano tape. Then she also sensed something else. She couldn't immediately put her finger on what this was, but she was certain that Jellicoe was hiding something. Something that she was certain was inside the smart black leather portfolio he carried. Something that she wanted to see.

He regained his composure. "I have no idea what you are talking about, Julianna. I am a businessman, who never accepts a job without having a fair certainty that I can successfully conclude it. As such, when I was approached by Mr. Romano, I carefully examined the situation and decided that you and," he said with a sneer, "your associates would be capable of accomplishing what was required, which you did for the appropriate fee. A fee that I have paid in full. Now I and my client are quite satisfied with the outcome. It would be a disaster for not only you, but also me, if Mr. Romano was to discover that we have been less than forthright with him in the conduct of this affair."

Julianna exhaled a cloud of smoke and said, "You do love the sound of your own voice, don't you, Ian." She stubbed out her cigarette in a glass ashtray on the conference table and leaned forward so that her hand rested on his portfolio. She watched with a satisfaction that she easily concealed as he pulled the portfolio away from her.

Julianna picked up the blue envelope from the table and placed it in her handbag along with her cigarettes and lighter. She stood up and walked to the door. Before leaving, she turned to him and said, "You're a smart, well-educated man, Ian. That's why I know that you also made a copy of that tape, because, just as you said, you're dealing with the Mafia. And with them, if you don't have some type of insurance to protect yourself, you'll end up just like that writer Greg Ennis. Have a nice day."

Ian Jellicoe remained seated at the conference table for thirty minutes after she left. During that time he considered, among other things, what the thief known as the Devil's Shadow had said. He was forced to admit that she was absolutely right on all counts.

When Julianna entered the Admirals' Club at O'Hare Airport, she had not planned to rob Ian Jellicoe. However, due to the fact that she had been cheated out of money she was owed in the past, she was prepared to do just that. The presence of Christophe and Hubert provided her with a certain degree of physical security, but she was a thief, not a strong-arm thug, and she didn't believe in violence. But she did want to see what the Englishman had in his portfolio.

She met with Christophe and Hubert on the main floor of terminal three a short distance from the private elevator servicing the Admirals' Club. A thin young man in his early twenties was seated at the end of a row of chairs a short distance away. This young man's name was Emil. He was British, had long platinum blond hair and large blue eyes. Emil was a male prostitute and would, by the design of *L'Ombre du Diable,* be Ian Jellicoe's seatmate in the first-class section of the nonstop British Airways flight from Chicago to London, which would be taking off in forty-five minutes. Christophe La Croix would also be on that flight, seated in the coach section.

"Does Emil know what he is supposed to do?" she asked Christophe in French. It was Christophe who had secured the young man's services.

Christophe smiled and responded in the same language. "Lord Jellyfish is crazy about little boys like Emil there. He'll slip Jellicoe the sedative before the flight reaches the halfway point. After he goes to sleep, Emil will bring the leather portfolio to me. Jellicoe won't wake up until the aircraft is on the ground and someone slaps an oxygen mask on his face. By then me and Emil will be long gone."

"Excellent," Julianna said. "Hubert and I will take the Concorde and be waiting for you at Heathrow."

"May I say something, Julianna?" Hubert said.

"What is it?"

"Why don't you let me go back up there and take that portfolio away from Jellicoe and save you all this trouble?"

The look she gave him transmitted how she felt about that option.

Leaving Christophe and Emil to make their way to the British Airways gate, Julianna and Hubert headed for the international terminal to board the supersonic transport for a three-and-a-half hour flight to London.

"May I ask another question?" he said.

"You are beginning to bore me, Hubert."

"What does Jellicoe's portfolio contain that's so important?"

"That's what I intend to find out."

7

DECEMBER 5, 2004
10:27 A.M.

Larry Cole, accompanied by Manny Sherlock, returned to the Metropolitan Bank Building. There was no sign left of the horrible death of Greg Ennis, which had occurred there the day before. Michigan Avenue was festooned with Christmas decorations, and people—conducting business, shopping, or sightseeing—bustled back and forth on both sides of the wide thoroughfare. At times some of these pedestrians stepped on the exact spot where Ennis's body had been pulverized on impact with the unyielding cement surface. For many, the tragedy had been noted and then, in a world in which tragedy was instantly transmitted into every home via cable television, quickly forgotten.

Sergeant Sherlock was driving the chief of detectives' black Mercury command vehicle and pulled to the curb in a red zone in front of the bank. Manny tossed a "Chicago Police Department— Detective Division Headquarters—Official Business" cardboard placard in black letters on a white background on the dashboard. Then he followed Cole across the sidewalk into the building entrance next door to the Metropolitan National Bank.

Today the detectives were attired in traditional conservative business garb consisting of neatly tailored dress suits, somber shirt-and-tie combinations, and trench coats. The only difference between Cole's and Manny's outer garments was that the chief of detectives wore a black Burberry and the sergeant a tan London Fog. Beneath their suit jackets they carried firearms: Cole a 9-mm semiautomatic Beretta pistol equipped with a Ram-Line nineteen-round clip, Manny a .357 magnum Colt Python revolver with a two-inch barrel. There were three speed loaders on the sergeant's belt holster.

As the detectives entered the bank building lobby, a white truck pulled up behind the police vehicle. The name on the side of the van proclaimed it to be one of a fleet of vehicles operated by the Bronson and Byrne Lock, Safe, and Vault Repair Company. Had Cole and Sherlock left the street thirty seconds later, they would have encountered retired Detective Lou Bronson, who had been Manny's first partner in the Detective Division thirteen years before.

Now Bronson, a gray-haired black man of medium height, was one of the senior founding partners in the Bronson and Byrne Lock, Safe, and Vault Repair Company. The retired detective had entered into this line of work after taking an extensive locksmithing course at DeVry Institute. He was currently responding to the Metropolitan Bank to repair the safe-deposit vault door, which had been damaged in an as-yet-unknown manner according to the call Bronson and Byrne had received from the bank manager.

Wearing white coveralls and carrying a tool case and laptop computer, Bronson entered the bank.

The twenty-first-floor office of Ennis Enterprises was padlocked and posted with the taped prohibition on the door:

CHICAGO POLICE DEPARTMENT
CRIME SCENE
ACCESS PROHIBITED
VIOLATORS WILL BE ARRESTED AND
PROSECUTED TO THE FULLEST EXTENT OF THE LAW

Cole and Manny were not "violators."

Cole produced a key and unlocked the door. Making sure not to break the tape, they entered.

The interior of the office was pretty much in the same condition as Cole and Blackie had found it the day before. The window from which Greg Ennis had begun the plunge to his death was closed and the telltale signs of the crime lab technicians' collection of evidence were apparent. Manny carried a folder containing all of the reports submitted to date on the mysterious death of author Greg Ennis. The sergeant stood by the window, while the chief of detectives, stepping gingerly over the debris, took up a position in the center of the room. They remained in those positions for some moments while maintaining a rigid silence.

There was a historian named Dr. Silvernail Smith over at the Field Museum of Natural History. Dr. Silvernail, as he demanded to be called, had a past which was as clouded in mystery as the death that Larry Cole was now investigating. Despite an impressive educational background encompassing doctorate degrees in the fields of medicine, law, and philosophy, Silvernail had also developed a number of abilities and skills, some of which dealt with magic and the occult. Although Larry Cole had no intention of practicing such exotic disciplines, he had picked up a thing or two from the historian, which aided him in conducting complicated investigations like this one.

Hands thrust in the pockets of his trench coat, Cole took a deep breath, willed himself to relax, and allowed his mind to drift into a passive mode. Then with his inner being, soul, or essence, he reached out to spiritually touch his surroundings.

Making no attempt to hide his fascination, Manny Sherlock watched his boss.

What followed for Larry Cole was a result of a combination of his experience, knowledge, and the metaphysical technique he had learned from Dr. Silvernail.

Yesterday, after the talk he had had in his office with Barbara Zorin and Jamal Garth, Cole had gone home with an armload of Ennis's paperbacks, which the authors had given to him. The chief of detectives had spent the evening browsing through them. This, other than the sight of the author's smashed body on the Michigan

Avenue sidewalk, was Cole's first exposure to Greg Ennis. Now Cole knew a great deal about the dead man.

Greg Ennis had been born in Warren, Ohio, in 1963. According to the bio supplied by his New York agent, his father, Alan Ennis, was an army helicopter pilot, who was killed in a crash in Vietnam in 1969. After his death and a full-honors military funeral, Greg's mother, Norma Jean, had packed up her only child and moved to the Windy City to seek her fortune.

The money from the military insurance had not gone far and Norma Jean Ennis was forced to take a job as a secretary in an investment brokerage house. That was where she met Thomas Soames, who became Greg Ennis's stepfather.

The name Thomas Soames became well known in financial circles and in the world of white-collar crime. He had embezzled two million dollars from investors in the Soames Investment Consortium, which he founded. He escaped before he could be arrested and a warrant issued for his arrest. Soames was suspected of having changed his name, and it was believed that he had taken up residence in either South America or Australia. Although the warrant was still on file, the United States law enforcement apparatus did not actively pursue the embezzler. So Thomas Soames remained a fugitive, while living a life of luxury. That had not been the case with the family he left behind.

At the time that Soames embezzled the funds from his consortium, Greg Ennis had been a teenager. In the police reports detailing the crime there was no mention of his family or how well they bore up under the media spotlight placed on them. However, there were indications that it did have an effect on Greg Ennis, as the young man soon followed in his stepfather's larcenous footsteps.

As Jamal Garth had told Cole yesterday, Ennis had been arrested, tried, and sentenced to prison for grand larceny. The young man, barely out of high school, had become employed as a teller for the Harlem Bank of Chicago. He had worked hard and over a period of four years obtained a position of trust. A bright future was forecast for him, which was quickly dashed when Greg Ennis stole seven thousand dollars in cash from the bank vault.

Initially the theft had seemed more an act of careless stupidity motivated by greed than an offense that was plotted and carried out by a cunning criminal. Only twelve hundred dollars was recovered from Ennis at the time of his arrest. During the trial of the *State of Illinois* v. *Gregory Ennis*, the defendant refused to reveal what he had done with the missing money. A factor that enraged the trial judge, who threw the proverbial book at Greg Ennis. He received a sentence of five years in the Illinois State Penitentiary at Joliet.

Standing in the ransacked twenty-first-floor office of the Metropolitan Bank Building, Larry Cole remarked to himself that despite his many years as a cop, the judicial system was still a mystery to him. Greg Ennis had received a stiff sentence for the theft of fifty-eight hundred dollars. The average minimum jail time for first-degree murder was seven years. Somehow it didn't seem fair, but Cole had long ago come to the realization that the American criminal justice system possessed many unfathomable intricacies. In the majority of cases, justice prevailed; in other cases, justice was not always served.

Larry Cole did not have enough facts about the 1987 case of the *State of Illinois* v. *Gregory Ennis*, and he didn't believe that a review of the court transcripts would help him discover anything about how the former embezzler had died. But one thing that Cole had discovered from the reports of the 1987 bank theft was that Norma Jean Ennis Soames had vanished just hours before her son's arrest. Cole asked himself, could her son have stolen the money to finance a search for and reunion with his fugitive stepfather?

In the contemplative state into which Cole had placed himself, he felt a strong tug in that direction. And if he was right, he had just discovered a very important piece of the puzzle that made up the dead mystery writer's life. A man whom Cole was beginning to understand better with each passing minute. Ennis never married and was very secretive about his personal life; however, the chief of detectives was determined to find out a great deal more about the dead writer. And Cole knew that when he did he would have a good idea of who killed him and why.

On the lower level of the Metropolitan Bank of Chicago, Lou Bronson had completed his inspection of the safe-deposit vault. The bank vice president, David Nicholas, a bland, impatient man who understood balance sheets and numbers better than he did security, stood by waiting for the repairman to finish. Nicholas was attempting to keep a lid on the vault malfunction. For the past two days they had been unable to engage the vault lock. This had necessitated the posting of a twenty-four-hour guard at the vault entrance. Now the vice president waited not so much for the vault repairman to tell him what was wrong as to provide an estimate of the charges prior to proceeding with expeditious repairs.

Bronson led the vice president a few feet away from the vault entrance so they would have a modicum of privacy.

"You've been burglarized," Bronson said in a low tone of voice.

Metropolitan Bank vice president David Nicholas's eyes went wide in shock. "That's ridiculous. No one could get in here and open that vault without the alarms going off."

Bronson smiled. "Well, that's just what the burglars did. Whoever carried this off was very good, but your vault has definitely been broken into."

The banker looked as if he was going to be ill. "This is really too much. First we have that homeless man die in the alley, then the death of Greg Ennis, and now this."

Lou Bronson had spent most of his life as a police detective, so he had a strong suspicion that the three events were related.

The State of Illinois Department of Corrections provided the CPD with a custody report on Greg Ennis. There was little of substance contained in the DOC document. Ennis had not caused any problems while in prison and was paroled after three years. There was no mention of any cell-mates.

After his release from prison, Ennis managed to get a job through the "Former Inmate Second Chance" Program. He began selling securities and writing articles on investments for a financial newsletter. Then he attended Barbara Zorin's mystery writing class.

Cole had stood motionless in the center of the room for twenty minutes. Finally he moved over to the PC on the desk against the wall opposite the door. Pressing the power button caused a menu of services to appear on the screen. He activated the word processing program and a listing of program titles appeared. Cole scrolled down to an entry listed as "DDI," dated 2 September 2004. Cole called up this title.

"THE DEATH OF THE DON—A NOVEL—BY GREG ENNIS," appeared on the screen.

"This must be the book that Ennis was working on before he died, Manny," Cole said.

The sergeant left his perch by the window and stepped up beside Cole. "I could make a copy of it, sir."

"Do that," Cole said, "but there's something wrong here."

"What's that, Chief?" The sergeant pressed the keys to activate the laser jet printer attached to the computer.

"There are no novels listed on his hard drive and no backup discs here. If he didn't save the data on the hard drive, where are the discs?"

"Maybe he kept them in his apartment."

Cole shook his head. "Judy accompanied a team of detectives from Area One to take a look at his Hyde Park place last night. It was a spartanly furnished studio apartment that Judy says doesn't appear as if Ennis spent a great deal of time in. From the looks of this office, he spent most of his time here. The detectives searched the apartment but didn't find much in the way of personal things. And there were no computer disks."

"Maybe he didn't save the data." The printer began running off copies of the pages of Greg Ennis's manuscript.

"I'd be willing to bet he saved everything, Manny," Cole said. "He started out in finance before he got into mystery writing. I also want to find out what kind of business this Ennis Enterprises did."

The printer finished the run. Ennis had completed sixty pages of *The Death of the Don* before his murder.

"We'll take the manuscript with us. But before we go, let's have one last look at the computer menu."

Cole once more began scrolling through the data directory. He stopped at the title "LstOAssts." He called up the data and read directly from the screen.

"This is a list of Greg Ennis's assets. He had two thousand shares of bank stock along with a money market account valued at two hundred fifty thousand dollars and a safety-deposit box downstairs at the Metropolitan Bank."

"Do you think he kept his disks in the safety-deposit box, Chief?"

"We're going to find out, Manny."

8

Paris, France
DECEMBER 5, 2004
4:45 P.M.

Julianna Saint owned a number of residences around the world. She had a villa built into the side of a mountain on the French side of Saint Martin in the Leeward Islands. A few of her neighbors were Bill Cosby, Diana Ross, and Sinbad, the African-American comedian. She maintained a small apartment in Geneva, Switzerland, because she did a great deal of business with the banks there. She also had an eight-room apartment on the boulevard de Courcelles in the Seventeenth Arrondissement in Paris. This apartment was staffed by two full-time servants year-round, and when *L'Ombre du Diable* was in Paris, four servants, including a chauffeur, attended to her needs. It was to this apartment that Julianna had gone after her commute from the United States to Europe.

In February 2001 O'Hare International Airport in Chicago had instituted nonstop supersonic transport flights directly to Europe. Flying Air France at first-class rates, passengers were whisked from the Windy City across the Atlantic at speeds of over 1,300 mph or Mach 2. Aboard the Air France Aérospatiale/BAC Concorde, Julianna and Hubert had flown from Chicago to London's Heathrow Airport in just a shade over three hours. It had taken Christophe, aboard British Airways flight 562, accompaning Ian Jellicoe and the male prostitute Emil, eight hours to travel from Chicago to London.

Christophe La Croix was good at appearing to be someone else. This was not to say that he used disguises. Instead he subtly altered his appearance and posture to become a different person. This had made him a very successful thief and enabled him to effectively elude pursuing police officers on more than one occasion. Primarily Christophe was an accomplished actor and a gifted mimic. By changing his posture, adopting various gaits, and donning distinctive headgear and glasses, the young Frenchman could significantly change his appearance. On the British Airways flight to London, Christophe walked with a stooped shuffle, donned a floppy, wide-brimmed hat, wore tinted glasses, and spoke German-accented French and English.

Ian Jellicoe and Emil were already in seats 2A and 2B, respectively, in the first-class section of the plane when Christophe boarded. Following slow-moving coach passengers entering the cabin section of the plane, Christophe was forced to stop in the aisle next to row two. But any worries the French thief had concerning Ian Jellicoe recognizing him were eliminated when he glanced down at the Englishman and his seat companion. Jellicoe had already consumed half a glass of white wine and was fawning over Emil.

Christophe smiled when he noticed that Jellicoe had one of his hands resting on Emil's knee.

From the aisle seat in the first row of the coach section, Christophe watched Jellicoe and his platinum blond seat companion. The Frenchman counted the number of times that the flight attendant filled Jellicoe's wineglass. The Englishman consumed four before the in-flight meal. Emil had been ordered to refrain from alcohol consumption. It hadn't taken Christophe much to get Emil to comply with these instructions, as the male prostitute had a crush on the tall Frenchman.

Somewhere over the Atlantic, the wine took its toll on Jellicoe and he got up to use the washroom. Christophe observed that the Englishman walked steadily and showed no signs of intoxication. Jellicoe also carried the black leather portfolio Julianna Saint wanted him to steal. While Jellicoe was absent, the flight attendant refilled his wineglass. When she was gone, Emil turned around to look at Christophe. The thief abhorred the scrutiny, but there was no better time for Emil to slip Jellicoe the sedative. Christophe nodded and Jellicoe's seat companion removed the small vial from his shirt pocket and poured the clear, tasteless liquid into the Englishman's glass.

Jellicoe returned from the washroom, took his seat, picked up his wineglass, and drained off half its contents. British Airways flight 562 continued on to England without incident.

Julianna Saint's Paris apartment was in a building that had been constructed at the beginning of the twentieth century. The eight-room second-floor walk-up was equipped with a great deal of varnished wood and frosted glass. Very little had been done to change the basic decor in the hundred years of the building's existence. During the World War II German occupation, the entire neighborhood had fallen into disrepair. A slow renovation had begun in the late 1950s, and by the time Julianna purchased her flat in 1999, the building had been maintained with the flawless perfection and attention of a museum. *L'Ombre du Diable* had spent a great deal of money furnishing her apartment and on its upkeep. Now it was one of the most stylish, tasteful residences of its kind in a city known for trend-setting fashion.

Julianna was seated on her glass-enclosed sunporch. Although it was raining in Paris, the room was equipped with sunlamps, which were bright enough to simulate natural light. The room temperature was a balmy, humid eighty degrees to accommodate the tropical plants she had transplanted from their natural habitat in the Islands. In contrast to the damp cold of the late afternoon outside, Julianna was dressed in a sleeveless white cotton dress and sandals. The only sound in the room was the tinkling of an artificial rock waterfall. The woman known in the world of international crime as the Devil's Shadow was quite relaxed in this environment. If she allowed her mind to unfocus slightly, she could easily imagine that she was back at home on Saint Martin.

A black Citroën pulled to the curb in front of the apartment building. Julianna's drowsy, semiconscious expression did not alter as she watched through the rain-streaked sunroom windows as Ian Fitzwalter Jellicoe got out of the car. There was a furious scowl on the Englishman's face and he was alone. Or at least he appeared to be alone.

As Jellicoe started for the entrance to the apartment building, the cellular telephone in Julianna's skirt pocket rang. Casually she placed the instrument to her ear.

"Yes?"

"There are two men in a beige Fiat parked at the end of the block," Christophe said. "They were following Lord Jellyfish and pulled over when he drove onto your street."

"Where is Hubert?"

"On the roof with a high-powered sniper rifle. He said he can take the two in the Fiat anytime that you want."

Julianna came out of her relaxed posture and opened her eyes. She now exuded tension. "Christophe, tell Hubert that he is to do nothing without a direct order from me. Do you understand?"

"Yes, Julianna."

Shutting off the telephone and returning it to her pocket, she stood up and walked rapidly from the sunporch just as the lobby rang up to announce Ian Jellicoe's arrival. She would receive her guest in the living room.

Ian Jellicoe was furious, but he was also frightened to the very marrow of his being. What Julianna Saint had done to him was more terrifying than any repercussions that could come from American gangster Jake Romano. There were forces in this world far more dangerous and formidable than the Mafia. Forces that *L'Ombre du Diable* had no idea even existed. Forces about which Ian Jellicoe possessed highly confidential information. Information that had been contained in the leather portfolio that Julianna Saint had stolen from him.

Most of the flight from America across the Atlantic Ocean had been a black void for Ian Jellicoe. He had become really turned on by his cute, sexy seatmate Emil. The job that Jellicoe had just done, or at least had ordered done, back in Chicago had been a tremendous success. As such, the Englishman felt that he deserved a break. A few days of relaxation, which he planned to enjoy with his new friend and anticipated soon-to-be lover. So Jellicoe had consumed a few glasses of an excellent white wine, as he began getting friendly with Emil. And then . . .

When Jellicoe regained consciousness there was an oxygen mask covering his nose and mouth, and they were lifting him out of his airplane seat to place him on a stretcher. A pair of ambulance attendants and a stewardess stood over him. He was dizzy, disoriented, nauseous, and had a splitting headache. Initially he had no idea what had happened to him, but he frantically fought to get up and retrieve his portfolio. However, he was too weak, and the medical attendants, believing Jellicoe to be delirious, strapped him down.

By the time they had transported him to a hospital a short distance from Heathrow, he had managed to regain enough of his equilibrium to communicate that he was in full command of his faculties. Against the advice of a severe-mannered female physician, Jellicoe had stumbled out of the hospital and into a taxi.

He was en route back to the airport when he discovered the white envelope in his inside suit jacket pocket. It was addressed to him in a flowing feminine script. Jellicoe knew that this envelope had not been in his possession when he boarded British Airways flight 562 in Chicago. When he opened it and read the brief note from Julianna Saint, an icy stab of fear sliced through him. The thief had his portfolio, and even though it was locked, Jellicoe knew that she was capable of opening it faster than he could with the key.

Ian Jellicoe was able to take little solace in the fact that Julianna Saint had stated in her note that he could retrieve his portolio free of charge at her Paris apartment the following day. By the time Jellicoe arrived in Paris, Julianna would not only have opened the portfolio, but would have made copies of its contents. Although the Englishman was not necessarily a violent man, he was a professional criminal. As such, he was not averse to the idea of killing Julianna Saint and that pair of petty crooks who always accompanied her. In fact, as he flew out of London, he realized that he actually relished the prospect of having them killed as revenge for the indignity he had suffered at their hands.

Jellicoe climbed the wide, winding marble staircase to the second floor. He had hired two strong-arm men from a local Paris-based criminal gang to back him up. They were not there to employ force against the thief, but were simply for show. If he did decide to eliminate the Devil's Shadow, he would find someone a great deal more efficient at dispensing violent death than a common street gang.

A slightly built, aging butler with black-dyed hair slicked back from a sharp widow's peak was waiting at the open door to Julianna Saint's apartment. A mocking grin creased Jellicoe's face. The butler was dressed in a red vest, black bow tie, and white shirt, but he had scarred hands and cracked fingernails. A servant's hands like his would never have been tolerated in a proper English household.

Without a word, Jellicoe surrendered his wet trench coat and umbrella to the little man and watched him hang them on a coat tree inside the entrance. Then the Englishman followed the butler down a long, high-ceiling hall to the living room. Julianna Saint was waiting there.

A varnished wooden cocktail table dominated the center of the room. Ian Jellicoe instantly noticed his portfolio lying on this table. Without a word of greeting to his hostess, he snatched up the portfolio and found it locked. He didn't think it had been in this secure state since it was stolen from him on the Chicago-to-London flight. Using his key, Jellicoe unlocked it and inspected the contents. Everything was there, including the tape of Victor Mattioli's assassination by Jake Romano and even his expensive Mont Blanc Oscar Wilde fountain pen. There was also the photograph in the sealed manila envelope. It was the contents of this envelope that had Jellicoe worried. Snapping the portfolio shut, he glared at the thief.

Julianna had taken a seat on a brocade couch on the other side of the room. She crossed her long legs, giving Jellicoe a view of bare flesh from knee to ankle. A view that was wasted on the Englishman.

"Have a seat, Ian," she said, pleasantly. "It's teatime."

On cue, the grubby-fingered butler entered with a tray containing finger sandwiches, buttered scones, and a teapot, which he placed on the table. His job done, the butler quickly left the room.

"I'm really not in a mood for chitchat, Julianna," Jellicoe said, acidly. "But I want you to be aware that I am very angry with you for what you did and I will not forget this insult."

He turned to leave.

Her voice stopped him.

"You really should sit down and have a cup of tea, Ian, There are a couple of things you need to know about Bishop Martin De Coutreaux of the Vatican before you become too deeply involved with him."

With his back to her, Ian Jellicoe stopped. The name she had mentioned had been on a slip of paper in his portfolio. Bishop Martin Simon Pierre De Coutreaux was not well known, but he was not a totally anonymous figure either. Julianna could have simply recognized his name when she went through the portfolio. But the Englishman did have important business pending with the Vatican-based Catholic prelate, so he needed to find out what, if anything, the Devil's Shadow wanted to tell him about Bishop De Coutreaux.

Turning, still clutching his recently recovered portfolio under his arm, Jellicoe crossed the living room and sat down on a love seat across from his hostess.

Picking up the teapot, she poured the hot liquid into a cup and inquired, "Tea, Ian?"

On the roof of the Paris apartment building on the boulevard de Courcelles in the Seventeenth Arrondissement, Christophe La Croix crossed to Hubert Metayer. Both men wore black-hooded rain slickers, which provided marginal protection from the elements.

Hubert had a Heckler & Koch PGS1 sniper rifle braced atop the two-foot restraining wall surrounding the flat roof. Despite the rain running down into his face, he was staring unblinkingly through the telescopic sight at the two men in the beige Fiat fifty feet below. These men had accompanied Ian Jellicoe, and Hubert had the sight's crosshairs lined up on the driver's brutal-featured face. Slowly he began to squeeze the trigger.

Nervously Christophe cleared his throat, "Hubert, Julianna said—"

"Shut up, Christophe," Hubert snapped. "I know what I'm doing."

The black Frenchman continued to slowly squeeze the trigger of the powerful weapon. The rifle emitted a loud click as the hammer engaged an empty chamber.

"Bang, you're dead," Hubert said.

Christophe was certain that he was going to faint.

9

M anny," Lou Bronson called from the side entrance of the Metropolitan Bank.

The familiar voice made not only Sherlock turn, but also Larry Cole. When the two cops saw the retired detective they both smiled and crossed the building lobby to greet him.

"What's with the white coveralls, Lou?" Cole asked.

Bronson turned around to show them the green-scripted lettering on his back.

"Wow, Lou," Manny said, excitedly. "When did you become a locksmith?" Next to Cole, Bronson had been the biggest role model of his police career.

Lou Bronson had a characteristic grin that was infectious. Now he smiled and said, "Just a little something I picked up in my spare time, Manny. So I guess the crime wave down here has brought the chief of detectives out to personally do some investigating."

Cole frowned. "Greg Ennis's death hardly qualifies as a crime wave, Lou."

"Then I guess you're not aware of the problems the bank has been having."

"What kind of problems?" Cole asked.

A few minutes later they were standing in the alley beside the delivery entrance to the Metropolitan Bank. Bronson had climbed the utility pole. When he descended he brushed the dirt off his hands and said, "Whoever did this job is not only the best I've ever seen, but the best I've ever even heard of. They attached a black box to the transformer up there and bled off just enough power to prevent the exterior alarm from being triggered. Then the burglar entered the bank through that door."

"But there have got to be backup alarms in there," Cole argued. "Infrared sensors, motion detectors, not to mention guards and closed-circuit TV monitors."

"All of those systems were bypassed, boss," Bronson said. "The burglar also got into the safety-deposit vault. They found a homeless man dead next to that Dumpster. Now, it could be just coincidence, but I'll bet an autopsy will reveal that he met with foul play after he eyeballed our burglars."

"There was no burglary reported at the Metropolitan Bank, Lou," Manny said.

Bronson removed his cap and scratched his receding hairline. "This is one for the books. According to the vice president who hired me, they didn't know they'd been burglarized."

A strange look came over Cole's face. "You mean nothing was taken?"

"Not that they can tell," Bronson responded. "And I would think that the bank could detect if there are any assets missing."

"Maybe they can't, Lou," Cole said. "Do you feel up to doing a bit of unofficial police work for us?"

"Anytime, Chief."

Police officer Joe Parker patrolled one of the highest-crime areas of the Windy City. Now he turned his marked police car off of Fifty-first Street and cruised south on Federal, driving past the vacant lots slated for development. At one time this area had been the site of a number of monstrous, crime-ridden, sixteen-story high-rise public housing developments.

Parker, a sturdily built black man with a shaved head and wise eyes, was a twenty-year veteran of the department and had seen more than his share of murder and mayhem on the streets of Chicago. Now, as midday passed, he was preparing to swing by a nearby grammar school to make sure there were no undesirables loitering on the grounds. But he was not going to make it to the school on this winter afternoon.

A garbage Dumpster had been left in the center of one of the vacant lots where a high-rise had once stood. Initially Parker thought that there was a fire inside the Dumpster, because a thick cloud of smoke billowed into the air. But it was not the Dumpster that was on fire, but the car parked behind it.

Pulling the police car into the lot, the officer got out and walked over to the burning car. The flames forced him to maintain a safe distance and he was very much aware of the possiblity that the gas tank could explode. He was reaching for his walkie-talkie to summon the fire department when he saw the body in the front passenger seat of the late-model Cadillac. Later, after the fire was struck, a second body would be found in the trunk.

Officer Joe Parker ran the still readable number on the blackened license plate. It came back registered to Peter E. Debenedetto of Cicero, Illinois. It was Debenedetto's body that was discovered in the Cadillac's trunk. His Mafia partner in crime, Joey Randall, was the corpse in the front seat. Before they were incinerated, both men had sustained large-caliber gunshot wounds to the head.

Another investigative lead into the murder of mystery writer Greg Ennis went up in smoke along with Pete Debenedetto's Cadillac.

10

Rome, Italy
DECEMBER 6, 2004
9:15 A.M.

Vatican City is in Rome and covers 108.7 acres. Established on June 10, 1929, the Vatican is a sovereign papal state from which the pope leads the millions of Roman Catholics worldwide. Saint Peter's Basilica and Vatican Square dominate the papal grounds. Twelve additional buildings make up the complex from which the business of the largest landowner in the world is administered.

In matters of faith, the pope is considered by his followers to be infallible. But the mortals who have exercised the awesome power that radiates from the head of the Catholic Church have made horrendous human errors in the past. Human errors that have often been criminal in nature.

Down through history the leaders of the Church have wielded immense power over the faithful. In the eleventh century Pope Urban II was reported to have taken a more secular than spiritual view in solving the known world's problems when he started the First Crusade to the Holy Land. Although there are many accounts of the words Urban II spoke on November 27, 1095, the rallying cry of "God wills it" was taken up by the Crusaders, who battled for the Holy Land over the next three centuries. Holy wars that resulted in thousands of deaths.

Besides having the objective of freeing the land of Christ's birth from the Moslem infidels who occupied it, Urban II is also believed to have had a number of secondary, more practical agendas. Among them were the reunification of the Eastern and Western Catholic churches by force, putting an end to the infighting among the various European nations by giving them a common, foreign, non-Christian enemy to fight, and asserting the influence of the Roman Catholic Church as an international power.

During the Renaissance, the Borgia popes gave a new meaning to the word *treachery*, and before, during, and after the Second World War, the Vatican under Pius XII collaborated with the Nazis and assisted a number of war criminals in escaping from Europe.

However, the Vatican managed to weather these storms of indiscretion and malfeasance. At the beginning of the twenty-first century it was still a very strong entity on the world stage, despite the relatively small size of the seat of papal power in Vatican City. Many of the members of the international brotherhood of the faith believed that this survival was based solely on the eternal message of goodness and strength passed down from Jesus Christ at the beginning of the first millennium. They believed that the words spoken by Pope Urban II, *Deus vult*, "God wills it," had sustained the Catholic Church through wars, religious oppression, and division from within. There were others who took a more earthly, practical view of the holy institution's longevity. One such person was Bishop Martin Simon Pierre De Coutreaux.

Bishop De Coutreaux was a striking man with sharp features and penetrating hazel eyes. In Vatican City, which was ornamented with the works of such world-renowned artists as Michelangelo, Perugino, and Signorelli, it was whispered behind the cleric's back that if an artist's rendering of the dark angel Satan were to ever grace the walls of this holy city, then Bishop De Coutreaux would make an excellent model. And the bishop's mind was as sharp as his nose or chin, and his eyes seemed capable of melting stone.

A very pale, thin man, Bishop De Coutreaux was the assistant to the cardinal chamberlain, who was the second highest-ranking priest beneath the pope in the hierarchy of the Catholic Church. e Coutreaux was French and had been educated at Oxford and the Sorbonne. He was a published author, who had penned a number of works on the histories of France and of the Church. His particular area of historical expertise was the Knights Templar, and he approached the study of these medieval Christian soldiers with an enthusiasm bordering on the fanatic. Bishop De Coutreaux's staunch belief was that an order within the Church based on the wealthy, monastic, military Knights Templar was necessary in the modern world in which Holy Mother Church was under constant assault from the forces of evil. And De Coutreaux believed that the machinations of such forces went beyond the demands for the ordination of women, permitting priests to marry, and calls for the Vatican to liquidate its worldwide holdings to help feed the poor and homeless. Of course, Bishop Martin Simon Pierre De Coutreaux was against any such radical changes of the centuries-old policies of the Vatican. But he also believed that a more demonic entity existed in the world. The physical embodiment of Satan—the Antichrist. A foe that

Bishop De Coutreaux had devoted his life to finding and destroying.

The bishop's official duties entailed him overseeing the administration of the Office of the Cardinal Chamberlain. The holder of that office was eighty-one years of age, could not see or hear very well, had a number of lingering ailments as a result of his advanced years, and tired easily. This left the fifty-six-year-old Bishop De Coutreaux in charge of one of the most powerful and influential offices in the papal hierarchy.

It was rumored that the pope was aware of the excellent work done by the relatively young bishop in such a quiet, unassuming manner. It was further rumored, through the extensive Vatican grapevine, that De Coutreaux would soon be elevated to the position of cardinal and made the papal nuncio (Vatican ambassador) to the United States.

Martin De Coutreaux was aware of these rumors, as there was little that went on within the walls of Vatican City that he was unaware of. Yes, the French bishop did his job in a quiet, unassuming manner; however, this was due to a lifelong inclination toward conducting all of his affairs in secret. As far as the appointment as papal nuncio of the United States, De Coutreaux would do all in his power to prevent any such thing from occurring. Oh, he did want to be named the Vatican ambassador to a foreign country, but not the United States. Especially not the United States.

The bishop's office, in comparison to the cardinal chamberlain's, was a closet-sized cubbyhole in an administrative wing of one of the twelve Vatican City buildings. De Coutreaux had no secretary, did all of his own typing, and even answered his own telephone. If he required any mundane clerical tasks to be performed, such as copying documents, faxing information, or journeying to the Vatican post office, a bright young priest would be summoned. Bishop De Coutreaux minimized any contact with nuns or, for that matter, women in general.

Now he was in his office working on a new book about the Knights Templar. In this volume he was chronicling the life of Jacques de Molay, the last grand master of the Knights Templar, who was burned at the stake in 1314. It is rumored that at the time of his death, de Molay cursed King Philip IV of France and Pope Clement II, who had orchestrated the destruction of the Knights Templar and the seizure of their assets. This curse was apparently effective, as King Philip and Pope Clement were dead within a year.

Martin De Coutreaux wrote all of his books in longhand on yellow legal pads before using an IBM Selectric typewriter to transfer the data onto twenty-pound bond paper. The bishop's handwriting was neat to the point of appearing to be mechanically produced. Each character was fastidiously formed to flow into the next. The completed handwritten text was almost a work of art; however, when De Coutreaux completed a chapter he would go back over the work and savagely edit it before the transfer to typed text. He possessed an extensive reference library in his office, and if he needed additional information, the main Vatican library was one of the most comprehensive in the world.

As with every other part of his life, the bishop's writing was compartmentalized into a neat cubbyhole of two hours every day. He rose at 6:00 A.M., said his morning prayers on the cold floor of his cell-like room, showered, shaved, and dressed before going to say mass in the Chapel of Saint James, which was beneath the cardinal chamberlain's suite of offices. After mass he breakfasted on cold porridge, black coffee, and a piece of fresh fruit. He was at his desk no later than 7:30.

Between 7:30 and 9:30 A.M. he went through the cardinal chamberlain's mail, prepared whatever correspondence was necessary, and promptly at 10:00 A.M. presented himself at the door of his superior's private quarters. If the cardinal chamberlain was up to it, which the eighty-one-year-old priest generally was not, Martin De Coutreaux would enter and be received in the sitting room of the spacious Vatican suite. Of late the cardinal chamberlain received the bishop in his bedroom, which nowadays he seldom left.

Bishop De Coutreaux was always brief and careful to make sure that the cardinal chamberlain did not become overly fatigued by the weight of the affairs of his office. The bishop would take down any directions his superior gave him and was generally back in his office by 10:30 A.M. After ensuring that the cardinal chamberlain's instructions were carried out and all Vatican business was taken care of, Bishop De Coutreaux would take one of the yellow legal pads from the center drawer of his locked desk, gather the necessary reference works in front of him, and begin to write.

The life and times of Jacques de Molay, who died in the early fourteenth century, were as real to Martin Simon Pierre De Coutreaux as were the events occurring in the twenty-first century in which he lived. But despite the gulf of nearly a millennium, De Coutreaux could see many similarities between then and now.

The bishop wrote for two hours. At exactly 1:00 P.M. he stopped. He had filled five of the yellow legal-sized pages with his precise script. Closing the pad, he placed it back in the drawer and locked the desk. He checked the time on the gold Swiss-made wristwatch he wore. The timepiece had been a gift from one of the devotees of his historical works and was the most expensive material item that De Coutreaux owned. The bishop took his priestly vows of poverty, chastity, and obedience very seriously.

Leaving his office, he descended to the Chapel of Saint James, where he had celebrated mass that morning. Now he was going to hear confessions, as well as confess his own sins to a fellow priest.

En route to the chapel, De Coutreaux passed a number of nuns, priests, monsignors, fellow bishops, and even a couple of cardinals. He spoke to each one, giving and receiving blessings, and inquiring as to their health and the well-being of their relatives. Despite his general reclusiveness and the severity of his appearance, Bishop De Coutreaux was known as a pious man with a deep spiritual resolve.

Arriving at the chapel, he went to one of the unoccupied confessionals. Before entering, he noticed that a line had already formed of people waiting for Bishop De Coutreaux to first hear and then absolve them of their sins. Most of those waiting were women, but there was a man present, who stood out from the other penitents.

This man was tall, thin, pale, and impeccably dressed in a Savile Row tailored suit. Bishop Martin Simon Pierre De Coutreaux recognized Ian Fitzwalter Jellicoe.

Ian Jellicoe did not go to confession, because he was not a Catholic. In fact, his religious beliefs were somewhere between those of an atheist and an agnostic. So he waited until Bishop De Coutreaux was finished with the penitents in the Chapel of Saint James. Then the tall Englishman accompanied the sharp-featured prelate on a walk across the ornate Saint Peter's Square.

"How did your business go in Chicago?" De Coutreaux asked, as they strolled along.

"Quite well," Jellicoe responded. "I hired a crew of thieves from your native—"

The bishop held up his hand. "We do not wish to hear about your more sordid pursuits, Mr. Jellicoe. We gave you a charge to carry out for Holy Mother Church. We trust that you were able to do so successfully."

"I managed to get a photograph of the man you wanted me to find while I was in Chicago."

De Coutreaux stopped. "May we see it?"

Jellicoe opened the leather portfolio, which had not been out of his presence since he had retrieved it from Julianna Saint in Paris. He handed a manila envelope to the bishop. With trembling fingers De Coutreaux opened it and extracted an 8½-by-11-inch black-and-white photo. De Coutreaux gazed at it for a long time. Finally he said in a whisper, "Now the devil has a face."

The Englishman could not help himself. "You think that man is the devil?"

De Coutreaux affixed his piercing gaze on Jellicoe. "If he is not the Dark Angel Satan himself, then he is one of his followers."

"Begging Your Eminence's pardon, but wouldn't a being, uh, that is, a human being who could summon up the power of the devil be something more than a historian in a dusty museum?"

Without responding, the bishop returned the photo to the envelope and secured it beneath his cassock.

They continued their stroll. "We will require an additional service from you, Ian, in connection with this so-called historian in Chicago."

"As always," Jellicoe said, formally, "I am at your service, Your Eminence. For the appropriate fee."

"Of course," De Coutreaux said. "We want to know more about this demonic personality. Actually what we need is a sample of his blood. A pint will do."

Jellicoe stopped. Bishop De Coutreaux proceeded a short distance past him before pausing as well. The two men were standing at the center of Saint Peter's Square with the sacred majesty of the Vatican surrounding them.

"I'm not a bleeding vampire, De Coutreaux. And I don't go in for rough stuff."

Martin Simon Pierre De Coutreaux smiled. "We know you're not a common criminal, Mr. Jellicoe. That is why we have employed you to represent us in various matters of this nature."

"But how am I supposed to get this historian's blood?" To say the least, the Englishman's voice was strained.

"We are sure there is someone in the criminal underworld that you could utilize to carry out our request." The bishop resumed his slow walk and the Englishman hurried to catch up with him. "But you must always maintain our anonymity in these matters."

Jellicoe cleared his throat. "I need to mention something to you that happened before I arrived in Rome."

De Coutreaux waited.

"A thief stole my portfolio, which contained the historian's photo and a piece of paper with your name on it."

Now it was De Coutreaux's turn to stop, and the look that he gave Jellicoe seemed capable of plunging his soul directly into hell. "Who is this thief?"

Jellicoe swallowed before continuing. "Her name is Julianna

Saint and she gave the portfolio back to me in Paris yesterday." At the mention of her name, the prelate's fiercely angry gaze was altered by another emotion. That emotion was fear.

Now Jellicoe proceeded more cautiously. "In Paris I did not disclose the nature of the business I had with you here in Rome, but Julianna, who is known in the underworld as the Devil's Shadow, said that she knows you. I assumed that since you are both French . . ."

De Coutreaux spun away from Jellicoe and hissed, "That is ridiculous. What would we have to do with a common criminal?"

They began pacing again, but maintained a lengthy silence. Finally the bishop said, "Perhaps the situation with this *L'Ombre du Diable* can be turned to our advantage, Ian. Do you think that she would be averse to taking this task of obtaining the blood from the historian in Chicago?"

"For the right price and if she was presented with the proper challenge, I'm sure she would consider it. But Julianna abhors violence, so she won't employ force."

"Make her an offer along the lines we have previously set down for you in the conduct of our affairs and get back to us as soon as you can."

"Your Eminence, it can be very dangerous dealing with the likes of Julianna Saint."

The Catholic prelate turned and graced the Englishman with a tolerant smile. "Then we're certain that you will be not only careful, but also discreet, Ian. Keep in touch."

With that Martin De Coutreaux walked rapidly across the square away from Jellicoe. Watching him go, the Englishman considered something that the bishop had just said. Jellicoe had referred to Julianna as the Devil's Shadow, but De Coutreaux had called her *L'Ombre du Diable*. The French churchman could have simply translated the thief's underworld title into his native tongue. However, Julianna Saint knew Martin De Coutreaux, and now Ian Jellicoe believed that the bishop also knew the Devil's Shadow. And De Coutreaux had also taken the photograph of the historian that he claimed was a disciple of Satan. But Jellicoe knew the man's name. It was Smith, Dr. Silvernail Smith.

11

Chicago, Illinois
DECEMBER 7, 2004
2:00 P.M.

The four bank robbers arrived at the Chatham Savings and Loan Bank in three separate cars. They parked in the lot off of State Street, which ran parallel to the Dan Ryan Expressway (I-94) at 7600 South. Wearing full-length overcoats, they entered the glass and brick building. They were all white, in their mid-thirties to early forties, and had on white shirts and dark ties beneath their outer garments.

A uniformed guard stood inside the front door. Although armed, the guard was a senior citizen who displayed a watermelon-sized gut that seriously strained the buttons of his shirt. His primary job on this winter afternoon was to pass out holiday calendars to customers entering the bank.

The first man in the quartet walked up to the guard and opened his overcoat. The smile on the guard's face faded when he saw the wicked-looking, compact, semiautomatic rifle the robber carried down at his side beneath the coat.

"Okay, pops," he said, "stay cool and you'll be home with your grandchildren for the holidays. How many other guards are on duty in the bank now?"

"Three," the old man managed with a trembling voice. "Fred

is behind the tellers' cage; Joe and Cynthia are waiting out back for the cash delivery."

The robber smiled. "Very good, pops. That jives with our intelligence. Now, you keep right on being cooperative and don't try to be a hero. *Capisce?*"

The guard managed to nod his head.

The other three men moved quickly through the bank, herding customers and bank employees before them without opposition. The guard named Fred, who was also a senior citizen, gave up even faster than his calendar-distributing counterpart stationed at the front door. One of the reasons for this quick capitulation were the weapons the robbers carried.

The formal nomenclature of the rifles was the Steyr-Mannlicher .223-caliber Universal Assault Rifle, containing a thirty-round clip. Nicknamed a "Bullpup," it was equipped with a telescopic sight and had the range of a high-powered rifle despite its relatively small size. The guards employed by the Chatham Savings and Loan Bank carried standard .38-caliber Smith & Wesson police specials with four-inch barrels. These weapons were the guards' own personal property, were seldom cleaned and never inspected by superiors. For all the good that a .38 could do against a Bullpup in a firefight, the guards could have been unarmed.

But the formidable firepower was only a portion of the operation. These men also had a plan, which was aimed at stealing $350,000 from the Chatham Savings and Loan Bank. Such a sum was not usually kept on hand in a neighborhood branch institution, but was being delivered by an armored car to provide cash for transactions to be conducted at nearby shopping malls. The armored car was scheduled to arrive at the bank at 2:15 P.M. One of the Bullpup-armed stickup men would be waiting to take delivery of the money before the robbers commandeered the armored car to make their getaway.

Within five minutes of the robbers' arrival at the bank, they were in complete control. Two of them covered the hostages, who had been corralled and forced to lie on the floor of the lobby. One of the stickup men went to the utility stairwell and climbed onto the roof. He crawled to the ledge overlooking the street and expressway below. From this position he commanded a field of fire up to 250 yards in all directions. On the roof it was cold and snow flurries blew out of a low-ceiling gray sky. However, the robber's adrenaline level was so high he could have been up there in his underwear and remain unaffected.

He had been waiting for less than a minute when the armored car turned off of Seventy-ninth Street onto State Street two blocks away and traveled north toward the bank. Cradling his rifle, he settled in to watch the streets below.

"Chicago Emergency, Callahan."

"Is this the police?" the elderly woman's cracked voice said over the line.

"Yes, it is," the operator said, examining the call location identifier (CLI) and discovering that this call was coming in from the 7700 block of South Wabash Avenue.

"This is Mrs. Warren. Mrs. Letitia Warren."

"Yes, ma'am. What seems to be the trouble?"

"Well, my house is right behind the Chatham Savings and Loan Bank on State Street."

"Yes, ma'am. Is there something wrong at the bank?"

"I don't know, Officer. But there's a man with a rifle on the roof."

The armored car pulled to a halt at the rear of the bank. The pair of savings and loan security guards were waiting for it. The car stopped and its back door opened. The armored car personnel were about to begin unloading the $350,000 in cash when the man with the rifle appeared behind the security guards.

The sniper on the roof saw the blue lights of the first police car when it was still a half mile from the bank. It was coming fast from the south. Then a second police car came into view, approaching from the west. How the cops had been alerted to the holdup was unknown to the sniper, but it really didn't matter. He was prepared for this contingency.

The sniper estimated that the car coming from the south would cross the intersection of Seventy-ninth and State Street first. He sighted the Bullpup on the grille of that car and waited. The police vehicle crossed the intersection and was followed closely by the one coming from the west.

"You're too close together, gentlemen," he said, with a sadistic grin. "You boys have got to maintain your intervals."

He fired two rounds from the thirty-round clip, which destroyed the radiator and engine block of the police car. The driver lost control and the vehicle went into a wild 180-degree skid. The trailing squad car was unable to prevent the collision and the two vehicles bounced off of each other before colliding again. They became a combined mass of twisted metal and came to rest less than twenty feet from the bank's parking lot entrance.

"It's time for you boys to vacate those cars," the sniper said, sighting in and proceeding to methodically shoot the Mars lights off the tops of both cars.

Initially the trapped officers ducked down as low as they could in the front seat. The sniper stopped shooting long enough for them to bolt from the cars and dash for cover behind a building from which a body and fender repair shop operated. The wrecked police cars, their engines still running, blocked State Street and vehicular access to the bank. This was by design.

"Now let's start a little fire," the sniper said, as he began to pump round after round into the wrecked cars until a gas tank ruptured with a roar and flames leaped into the air.

The sniper smiled at his handiwork. Then more police cars began showing up.

"Come to Papa," he said, his grin never diminishing.

Jake Romano and his wife, Alicia, were hosting guests for lunch. The vice president of the Abco Oil Company and his wife, Attorney

Sol Engstrom and his current girlfriend, the golf pro who gave Romano and Alicia lessons at the North Shore Country Club and his wife, were some of the guests in attendance. The remainder of those present were Chicago Mob underbosses with their spouses or girlfriends.

The guests had arrived at noon, and lunch was served in the spacious dining room of the Lake Shore Drive brownstone. The menu consisted of clam chowder, tossed salad, smoked salmon, new potatoes, and creamed spinach, with baked Alaska for dessert. The guests had their choice of beverage, including hard liquor, but everyone followed Jake Romano's lead and had no more than one glass of white wine before the meal and either coffee, mineral water, or soft drinks during lunch.

Afterwards they retreated to the music room, where Alicia Romano entertained her guests with a selection of classical music and show tunes on the piano. The guests broke into groups and engaged in polite conversation.

"I don't see why we can't adopt a concealed-weapon carry law for qualified citizens in Illinois," Attorney Sol Engstrom was saying to Romano and the wife of the oil company exec. Engstrom was a comparatively young man of thirty-eight and had a receding hairline creeping rapidly toward the top of his head. He was a graduate of Yale Law School and the nephew of the late Frank Kirschstein, who had been the mouthpiece for Tuxedo Tony DeLisa. Although he was a bit pompous, Engstrom was one of the best attorneys in the country.

"Look what we have now," the attorney continued. "Every low-life punk out there is carrying a gun, while the law-abiding citizen goes unarmed and ends up becoming the victim of these armed thugs."

"I think you might have something there, Sol," said the oil company vice president's wife, a stunning green-eyed redhead. "I know I would feel a lot better if I had a gun with me when I'm going into the house at night."

"But you live in Lake Forest, which is one of the most exclusive and, I must say, safest neighborhoods in the country," Romano said.

The woman colored slightly. "Well, I don't spend all of my time in the suburbs, Jake. After all, we are in the city now."

"Yes, we are," the handsome mob boss said, "but we're on North Lake Shore Drive, which is probably just as safe as Lake Forest. And, Sol, I must disagree with you about this concealed-carry law. We can't have people running around out on the street with guns. It's contrary to the rule of law. Our society would rapidly deteriorate into a Dodge City, shoot-to-kill mentality. Then where would we be?"

The attorney and the oil company executive's spouse considered pursuing the argument, but quickly changed their minds. The new Chicago Mob boss was a man who demanded the utmost respect. Therefore it was not wise to argue with him. In fact, to do so could be quite dangerous.

An underboss crossed the music room and motioned to Romano.

"Excuse me," he said to his guests, and walked over to join the man. They exchanged brief whispers before the Mob boss left the music room and entered the study. After locking the door securely behind him, Romano turned on the television. He selected WGN, which was covering the in-progress robbery of the Chatham Savings and Loan Bank. Jake Romano was very interested in this crime since he was the mastermind behind it.

After taking over as the new head of the Chicago Mafia, Romano decided that it was time to go back to what the criminal underworld did best: commit crimes. Yes, they would continue to dabble in the area of white-collar crime, as well as remaining the largest purveyor of vice in the United States, but they would also engage in violent criminal acts as the Mob had done back in the 1920s and 1930s. One of these acts was unfolding before Romano on the television. And the head of the Chicago Mafia planned to plague the Windy City with a great many more of these violent acts.

*   *   *

The area for blocks around the Chatham Savings and Loan Bank had become a war zone. Six police vehicles had been damaged by sniper fire from the bank roof. Two officers had been injured by flying glass, and a cop over the age of sixty had suffered a heart attack induced by the stress of the incident.

No police officer or police vehicle was able to get within a hundred yards of the bank without coming under intense sniper fire. And the Chicago Police Department field units were completely outgunned. The only weapons they possessed were sidearms, and what fire they had been able to return had no effect on the sniper.

The first field sergeant to arrive on the scene initially attempted to assess the situation from the west side of the Dan Ryan Expressway over one hundred yards away from the bank. However, when the back window of his police vehicle was shattered by sniper fire, he quickly put a great deal more distance between himself and the scene of the robbery in progress. He ordered the responding units to maintain a safe distance from the sniper, which virtually placed the police out of visual contact with the bank.

The Chatham Savings and Loan Bank was in the Sixth Police District. As of 2:27 P.M. on December 7, every police car on patrol in that district had responded to the bank. Having no idea what to do next, the sergeant requested that the Sixth District field lieutenant respond to the scene. Actually he was already there, but had taken cover on the east side of the expressway in a gas station.

Now the field lieutenant sized up the situation and, seeing that they were severely outgunned, requested that the watch commander come to the scene. This was followed by requests for the district commander and the assistant deputy superintendent, who was the highest-ranking field officer on duty in the city.

The ADS radioed that she was on the way, but after being apprised of the fact that they were up against high-powered semi-automatic weapons, she ordered the Special Weapons Unit to respond. Then the shooting stopped.

None of the cops moved for a full ten minutes after the firing ceased. Then slowly they came out and began approaching the bank. They found the hostages still lying on the floor of the bank lobby. The security guards and the armored car operators were among them. The robbers and the armored car containing the $350,000 in cash were gone.

Larry Cole and Blackie Silvestri followed the path that the robbers had taken to leave the bank. From the loading dock area behind the Chatham Savings and Loan Bank, the robbers had driven to the six-foot-tall, black wrought-iron fence surrounding the bank parking lot. Using the armored car as a ram, they had broken through the fence, severely damaging the front end and rupturing the radiator. Spewing steam and leaking coolant, they had driven north through the alley to Seventy-fifth Street. A marked police car was parked in the alley and the truck crashed into it, knocking the officer assigned to Beat 622 unconscious.

The stolen vehicle then proceeded east from the alley behind Seventy-fifth and State to the 7400 block of Indiana Avenue. There the trail of leaking coolant stopped.

Cole and Blackie got out of the police car and examined the street.

"They had to have a truck parked here, boss," Blackie said, squatting down to examine the last drops of coolant visible on the pavement.

"Yeah, Blackie," Cole responded, "and it must have been a pretty big truck."

Cole looked around. This was a quiet residential neighborhood called Park Manor. When Cole was a rookie cop, he had lived a couple of blocks away in a one-bedroom apartment. The people who lived in Park Manor were home-owning solid citizens who took care of their property, voted in every election, and knew that the key to effective crime fighting was the establishment of a good police-community partnership. So the chief of detectives was certain that they would find witnesses who would be able to tell the police what had happened to the armored car. And witnesses would indeed come forward to give a description of the large moving van into which the coolant-leaking vehicle was driven. No license plate numbers were taken. However, this was only the first step in the investigation of the robbery of the Chatham Savings and Loan Bank.

A short time later Cole, Blackie, Manny, and Judy stood on the roof of the bank from which the sniper had commanded a devastating field of fire. The crime lab had finished collecting over one hundred shell casings from the Steyr-Mannlicher .223 Universal Assault Rifle, which the sniper had used to pin down over fifty of Chicago's finest for over thirty minutes.

There were six Special Weapons Unit teams on the Chicago Police Department. Five of them were assigned to each of the detective areas in the city, and one to the Thirty-fifth Street headquarters complex. Since the SWU teams were established in 1999, they had only been called out twice. This necessitated the officers assigned to this unit to have other jobs within the department. The majority of them were detectives. Cole and his personal staff made up the SWU team assigned to police headquarters.

The SWU teams had been established after a series of bank robberies on the West Coast, which had been perpetrated by groups of heavily armed men. Robbers who had the responding police units outgunned. This had never before happened in Chicago. That is, until today.

Cole, Blackie, Manny, and Judy had been trained by the FBI. They were qualified with a number of high-powered semiautomatic and automatic weapons. They had been less than ten minutes away from the Chatham Savings and Loan Bank. If they had received a timely notification, Cole's team could have responded to the scene and offered some degree of resistance to the heavily armed robbers. Perhaps they might have even foiled the effortless escape.

Now Cole and his staff would make a thorough investigation of what had occurred. Their primary objective would be to identify, arrest, and prosecute the perpetrators of this crime. However, they were also charged with examining the incident prior to conducting a debriefing for all SWU personnel. This debriefing would be aimed at ensuring that the next time something like this happened, the CPD would be prepared to respond more effectively.

When Judy Daniels reported for work that morning, she was wearing a dark blue pants suit and horn-rimmed glasses, and wore her hair hanging to her shoulders. When Cole's crew had been alerted to the situation at the Chatham Savings and Loan Bank she had dashed to the ladies' room and changed into a black military-style jumpsuit with multiple pockets and tied her hair back into a severe ponytail. As they piled into police cars for the ride to the scene, Manny had called her "Rambolina."

She was the best shot on Cole's team and was capable of hitting a target with a high-powered rifle at a distance of 750 yards. Now she examined the scene with an eye toward how they could have gone about dealing with the rooftop sniper, who had held the police at bay.

"The only place that we could have set up that would give us a view of this rooftop is that four-story building down on Seventy-ninth Street."

Blackie and Manny looked off into the distance at the structure she had mentioned. Manny said a disbelieving, "But that's got to be at least a thousand yards away, Judy."

"At least," the Mistress of Disguise/High Priestess of Mayhem repeated. "But there is no place else in the area where we would have had even the most remote chance of having a clear shot at anyone up here."

"The robbers really knew what they were doing," Blackie said.

Cole had remained silent since their arrival at the bank. Now they turned to look at him. It appeared that he hadn't heard a word they'd said.

"You okay, boss?" Blackie asked.

It took Cole a moment to respond. He glanced at the building down on Seventy-ninth Street. "Our bad guys selected this bank because it was easy to defend while they committed the robbery and made their getaway. They'll choose their next job with the same factors in mind. We need to anticipate their next move." Now he became more focused. "Go back to headquarters and compile a list of financial institutions which have similar vulnerability factors to the Chatham Savings and Loan Bank."

"Why do you think they'll go after another bank, boss?" Blackie asked.

Cole shrugged. "Just a guess, but they netted three hundred fifty thousand here, and that will give them confidence. They'll be looking for another big payday, and the only place they can make a score like that is from a bank."

"I can tie in to the Municipal Department of Buildings computer to begin the search, Chief," Manny said. "They'll have blueprints of every financial institution in the city and the buildings surrounding them, but it's going to take time."

"I understand that, Manny, but the sooner you get started, the quicker we'll have the data. I'll call to see how you're doing later."

"You're not coming back to headquarters?" Blackie said.

Cole shook his head. "Not right now. I'm going to take a ride over to the Museum of Natural History to talk to Dr. Silvernail."

"About what happened here?" Judy asked.

"No," Cole said. "I want to talk to him about Greg Ennis."

12

DECEMBER 7, 2004
4:45 P.M.

During his years as a Chicago police officer, Larry Cole had handled a lot of cases. More than once his personal life had collided violently with his professional one. However, never before had the man who had risen to the rank of chief of detectives of the second largest police department in the country ever become so obsessed with a case as he was with the investigation of the murder of mystery writer Greg Ennis.

In the past few days, Cole had read everything written by and about Greg Ennis that he could get his hands on. Some of the novels were actually ludicrous in the crude way that the author caricatured Mob guys, with them spewing expletives, killing indiscriminately, and engaging in excessive violence while adhering to a Boy Scout–like code of *Omertà*, or silence. However, that pattern was only discernible in the first five novels. The tone changed in the sixth through the eighth books, the latter of which Cole had obtained a galley of from Ennis's New York publisher.

The novel *Dark City* was scheduled for publication in February 2005. In the author's later works, wise guys were not portrayed as cheap hoods with oily hair and garish suits, but as more intelligent, infinitely more cunning, and extremely more dangerous. Then there were the remarkable similarities between Greg Ennis's fictional characters and real-life Mafia types whom Cole had come in contact with over the years.

Paul "the Rabbit" Arcadio, Antonio "Tuxedo Tony" DeLisa, and Victor Mattioli were all thinly disguised fictional characters in the author's last three published novels. But it was *The Death of the Don,* which Ennis had completed sixty pages of before his death, that contained the most chilling portrayal of a Mob boss.

The character of Roman Jacobi was Jake Romano. Ennis's fictional description of the mobster, his background biography and lifestyle, closely mirrored that of the current Chicago Mob boss. In the few pages that had been completed, the tale of the Roman Jacobi character was told. It began with his release from the Joliet State Penitentiary after serving a seven-year sentence for manslaughter, which Cole knew was exactly what had happened to Jake Romano. Upon Jacobi's return to Chicago, he had been accepted with open arms by the Mob and rose rapidly to the position of underboss. Jake Romano had risen quickly within the ranks of the Mattioli family. By page fifty of the manuscript, Ennis had established that a black street gang had begun muscling in on Mob rackets, which was exactly what had happened in the real world with the Black Gangster Disciples. In the novel the indecisive Mob boss had refused to retaliate against the black street gang, which had enraged the underbosses. Again fiction bore a close resemblance to reality. That concluded chapter five. Chapter six of *The Death of the Don* dealt with Roman Jacobi meeting a North Shore socialite named Alice La Fleur, a woman who bore a close resemblance to Alicia Holland Romano, the mobster's wife. It was with this episode in the life of fictional character Roman Jacobi that the manuscript ended.

Larry Cole turned the black Mercury off of Lake Shore Drive onto McFettridge Drive behind the Field Museum of Natural History. He found an "emergency vehicles only" spot, locked the car, and carried his burgundy attaché case with him as he entered the gray stone building. Cole had called ahead to alert Dr. Silvernail Smith that he was on the way. The historian promised to be waiting for Cole in his lower-level office.

Cole crossed the main rotunda. On this cold winter afternoon there were few visitors taking in the exhibits. A woman was seated on a stone bench adjacent to the Tyrannosaurus rex skeleton on display. There was a sketch pad open on her lap and she was sketching the immense fossil. A grim smile crossed the cop's face. He wondered how the woman would react if she ever saw this monster move. Cole had experienced this a few years ago when mad scientist Jonathan Gault attached powerful remote control devices to the skeletal frame and made the entire thing move with a terrifying ease—to attack Larry Cole.

The policeman continued on to the lower level of the museum. As he walked along, he found the galleries down here to be eerily quiet and absent of any human presence. Again Cole recalled the incident on that summer day when he had not only been chased by the dinosaur skeleton, but also attacked by a stuffed gorilla—again courtesy of Jonathan Gault's twisted genius—and forced to kill a live cobra. While in the museum during that incident, Cole had experienced a strange unease similar to what he was feeling now.

He remembered characterizing it at the time as the sensation someone would experience walking through a graveyard at midnight.
Later Silvernail had told him that the museum was haunted by a
legion of ghosts.

Pushing things that go bump in the night out of his mind, the
cop continued on to Dr. Silvernail's office. The door marked "private" was situated between two large glass cases displaying artifacts
from the Navajo Nation. The office entrance went unnoticed by
most museum visitors, and only the invited were ever permitted
entry. Cole saw the note thumbtacked to the frame. "Larry, I'll be
back in a jiff. Make yourself at home." It was signed "Dr. S."

Cole entered.

Silvernail Smith was a tall, slender man with the stamp of the Native American on his features. He wore his long silver hair in a
ponytail tied with a gold coiled snake clasp with emerald eyes.
Because his job called for him to work inside of dusty display cases,
he generally dressed in flannel shirts and denim trousers. His feet
were clad in hand-tooled moccásins and he seldom wore socks. He
walked with the graceful, silent strides of the North American plains
hunter of a bygone era. Now he was returning to his office with a
paper bag containing two cups of hot water for him and his guest.
The historian, who was also a naprapath, had developed a herbal
tea that he wanted Cole to try. During the years of their friendship,
Silvernail had advised the cop on matters of nutrition, which made
the chief of detectives look and feel twenty years younger than his
actual chronological age.

The historian was passing the lower level of the two-story,
centuries-old tomb of an Egyptian nobleman, which had originally
been constructed at the base of one of the great pyramids. The Field
Museum had purchased the tomb and had it shipped to Chicago. It
stretched from the lower level of the museum to the main rotunda
above and was one of the most impressive historical exhibits in the
world. Silvernail had worked within it many times and knew each
square inch of the interior. Now, as he walked past the lower-level

entrance, he felt an odd chill at the same time that he heard a strange noise coming from inside the tomb. He stopped.

To enhance the eerie effect, the tomb was dimly lighted and contained a labyrinthine maze of narrow corridors. Silvernail was unable to see inside the entrance, and despite his familiarity with the exhibit, he now felt as if he were in an alien environment. He shook off the odd feeling and forced himself to concentrate. Then the sound came again. It was a whisper.

"Silvernail, it is time."

The historian was schooled enough in the fields of magic and the occult to realize that what he was hearing was not a human voice. He reached out with his spirit to touch what was there, but was unable to make contact with the origin of the voice. For a magician as powerful as Dr. Silvernail Smith, this was unusual. Then it was gone.

He remained standing outside the tomb for a moment longer before remembering that Larry Cole was waiting for him. He continued on to his office. The eerie feeling and the strange voice he had heard were forgotten.

Silvernail's herbal tea was exceptionally good. Sweetened with a few drops of honey, it had a tangy aroma and taste.

"It will give you an energy boost if you drink it during the day," Silvernail said, "but I wouldn't suggest that you consume it before going to bed because you'll be up all night."

Cole smiled. "With my job I lose enough sleep as it is."

"So what can I do for you, Larry?"

While he had been waiting, Cole had once more examined the plethora of drawings and photos lining the walls of Silvernail's office. There were pictures of the historian that, if accurate, indicated that he had either been alive for at least two centuries or had relatives over five generations who bore a remarkable resemblance to him. Once Cole had asked him about this and Silvernail had deftly evaded providing a direct response. This created an aura of mystery about the multitalented historian, which he neither cultivated nor discouraged. The impression Silvernail gave Cole was that the historian simply wanted to be accepted for who and what he was.

It took Cole half an hour to narrate the details of the Ennis murder investigation, starting with the telephone call from Jamal Garth, to Blackie and Cole watching the author's body plummet to the ground outside the Metropolitan Bank Building, to what Cole had discovered about the burglary at the Metropolitan Bank.

"We know that a very sophisticated thief managed to bypass all of the bank alarm systems, break into the vault, and, despite there being a fortune present, apparently steal nothing. A homeless man was found dead in the alley beside the bank. The initial investigation listed him as having died of exposure. His body was taken to the morgue, but wasn't autopsied until I called the ME's office yesterday. That's when they discovered that he had sustained a broken neck."

Cole sighed and concluded with, "So I've got three felonies, two homicides and a burglary, which all occurred at the same location. There is nothing linking the crimes together, but somehow I've got a feeling that they are related."

Silvernail had been listening closely. Now he said, "You did say that the murdered writer had a safe-deposit box in the burglarized bank vault?"

"That's right. We had to get a court order to open it, but it was empty. I believe that is another part of the puzzle."

Silvernail closed his eyes. When he spoke, his voice was soft and sounded as if it came from a great distance. "The burglar breaks into the vault and either takes nothing or something which no one is aware is missing. Greg Ennis receives a death threat and is subsequently killed. The homeless man is found dead."

"That's about it," Cole said. "Then there were the two Mafia suspects we grabbed at the scene, who very conveniently end up dead as well."

"What are you looking for specifically, Larry?" The historian had not opened his eyes.

"A connection between the various elements in this case."

"I see." Silvernail began to sway slightly. "There is a woman involved in this. In fact, there are two. One of them used the writer to seek revenge. This woman is now very frightened in the light of what happened to Greg Ennis. The author did have something in his safety-deposit box. Something which was of great importance to him and the frightened woman. Something that led directly to his death. The other woman is a thief. She is . . ."

As Larry Cole looked on, Dr. Silvernail Smith opened his eyes wide, emitted a gasp, and passed out.

Field Museum of Natural History curator Nora Livingston rushed out of her office and down the stairs from the second level across the main rotunda. Before she reached the dinosaur skeleton exhibit, an ambulance crew was rolling a stretcher bearing the unconscious Silvernail Smith toward the south exit. Larry Cole walked rapidly beside this stretcher.

"What happened, Larry?" she questioned, as they swept past her.

Cole stopped to explain.

Nora Livingston, a pretty black woman dressed in a gray suit, frowned at the news that Silvernail had mysteriously passed out. During the years that the curator had known him, he had never shown the most remote signs of illness. In fact, despite the long hours that he often worked every day, he had never even shown any signs of fatigue.

"One minute we were discussing this case I'm working on and the next he just keeled over," Cole said.

The Chicago Fire Department ambulance attendants exited the rotunda with the stretcher.

"But Silvernail is never sick," she argued. "He has the constitution of an ox. Even that time a few years ago when we were trapped in here by Jonathan Gault and Silvernail injured his leg when he was forced to jump off the roof of the Egyptian tomb, he was back at work the next day and wasn't even limping."

Cole nodded. The chief of detectives was also aware that

Silvernail was not only quite durable, but virtually indestructible. Searching for some explanation that would explain what had occurred, Cole said, "Maybe it was the tea."

"The tea?" the curator questioned.

Cole was just about to explain that they had been drinking a new herbal tea before Silvernail collapsed when one of the attendants rushed back into the rotunda and frantically motioned to Cole.

The policeman and the curator ran over to him.

"He's gone," the attendant said, breathlessly.

"But he was unconscious," Cole said in a tone that bordered on the edge of anger.

Defensively the attendant responded, "And he had a weak, irregular pulse and extremely low blood pressure. But when we got him outside he came to, stood up, and just walked away."

"Show me which way he went," Cole demanded.

Once outside, they found the other blue-uniformed ambulance attendant staring off toward the western shore of Lake Michigan a block away. Snow fell heavily and visibility was very poor.

Cole looked down at the accumulating snow on the sidewalk and saw the prints left by the missing historian's moccasins. Yelling for Nora Livingston and the paramedics to wait for him, the cop trudged off into the heavy snowfall that was rapidly turning into a blizzard.

Gale-force winds were blowing off the lake, and after traveling only a short distance, Cole realized that he would be unable to find Silvernail Smith by himself. Returning to the ambulance parked behind the museum, he removed his portable radio from his coat pocket and summoned additional police assistance.

Standing at his side, a half-frozen curator asked, "Do you think he'll be alright, Larry?"

With falling snow accumulating in his hair, Cole said, "I hope so, Nora. I hope so."

13

The black Lincoln Town Car pulled off of Interstate 80 145 miles south of Chicago. Despite the heavily falling snow, the Lincoln made good progress because they were able to follow a salt-spreading snowplow for the last fifty miles of the journey. Jake Romano, seated in the backseat of the black car, had referred to the snowplow as "our personal escort provided by the good taxpaying suckers of the State of Illinois."

The two officially licensed bodyguards, who were always with Romano when he went out in public, were in the front seat. They did not respond to the mobster's remark.

Gilford was a farming community that had seen better days. The principle crop was corn, but extremely dry summers the past two years had caused a drought. The town managed to hang on, but just barely. Another summer like the last two and Gilford, Illinois, would become a ghost town.

Some vestiges of the drought were evident on the main street of this farming community with a population of 2,500. A number of businesses had failed, leaving vacant storefronts dotting the shopping district like tombstones in a cemetery. On this winter day there were few people out on the streets, and the Christmas decorations failed to brighten the dismal facade of the dying town. The few Gilford citizens who observed the out-of-place black luxury car cruise down the main drag didn't give it much thought. They figured that the driver had pulled off the highway to get gas and would soon be gone. If any of them had known that the Mafia had come to Gilford, they would have been dumbfounded.

At the edge of town was a building that had once housed a farm tractor dealership, which had moved to nearby Crystal City.

The building was now vacant and had been boarded up for the last six months. In November the property had been leased by a Chicago firm, but none of the locals had been able to find out what type of business would be moving in. Belying the myth of small-town nosiness, the citizens of Gilford took no interest in the potential new arrival, as they had too many problems of their own to deal with.

The Lincoln pulled up to the rear overhead door of the boarded-up building. The horn was sounded once. A side door opened and the head of a man appeared. He studied the Lincoln before vanishing back inside. A moment later the overhead door began to rise. The Lincoln drove inside and the door shut behind it. The area the car entered had been the tractor dealership's maintenance garage. The large room had been stripped of all equipment and furnishings. Only the bare cinder-block walls remained. There were two trucks parked on the stone floor. One was a tractor trailer, the other an armored car with a damaged front end, which was still leaking coolant.

Romano got out of the Lincoln and, flanked by his bodyguards, approached the armored car. Five men, the four who had robbed the Chatham Savings and Loan Bank and the driver of the tractor trailer, were standing outside the vehicle. The back door of the armored car stood open and the $350,000 in cash from the robbery was stacked neatly inside.

The mobster looked in at the money and smiled. "You have any problems getting here?" Romano asked of no one in particular.

The tractor trailer driver, who sported broad shoulders and a thick waist beneath a red-and-black checked flannel shirt, responded, "The roads are icing up pretty bad, so it took us a while to get here. Other than that, the entire opertion went off without a hitch."

"Good," the mobster said. "We'll take the money back to Chicago in the trunk of the Lincoln. You guys ditch the armored car outside of Gilford and head back to Chicago. Take a week off and go down to Miami, but keep a low profile. I want you back in town by the fifteenth. Leave the guns at the safe house. You're going to pull another job before Christmas."

As one, the five men nodded. Jake Romano had chosen them well for the series of robberies he planned to inflict on the Windy City. Each of them had a military background and was trained extensively in the use of high-powered automatic weapons. They were all "made" wise guys in the Chicago Outfit and would die before they violated their oath of *Omertà*. However, more than anything else, they were slavishly loyal to him and followed his orders to the letter.

Momentarily Romano remembered Joey Randall and Pete De-benedetto. They had made a mess of Greg Ennis's murder. Romano had known that Cole and Silvestri would eventually manage to put enough pressure on the hit men that they would give him up. This he couldn't permit, so the first job the men in the Gilford, Illinois, garage had done for him was the elimination of Randall and De-benedetto. Everything was neatly tied up in Big Jake's estimation. At least almost everything. He still had to find Vivian Mattioli, the daughter of Romano's predecessor, Victor Mattioli. She was the last link between Romano, the death of Mattioli, and Greg Ennis.

As he watched his bodyguards load the bundles of money into the trunk of his car, Jake Romano smiled. He was having a good week. A very good week indeed.

14

Paris, France
DECEMBER 8, 2004
8:00 A.M.

Ian Jellicoe had an estate in England which he had inherited from his father. The main house, stable, servants' quarters, and grounds were modest in comparison to some of the other properties in the area of the country where it was located. But since Ian had taken over, he had shown little interest in being a landowner and the Jellicoe estate north of London had deteriorated into a state of abject disrepair. Jellicoe seldom visited the property and would have sold it if he could find a buyer. As the buildings and grounds were unkempt, the prospects for a sale were slim.

So Ian Jellicoe lived in hotels. All of his possessions, which consisted largely of his tailor-made clothing, were shipped in trunks via air express to the next five-star hotel in which the Englishman would be staying. Now he resided at the Palais Royale Hilton in Paris.

Jellicoe always occupied suites and, if he was entertaining clients, had been known to lease entire floors. Such a lifestyle was expensive, but Ian Jellicoe could definitely afford it.

He had rejected a great many things about his British civil servant heritage, but there were some practices that he retained. Despite being a man with a great deal of leisure time on his hands, he rose every day at 7:00 A.M. no matter what world time zone he happened to be in. After a brisk five-mile walk, he would return to the hotel, shower, dress for the day, and be prepared for breakfast at exactly 9:00 A.M. In the luxury hotels in which Jellicoe resided around the world, he was well known and his needs carefully catered to.

When he emerged from the bedroom of his three-room suite at the Palais Royale Hilton, his breakfast, consisting of half a grapefruit, a three-minute egg, plain yogurt, white toast with peach marmalade, and black coffee, was waiting fo him. Jellicoe was clad in a navy blue single-breasted suit, white shirt, and burgundy tie. His black slip-ons were brilliantly shined and the only jewelry he wore was a solid gold Rolex Chronometer Oyster Perpetual strapped to his right wrist. Unfolding the white linen napkin and placing it on his lap, he began to slowly consume his breakfast, savoring each bite. As he ate, his mind worked.

Ian Jellicoe had returned to Paris to carry out the charge given to him by Bishop Martin Simon Pierre De Coutreaux of the Vatican. But he was looking at his situation, particularly as it applied to the problem of Julianna Saint, from a more holistic perspective. He needed the Devil's Shadow to remove a pint of blood from the historian in Chicago by whatever means necessary short of killing him. But in the process, after Jellicoe took delivery of the grisly proceeds of the act, he planned to eliminate not only Julianna Saint, but also her two henchmen—Christophe La Croix and Hubert Metayer.

Jellicoe finished his grapefruit, daintily dabbed his lips with the napkin, and began cracking the shell of his egg. Spooning the soft-boiled contents onto a slice of toast, he mentally examined the two methods at his disposal to rid himself of the meddling French-woman. These methods varied greatly in application, but were represented by two Americans: gangster Jake Romano and police officer Larry Cole.

The key to any plot that Jellicoe might hatch involving the Mafia boss would be guaranteeing that the Englishman would be personally protected from any possible backlash. His manipulations in such a matter would have to be delicate, but were not impossible. And having the beautiful thief and her wretched minions fall into the hands of a hostile criminal organization like Jake Romano's Mafia would be a fitting revenge for the indignity that the English-man had been subjected to on the British Airways flight.

Jellicoe finished his egg and toast, sipped coffee for a time, and then started on the yogurt.

The other alternative for dealing with the Devil's Shadow and Company was a great deal more civilized. Yet, despite his mask of breeding and cultured intelligence, Ian Jellicoe was still a vicious criminal. However, he forced himself to explore this option.

The name and reputation of Chicago police chief of detectives Larry Cole had grown to legendary proportions in the world of international crime. As a rookie plainclothes cop, Cole had burst onto the crime-fighting scene by engaging in two separate gun battles on the same day with members of the Chicago Mafia. When the cordite stench cleared, Cole didn't have a scratch and four Mob soldiers were dead. A few years later, Cole was a detective commander and put the late Mafia don Antonio DeLisa through enough changes that it shook the entire organized criminal structure of the United States. The cop hadn't only plagued the Mafia, but had also done damage to a pair of storied international criminals with whom Ian Jellicoe had more than a passing acquaintance.

Karl Steiger, a descendant of a long line of German military officers in the Prussian tradition, had accepted a contract to assassinate United States Senator Harvey Banks of Illinois. Steiger was considered the best at what he did in the world and was known within international crime circles as the Mastermind. And although Cole had been unable to thwart the assassination, Steiger had not made it out of Chicago alive.

Then there was the case of one of Jellicoe's mentors, Baron Alain Marcus Casimir von Rianocek of the German state of Bavaria. When Jellicoe was first starting out, he had been an employee of RanCorp, an international high-tech security firm founded by von Rianocek. However, the security angle was merely a front for an extortion and assassination-for-hire operation. The Englishman had not been on the violence end of the business, but started out as a researcher and quickly worked his way up to the position of event planner. Under Baron von Rianocek's tutelage, Jellicoe had learned to examine a proposed objective and put together a sound plan of action for its implementation. During his tenure with RanCorp, Ian Jellicoe had plotted kidnappings, arsons, the burglary of a Spanish museum, for which he had employed Julianna Saint for the first time, and even an occasional murder.

Then two years ago, Alain von Rianocek had taken a mysterious trip to the United States. The reason for this journey was never disclosed and the Bavarian baron never returned. The international assassin was killed inside the massive Sears Tower in Chicago by Larry Cole, assisted by his little band of cops. Nigel Armbruster, a fellow countryman of Jellicoe's and the executor of the von Rianocek estate, had dispatched Jellicoe to the United States to claim the baron from the Cook County medical examiner's office. On that occasion Jellicoe had been unable to retrieve the body until Larry

Cole and his perennial sidekick Blackie Silvestri arrived at the morgue to give the okay. Because of what Cole had done to his former employer, which put Jellicoe temporarily out of a job, the Englishman hated the American cop. A hatred that still smoldered with a hot fury within him. Yet Cole could indeed be utilized to dispose of the infamous Devil's Shadow. That is, if Jellicoe played this just right.

He finished his breakfast and rang for a steward to remove the tray. After the suite had been tidied, Jellicoe came to a decision on the exact means he would utilize to rid himself of Julianna Saint. But first things first.

Picking up the telephone in his sitting room, he called the thief's apartment.

"Allo."

The Englishman guessed accurately that this was Julianna's grubby-fingered butler.

"Ian Jellicoe here, my good man. I wonder if I could speak to the mistress of the house."

"Just a minute, sir."

While he waited, Jellicoe whistled "Hail Britannia."

15

Chicago, Illinois
DECEMBER 8, 2004
5:37 A.M.

Larry Cole was cold and dead tired when he arrived at his apartment overlooking Grant Park. It was not unusual for him to have been up all night; for his entire career he had been the type of cop who stayed on a case until it was solved, no matter how long it took. However, the case that had caused his lack of sleep had not been the hunt for a criminal, but instead the search for a missing friend. After walking away from the Chicago Fire Department ambulance, Dr. Silvernail Smith, in shirtsleeves and thin moccasins, was still missing. But that was only one of Cole's problems on this winter morning.

After summoning assistance from the First Police District, Cole had commanded a search for the missing historian. In his condition, which the chief of detectives could only describe as dazed and disoriented, it was not believed that Silvernail could have gone far. With a sergeant and six police officers at his disposal, Cole had directed a systematic search along the lakefront of Museum Park, Burnham Harbor, Meigs Field, Soldier Field, and as far south as McCormick Place. The results were negative. The few people who were out on such a wretched day, who consisted mostly of emergency city work crews, were interviewed, but no one had seen the missing man.

Cole extended the search grid down into the Chicago Historical District, north into the Loop, as far south as Cermak Road and up to the Chicago River. The First District shift changed and Cole obtained replacements for the officers who had been conducting the search. He was about to expand the search area once more, as well as put out an APB in case Silvernail had been taken to a hospital or picked up by a good Samaritan—at least Cole hoped that anyone who had picked up his friend was a good Samaritan—when Blackie Silvestri called him on the radio.

Cole was on his way back to the Field Museum, in case the curator had heard from the missing man, when Blackie requested his location. They arranged to meet behind the museum. Four inches of snow had fallen by the time they rendezvoused on McFettridge Drive, where the ambulance crew had lost Silvernail.

The lieutenant got out of the unmarked gray Ford he was driving and got in with the chief. Cole took one look at Blackie's face and could easily detect the strain.

"What's going on, Larry?" When they were alone, Blackie, who was Cole's best friend, was allowed to use the chief of detective's first name.

Cole explained about Silvernail having gone missing in the blizzard. Blackie listened attentively, and when Cole finished, the lieutenant exhaled a heavy sigh.

"What's wrong?" Cole demanded.

Blackie removed a twisted Parodi cigar from his inside pocket and stuck it in the corner of his mouth. He was trying to give up smoking completely, but he had been unable to break the habit of holding and chewing on the crooked black tobacco tubes.

"I got a call from the superintendent's office asking where you were. He wants to hold a press conference at six o'clock this evening and he wants you there."

"That's not a problem, Blackie," Cole said. "I'll go to the press briefing and then I'm coming back out here until we find Silvernail."

This did not ease the lieutenant's anxiety. "There's more going on at headquarters than just this press conference, Larry."

"Such as?" Cole said with a frown.

"Malcolm Towne is involved."

The upper command structure of the Chicago Police Department is based on a pyramid corporate model. At the top of the pyramid is the superintendent or CEO of the CPD. He is appointed by and serves at the pleasure of the mayor, with the approval of the majority of the fifty-member city council. The superintendent in turn is responsible for appointing his own personal staff of one hundred "exempt" members, who command the thirteen thousand sworn police officers of the second largest department in the country.

Larry Cole had been on the command staff of each Chicago police superintendent for the past sixteen years. For most of that time he had been in the detective division, occupying the post of chief of detectives since 1998. Only once had Cole ever aspired to the Windy City's top police job, but such ambition was short-lived. He had come to the decision a long time ago that the best job for

him in the department was the one he currently occupied. And he
had done his job with such brilliance that he had become a living
legend. However, some of his peers on the command staff envied
him to the point of hatred.

More than once Cole had survived attacks from corrupt politicians. Each of these he had defeated with seeming ease, which
had been carefully monitored by the high-ranking officers inside the
department who either had ambitions to replace Cole or saw him
as a threat they couldn't afford to ignore. But no one—including
the superintendents, who averaged three-year terms in office—
would dare make an overt move to replace the man many thought
to be the best chief of detectives of any major police department in
the last fifty years. However, if Cole did something to discredit
himself, that would be a different story.

The press briefing concerning the robbery of the Chatham Savings
and Loan Bank was held in the auditorium of the police headquarters complex. The news media had begun gathering thirty minutes
prior to the announced time. Cole and Silvestri made it back to
headquarters fifteen minutes before the briefing was scheduled to
begin.

On the way, Blackie had filled Cole in on the rumors pulsing
through the department grapevine. The chief of detectives had listened patiently, but had said nothing. Any negatives aimed at him
were undoubtedly coming from the allies of Malcolm Towne, the
current executive assistant to the superintendent.

Malcolm Towne had not come up through the ranks of the police department, but had instead been appointed by a previous may-
oral administration to be the director of the CPD's Office of Legal
Affairs. This office dealt with internal legal issues as they affected
the department in the areas of law enforcement and labor affairs.
Towne, a bland, overweight man with thinning hair and a perpetual
phony politician's smile, had attended law school in his native state
of Florida and still possessed a slight southern accent. He had re-

portedly worked briefly in the Dade County criminal prosecutor's office before moving north to Chicago.

Prior to being appointed to the CPD, Malcolm Towne had worked for a LaSalle Street law firm with City Hall connections. The southern attorney's legal area of expertise was a mystery, but apparently sufficient to secure his political appointment to the legal post within the police department. A short time later he'd had a run-in with Larry Cole over the placing of felony charges for aggravated sexual assault of a juvenile against one of Towne's former colleagues. Towne lost.

Now Towne accompanied the superintendent to the auditorium for the press conference. Cole was waiting for them outside the entrance. The superintendent graced his chief of detectives with an emotionless gaze. There was no mistaking the look of triumph on Malcolm Towne's face.

"We don't have much on the Chatham Savings and Loan robbery, boss," Cole began. "But I will be able to provide the press with the details of what we have so far."

Without a change of expression, the superintendent said stonily, "Deputy Towne will assist me with the briefing, Chief Cole. I think we have everything that your people have been able to come up with."

Towne added, "But if you have anything to add during the briefing, Cole, please feel free to jump in."

Now in his apartment at dawn the following day, Larry Cole shrugged out of his trench coat, tossed it on the couch, and collapsed into an easy chair. The sky over the lake was brightening rapidly on another gray winter day in the Windy City. A gray day that mirrored Cole's emotional state.

Yesterday's press briefing, conducted by the superintendent of police and executive assistant Malcolm Towne, had been not only vague, but also inconclusive. Towne had done most of the talking and, using stilted legalese, accomplished little more than reiterating the fact that the Chatham Savings and Loan Bank had been robbed by four heavily armed men. The executive assistant had been unable to answer any of the follow-up questions posed by the press, and when the superintendent failed to ask Cole to clarify any of the issues raised, the chief of detectives remained silent.

Then the real message behind the press conference became clear when the superintendent closed the briefing by reading from a prepared statement. "The incident that occurred earlier today on the South Side was not merely a simple robbery, but also a frontal assault on not only the police department but this entire city. As the chief executive officer of this law enforcement agency, I pledge that every sworn officer will do all within his power to bring these criminals to justice in an expeditious manner. And any member of this organization, regardless of rank, who fails to do his duty or who feels that he can rest on his laurels and give attention to more personal matters will no longer have a place in this administration. Thank you."

With that the superintendent left the auditorium with Malcolm Towne following close behind. When Towne passed Cole, he shot the chief of detectives a mocking glare.

Larry Cole was not the type of man who could be easily frightened by a veiled threat. Even a threat from the man who could end his career as the chief of detectives. Actually, the superintendent's statement had angered him. Cole had done all that he could under the circumstances by assigning his very competent staff of Blackie, Manny, and Judy to specific tasks in connection with the bank robbery. And if Cole's superiors had any problems with his work, it would have been infinitely more professional to personally confront him rather than make veiled threats at a public press conference.

There was nothing he could do about that now, but he did have a course of action to deal with the bank robbery. Larry Cole planned to find the stickup men and arrest them.

Back in his office, Cole had prepared a comprehensive report to the superintendent regarding the bank robbery. He had Blackie proofread the six-page document prior to having Manny deliver it to the superintendent's office. Cole made sure that Malcolm Towne received a copy. Then, with no other official duties facing him at headquarters, Cole had returned to the Field Museum of Natural History and the search for the missing Dr. Silvernail Smith.

Cole dozed off. He was asleep for ten minutes until his head dropped onto his chest and he snapped himself awake. He realized that he would have to get a few hours sleep or he wouldn't do himself or anyone else any good today. Dragging himself up, he made his way to the bedroom, pulling his clothes off along the way. After changing into pajamas and brushing his teeth, he got into bed. Before sleep took him, he went back over the last twelve hours.

They had still been unable to find any trace of Dr. Silvernail Smith. As the night wore on into the early hours of the morning, Cole had remained at the museum with curator Nora Livingston. The search for the historian had become a citywide lookout alert issued on the authority of the chief of detectives. But as time passed and they heard nothing, Cole and Nora began to fear the worst. Although he didn't say anything to her, Cole was afraid that the reason they couldn't find Silvernail, after such an exhaustive search, was that he was in the one place nearby where they had been unable to look. That place was Lake Michigan. And if he had gone into the icy water in the dead of winter, there was no way that he was still alive.

Finally, Cole had gone home after leaving instructions with Nora Livingston and Operations Command at police headquarters to contact him immediately if any word was received about the missing man. Now he succumbed to the exhaustion and slipped into a deep sleep. A deep sleep filled with vivid dreams.

Nora Livingston was asleep on the couch in her office in the administrative wing of the Field Museum of Natural History. The huge building was as silent as a tomb, but she slept fitfully. Then something awakened her with a start.

Sitting up, she looked around. She had left all the lights on and was able to see quite clearly that she was alone. Getting up and slipping her shoes on, she went into the outer office. Here the lights were also on and the room empty. But there was still something bothering her. Now she wished that Larry Cole had stayed.

Leaving the office, she went out onto the gallery overlooking the main rotunda. The silence was so absolute here that it was eerie. She felt a chill and wrapped her arms around herself. Then she heard a noise.

The curator stood stock-still and listened. A low humming sound was coming from the Native American exhibit hall a short distance away. Although she was terrified, this was her museum, and if something was wrong, she planned to find out. To take the edge off her fear, she returned to her office, went to the electrical and PA control panel, and switched on all of the museum's lights. Then she headed out.

This exhibit had been assembled artifact by artifact by Dr. Silvernail and was dominated by a twenty-foot-tall canvas wigwam at the center of the display chamber. Now the noise that the curator had heard sounded like chanting, and it was coming from inside the canvas structure.

The curator slowly approached the display, stepped under the restraining rope, and pulled back the tent flap. There, squatting on a ceremonial prayer rug with his eyes closed, was the missing Dr. Silvernail Smith.

16

Vivian Mattioli had been on the street since dawn. This time Romano's soldiers had almost caught her. She had been hiding in her deceased maternal uncle's cabin twenty miles north of Lansing, Michigan. Because the property was on her mother's side of the family, she didn't think they could find it. But she should have known better. *They* could find out anything about anyone in the world.

She had managed to escape because the only access road to the cabin was via a gravel road, which was a half mile long. They had come in a late-model, four-door Buick. She was able to see them long before they reached the cabin. This had given her enough time to pull on her parka, dash out the back door, and make it to her four-wheel-drive Jeep Eagle. She had taken off across the snow-covered countryside and they had been unable to pursue her. However, they had the Jeep's license plate number and would have the army of organized crime minions under their control looking for it and her. But she had learned a thing or two since Jake Romano had assassinated her father. Some of these things she had picked up on her own; the others Greg Ennis had taught her.

For most of her life Vivian Mattioli had been a shy wallflower. Since she was an only child, her father, Victor, and her mother, Frances, had spoiled her, but were unable to bring her out of her shell in public. When she was growing up, Vivian had preferred being alone in her room with her dolls or reading novels to playing outside with other children. In school she was an above-average student and could have shown genuine genius if she had managed to overcome her shyness.

A frail, pale woman with dark brown hair that she kept trimmed in a boyish-looking cut, Vivian had grown into adulthood without ever being kissed by a boy, making love, or even being alone with a member of the opposite sex other than her father. Because of Victor Mattioli's position, which she became aware of when she was ten years old, Vivian was required to attend various Mob social functions. Looking at it as more of a painful duty, comparable to a root canal or an appendage amputation, she had obediently accompanied her parents and done all that she could to blend in to the background so that few paid her any attention. Occasionally a young man would approach her, considering her a challenge, only to find that she spoke in a monosyllabic whisper, which few could hear or tolerate for very long.

After her mother's death she began to blossom. Perhaps it was because she had the responsibility of taking care of her father. She was now the woman of the house, charged with overseeing the cleaning, laundry, and preparation of meals. She gained weight, started wearing light makeup, and even began enjoying the attention she received when her father was appointed the head of the Chicago Mob. Then at a Christmas party given by Carmine Giordano, Vivian Mattioli met Greg Ennis.

When she first set eyes on the writer, she thought that he was a soldier on underboss Jake Romano's crew. Ennis looked and postured himself like the other wise guys at the party. Then she noticed that there was something different about him. He exuded more intelligence and polish than the others, with the exception of her father and Jake Romano. She had even gotten up the nerve to ask her father who Ennis was. When she discovered that he was a mystery writer instead of a Mafia soldier, she was thunderstruck.

During the years of her very lonely childhood and adolescence, she had been an avid reader. Often she had fantasized what it would be like to write a book about her life as a Mafia princess. But she had no idea where to begin. The fact that Greg Ennis was a real published author fascinated her.

That night at the Giordano Christmas party, Vivian Mattioli

shocked her father when she asked him to provide an introduction for her to the mystery writer.

After being introduced to him, Vivian didn't think a great deal of Greg Ennis. He had come to the party with some low-ranking members of the Romano crew. Most of them proceeded to get quite drunk, and the author was attempting to emulate their every action, including the swilling of booze. Ennis was hardly paying the shy, smitten young woman the slightest attention when Jake Romano came over, grabbed the writer roughly by the arm, and whispered angrily in his ear. Ennis went pale with fright, and when Romano let him go, he became a great deal more polite and attentive to Vivian. And although she was aware that it was because Victor Mattioli was her father, she didn't care. She found herself drawn to him and they spent the rest of the evening together.

A couple of days after Carmine Giordano's Christmas party, they went out to dinner. On New Year's Eve they became lovers.

Looking back, Vivian Mattioli realized that her life actually began the day she met Greg Ennis. She had never had a sexual relationship before, and the experience filled her with unbridled ecstasy. But sex was only a part of their relationship. Greg Ennis also became her friend. They could talk for hours and she found herself telling him things that she had never disclosed to another human being. But despite their closeness, Greg made Vivian keep their relationship a secret. His reason for doing this was that if it became known that he was dating the don's daughter, it would jeopardize his contacts within the Mob. Contacts that he depended upon for the information that he used to write his novels. Despite her wanting to shout her love for him from the rooftops, she respected him with the same devotion that her mother had given to her father for over thirty years. Then she came up with a plan.

Victor Mattioli was a loving father and had been a good, faithful husband to his dead wife. But he was very suspicious and fearful of his Mafia subordinates, which later proved to be justified. As such, he cultivated spies on each of the crews run by the underbosses, was constantly micromanaging by checking up on Mob operations that were under the direct control of the underbosses, and, finally, installed secret video and audio suveillance devices in his downtown office, his car, and his home. The only person who knew about these devices was Vivian. She had access to the records of every private conversation and meeting held at the top echelon of the Chicago Mob. Information that she decided to share with Greg Ennis.

After escaping from the Michigan farm, Vivian had driven back to Chicago. She was forced to abandon the Jeep, because *they* would be looking for it. Every Mob soldier in the city was out to get her, and she was known to the cops and a number of Chicagoans simply because her last name was Mattioli. She realized that she couldn't stay out on the street indefinitely. She had been forced to abandon her transportation and was running out of money. There were few places where she would find safety. In fact, there was only one person she could trust. She would go to him, an act that would place her life in his hands. But she was cold, tired, hungry, frightened, and had no choice.

She began making her way to the west end of the Chicago Loop where the Presidential Towers apartment complex was located.

Vivian Mattioli's sharing of her father's secret tapes with mystery writer Greg Ennis had as great an impact on his life as he'd had on hers. By this stage in their relationship, she had read everything that he had published, and one of the happiest times was when they spent an evening alone together. First they would have a quiet dinner, followed by making love. Then they would lie in bed, side by side, and he would read to her from the current novel he was working on.

Vivian had done a great deal of reading in her life. She considered Greg a good writer. Maybe not a great one and perhaps not even in the same league as his fellow Chicago mystery authors Barbara Zorin and Jamal Garth, but Greg was more than just adequate. And when he read to her, Vivian felt as if she was actually a part of the creative process. Then, after she began supplying him with confidential information about the internal workings of the Mattioli crime family, Greg's writing ability improved to the point of becoming nearly phenomenal.

It was as if a lightbulb had been switched on in the author's head. From the shallow, formulaic tales of the Mob Greg had written before, his novels became well-written crime fiction, which reviewers favorably compared to Mario Puzo's *The Godfather* and Lawrence Sanders's *The First Deadly Sin.* For the first time in his writing career, he made *The New York Times* best-seller list and was nominated for an Edgar, the award named for Edgar Allan Poe and bestowed by Mystery Writers of America. He became something of a celebrity and appeared on a few national talk shows. Despite his newfound fame and fortune, he remained faithful to Vivian, but their relationship continued in secret.

Then they decided to take a trip abroad. They would travel separately and meet someplace where they could spend a few days alone together. To make the ruse work, Greg Ennis, ever the master plotter, had Vivian tell her father that she was going to visit distant relatives in Italy. Greg would wait a few days and follow. He had rented a villa in Greece, where she would meet him after an abbreviated visit with her relatives. It was while they were gone that Jake Romano killed her father.

Jamal Garth and Angela DuBois were about to leave their apartment to go to Greg Ennis's funeral when the doorbell rang. The author went to the intercom.

"Yes."

"Mr. Garth?" a soft female voice came over the speaker.

"Who is this?"

"Vivian Mattioli. I need your help."

Angela DuBois looked as startled as the man she had lived with for the past twenty years.

"I don't know how I can be of help to you, Ms. Mattioli," Garth said. He had also been in the dark about the relationship between Ennis and the Mafia princess. All the black author knew about her was that her dead father was the former boss of the Chicago Mob. As far as Garth was concerned, she was bad news.

"Please, Mr. Garth," she pleaded, obviously on the verge of tears. "Greg told me that if anything ever happened to him and I was in trouble, I was to come to you."

Still Garth hesitated. Then Angela DuBois stepped over to the downstairs door-release button and pressed it.

"What are you doing?" he demanded.

"That woman is terrified and obviously in trouble," she responded, defiantly. "Many years ago you were in the exact same position and someone helped you."

Her comment hit home. Not only was she right, but she had been the one who had helped him.

Forty-five minutes later, Vivian Mattioli was seated on the couch in Garth's living room. Angela had fixed her a cup of coffee, which she occasionally sipped from as she finished the tale of her clandestine relationship with the late Greg Ennis.

"My father's death would have killed me if it hadn't been for Greg. We were in Greece when word reached us that Daddy was dead. I wanted to start back right away, but Greg convinced me to wait, because returning could be dangerous. When we did make it back to the States, Jake Romano had been installed as my father's replacement. But Greg knew that Romano had killed my father."

Garth and Angela exchanged questioning looks. "You mean that Romano had your father killed?" Garth said.

Vivian shook her head. "No," she said in a near whisper, "he did the deed himself. And Greg . . ." her voice trailed off and she came close to tears, which she managed to blink away ". . . had proof."

"What kind of proof?" Garth asked.

"It was our insurance policy against Romano. A few days ago,

Romano managed to steal it. Then he killed Greg and came after me."

"We need to let Larry Cole know about this," Garth said.

"No!" Vivian Mattioli leaped to her feet, her fear evident. "You might as well turn me over to Jake Romano if you call the police."

"But Cole is an honest cop, Vivian," Garth argued, "and if Greg told you anything about me, you should know that I have no love for the police."

She sank back down on the couch and cried softly, "Please don't. At least not yet."

Angela gently grasped Jamal's arm. "Maybe we need to give her some time to rest. Then you can talk to her again and see if you can convince her to go to Chief Cole."

Sighing, he said, "Okay, Angela. But I'd better go to the services for Greg. You stay here with her."

When he was gone, Angela sat down next to the distraught woman. "It will be alright, Vivian. This too will pass."

"I've lost Greg," she said in a voice she fought to bring under control. "I will never find another man like him again."

17

DECEMBER 18, 2004
12:45 P.M.

DeWitt Plaza was located on North Michigan Avenue not far from the John Hancock Center and the historical Old Water Tower monument, which had survived the devastating Great Chicago Fire of 1871. The fifty-story building was separated, the top forty floors devoted to residential living—twenty floors of which had been converted into a luxury hotel—and the remaining ten floors to commercial endeavors. The commercial floors were open to the public and consisted of businesses catering to the elite, super-rich types, who shopped on Michigan Avenue from the Chicago River up to Oak Street, an area known as the Magnificent Mile.

The plaza had once been the sole property of Neil and Margo DeWitt, a couple who rewrote the FBI profiles on serial killers. Now they were dead, having been killed in the act of attempting to murder innocent victims, one of whom was Butch Cole, Chief Larry Cole's son. Now, as one of the most valuable properties in the United States, DeWitt Plaza was managed by the law firm at Franklin Butler and Associates, which was a subdivision of the multinational DeWitt Corporation.

There were a number of businesses inside DeWitt Plaza. Most of them were high-yield financial operations, which, despite this age of credit card use, took in a great deal of cash every day. Cash that was deposited in the DeWitt National Bank on level six of the plaza's commercial area. The bank occupied the smallest square footage of any business in the plaza. It did not give out loans, issue credit cards, provide checking or savings accounts, or offer any other commercial banking services that similar institutions did. The DeWitt National Bank did convert secure financial instruments, such as checks and credit card cash advances, into currency. However, primarily the bank was a receiving station for the large amounts of cash taken in by not only the commercial businesses inside the plaza, but also the hotel. Seldom did shoppers enter the establishment. It was estimated that the DeWitt National Bank took in over a million dollars in cash a day. Cash that was not held overnight at DeWitt Plaza but was instead shipped by armored car to the First National Bank in the Loop.

Since the robbery of the Chatham Savings and Loan Bank, private security guards in marked vehicles, equipped with shotguns, were hired to escort the armored cars. This meant that the easiest time to rob the DeWitt National Bank was while the money was still in the bank.

*   *   *

This plan was a great deal different from the one utilized to steal $350,000 from the Chatham Savings and Loan Bank. This time there would be eight members of the robbery crew: six men and two women. They were broken down into four teams, with each armed robber being assigned a driver.

Two of the robbers registered as man and wife in the DeWitt Plaza Hotel on the evening of the seventeenth of December. A middle-aged couple, they made sure that they were noticed by hotel personnel when they checked in.

"Name's Clyde Garner," the man in the western-cut suit, cowboy boots, and beige Stetson said expansively. "Clyde Garner from Fort Worth, Texas. This here's my wife, Annie."

The heavily made-up woman with the blond beehive hairdo said with a heavy southern accent, "Howdy," to the young desk clerk.

"We came up here to Chicago from Texas to spend our second honeymoon in this fair city," Garner virtually shouted, making other guests present in the lobby turn to look at him.

His wife gave him a hug and drawled, "And me and Clyde are as much in love now as we were twenty-two years ago on the day we were married."

The bellboy who carried their suitcases and garment bags to their eighteenth-floor room remarked to himself that the luggage was extremely heavy. But a ten-dollar tip quickly made him forget the effort he expended. Once the room door was closed, the Garners dropped their congenial southern personas and became the hardened professional criminals that they actually were. Opening their suitcases revealed a pair of Bullpups with a hundred rounds of ammunition for each weapon and two walkie-talkies. Then they settled in for the night, doing everything that was necessary to keep up the facade of them being on a second honeymoon.

The others began arriving at DeWitt Plaza at noon the following day. A late-model silver Lexus pulled into the twelve-story parking garage. The driver was a thin black man with a shaved head. In the criminal underworld, he was touted as one of the best getaway-car drivers in the country. Once he had eluded eight Illinois State Police cars during a high-speed pursuit across three northern Illinois counties. Negotiating heavy traffic in downtown Chicago would be difficult if the cops did get on to him; however, the getaway driver had an advantage. He had no regard whatsoever for human life and no compunctions about driving onto a sidewalk and running down a few pedestrians. That would give the Dudley Do-Right cops chasing him second thoughts about continuing the pursuit.

The driver found a space on level nine of the parking garage and switched on his walkie-talkie.

"Car One to Asset One."

"Asset One," the man posing as Clyde Garner of Forth Worth, Texas, responded.

"I'm in place."

"Roger."

The Yellow Cab had been stolen, but the theft had not been reported to the police. The assigned driver, who was in hock to the Mob for a heavy juice loan, had been easily persuaded to leave the keys in the ignition and look the other way while the Mafia wheel man pilfered the taxi.

The wheel man had driven the tractor trailer containing the armored car taken from the Chatham Savings and Loan Bank. Although he was not in the same league as the black driver who was parked on the ninth level of the DeWitt Plaza parking garage, he was skilled enough to escape if he had to. But this operation was so well planned it was doubtful that he would have a problem.

The stolen cab driver's assignment was to cruise around the plaza until the woman posing as Annie Garner was ready to make her escape. Then he was to pick her up and drive to the rendezvous point. He raised the walkie-talkie lying on the seat beside him, activated the transmit button, and said, "Car Two."

"Asset Two," she replied.

"In place."

"Roger."

Activating the "occupied" light on the roof of his cab, the driver cruised north on Michigan Avenue and made a left turn onto Chestnut Street.

The Lincoln stretch limousine pulled up at the front entrance to the plaza and a uniformed chauffeur got out. He rushed around to open the rear door. A stunning woman of sixty, wearing a full-length ranch mink coat, got out and crossed the sidewalk to the building entrance.

Team Three, consisting of the driver designated Car Three and the armed robber designated as Asset Three, had arrived.

A delivery van for Metro Flowers of Illinois stopped in the loading zone at the south end of DeWitt Plaza. There were two men in the van. Both were clad in white coveralls with matching white ball caps. The passenger, carrying an oblong cardboard flower box, got out of the van and walked into the delivery entrance. Team Four had arrived. The bank robbery was proceeding as planned.

Besides the DeWitt National Bank, level six of the plaza was home to a number of businesses. There was a chain bookstore, a restaurant, a men's apparel store, a combination television/computer outlet, and a motorcycle dealership, which was right next door to the bank. As the four armed "assets" converged on their objective, two customers inside the motorcycle showroom were looking at a fire-engine red Honda SJ7 motorcycle. Larry Cole was about to purchase this vehicle for his seventeen-year-old son, Larry "Butch" Cole Jr.

"Now, you're sure your mother won't have a problem with this, Butch?"

The young man, who bore an uncanny resemblance to his father, replied, "I've already got a motor scooter in Detroit, Dad. This has a lot more horsepower, but I'm sure I can handle it."

Cole looked at the slick-looking bike a moment longer. He had never been interested in two-wheel motorized vehicles, but he realized that his son was an individual with his own tastes, desires, and needs. Butch was spending the Christmas holidays with his father and would return to Detroit in early January. Since his son had been in Chicago, Cole had pushed to the back of his mind the professional problems that had plagued him earlier in the month. He planned to enjoy the holidays and not worry about police work for a while.

"Okay, Butch," Cole said, "you can have it."

"Great!" The young man jumped into the air and then grabbed his father in a bear hug. "You're the greatest, Dad."

Cole was surprised at his son's strength. The young man was rock-hard with shoulder, arm, and chest muscles that bulged from beneath the knit shirt he wore. Then the cop happened to look up through the showroom window just as a man in a white jumpsuit and white ball cap walked past the entrance to the motorcycle dealership. Cole noticed that this man was carrying a flower box perpendicular to the floor. As the man disappeared from view, Cole became aware that his son was talking to him.

"I'm sorry, Butch, but I didn't hear what you said."

The man carrying the flower box in the odd manner was still on Cole's mind.

The four armed robbers reached the bank at precisely the same time. The two females—Annie Garner and the woman dressed in the full-length ranch mink coat—entered first, followed by Clyde Garner and the flower delivery guy. Once inside, they each had a specific objective.

Annie Garner went for the lone security guard, who was a young off-duty Chicago police officer. The woman was wearing a trench coat with the compact assault weapon concealed beneath it. When she approached him, he merely glanced up, expecting her to ask him a question. Before he came to the full realization of what was happening, she had placed the barrel of the Bullpup beneath his chin and removed the Glock 9-mm semiautomatic pistol from his holster. In less than thirty seconds, he was handcuffed with his own cuffs and completely immobilized.

The woman in the mink coat walked the length of the narrow bank lobby to the location where the security cameras were mounted on walls above the tellers' cages. She had carried her weapon beneath her coat in the same manner as Annie Garner. Now she displayed it and shot out each camera. Of the four weapons being used by the robbers, hers was the only one equipped with a silencer. This was because if a firefight did ensue in the cavernous, marble-lined plaza with its multistoried atrium, the horrendous noise made by the assault weapons would be terrifying to civilians and cops alike. The resulting confusion would make the robbers' escape easier.

The two men went for the tellers' cages. There were two clerks and a bank manager on duty. Before they knew what was happening, the robbers had them covered.

The woman in the mink coat with the silenced weapon headed for the vault, followed by Annie Garner, herding the handcuffed security guard in front of her. The money was wrapped in bundles by denominations and shoved into canvas bags, which were not to be locked until it was time for the money to be transported to the First National Bank. Forcing the guard to face the wall at the rear of the vault, the two women dumped the contents onto the floor and began transferring it into specially constructed pockets sewn into the linings of their coats. The transfer took ninety-two seconds and the haul was $1.3 million.

The men forced the tellers and the manager into the vault with the guard. They shut the inner vault door and secured it with a padlock they had brought with them. There would be enough air to sustain the captives until a rescue could be mounted. According to the plan, the "assets" would reach their "cars" and be long gone before anyone even became aware that the robbery had occurred.

The flower delivery man turned off the interior lights and they headed for the door. At that moment a young woman carrying a cash deposit bag from Burton's Toy Emporium on level four entered the bank.

*   *   *

Jake Romano was attending a Christmas benefit concert at the Chicago Cultural Center approximately a mile and a half south of DeWitt Plaza. His wife at the piano accompanied a string quartet with a medley of Christmas tunes. The Mob boss was seated in the front row of the audience. His ever-present bodyguards were standing in the back of the room keeping a watchful eye on their charge and those around him.

Romano had donated ten thousand dollars to the benefit to provide food baskets and toys for the needy during this "season of giving." As he listened to a soothing rendition of "Silent Night," a smile creased the corners of his mouth. He would be repaid many times over for his generosity this Christmas season. A recompense that would come courtesy of the DeWitt National Bank.

He glanced at his watch. By now his carefully conceived plan had been carried out and his "assets" would be making their escape with a cool million in cash. And, like the Chatham Savings and Loan Bank robbery, Romano expected the operation to go off without a hitch. However, this time Romano had not taken all of the possible variables into account.

One such variable was the clerk from Burton's Toy Emporium. The other was Chief of Detectives Larry Cole.

18

DECEMBER 18, 2004
1:00 P.M.

The clerk in the motorcycle dealership was processing Cole's bank debit card for the purchase of the red Honda SJ7.

"We have a test-drive area on the top level of the parking garage, if you'd like to take it for a spin," the young clerk was saying to Butch Cole.

"That would be great," Butch said, exuberantly. "You gonna try my new bike out, Dad?"

"I don't think so, Butch. I prefer four wheels to two. You go ahead and give it a spin. I'll wait down here."

The clerk unlocked the Honda and, with Butch's help, rolled it to a freight elevator that would whisk them to the twelfth-floor demonstration area. Cole waited until they began their ascent before he walked to the showroom entrance. He was about to step out onto the sixth-floor gallery when the man carrying the floral box walked past. Now he had a woman by the upper arm, who was obviously being forced to accompany him.

Cole exited the motorcycle dealership and looked up and down the gallery. Three people—a man wearing a beige Stetson and two women in long coats—were coming out of the DeWitt National Bank. Maintaining a casual air, Cole glanced through the plate-glass windows of the bank. There was no movement inside and the lights were out. As adrenaline flooded into his system, making his heart beat discernibly faster, he realized that a bank robbery had just gone down.

Forcing himself to maintain his relaxed scrutiny, Cole studied each of the robbers. It was obvious that they were all heavily armed, with weapons carried beneath their outer garments. The cop quickly ran the Chatham Savings and Loan Bank robbery through his mind. High-powered assault rifles with multiple-round magazines had been employed. It was easy enough to guess that these four were similarly armed. On this day, as he was off-duty, Cole carried a .38-caliber Smith & Wesson blue steel snub-nosed revolver. The only ammunition in his possession was the six rounds in the cylinder. He would be no match for the four heavily armed robbers. But he didn't plan to just let them go.

Larry Cole began implementing the plan to deal with the robbery while it was still being formulated in his mind. Pulling his combination portable telephone/radio from his pocket, Cole stepped back inside the motorcycle dealership showroom, switched to the citywide emergency frequency, and pressed the transmit button.

"Car Fifty, emergency," he said in a steady voice, which transmitted the proper degree of urgency and succeeded in clearing the frequency of cross traffic.

"Go ahead with your emergency, Car Fifty," the dispatcher responded.

The chief of detectives calmly announced to every on-duty Chicago police officer equipped with a radio that an armed robbery had just occurred at the bank on the sixth level of DeWitt Plaza on North Michigan Avenue. He provided a detailed description of the four suspected robbers and informed those listening that he suspected that each of them was armed with the same high-powered weaponry that had been employed at the earlier South Side bank robbery. He emphasized that the robbers should be considered "armed and extremely dangerous."

Now the cavalry had been summoned and were charging to the rescue. But Cole wasn't going to sit back and wait for them to arrive. Of course, it would be suicide to take the robbers on in a frontal assault by pulling his gun and shouting, "Police! Freeze!"

However, he could keep one of them under surveillance and, if he was lucky, manage to get the drop on him. Because there was the strong possibility that a hostage had been taken, Cole decided to go after the man carrying the flower box. Removing the revolver from its holster and placing it in his trench coat pocket, Cole followed the armed robber and the kidnapped clerk.

The man carrying the flower box, in which the compact assault rifle was concealed, had been the sniper who had climbed to the roof of the Chatham Savings and Loan Bank and kept the responding police units at bay. He was ruthless and psychotic. But his boss had given them strict instructions to avoid killing anyone unless it was absolutely necessary. The DeWitt National Bank vault was locked and he didn't have the time to unlock it and shove the clerk inside. So he decided to take her with him.

The others hadn't liked this decision, because it was not in Romano's plan. However, without an alternative course of action, they didn't argue. The clerk would be his problem, and those who knew the stickup man were aware that he didn't plan to just let her go. Before he was through with her, if she survived, she would wish for the rest of her life that she had never heard of DeWitt Plaza.

He had a firm grip on her arm as they traversed the sixth level and went to the west elevator bank. As they approached the elevators, there were three people already waiting. He tightened his hold and whispered, "Keep your mouth shut and don't make any funny moves or I'll kill you and them too. *Capisce?*"

"I understand," she said in a terrified voice. "But you promised to let me go when we get outside."

A cruel smile crossed his face. "Sure, doll. I promised."

The elevator came and they boarded along with the others. The doors were just about to close when a broad-shouldered black guy slipped inside. He quickly turned around to face the front of the car.

The robber wasn't concerned about him or any of the others. With the weapon he was carrying, he could take them out along with half the cops in this town.

The instant the elevator doors opened, the sound of sirens echoed through the winter air from outside as police cars rushed to the plaza. Elbowing the black guy and an elderly woman out of the way, the robber forced his hostage from the car. He snatched her brutally toward the exit where the phony delivery van was parked. Dropping any effort to conceal who and what he was, he yanked the Steyr-Mannlicher assault rifle from the flower box. Hefting the weapon, he forced the woman ahead of him out onto the street. The hordes of Christmas shoppers entering and leaving the plaza took one look at the wicked-looking weapon and scrambled out of the gunman's way.

A pair of marked police cars came screaming down the street toward the south exit. Their assignment was to seal off this area in an attempt to bottle up the robbers. The phony flower delivery van, its engine running, was parked a few feet from the exit. Now, forgetting his hostage, the gunman leveled the assault rifle on the approaching police cars, snarled, "Yeah! C'mon, assholes!" and opened fire.

The bullets tore into the cars, smashing windows and engine blocks and flattening tires. Of the four officers aboard the two police cruisers, three were wounded—one critically. The lead car jumped the curb and crashed into the wall of DeWitt Plaza. The other smashed into a lamppost.

Grinning at his violent handiwork, the gunman turned to locate his hostage when he spied the black guy who had been on the elevator. He was standing on the sidewalk a few feet away holding a snub-nosed revolver, which was pointed right at the gunman's head. There was no doubt that the black man was a cop.

"You can decide how we're going to do this, friend," the cop said. "The easy way or the hard way."

The gunman still held the smoking assault weapon in his hands. It took him only a second to come to a decision. He swung the weapon around through a ninety-degree arc to come to bear on the cop. And he almost made it.

Larry Cole fired one round from the Smith & Wesson .38 into the gunman's right temple. He was dead before he hit the ground.

The phony delivery van roared to life as the driver yanked it in gear in an attempt to escape. Cole took aim at the windshield and fired two rounds at the driver, whom he could only see as a silhouette behind the steering wheel. The windshield shattered into a glass spiderweb mosaic. The van spun out of control and crashed into the right rear quarter panel of the already damaged police car that had struck the lamppost.

Cole rushed over to the van and yanked open the door. The driver's white coveralls were stained red from the blood gushing from wounds in his chest. But he was alive, and the chief of detectives planned to keep him that way.

The woman in the ranch mink coat exited DeWitt Plaza onto Michigan Avenue and found her limousine driver spread-eagle against the hood of the Lincoln. Four police officers had him covered, and before she could do anything to help him, she found herself surrounded by six officers, all of whom had guns pointed at her. With an ironic smile, she dropped the rifle on the ground and raised her hands in surrender.

Annie Garner, carrying over a half million dollars in stolen cash tucked into the lining of her coat along with a compact assault rifle, exited the north doors of the plaza just as gunshots erupted on the opposite side of the building. Maintaining an icy calm, she crossed the sidewalk and looked up and down the street for her escape vehicle.

The Yellow Cab turned the corner off of Michigan Avenue and sped toward her. A fraction of a second later, three marked police cars raced down the street and skidded to a stop. Police officers bounded out of the cars and began sealing off the north entrance to DeWitt Plaza.

She managed to enter the taxi without being noticed by the cops, who possessed a description of her provided by Larry Cole.

"Something's gone wrong," she said. "Get us away from here, but don't rush. I don't want to get stopped."

"Yes, ma'am," the driver responded, dropping the flag and putting the cab in gear.

Clyde Garner reached the gray Lexus on level nine of the DeWitt Plaza parking garage less than five minutes after he'd left the bank. Jumping in beside the driver, he said, "Let's go."

"Everything okay?" the black wheel man asked as they began their descent.

"There was a slight problem at the end, but it should work itself out."

The wheel man handled the sleek car with ease as they wound their way down to level six. There they were forced to stop.

"What the hell?" the wheel man said, as he studied a barricade manned by two DeWitt Plaza uniformed security guards.

Clyde Garner slid the assault rifle from beneath his coat.

One of the guards walked over to the driver's window.

"What seems to be the problem, Officer?" the wheel man asked.

The middle-aged guard responded, "The DeWitt National Bank has just been robbed and the police have ordered all exits to the complex sealed. The robbers are still believed to be inside." Then the guard noticed the outfit that the Lexus's passenger was wearing. The guard was an ex-cop who had spent twenty-two years with the Milwaukee Police Department. The wanted message that they'd received concerning the bank robbers described two females and two males. One of the males was reportedly wearing western-styled clothing and a Stetson.

Stepping back from the car and reaching for his gun, the guard ordered, "Would you gentlemen please step out of the car?"

The bank robber extended the rifle across the driver's chest and opened fire, stitching the curious security guard with bullets. The other guard, who had no prior law enforcement experience and had never heard gunshots fired other than on the pistol range, was initially frozen into immobility. By the time he did come to the realization that his life was in danger, the bank robber had stepped out of the car, leveled the assault rifle, and fired a burst of ten rounds. The horrendous sound of gunshots echoed through the multistoried parking garage as the bullets knocked the security guard's body onto the hood of a parked car.

When the robber was back inside the car, the wheel man rammed the wooden barricade out of their path and continued their descent to the street. Using a key card, they got through the exit gate and drove onto the street on the north side of the plaza. The din of approaching sirens was deafening, but they negotiated the heavy traffic without incident.

The Lexus proceeded west to Rush Street, north to Oak Street, and then east back to Michigan Avenue. After a brief wait for a red light, the wheel man turned north on Lake Shore Drive, leaving the confusion at DeWitt Plaza behind.

"So far, so good," the armed robber said, as they passed the North Avenue exit.

"I wouldn't be too quick to count your chickens, my man," the driver said, glancing in the rearview mirror. "I think we're being followed by a kid on a red motorcycle."

Clyde Garner, still holding the automatic weapon, spun around in his seat to look out the back window. There, following the Lexus about five car lengths back, was Butch Cole on his new motorcycle.

19

DECEMBER 18, 2004
1:22 P.M.

The streets around DeWitt Plaza were completely gridlocked. The only traffic capable of moving was on foot, and even then, few of the spectators to the strange and violently exciting events were not going far until the legion of cops surrounding the building gave them some indication as to what had gone down inside. No news media crew had been able to get within half a mile of the prestigious North Michigan Avenue location before everything was shut down. A couple of the more enterprising camera crews from the local WGN superstation and the NBC affiliate in Chicago had abandoned their vehicles and proceeded on foot. The Minicam crews were forced to come to a complete halt before the plaza even came within sight.

The first member of Cole's crew to make it to the scene of the bank robbery was Manny Sherlock. He had been shopping with his wife, Lauren, in the Water Tower shopping mall, a short distance from DeWitt Plaza. Lauren Sherlock, a pretty woman with light brown hair and blue eyes, had been in the process of selecting a set of crystal goblets as a Christmas gift for Manny's aunt when the device attached to her husband's belt went off. She took it in stride, but Manny, thrilled to escape the shopping, grabbed the phone when it rang.

"I've got to go," he said, heading for the store's exit.

Returning the crystal goblets to the display, she hurried to catch up with him. "What happened?"

"Chief Cole just foiled a bank robbery down the street at DeWitt Plaza," he said, as they entered the crowded mall. "The perpetrators were heavily armed and used a similar MO to that of the robbery a couple of weeks ago at the Chatham Savings and Loan Bank."

She continued to keep pace with him all the way down to the main floor. Finally he stopped and turned to her. "Lauren, where are you going?"

"With you, Manny," she said with excitement. "I'm getting tired of you having all the fun."

"But . . ." However, she was already on her way through the revolving doors out onto Michigan Avenue.

With a shrug of resignation, he followed.

The Sherlocks made it through the traffic jam, the police barricades, and the security and perimeter checkpoints to the DeWitt National Bank. The last obstacle they encountered was a uniformed sergeant and a police officer stationed outside the sixth-level bank entrance. The sergeant was arguing with a young man wearing a Honda motorcycle jacket.

"I'm not going to tell you again, buddy," the sergeant railed. "Chief Cole is busy right now."

"But it's about his son and the motorcycle that Mr. Cole just purchased."

"Just take it easy and when things settle down, I'll tell him you're here," the sergeant said, his face flushing and sweat beginning to run in rivulets down into the tight collar of his uniform shirt.

Manny, with Lauren hanging close at his side, stepped forward, flashed his badge, and announced, "I work for Chief Cole. What was that you said about his son and a motorcycle?"

* * *

The bank personnel and the security guard had been rescued from the vault. Half of the money had been recovered and the police had captured four of the robbers, although one of them, who would later be identified as part of the robbery gang from the Chatham Savings and Loan Bank, was dead. Cole had talked directly to the superintendent on the phone, and the CEO of the CPD had dropped the frigid attitude he had assumed whenever he had been around the chief of detectives of late. The superintendent had actually been exuberant as he shouted, "Wrap things up there as soon as you can, Larry. This afternoon I'm going to hold a press conference that will make this department the toast of the international law enforcement community!"

After breaking the connection, Cole took a moment to stare at the small communications device. Once again he had gone from goat to hero within the seeming blink of an eye. Cole was about to return to the investigation when he paused for a moment. The policeman was experiencing a familiar "high," a result of adrenaline and knowing he'd done a good job. In fact, what he had managed to single-handedly carry off today was phenomenal by anyone's standards. So he would go to the press conference with the superintendent of police this afternoon and perhaps allow himself to gloat just a bit at the expense of Malcolm Towne.

Cole was about to return to the investigation when Manny, followed closely by Lauren Sherlock and the clerk from the motorcycle dealership, rushed across the bank lobby toward him. The chief took one look at Manny's face and knew that something was wrong.

Involuntarily Cole said out loud, "Butch."

Butch Cole had been enjoying the demonstration ride on the SJ7 motorcycle when he heard gunshots echoing up from the streets far below the twelfth level of the parking garage. The motorcycle clerk had displayed no reaction to the noise, possibly believing the sounds to be caused by truck backfires. However, Butch knew the difference, because he had been around guns all of his life.

Steering the motorcycle to the edge of the twelfth-level demo area, he dismounted, but was unable to see much of the street far below. Then there were more gunshots. Butch recognized instantly that these came from inside the parking garage only a few levels beneath them. Even the oblivious clerk began to display some degree of apprehension.

Butch, clad in his hooded black parka, walked back to his new bike. Officially, as the motorcycle was paid for, the Honda belonged to him. They had also filled out a temporary insurance form, which had been necessary before the younger Cole could test-drive the bike. The clerk had even sold them a visored helmet, which matched the red color of the motorcycle. All of this Butch took into account before getting back on the bike.

"I'm going to take a look downstairs and see what happened," he said to the clerk. "I want you to move that barricade." He pointed to the yellow wooden sawhorse blocking egress from the demo area onto a ramp leading to the lower floors.

The clerk hesitated. "Are you some kind of cop?"

"Just move the barricade," Butch said in a commanding tone.

After another brief hesitation, the clerk went to do as he was told. He rationalized that the sale had been made, and after all, "the customer is always right."

Pulling the visor on his helmet down, Butch roared out of the demonstration area onto the descending ramp.

Butch Cole reached the sixth level of the parking garage to find the bodies of the two DeWitt Plaza security guards. He could hear the squealing tires of a rapidly moving vehicle some two levels below him. Without hesitation, the young man steered around the bodies and smashed a barricade to continue down the ramp.

Larry Cole Jr. had been in dangerous, life-threatening situations before. When he was a child, Margo DeWitt—the serial killer who had owned the North Michigan Avenue building that he was in right now—had kidnapped him with the intention of murdering him and then dismembering his corpse. Just that previous summer, while he was visiting his father, a gangster named Jack Carlisle had held him at gunpoint, intending to kill him as well. Each time the young man had indeed been frightened, but then there had also been another emotion present. That emotion was anger.

In his seventeen years of life, Butch had observed his father closely and come to the realization that they were very alike in temperament, appearance, and intellect. They both had an overwhelming desire to see that justice was done. Now the young man was descending through the DeWitt Plaza parking garage in pursuit of justice. He was not necessarily being foolhardy in this endeavor and realized that he couldn't stop whoever had killed the guards. But he could keep them under surveillance until he spotted a police car. This strategy was remarkably similar to the one his father had used only moments before to spoil the bank robbery.

He caught sight of the silver Lexus as it descended to level two. Butch slowed his speed to remain out of sight. When the driver used a key card to exit the garage, Butch was at the top of the first-level ramp. Before the wooden gate could return to the lowered position, he gunned the motorcycle down the ramp and barely managed to slip beneath it. Once out on the street, he began following the silver car at a discreet distance.

Now they sped north on Lake Shore Drive approaching Fullerton Avenue. Butch had changed lanes on the four-lane thoroughfare three times and attempted to keep larger vehicles between him and the Lexus. So far Butch thought he had been successful, but as they passed Belmont, the traffic thinned, leaving the motorcyclist exposed. He dropped back to five car lengths, but suddenly it was as if the Lexus and the Honda were the only two vehicles traveling on the Drive.

Butch was just about to abandon the pursuit when the sunroof of the silver car opened and a man wearing a western suit climbed up out of the vehicle. As the young man looked on in horror, the cowboy aimed a rifle at him and opened fire.

20

Lake Shore Drive was backed up from Chicago Avenue in both directions and there was no way that a vehicle of any type, emergency or otherwise, could enter the downtown area. Lieutenant Blackie Silvestri and Sergeant Judy Daniels had rushed from police headquarters and raced north to DeWitt Plaza. Now, with Judy behind the wheel of the unmarked burgundy police car, they were stuck in a traffic jam.

The lieutenant drummed his fingers nervously on the dashboard. "We can't just sit here. We've got to get over to Michigan Avenue."

The Mistress of Disguise/High Priestess of Mayhem was wearing her hausfrau disguise, which consisted of a flower-print dress, thick-soled brogan shoes with argyle socks, a red wig tied into two long braids that hung to her shoulders, and a smattering of freckles across her nose. In response to Blackie's statement, she said, "The only way we're going to get to DeWitt Plaza in this mess is to fly or walk."

Blackie fumed for a moment before saying, "Go north."

Staring at the unmoving traffic, she said a dismayed, "How?"

"Head up to the North Avenue exit, Judy. We'll try to get to the plaza from the opposite direction." With that he reached beneath the dashboard and flipped the switches to activate the police car's emergency alternating headlights and electronic siren. The noise was nearly deafening, but it did succeed in parting the wall of traffic and allowing the police car to squeeze through. Once they were north of Chicago Avenue, the traffic thinned and they were able to make rapid progress. Judy cut the siren and lights.

The police radio had been alive with cross traffic since the shootout at DeWitt Plaza. Now a message came across the air about a red motorcycle that shocked the two veteran detectives.

Blackie glared at his radio and said, "What in the hell is Butch doing on a motorcycle?"

"Didn't they say that the bike is a red Honda?" Judy asked.

"Yeah. And he's wearing a red helmet."

"There's a red motorcycle up ahead."

"Let's check it out."

She accelerated after the motorcycle and was closing the distance between them when the man standing in the Lexus's sunroof opened fire. The volley of bullets bounced off the asphalt and struck the concrete guardrail at the center of Lake Shore Drive, but did not strike the motorcycle or the rider.

"You've got to catch that car, Judy," Blackie shouted.

She floored the accelerator and the police cruiser leaped forward. Blackie pulled a .357-magnum Colt Python revolver from its holster beneath his coat and rolled the window down. He took aim at the Lexus.

North Lake Shore Drive curves sharply at Belmont. As the getaway car driver negotiated the roadway, the gunman lost his balance and nearly fell back inside the car.

"Keep this thing steady, dammit!" the gunman shouted.

"Just blast that kid on the motorcycle!" the driver yelled back.

The gunman braced himself and looked through the telescopic sight. He was about to squeeze off another burst at the motorcycle when Blackie opened fire from the approaching police car. Of the four bullets fired from the .357 magnum, only one hit the gunman. But it struck him in the chest, tearing through the rib cage, puncturing the left lung, and destroying his heart. He dropped back inside the car, still clutching the rifle. As his body spasmed in death, the gunman's finger tightened on the trigger, causing the weapon to continuously discharge. The remaining twelve rounds in the thirty-round clip were fired inside the car. Most of them tore into the driver and ricocheted around to knock out all of the windows. A red cloud escaped into the air as the Lexus jumped the curb, rolled across the parkway grass north of Montrose, and slammed head-on into a tree.

Butch had hit the brakes and dropped back when the first burst of rounds was fired from the Lexus. However, he wasn't about to abandon the pursuit. When the man in the western suit appeared in the sunroof a second time and began taking aim at him, the younger Cole was about to steer the motorcycle off of Lake Shore Drive into the park. There he could take cover behind the trees lining the lakefront. He wasn't even aware that Blackie and Judy were behind him until the gunman inside the Lexus was shot.

As the luxury car careened off the Drive into the park, Butch slowed the motorcycle. He came to a halt on a rise overlooking the spot where the destroyed vehicle had come to rest. A moment later Blackie and Judy rushed over to him. Removing his helmet, the young man grinned and said, "I guess we got them."

The lieutenant and the Mistress of Disguise/High Priestess of Mayhem were speechless.

21

DECEMBER 18, 2004
2:00 P.M.

Jake Romano and his wife, Alicia, posed for photographs with the mayor of Chicago in the immense, ornate rotunda of the cultural center. The bodyguards of the two men—one the elected leader of a major American city and the other a United States crime lord—mingled a short distance away, staunchly ignoring each other, but keeping a close eye on the men they were employed to protect. The Chicago Chamber of Commerce Annual Christmas Benefit Reception and Concert concluded amicably, and by the time Jake and

Alicia Romano stepped out onto Randolph Street west of Michigan Avenue, the black Lincoln Town Car was waiting.

"Begging your pardon, Mr. Romano," the bodyguard riding shotgun in the front seat said, "there's been a robbery at DeWitt Plaza and the cops have got North Michigan Avenue and Lake Shore Drive all screwed up."

The other bodyguard was driving and added, "I was thinking of going over to the Kennedy Expressway and trying to get back to the brownstone from there."

"Oh, Jake," Alicia said, "I'm hosting the Ladies' Poetry Reading Circle today. We're scheduled to meet at three."

"Don't worry, dear," Romano said. "If the traffic is bad for us, it will be equally disastrous for your poetry-reading group." He squeezed her hand. "We'll make it in time."

Alicia clutched her husband's arm and kissed him on the cheek. "That's one of the things I love about you, Jake. You're always so confident."

He smiled, because Alicia Holland Romano was absolutely right. As they rode down Randolph, Romano said to the bodyguards, "Turn the news on, boys. I want to know what happened at DeWitt Plaza."

By the time they got through the heavy traffic north of DeWitt Plaza, Alicia had ten minutes to go before her scheduled poetry-reading circle and none of her guests had arrived. After escorting his wife inside, Romano remained at the front door, flanked by his bodyguards. "I've got to go back out for a while, dear. I should be home in time for dinner."

The pretty socialite frowned. "Jake, you know how much the ladies in the poetry circle enjoy your sitting in on our readings. They will be terribly disappointed."

"Please make my apologies to them, but duty calls."

She came over to kiss him, but when she got closer, she frowned. "Are you feeling okay, honey? You look pale."

"Probably a combination of that rich eggnog and those hot chicken wings I had at the reception. I'll be fine."

But eggnog and spicy chicken wings had nothing to do with the physical and emotional state of cultured Mob boss Jake Romano.

The news broadcasts did not have all of the facts concerning what had occurred at DeWitt Plaza, but they had told Romano enough. Of the eight people—broken down into four two-person teams—he had dispatched to rob the DeWitt National Bank, three were in custody and three were dead. The Mob boss's carefully conceived plan had turned into a disaster. Especially since three of the robbers had been taken alive.

Of all the bosses in the history of the Chicago Mob, dating back to Big Jim Colisimo—the predecessor of Al Capone—Jake Romano had the highest IQ and was the best educated. Under the alias of John Roman, he had obtained a masters degree in business administration from the University of Chicago. Romano was still in the habit of reading four to six books a week and scanned all of the Chicago daily newspapers and *The Wall Street Journal* from cover to cover every day. Had he chosen a legitimate line of work, he would have been successful. As the head of a criminal organization, he was extraordinarily cunning.

Romano had plotted the bank robberies with meticulous precision. He'd dispatched members of his organization to conduct highly detailed research for him, and utilizing the personal computer in his study, Romano had put the plots together.

The Chatham Savings and Loan Bank had been a work of art; the DeWitt National Bank had turned into an amateurish debacle. And the media had provided Romano with enough information so that he knew what had happened to his brilliant criminal strategy. Chief of Detectives Larry Cole had interfered.

The rendezvous location following the robbery of the DeWitt National Bank had been carefully selected by Romano, because it was literally the last place that the cops would expect the robbers to meet. Of course, that was before Larry Cole had broadcast a description of the criminals.

The McDonald's fast-food, drive-thru restaurant was located on Fifty-first Street at Wentworth Avenue on the South Side of the city. The Yellow Cab designated as "Car Two" pulled into the drive-thru lane. The female passenger was in the backseat. When their turn came, the burly driver ordered two cups of black coffee. Then he drove to a remote corner of the parking lot and positioned the taxi so that it was facing south. He handed a cup of coffee to his passenger before producing a half-pint bottle of bourbon from the glove compartment. After pouring a shot into his own cup, he passed the bottle to the woman. Taking it, she poured a generous portion into her coffee. Then they settled in to wait in silence.

The location of this clandestine meeting could be considered from two very contradictory points of view. On one hand, it could be an act of pure genius; on the other hand, it could be insanely foolhardy. That was because the McDonald's restaurant where Car Two and Asset Two were waiting for Jake Romano to arrive was right across the street from the Area One Police Center, which was one of the largest, most heavily staffed Chicago Police Department facilities in the city. As the pair in the stolen Yellow Cab looked on, a steady stream of officers entered and exited the police station. None of the cops paid any attention to the parked taxicab.

Jake Romano's Lincoln Town Car pulled into the fast-food restaurant parking lot a few minutes later.

The luxury car was parked facing west thirty feet from the taxi. The occupants of the Lincoln remained inside. After a moment, the taxi driver exited the Yellow Cab and crossed to the Lincoln. He opened the back door and got in next to Romano.

"We managed to get away before they sealed the building," the big man said. "She's got half the money from the haul in the lining of her coat."

Romano simply nodded at this information. He was silent for a time before saying, "Cole was somewhere inside the plaza and broadcast a description of each of our people, including her."

The big man responded, "So I understand."

The Mob boss looked through the windows of his car over at the stolen taxi. The silhouette of the woman, seated in the backseat drinking spiked coffee, was visible.

"Are you packing?" Jake asked the driver.

He patted his right side. "Forty-four Colt Auto Mag."

"It's unfortunate that she was seen. Go back over there and get my money. We'll leave the cab here. You will come with us."

"As you wish, Don Romano," the taxi driver said formally before getting out.

There had been no need for Romano to go into detail concerning what he wanted done. Less than two minutes later the taxi driver returned to the Lincoln carrying the coat of the woman who had been known as Annie Garner of Fort Worth, Texas. Inside the lining of this coat was over a half million dollars in cash and a .223-caliber Steyr-Mannlicher assault rifle.

Slowly the Lincoln pulled from the McDonald's restaurant parking lot at Fifty-first and Wentworth. No one, not the fast-food restaurant patrons nor the legion of cops entering and leaving the police facility across the street, noticed the black car at all. The body of the dead woman in the stolen cab was not discovered until eighteen hours later.

22

DECEMBER 24, 2004
8:32 A.M.

Chief of Detectives Larry Cole conducted a debriefing for the senior command staff in the vendeteria of the Timothy J. O'Connor Training Academy at 1300 West Jackson Boulevard in the shadow of the Sears Tower. The police academy was a campus devoted primarily to the mental and physical education of recruits and preservice detectives, sergeants, lieutenants, and captains. Once a month the police superintendent held his command staff meeting in the automated cafeteria of the training facility. The meeting for December had already been held, but the superintendent had deemed a second meeting necessary. This was due to the sophisticated bank robberies that had recently taken place in the Windy City.

Every member of the command staff, the majority of whom were in uniform as their assignments required, was present. Grudgingly a subdued Malcolm Towne, on the orders of the superintendent, rose to introduce Cole.

"Could I have your attention, please?" he drawled. "This morning we are going to have detailed analyses of the robberies of the Chatham Savings and Loan Bank, which occurred on December seventh and the DeWitt National Bank, which was committed on December eighteenth. This presentation will be given by Chief Cole of the Detective Division." Towne barely concealed a grimace as he said, "Chief Cole, you have the floor."

Cole, clad in a black camel-hair blazer and gray houndstooth slacks, rose from his seat and walked to the podium at the front of the room. He nodded to Manny Sherlock, who would operate a slide projector set up in the center aisle. A white screen on a tripod was next to the podium to receive the images from the projector. Judy Daniels and Blackie Silvestri were also present, and all of them had been working around the clock with Cole to prepare for this morning's presentation. Manny turned the projector on and a diagram of the Chatham Savings and Loan Bank and the surrounding area appeared on the screen.

Cole began, "On December seventh at fourteen hundred hours, four armed men entered the Chatham Savings and Loan Bank."

While the chief of detectives ran through the events of that first robbery, Blackie and Judy handed out folders containing all of the information that had been compiled concerning the robbery investigations. There were detailed diagrams; biographies of the known career criminals involved, who were either dead or in custody; photos and schematic drawings of the weapons the robbers had used; and a written summary of each incident.

Larry Cole took the audience through the Chatham Savings and Loan Bank episode. He mentioned, but did not dwell on, the confusion that ensued among the responding police units after they had come under fire. That was when Malcolm Towne interrupted the presentation.

"There's a couple of things I don't understand here, Chief Cole," the executive assistant said, deepening his southern accent. He stood up and pointed to the diagram of the Chatham Savings and Loan Bank. The area surrounding the bank, from Seventy-fifth Street on the north, Eightieth Street on the south, Michigan Avenue on the east, and Perry Street on the west, was displayed. Each of the structures where relevant incidents occurred in connection with the robberies was accurately drawn to scale.

"May I?" Towne asked, as he stepped in front of the white screen.

"Feel free," Cole said with a patient smile.

Approaching the diagram, Towne adopted his courtroom prosecutorial manner. "Correct me if I am in error, Chief Cole, but after the sniper opened fire on the responding police cars, all of the units retreated to one of three locations?" Towne indicated the body and fender repair shop on State Street, a Shell gas station on Seventy-ninth Street, and a convenience store on the opposite side of the Dan Ryan Expressway in the 7900 block of South Wentworth.

"That is correct," Cole responded.

Malcolm Towne paused a moment to glance in the direction of the assistant deputy superintendent and the Sixth District commander, who were both seated in the audience. They had been the highest-ranking police officers on the scene of the first robbery. "Now, each of these locations placed the responding officers out of visual contact with the bank."

Cole could see where the civilian executive assistant was going with this line of inquiry, but he didn't respond.

Towne's voice rose. "And there was not one single, solitary attempt by the police to assault the held position."

Some of those present were aware that Malcolm Towne had spent some time in the Florida National Guard, where he had attained the rank of major. Periodically the executive assistant used terms that were inappropriate for American law enforcement operations, such as "assaulting positions," "laying down suppressing fire," and "taking acceptable casualties."

"We have to give the robbers some degree of credit, Mr. Towne," Cole said, calmly. "The selection of the Chatham Savings and Loan Bank was carefully done by whoever put this plan together. They had the high ground and possessed superior weaponry, which they utilized with devastating results. We should consider ourselves lucky that none of our officers were killed or seriously wounded."

"That is unacceptable in my opinion, Chief Cole," Towne countered. "The perimeter was porous, which allowed the robbers to escape with the proceeds in an armored car with little or no difficulty. Then there was not one round fired by the police in response to the rooftop sniper firing over one hundred bullets in a densely populated area of this city."

Cole, maintaining his composure, was about to respond to the executive assistant's allegations when the superintendent intervened. In a quiet voice he said, "Where would you have returned the sniper's fire from, Mr. Towne?"

The executive assistant, aware of the superintendent's disapproving tone, hesitated momentarily. But then Towne had not been appointed to his post by this man, and sincerely believed that he couldn't be removed from that position by him either. Malcolm Towne was also very arrogant, and possessed a certain disdain for police officers, whom he considered to be menials. However, he had a definite dislike for one particular Chicago police officer. That officer was currently the chief of detectives and his name was Larry Cole.

"It should be quite obvious where the most defensible position is," Towne said, in response to the superintendent's question. "The roof of this building on Seventy-ninth Street provides a number of logistical advantages. It would provide the police with—"

The superintendent stopped him. "Chief Cole, how far is that building from the bank?"

"Approximately one thousand yards, sir."

"What caliber weapons were the officers responding to the robbery carrying?"

"Mostly nine-millimeter pistols, but there were a few .45s and .357 magnums," Cole answered.

"I see," the superintendent said. "Could you give us the approximate range of those weapons?"

The chief of detectives considered the question for a moment. Finally he responded. "In the hands of an expert marksman, a nine-millimeter pistol is probably accurate up to seventy-five yards. A .45 or .357 magnum would have a greater range of, say, from seventy-five up to one hundred yards maximum."

"That's nonsense," Towne railed. "A simple .22-caliber round has been known to travel over a mile."

Now the superintendent's face contracted in anger. He glared at Malcolm Towne. "Are you aware that officers on this department are prohibited from firing at a target that they cannot hit accurately? We don't take wild shots, Mr. Towne. That's a good way to get an innocent bystander killed."

But the executive assistant had another card to play. "The rooftop of that building is not the only place where the police could have returned the sniper's fire. What about the home of that woman who called the Office of Emergency Communications about the sniper being on the roof of the bank?"

Cole could see what was coming now, but remained silent.

There was an uneasy stirring within the ranks of the command staff. The superintendent's scowl deepened. Towne forged ahead.

"This Mrs. Letitia Warren lives here on Wabash." Towne pointed to the location of her house on the projected diagram. "How far is that from the bank, Chief Cole?"

"Between seventy-five and one hundred yards," Cole responded.

"That's it," Towne said, triumphantly.

"That's what?" the superintendent asked.

Malcolm Towne had a look of triumph on his face. "I think it would be fairly simple. The responding officers should have commandeered that woman's house, found the best marksman at the scene, and had him blow that sniper's head off."

A deafening silence fell over the police academy vendeteria.

The superintendent cleared his throat and leaned forward to place his elbows on his knees. "Mr. Towne, we have no right to 'commandeer,' as you term it, that woman's home. In fact, under any circumstances, I would discourage our officers from entering a citizen's house in a densely populated residential area and firing shots at a heavily armed assailant. An ensuing gun battle could result in not only innocent bystanders being killed, but also a number of our officers."

With a condescending snort, Towne shook his head. "Begging the superintendent's pardon, but we had a sniper on the roof of a bank with a high-powered rifle, who had initiated a state of war on our streets. The police cannot conduct themselves according to an antiquated law enforcement officers' code of conduct, but must—"

The first time it was uttered too softly for Towne to hear, although Cole picked it up. The second time, the superintendent virtually shouted, "Sit down and be quiet, Mr. Towne!"

The executive assistant stopped in midsentence with his mouth open. When the impact of his situation dawned on him, he flushed crimson, lowered his head, and returned to his seat. He didn't make another comment.

Regaining his composure, the superintendent said, "You may continue, Chief Cole."

Before resuming his presentation, the chief of detectives glanced around the room and noticed that a number of the command officers present were unable to conceal their looks of satisfaction after the pompous lawyer had finally been put in his place.

"The incident at the DeWitt National Bank on December eighteenth at thirteen hundred hours had a much different outcome than was the case at Chatham Savings and Loan," Cole said, motioning for Manny to switch the slides.

"Did you see the look on Towne's face?" Blackie howled, as they rode back to police headquarters in Cole's car.

Judy, who was dressed for the season in a red and green outfit trimmed with white fur, said, "I could actually hear the whistle of the hot air coming out of that old windbag."

"As always, you did a great job, boss," Manny added.

Cole couldn't stop grinning. "Actually, Towne put his foot in his own mouth without any assistance from me. But he did provide some interesting holiday entertainment."

Back at the Thirty-fifth Street headquarters complex, Cole gave his staff the rest of the day off and was about to head home himself when Blackie knocked on the office door. "Can I talk to you a minute, boss?"

"Sure, Blackie, come on in."

The lieutenant closed the door behind him. He held two gift-wrapped packages in his hand.

"Now, what have we got here?" Cole said.

"Christmas gifts for you and Butch."

"You didn't want to wait until tomorrow when me and Butch came over for dinner?"

Blackie shrugged. "I wanted you to open yours now, if you don't mind?"

Cole gave his old partner a questioning look. "I thought you were always a big one for waiting until after Santa Claus comes down the chimney."

Blackie sunk down into a chair in front of the chief's desk. "Just consider me one of Santa's little helpers."

Both gifts were wrapped in silver holiday paper with cards at-

tached. Cole laid the one for his son down on the desk and unwrapped the other. A flat, white cardboard box contained a
photograph in a gold frame. The instant Cole set eyes on it, memories from a quarter of a century ago came rushing back.

The photo was of Cole and Blackie when they were Nineteenth
District tactical officers. The picture had been taken in the late seventies. Actually Cole could remember the day, if not the exact date.
Blackie had just returned to duty after being on medical leave. He
had been shot by Frankie Arcadio, the nephew of former Chicago
mob boss Paul "the Rabbit" Arcadio. The picture was taken in front
of the police station at Addison and Halsted, a short distance from
Wrigley Field.

"You remember those guys?" Blackie said.

"I'll never forget them." Cole beamed. "They were two pretty
tough cops. Whatever happened to them?"

"They're still around. In fact, they're as tough now as they were
then."

"Yeah," Cole said, sinking down in his desk chair without taking his eyes off the picture. "But they're a lot older."

"And wiser," Blackie added. "Remember the time they chased
Martin Zykus into the abandoned Sherman House Hotel in the
Loop?"

Cole laughed. "They even disobeyed the direct order of a First
District sergeant who told them not to go inside."

"But they went in anyway. If it wasn't for Commander O'Casey,
they could have ended up being suspended and kicked off the tactical team."

"Yeah," Cole said, lost in the memory. "They lucked out on
that one. And it took them fifteen years to catch Zykus."

Blackie pointed at the picture. "That young guy sure made a
name for himself, but he took a lot of chances."

"He sure did. After that shootout with Arcadio, he ended up in
a gun battle with another Mob lieutenant named Sal Marino and a
couple of Mafia soldiers down at Marina City Towers."

"And he came out on top," Blackie said. "Didn't even get a scratch. Things like that have a tendency to run in the blood from generation to generation. Kind of a danger gene."

Now Cole understood what this was all about. "Blackie, after risking his life on Lake Shore Drive, Butch is not getting back on that motorcycle. I'm sorry that I even bought it for him in the first place."

"Look at the photo again, Larry."

Cole did.

"That young cop and Butch are as alike as any two human beings could ever be," Blackie said. "So each should be able to understand the other."

The lieutenant got to his feet. At the door he stopped and turned around. "You didn't ask what me and Maria got Butch for Christmas."

"I guess you're going to tell me, aren't you, Santa?"

"A pair of red leather driving gloves."

With that Blackie Silvestri let himself out.

Cole looked back at the photo. Blackie was right about one thing. Larry "Butch" Cole Jr. was the spitting image of that Nineteenth District tactical officer twenty-five years ago.

That afternoon Butch Cole's motorcycle-riding privileges were restored.

23

DECEMBER 24, 2004
1:51 P.M.

After the meeting of the command staff at the police academy, Malcolm Towne was driven back to police headquarters by his assigned chauffeur. Once in the three-room suite reserved for the executive assistant, Towne went into his private office, slammed the door behind him, and, in an uncontrollable outburst of rage, swept everything off the top of his desk onto the floor. There was not much on the desk to begin with: a telephone, desk blotter, jar of paper clips, and a message pad. Towne's job required little effort.

The noise he made was not loud, but his secretary, a matronly type who was as much a fixture in the office as the walls and floor, knocked softly before calling through the door, "Are you alright, Mr. Towne?"

The executive assistant responded, "I'm fine. Don't concern yourself, madam."

Then he plopped down in his desk chair and proceeded to brood until it was time for lunch. When he emerged from his office, the secretary was still at her desk.

"I won't be back this afternoon," he said. "You can take the rest of the day off, and Merry Christmas."

She didn't tell the Florida-born attorney that on Christmas Eve it was traditional for the civilian staff assigned to headquarters to be given the afternoon off unless there was some pending emergency. She wished him a Merry Christmas as well and began tidying up the office.

The executive assistant had his police chauffeur drive him to the New Sandy's jazz club in Hyde Park. There the chauffeur was dismissed. The club had become one of Towne's favorite wateringholes since he'd been living in Chicago. He liked the jazz music and the ambiance, which reminded him of the South due to the proliferation of tropical plants arranged around the club. The tables had ornamental wrought-iron legs and marble tops. The waiters and waitresses did their jobs in an attentive, soft-spoken manner, which Madam Sandra Devereaux, the club owner, demanded. Malcolm Towne considered the service only a shade less than what could be considered true "southern hospitality."

When Towne arrived, the New Sandy's was doing a brisk preholiday business. There were drinkers packed three deep at the bar and the tables were filled. A sextet was on the stage playing a medley of Christmas tunes with a jazz beat. A maître d' in a black tuxedo was stationed by the door.

"Good afternoon and a Merry Christmas to you, Mr. Towne," the maître d' said.

"Merry Christmas to you, my good man. Is Madam Devereaux in?"

"No, sir. She's visiting relatives down south for the holidays."

"Alas," the executive assistant said, expansively, "our lovely proprietress is in the land of magnolias and orange blossoms, while we are stuck here in this cold Yankee city."

The maître d' smiled, which his job required. He did not like Malcolm Towne. He was aware that Towne was the executive assistant to the superintendent of police, but was not a real cop. He also realized that Towne was actually more of a politician than anything else, and the maître d' considered politicians to be of a species of critter that was slimy, crawled on its belly, and that you never turned your back on. The maître d' at the New Sandy's was also aware, from the times that Towne had had a few too many martinis, that the executive assistant was not very fond of Chief of Detectives Larry Cole, who was considered a bona fide hero around the New Sandy's jazz club.

But the maître d's job was not to pass judgment on the customers, but to see to their needs.

"We're a bit crowded right now, but I think I can squeeze you into a table in the corner near the stage."

"That would be fine, my good man," Towne said. "And have the waiter bring me a pitcher of those excellent vodka martinis." As he was escorted across the club, he added, "To start."

There was a man standing at the crowded bar nursing a beer. By profession he was a private detective, but his license had been revoked by the State of Illinois because he had been caught engaged in what were termed "unethical business practices" by the Professional Licensing Commission. Actually the PI had been lucky, be-

cause he barely avoided criminal charges. When he was plying his
official trade on the streets of Chicago, he had worked for Jake
Romano. Now, without a license, he was still on the Mob payroll.

The unlicensed PI recognized Malcolm Towne and on a hunch
decided to keep him under surveillance. The maître d' had a small
table with a single chair squeezed into a corner next to the stage.
A few moments later a waiter came to the table with an iced pitcher
containing a clear liquid that the PI initially thought to be water.
But when a cocktail glass containing four green olives was placed
on the table, there was no doubt what was inside the pitcher.

The PI ordered another beer and settled in to watch the executive assistant to the superintendent of the Chicago Police Department get sloppy drunk.

24

Paris, France
DECEMBER 25, 2004
12:20 A.M.

The archbishop of Paris celebrated midnight mass at Notre Dame
Cathedral. The mass was already in progress when Ian Jellicoe's taxi pulled up in front of the historic church. The Englishman
paused a moment before going inside. It seemed that he spent a
great deal of time in Catholic churches lately.

A choir was singing when Jellicoe entered the vestibule. He did
not proceed into the main section of the church, but went to one of
the bell towers. A spiral staircase led up into the tower made famous
in the Victor Hugo novel *The Hunchback of Notre Dame.* Jellicoe
had expected an attendant to be on duty, but he encountered no one
until he reached the halfway point of the climb.

He smelled the cigarette smoke before he saw them. Christophe

La Croix was seated on the steps, and Hubert Metayer, with a cigarette dangling from his lips, lounged against the wall. The Englishman stopped when he saw them. No words were exchanged, and after a moment's hesitation, Jellicoe stepped around them and continued the ascent. Julianna Saint was waiting for him in the belfry.

The tower of Notre Dame provided a panoramic view of the Seine, and the City of Light was spread out beneath them. The Devil's Shadow was wearing a black bolero hat adorned with a silver band and a full-length black cape. She was standing with her back to the staircase, and when she heard Jellicoe behind her, she turned around.

Although Ian Jellicoe was gay, he was forced to admit to himself that she presented a stunningly beautiful sight with the backdrop of Paris behind her. But the thought was fleeting, because he was here on business, not to view the scenery, landmark or otherwise.

"Couldn't you have arranged a more comfortable and convenient place for us to meet?"

"Why, Ian," she said, flashing him a dazzling smile, "I thought you'd welcome a chance to go to church on Christmas morning."

"I don't believe in such things, Julianna. I have a new proposal for you in addition to the one we discussed a few weeks ago."

L'Ombre du Diable turned to look back at the lights of the city below. Ordinarily she would not have given a second thought to a task such as the one Ian had offered her. However, she had managed to get him to tell her who the job was for. Although it wouldn't have taken any great feat of the imagination for her to guess. Bishop Martin Simon Pierre De Coutreaux.

"Bishop De Coutreaux is undoubtedly engaged in another search for the Dark Angel, Satan," she said. "That's why he wants the Chicago historian's blood."

With a snort, Jellicoe replied, "I haven't the slightest idea what you are talking about, Julianna. And, as I am well paid by my clients, I don't inquire too deeply into their motivations for wanting a particular assignment carried out."

Without turning around, Julianna said, "Don't insult my intelligence. I am also aware that you no more believe in the devil than you believe in God."

As if to emphasize her statement, the voices of the choir rose from the cathedral into the belfry.

"However, I don't believe in the devil either, so I will take the assignment." Now she turned to face him. "For one hundred thousand dollars, plus expenses."

Jellicoe did not flinch as he responded, "Your fee will be paid in the usual manner. May I ask how you are going to obtain the blood?"

"Of course you may ask, Ian."

But when she did not elaborate, he said an irritated, "De Coutreaux does not want him killed."

Now she laughed. "If I did manage to kill this suspected 'devil,' your devout, holier-than-thou Bishop de Coutreaux would undoubtedly believe that he had proof that I am Satan." She again turned to admire the view. "Don't worry, I won't kill this Dr. Silvernail Smith."

"What is it between you and De Coutreaux, Julianna?"

"I thought you didn't pry into your clients' affairs, Ian."

"I'm not prying. I simply asked you a question."

"I could almost believe from your tone that I hurt your feelings, but I know better. You don't have any feelings." Then she paused and added, "I actually don't know the bishop at all." Under her breath she added, *"Mais pas maintenant."* (At least not anymore.)

"What is the other job you have for me?" she asked.

"It is also in Chicago and is once more for our friend Jake Romano."

"Does he want another bank burglarized?"

"Actually, what he is contracting for, if you are able to carry it off, is so exotic and difficult that it will make you a living legend in the criminal underworld."

"What does he want stolen?"

Ian Jellicoe looked out from the belfry of Notre Dame Cathedral at the Eiffel Tower sparkling in the distance and responded, "The one thing that no one in the United States would ever think could be stolen."

PART 2

"You lied to me, Mr. Cole."
Julianna Saint

25

Field Museum of Natural History curator Nora Livingston parked her white four-by-four in the parking lot on the east side of the museum. The winter had been extremely mild, and even now, with February having just passed, the temperature was in the mid-sixties under a cloudless sky. By rights the young woman should have been in high spirits. However, she was not, because she was worried about the museum's star historian, Dr. Silvernail Smith.

The museum did not open to the public until 9:30 A.M. Now, as the curator entered the building, maintenance and service personnel were busily going about their tasks preparing one of the largest such institutions in the world for viewing.

The curator stopped to talk briefly with a crew working in the Neanderthal Era exhibit. They were being careful with each of the ancient items they were handling, and there was really no need for her to say anything to them at all. Ordinarily she would not have engaged in such "hands on" supervision, because Silvernail would have personally overseen the work. But the historian had not been himself lately. In fact, since the episode in early December when he had mysteriously disappeared in the snowstorm, Silvernail had been behaving in such a detached manner as to almost appear to be sleepwalking. For another, less valuable museum employee, such conduct would be grounds for dismissal. However, he was not an average museum employee, to say the least.

The curator proceeded to her office, where she checked with her secretary to see if there were any matters requiring her immediate attention. Then she headed for the Native American of Yesteryear exhibit.

Dr. Silvernail Smith had experienced a great deal during a long, exciting, and unusual life. For the majority of his time on earth he had been a soldier or, more appropriately, a warrior. He had fought in conflicts all over the world and many times had barely escaped death. He was also gifted with "second sight," which in the past had served him well. Now, since the incident in December, he viewed his psychic ability as a curse. This was because he had seen his own death at the hands of the female thief Larry Cole was searching for. A woman whom death followed with the affection of a smitten lover.

Silvernail knew that the thief did not kill directly; nevertheless, the items that she pilfered led to the deaths of others. One such death was that of mystery writer Greg Ennis. And despite her being nonviolent, preferring stealth and cunning to accomplish her ends, people died because of her.

Although the historian had foreseen his own death, he was not about to blindly accept his fate without doing everything he could to prevent it. So each day since he had experienced the initial vision, he had entered the museum in the predawn hours and gone to a canvas structure in the Native American of Yesteryear exhibit hall. For Silvernail this was a holy place embued with a high degree of spiritual energy. It was this energy that he had been tapping into for the past three months. Energy that he hoped would help save his life.

But what had served him so well in the past was simply not working anymore. It was as if the well of psychic energy he had relied on had simply dried up. But there was one thing that did remain. That was the voice that he had heard from inside the Egyptian tomb on that wintry day back in December. The voice that had whispered through his consciousness, "Silvernail, it is time." The historian now recognized this voice. It came from the grave of a man who had been dead for five years and belonged to his brother Jonathan Gault.

Silvernail continued to chant a prayer in the ancient language of the Navajo Nation. He was praying for help for his spirit. At another time and place the incantations would be utilized to summon good magic to conquer evil. Now the historian was asking the spirits to restore his ability so that he could protect himself from the woman who was coming to kill him.

He became aware of someone approaching the canvas structure. His keen sense of sound told him that it was Nora Livingston. Silvernail realized that he would have to go to work, although he would not be very effective in his role as a museum historian. The option was always available for him to resign and go someplace far away from this museum and the Windy City. But that wouldn't alter his fate. At least not for long. If it was his "time," as the spirit of his dead brother was telling him from the grave, then he would face it when it came, from this place.

In one smooth, effortless motion, Silvernail Smith broke out of his trance and stood up. Before the curator reached the exhibit, the historian stepped out of the wigwam and said, "Good morning, Nora."

26

MARCH 1, 2005
7:38 A.M.

The doorman at the Presidential Towers apartment complex liked to play the horses and was seesawing between opulence and bankruptcy as his gambling fortunes fluctuated. He, along with every cab driver on the make, small-time crook, and dishonest cop in town, had been on the lookout since before Christmas for Vivian

Mattioli. Pictures had even been made available, and a couple of Outfit types from the Romano family dropped around occasionally to see if the doorman had any information about the hunted woman. Only once had the Presidential Towers employee considered mentioning to them anything out of the ordinary at the apartment complex. There was a fifty-thousand-dollar bounty on the Mattioli woman's head, which could come in very handy for a man who lived from paycheck to paycheck.

However, he realized that if he gave the mobsters false information, Jake Romano might not take a too favorable view of him. Being placed in such a position could result in him ending up with a broken leg, a few smashed fingers, or worse. So he kept his mouth shut and kept an eye on Jamal Garth and Angela DuBois's new maid. And the more the doorman saw her, which was seldom, the more he breathed a sigh of relief that he hadn't said anything about her to Romano's people.

The woman was basically of the same physical type as Vivian Mattioli: slender build and medium height. But that was where any resemblance between the black couple's maid and the former Mafia don's daughter ended.

When the doorman first set eyes on the maid back in mid-January was when he became suspicious of her. She was going out with Garth and DuBois. It was a bitterly cold day and the trio were bundled up in hats, scarves, and heavy coats. The doorman was unable to see the woman's face, but he did notice her build and the fact that she kept her head down when she walked past his lobby station. He rushed to open the door for them, and the heavily clothed woman virtually curled herself into a ball as they went out into the cold.

The doorman had been off-duty when they returned, but the building was equipped with closed-circuit TV cameras, and twenty-four-hour videotapes were kept by the security service for thirty days. It had been simple enough for the doorman to obtain a copy of the tape in exchange for a few dollars in the right security supervisor's pocket. The tape displayed them returning to the complex later in the evening.

But the suspect woman had been equally as covered up coming back in as she had been on the way out. This was what initially made him suspicious, because she wore the scarf covering the lower part of her face, like a mask.

At the time, the doorman was in to the Mob for two grand in connection with some bad bets he had placed on California horse races. They were putting pressure on him, which could turn ugly if he didn't pay up soon. He saw his salvation in the woman living with Garth and DuBois. A woman who he hoped, but did not really believe, was the wanted Vivian Mattioli.

He began keeping the occupants of the ninth-floor apartment under a careful watch. Initially he attempted to enlist his fellow doormen's support in this scheme, but they either refused to co-operate or asked too many questions about what they were doing and why. Not wanting his antics brought to the attention of building management, he was forced to do it alone.

He tried making up excuses to go to Garth's apartment, but when the DuBois woman answered the door each time, his ruses for personal visits wore thin. He was forced to abandon this area of inquiry. Then on a day in mid-February, he got a good look at the mysterious maid.

The doorman had just put an old lady who lived on the twelfth floor in a taxi when a woman with flaming red hair walked toward the entrance. He frowned, because she didn't look like the type of person who belonged at the Presidential Towers.

"Excuse me, ma'am," he called to her.

She stopped just shy of the revolving door and fixed him with a blank stare.

He came up to her. "Can I help you?"

"Help me do what?"

He noticed that she spoke with an accent. It could have been German or even Swedish for all he knew. But he wasn't much of an expert on such things.

"I mean," he said, placing the proper degree of polite irritation in his voice, "who do you want to see?"

"I work here."

"I've never seen you before."

"Sure you have," she argued. "Lots of times."

He studied her face. Something about her did seem familiar, but he couldn't put it together. She was kind of plain, had bland features and a large, odd-shaped nose.

Then she dropped a bombshell. "I work for Mr. Garth and Ms. DuBois."

Stunned, he recalled the picture of Vivian Mattioli in the desk drawer at his lobby station. Yes, there was a resemblance between the two women, but a remote one at best.

"I'll have to clear you to go upstairs," he said, although she could have simply rung the lobby bell and requested access through the buzzer-operated inner lobby door.

"Whatever you say, dad," she said with a shrug.

The "dad" remark caused the back of his neck to redden. A few minutes later the woman had been cleared by Angela DuBois and was boarding an elevator for a ride to the ninth floor. When she was out of sight, he removed the photograph of Vivian Mattioli from his desk drawer, ripped it in two, and tossed it in the trash basket. After that the maid entered and exited the Presidential Towers complex without incident.

What the doorman didn't realize was that the Garth/DuBois maid had been auditioning for him. Her hair had been dyed and permed, and a fake nose applied over her daintier one. Angela DuBois had helped with the transformation after the doorman had come to the apartment, obviously attempting to get a glimpse of their house-guest. Luckily, on the day that Vivian Mattioli had sought refuge at the Presidential Towers, the nosy, horse-betting doorman was not working. But as the days turned into weeks, and the weeks into months. Jamal and Angela realized that the chances of Vivian being discovered increased.

The author and his companion had been unable to convince the hunted woman to go to the police, and there was no way that they were going to kick her out. They had also grown very fond of her. So a way would have to be conceived to enable her to remain with them and at the same time throw off the people who were looking for her. Jamal Garth, the internationally known, best-selling author, had come up with a plan.

He took Judy Daniels to lunch on the pretext of doing research for a novel and questioned her carefully about disguises. When Jamal returned to the apartment, he sat down with Angela and Vivian to explain the plan. When he was finished, Vivian looked down at her hands and said, barely audibly, "I can't do that."

They convinced her. It took weeks of practice and they managed to transform Vivian Mattioli from a Mafia princess into a foreign-born domestic. However, there were problems.

"According to Judy, the cosmetic end of any disguise is a small part of changing your persona, Vivian. You've got to actually become a different individual," Jamal explained.

"But who can I be other than myself?" Vivian argued with dismay.

That had stumped both Jamal and Angela. Then one night they were watching a rerun of the *I Love Lucy* television series.

The episode, like all those in the long run of the classic series, was funny and the three viewers were amused. However, Vivian Mattioli's laughter went far beyond simple amusement. Jamal and Angela ended up spending more time watching the hysterics of their guest than paying any attention to the program. Vivian was convulsed to such an extent that her face became flushed, tears ran freely down her cheeks, and she clutched her sides to seemingly keep herself from exploding.

When the program ended, Angela asked, "Haven't you ever seen that episode before, Vivian?"

Wiping moisture off her face, she answered, "Many times, but it still breaks me up. Greg always said that I was a nut for Lucille Ball." With that she puckered her lips and crossed her eyes, sending her hosts into fits of laughter themselves. When they recovered, the idea dawned on them and the look they gave their houseguest made the humor dissolve from her face.

Vivian Mattioli did not become Lucy, but what she did become effectively disguised who she actually was.

On the morning of March 1, Jamal returned to the Presidential Towers after giving a lecture, accompanied by a signing for his new book, at the University of Wisconsin. He had spent the night at a Ramada Inn in Madison and risen at dawn to drive the 170 miles back to Chicago. The author did not like long drives and would have taken alternate transportation if it had been more efficient. However, when it came down to it, going by car was the fastest way to travel the relatively short distance.

He was in a less than cheerful mood when he walked into the apartment and dropped his bag by the door. He could smell the aroma of freshly brewed coffee coming from the kitchen. Expecting Angela, he opened the door to find Vivian, in the disguise that she now never took off, standing at the stove.

Despite himself, Garth frowned before he managed, "Good morning, Vivian."

She noticed his frown and lowered her head. "Good morning, Jamal. Angela asked me to get breakfast for you. She went to the health club. She said she'd be back at noon."

He poured himself a cup of coffee. "How are you today?" He felt guilty over the way that he'd reacted to seeing her.

"I'm fine," she said in a small voice without raising her head. "Do you want your eggs scrambled or over easy?"

"Over easy, please."

He tried to make small talk with her, but she only answered him in monosyllables. When his breakfast was ready, she set it down in front of him and quickly left the kitchen. He managed a couple of bites before giving up in disgust. By his callousness due to fatigue, he had hurt her feelings. He was sorry and would do anything to make amends for what had occurred. But he also realized that something would have to give soon. Vivian Mattioli couldn't hide here in disguise forever.

Pushing the plate away, he poured another cup of coffee. As he sipped the black liquid, he mumbled to himself, "You're the mystery writer, Garth. Think of something."

A short time later, when Angela returned from the health club, he had come up with a plan.

27

MARCH 1, 2005
10:03 A.M.

The Lakefront Casino Project board of directors met in the law offices of Peck, Goolsby, Engstrom and DeLacey on Wacker Drive overlooking the Chicago River at LaSalle Street. The conference room where the meeting was held could easily hold seventy-five people. However, the board of directors had only four active members: alderman Sherman Ellison Edwards, former alderman Walter Blumenberg, attorney Alexander Peck—the senior partner of the LaSalle Street law firm—and Sol Engstrom—the chairman of the Lakefront Casino Project board of directors.

Of the four men present, only three actively participated in the proceedings. Alexander Peck, who was eighty-four years old and a founding partner of the host law firm, was present only as a courtesy. He was becoming increasingly senile and didn't have much to contribute. Actually, the others were only present for show. The Lakefront Casino Project was no more than a Mob front. Using the men in this boardroom, the Mafia planned to construct and secretly operate one of the largest gambling establishments in the country. Because he was a convicted felon, Jake Romano could never get a license from the State of Illinois. His name would never appear on any of the documents of incorporation or ownership, but he would indeed own the casino and adjoining hotel lock, stock, and barrel. All of the money, which would be laundered through a bank in Switzerland via a legitimate New York investment company, would come from bank robberies.

A stenographer took copious minutes of the meeting in case these deliberations were ever examined by any investigating body. The board members had been selected because they all had a certain degree of political clout and were savvy enough to keep their mouths shut if things got tough. They would also be cut in for a major share of the action, which would make each of them, and their heirs, extremely wealthy.

At the center of the conference table was a scale model of the planned lakefront gambling facility. It was of ultramodern, state-of-the-art design and would cost $300 million to build. Now the chairman of the board, using a metal pointer, went through a detailed description of the complex.

All present, with the exception of the octogenarian, who was dozing, were politely attentive to the presentation that would result in them becoming very rich men for a relatively minor effort and minimal risk. However, there was an additional party listening in by way of a concealed speaker phone beneath the conference table near the chairman's seat.

Some miles away, in the finished basement of his Lake Shore Drive brownstone, Jake Romano was listening. An exact duplicate of the model set up in the conference room was on display on a table in the center of the wood-paneled recreation area. The concept for the arrangement of the four connected structures of the complex was the Mob boss's own idea. Now Romano listened as Sol Engstrom described the property.

"The main entrance to the complex will be here off Lake Shore Drive at Wacker." Engstrom's voice came over the instrument with such clarity that the lawyer could have been standing in the room with Romano. "Four lanes will lead up to the main entrance, where valet parking will be mandatory. There will be no public parking at the facility for security reasons. All guests will be directed into the ornate lobby here." Romano studied the glass-domed building at the center of the model. His eyes glistened with anticipation of what the lakefront gambling complex would be once it was completed. He had dreamed of this for years.

"The casino will be at the north end of the main entrance," Engstrom droned on. "It will be the largest gambling facility in the world and will be capable . . ."

Jake Romano did not need the attorney's description now, nor even the model before him, to envision the structure that would rise on the western shore of Lake Michigan in the next two years. Originally he had wanted to call it Romano's, but the Gaming Commission would never go for that. So he had permitted the phony board of directors to come up with a name. The casino would be called The Star of the Great Lakes. Romano had grudgingly accepted the name. It didn't matter what the casino/hotel complex was called anyway. It was what the establishment would mean to the Mob boss personally.

"Each room in the hotel will be of four-star quality and not for bargain-basement, Las Vegas–junket pocketbooks," Engstrom was saying. "The restaurants will cater to the gourmet palate. We will only allow the most cultured, sophisticated gambler of means into the establishment."

The chairman of the Lakefront Casino Project board of directors had just used a phrase that transported Jake Romano back through the years. The first time he had heard the words *sophisticated gambler of means*, he had been in prison and they had been spoken by his cell-mate in the Joliet State Penitentiary, Greg Ennis.

As an Arcadio family lieutenant, Jake Romano had been ordered to eliminate the owner of a Rush Street bar. The bar owner, in exchange for a grant of immunity from the Cook County state's attorney's office, was going to testify before a grand jury concerning Mob extortion and intimidation in the bar and restaurant industry. The potential witness was placed under police protection, which would make the carrying out of a murder contract very difficult.

The young mobster, who had come up hard on the streets of Cicero, Illinois, saw this opportunity as his ticket to the top of the Outfit. So he sat down and came up with a plan. Later he would discover that his brain made him far more formidable than his muscles ever could. And in order to make sure that he was given total credit for the job, Jake Romano planned to do it alone.

On a Saturday night in June, while the Rush Street area was doing a brisk business, the lone gunman walked into the club. He approached the potential fink, who was standing at the bar flanked by two Chicago cops detailed to the state's attorney's office, and opened fire with a .45-caliber semiautomatic pistol. The sound of the discharging weapon, along with the blood of the three murdered men spattering patrons, caused the nightclub to erupt in bedlam. Then, as he would do in the future when he executed Victor Mattioli, Romano dropped the gun to the floor and calmly walked out.

By the time the Chicago Police Department and the Cook County state's attorney's office completed their investigation, seventy-two hours had passed. Of the over 150 people present in the Rush Street bar at the time of the shooting, only ten could be found who could say that they actually saw the gunman. Of that number, only three claimed they could accurately identify the trigger man. From a photo lineup, all three witnesses picked out Jacob Romano. But before he could be arrested, the Mafia soldier, accompanied by Mob attorney Frank Kirschstein, made an appointment to surrender at the Twenty-seventh and California Criminal Courts Building. Then the legal maneuvering began.

The case of *The People of the State of Illinois* v. *Jacob Romano* would be based solely on the testimony of the three eyewitnesses. The recovered .45 yielded no fingerprints and was worthless as evidence. To say the least, the case was weak; however, there was never any doubt that the current state's attorney was going to proceed to trial with the case against Jake Romano. This was because not only had a government potential state's witness been murdered, but also two Chicago police officers.

Jake Romano sat in jail until his case was scheduled for trial nine months after the Rush Street murders occurred. The mobster would not testify in his own behalf. The state would be forced to prove him guilty. Frank Kirschstein, Sol Engstrom's uncle, was the attorney of record for the defense and did a Perry Mason–like job of attacking the prosecution's case. And he almost carried the day, but was unable to shake the witnesses' identification of Romano. The mobster was found guilty and sentenced to life in prison.

Then Kirschstein went to work to get the verdict overturned.

During the next four years Romano was an inmate of the Illinois State Penitentiary at Joliet. The state penal system comes under the Illinois Department of Corrections; however, penologists familiar with the operation were aware that it did little to *correct* the inmates entrusted to the system's care. Actually, what those convicted of crimes discovered, upon being ushered through the gates of the Joliet State Penitentiary, was that they had been dropped into a jungle occupied by the worst human predators known to man. And *correction* was not the objective, but rather *punishment*.

Jake Romano was transferred by bus from the Cook County Jail in Chicago to Joliet to begin serving his life sentence. He was handcuffed to one of the other three Caucasian inmates making the trip. The bus had a capacity of thirty-five inmates and the windows were covered with iron mesh. All of the others were either African-American or Hispanic. The white prisoners, along with some of the younger, less-experienced inmates, were being sized up by the older, more experienced convicts. When they reached the prison, the weaker, unprotected ones would become victims of the stronger unless they allied themselves with a criminal faction.

Jake Romano had no problem in this regard, as the Mafia was the most powerful criminal organization inside of any prison in America. The other gangs inside Joliet—such as the Black Gangster Disciples, Vice Lords, Latin Kings, and the White Aryan Nation— gave Mafia members a wide berth and tremendous accompanying respect. Already, as the prison bus pulled onto the expressway and sped southwest toward the suburban prison, his rep was being circulated among the inmates. He was touted as a stand-up guy whom the Chicago Mob had its arms around. Anyone crossing Romano inside the joint would get very dead, very quick.

On the ride to the prison, Romano got to know the young white guy he was handcuffed to. It was obvious that the kid was a new "fish" and scared to death over the prospect of what awaited him. As an example of his power within prison walls, Romano let it be known that the kid was under his personal protection. Exercising his influence with prison officials, the mobster even got the new fish assigned as his cell-mate. This new prisoner's name was Greg Ennis.

Romano and Ennis were assigned to Cellblock H of Building Three, which was considered the executive wing of the maximum security prison. Here only "special" inmates were housed. The stark penal accommodations were kept unusually clean, the beds were plush by prison standards, and there were also certain perks available for those who could afford them, such as gourmet food, alcohol, drugs, and women. Even during frequent lockdowns, the prisoners in Cellblock H were not affected. Their status inside the institution made them minimal security risks.

Jake Romano and Greg Ennis got along well. The young embezzler realized that the Mafia soldier was his benefactor and kept him from being thrown unprotected into the general population. There his youth, lack of muscle, and powerlessness would succeed in making him the victim of the most bestial, subhuman forms of abuse. As such, Ennis treated Romano with the utmost respect, which the mobster acknowledged with the casual deference that his superior status demanded.

The two inmates were seldom apart and were at times derisively referred to behind their backs as a prison "couple" in a sexual sense, which was untrue. But they were good friends and shared many confidences.

Romano found Greg Ennis to have a sharp mind and a phenomenal memory. They began making plans as to what they were going to do after their respective releases from prison.

"I always wanted to write," Ennis said, as the two prisoners walked across the prison yard.

"Write what?" Romano inquired, while acknowledging the respectful nod from the leader of the Gangster Disciples, who was accompanied on a stroll by an entourage of six inmates.

"I don't know, boss. Articles, stories, maybe after I get the hang of it, novels."

Later they were in a corner of the prison weight room, which was reserved for the Mafia lieutenant and his guest's exclusive use for two hours every other day. Romano finished a set of ten reps of a bench press with two hundred pounds. Toweling his muscular upper body, Romano turned to his training partner, who was removing plates from the bar to do a less substantial bench press.

"Well, I'm going to make a lot of money," Romano said, continuing the conversation the cell-mates had started out in the yard.

"Doing what?" Ennis said, beginning his reps.

"The usual. Loan-sharking, gambling, prostitution. Maybe open a gambling casino. There's a lot of cash in those rackets."

Ennis completed the exercise and returned the barbell to the overhead rack. Sitting up on the bench, he said, "There is a lot more money in banks. I know because I used to work for one."

"Yeah," the mobster sneered, "and that's why you ended up in here."

Ennis didn't respond out of fear of angering his protector. But later, back in their cell, Romano brought up the subject of banks again.

"How would you do it?"

"Do what, boss?" Ennis asked. The younger man was shining Romano's shoes.

"Get large amounts of money out of a bank."

Continuing to spit-shine the brogans, Ennis began, "I would start by robbing one of the smaller neighborhood branch institutions on the day that it receives a large cash deposit."

*　　*　　*

Romano's appeal took time—four years, in fact, during which he continued his privileged status as an inmate in the Illinois Department of Corrections system. Finally Frank Kirschstein managed to get the guilty verdict from the initial trial overturned. A new trial was granted, and away from the glare of the publicity that had accompanied the previous proceeding, Romano was again found guilty. However, this time the charge was voluntary manslaughter. The four years he had already done in prison were considered as time served and he was released.

In the basement of his Lake Shore Drive brownstone, a vicious scowl turned Romano's face into a mask of intense fury. Greg Ennis had never been what the Mob boss would have considered a friend. In fact, Romano had no one he could really refer to as a friend, not even his wife. And he didn't need companionship or a confidant. What he required of all of his Mob subordinates, acquaintances, and the miscellaneous others in his life was total loyalty. And Greg Ennis had betrayed that loyalty. However, the thing that infuriated Romano most of all was that his old cell-mate really thought that he could get away with it.

Ennis was released from jail six months before Romano. When the future Mafia boss returned to Chicago, Victor Mattioli gave him a huge party. Romano made sure that Greg Ennis was invited.

The affair was a drunken orgy, with hookers, free-flowing booze, and plenty of nose candy available. It hadn't taken long for the two prior Joliet State Penitentiary inmates to get completely smashed. At one point Romano embraced Ennis and said a slobbery drunk, "I love you, Greg, and I'm gonna take care of you, kid."

Over the din of the party raging around him, Ennis shouted a reply that Romano couldn't here. A couple of days later, after they had both sobered up, the mobster found out.

"I want to write a book about the time we spent in the joint."

They were in the North Side luxury apartment the Mattioli family had temporarily leased for their returning lieutenant. Needless to say, Romano had not been very fond of the idea.

"Look, kid, that's ancient history. There's a lot more interesting stuff to write about out here in the world. I'll even help you get started."

Ennis was introduced to some low-ranking Mob soldiers, who shared their somewhat exaggerated tales of life inside the Mafia with the fledgling writer. With the assistance of Barbara Zorin and Jamal Garth, the first manuscript, *Street Wars*, was completed by Ennis and published to moderately encouraging reviews.

Then, as Jake Romano rose within the ranks of the Chicago Mob, he forgot about his old cell-mate. Occasionally he would run into Ennis, such as the time at Carmine Giordano's Christmas party when Romano had provided the introduction of the mystery writer to Vivian Mattioli. By this time Romano was already setting his sights on the top post in the Chicago Mob. Then, after the assassination of Victor Mattioli had been carried out, he got a call from Ennis.

Romano was now married and had just moved into the Lake Shore Drive brownstone. He was on top of the world and was actually glad to hear from his old friend. But the instant he heard the insolent tone in the mystery writer's voice, Romano knew that something was wrong.

"How you doing, boss?" the writer asked, sarcastically.

Romano responded curtly, "Good, Greg. What can I do for you?"

"Get together a hundred and twenty-five thousand dollars in cash, which you will have delivered to my office in the Loop."

Romano laughed. "Why should I do that?"

When Ennis told him, Jake Romano's blood ran cold. But there was an icy rage present. His former cell-mate had the upper hand, but Romano swore that the day would come when the mystery writer would pay.

The meeting of the Lakefront Casino Project board of directors was breaking up. It had been some minutes since the man listening in the basement recreation room of the Lake Shore Drive brownstone had been paying any attention to the proceedings. He was lost in a memory of treachery and betrayal. Now he picked up a black remote control device from a table next to the model and pressed a button on its face. The model of The Star of the Great Lakes casino and hotel complex was electronically lowered into the housing of the table and another scale model swung up in six sections to take its place.

The casino model was a work of art; what replaced it was a masterpiece wrought by genius. The genius of Jake Romano.

There were three primary structures on this model: the Federal Reserve Bank, the Richard J. Daley Civic Center, and Union Station. All of them were the targets of Romano's next robbery plan. This was going to be the most ambitious felony ever attempted on American soil and would be the subject of legends that would last for generations.

But as the Mob boss continued to examine the model, he recalled how dangerous the situation with Greg Ennis had actually been to him. As he reached down to adjust the plastic figurine of the Picasso statue in Daley Center Plaza, he again drifted back into the past.

Greg Ennis finally got the upper hand on Jake Romano. The Mafia boss knew he had screwed up the Mattioli hit, because he had been videotaped. But mistakes of this type could always be rectified. That was why they made hit men who tossed people out of skyscraper windows.

The blackmailing mystery writer sent Romano a copy of the tape. Ennis let him know that there were additional copies and that he also possessed the weapon used to kill Victor Mattioli. At the time there was nothing that Romano could do but pay up.

However, despite Greg Ennis's brains and imagination, he really had no idea what he was up against. Jake Romano had the entire organized criminal apparatus of the United States at his disposal.

An apparatus that had tentacles extending around the world. An apparatus utilized to find out everything there was to know about Greg Ennis, ex-convict and best selling author.

The blackmail was half a million dollars a year, which Romano was told to pay in quarterly installments. After the second payment, Romano discovered that the .44-caliber Smith & Wesson revolver he had dropped at the scene had been recovered by the maid who discovered Mattioli's body. The aging domestic had been born and raised in Sicily and spoke little English. But she did understand the ways of revenge for the murder of a family member. Especially when that family member was a Mafia Don. The woman had hidden the gun and later had given it to Vivian Mattiolli, so that she could someday use it to avenge her father's death. In turn, Vivian Mattioli had given the gun to Ennis.

The romance between the mystery writer and the Mafia princess was discovered. Romano had found their clandestine relationship intriguing, because he had introduced them. Now they were coconspirators who would suffer the same fate.

It took more than a year for Jake Romano to find out where Greg Ennis was keeping the incriminating evidence against him. When he discovered that it was in a safety-deposit box in the vault on the lower level of the Metropolitan Bank of Chicago in downtown Chicago, his memory took him back behind the walls of the Joliet State Penitentiary.

"But where does it say that banks are impregnable?" Greg Ennis argued when his cell-mate said that attempting to rob a bank was a good way of ending up permanently in their current domicile. "Back during the thirties, bank robberies were common. Then it became a federal offense, giving the FBI jurisdiction, and the crooks began looking for safer crimes to commit. But banks are where the money is and there's no such thing as an impregnable bank anywhere in the world."

* * *

Robbing a bank on North Michigan Avenue to obtain the contents of one safety-deposit box was too messy. So Romano explored alternate avenues.

RanCorp was an international security consulting firm based in Germany. The firm's consulting end extended to carrying out assassinations and plotting criminal enterprises with comprehensive precision. It was through RanCorp that Romano was put in touch with Ian Jellicoe. The Englishman had charged the Chicago mobster three-quarters of a million dollars, which was more at that point than Ennis had extorted from Romano. But to him it was worth it.

The videotape and the gun were now in Romano's possession. The burglary of the Metropolitan Bank had been carried out with such finesse that not a word about it appeared in any media account. Then Romano called Greg Ennis.

His message was simple. "You're a dead man, kid. A very dead man."

After that, everything had fallen into place, with one exception: Vivian Mattioli had not been located. But he was confident that she would be found eventually.

Jake Romano went back to examining the model. Studying each of the small, made-to-scale structures, he counted off, "one" for the Daley Center, "two" for the Federal Reserve Bank, and "three" for Union Station. The Robbery of the Century was about to take place in Chicago.

28

MARCH 2, 2005
NOON

W e have experienced a significant crime reduction during the first quarter of the year," Malcolm Towne said, as he read from a sheet of crime statistics at the daily meeting in the superintendent's office. "Also, the clearance rate for the Detective Division, for crimes which have already been committed, exceeds last year's ratio by seventeen points. I would say that is acceptable."

"I would say 'acceptable' is a gross understatement, Mr. Towne," the superintendent snapped.

There were five command officers seated around the conference table in the CEO's office at Chicago police headquarters. Each of them represented one of the department's five bureaus. Lieutenant Blackie Silvestri from the Detective Division was the representative of the Bureau of Investigative Services.

When Towne made the condescending remark about the Detective Division's clearance rate, Blackie scowled. However, after the superintendent's admonishment, the lieutenant didn't dwell on the insult. Towne was a jerk and rumors were running rampant through the headquarters complex that the executive assistant's days with the CPD were numbered. Due to the political clout he still managed to maintain, he was supposed to be transferred to another city department by summer. It was also going around that Towne had been observed dead drunk at a couple of bars in the city. It would only be a matter of time before one of his drunken escapades became the subject of an item in a local gossip column.

The meeting broke up in time for the superintendent to make a chamber of commerce luncheon at McCormick Place. With a desk full of paperwork waiting for him, Lieutenant Silvestri headed back to Detective Division headquarters.

Blackie was in charge of the administrative duties at headquarters while Larry Cole was on vacation. As such, he had moved into the chief's office in order to more efficiently handle the volume of paperwork that passed through the investigative arm of the department.

Manny had placed a sandwich, an apple, and a glass of iced tea from the headquarters cafeteria on the chief's desk. Blackie would probably be wading through the mountain of orders, case report follow-ups, and statistical printouts until well after six o'clock that evening. When Cole was here, he had a system that usually got him through these administrative duties by early afternoon. But Larry Cole had been the chief of detectives for eight years.

Blackie unwrapped the sandwich. It was cold roast beef on rye with mustard, which wasn't one of the lieutenant's favorites. He would have preferred a Mama DeLeo's special submarine sandwich with Italian cold cuts and sweet peppers over this bland delicatessen fare. But it didn't look like he was going to be able to get away from this desk for a while, so if he was going to eat, the cold roast beef was it.

The chief's correspondence had been delivered while Blackie was at the superintendent's meeting. A couple of postcards from the Leeward Islands had arrived. One was from Judy Daniels writing from someplace called Pelican Key on the French side of Saint Martin. The other was from Larry Cole, who was at the Oyster Bay Beach Resort, which was also on the French side of the Caribbean island. The lieutenant was aware that they had not selected the same area of the world to take a vacation by coincidence. In fact, the Chicago police chief of detectives and the infamous Mistress of Disguise/High Priestess of Mayhem were not actually on vacation, but engaged in an unofficial investigation. A case that had taken them out of the country to investigate an international thief known as the Devil's Shadow.

The lieutenant finished his sandwich and idly wondered how Cole and Judy were doing. Then he went back to work.

29

Saint Martin
MARCH 2, 2005
2:05 P.M.

The village of Marigot is located on the French side of Saint Martin in the Leeward Islands. On Simpson's Bay, Marigot is geared toward serving the tourist trade, which is the main source of income for the Caribbean island. There were souvenir shops, stores selling native products, and restaurants and bars catering to a wide variety of appetites and tastes, from the gourmet to those of the fast-food aficionado.

The weather in the South Atlantic was usually mild throughout the year; however, periodically severe storms swept through the area with extreme force, threatening lives and inflicting severe property damage. Over the past few years there had been no hurricanes and the native islanders had prospered.

On this afternoon it was hot and a shade muggy as tourists from the cruise ships lying at anchor in the harbor circulated through Marigot. There were a number of popular places in the town. Most of them were known for the exotic spirits and native dishes they served. One of the spots the tourists gravitated to was Mama Johnnie's. A relatively small restaurant and bar, it was located a bit off the main drag, but had a native flair. The drinks were potent, the food good, and the entertainment exciting.

At four o'clock daily, a trio began playing jazz and calypso tunes. A pair of vocalists—male and female—sang popular songs, and at eight o'clock, when most of Mama Johnnie's patrons were feeling little or no pain, the dance floor was cleared and an exotic dancer took center stage. A tall, exquisitely built young woman, the dancer began her number in a costume consisting of a bikini, wrap-around skirt, and native headdress. Twenty minutes later, when the dance concluded, she was totally nude and drenched with sweat.

The men and women, both tourist and native, walked away astounded over not only the sensuality and wanton abandon of the dance, but also the manner in which the dancer was able to contort her voluptuous body into seemingly impossible positions.

Partying at Mama Johnnie's had been known to go on until dawn, and more than once, nightly festivities had spilled out onto the streets of Marigot.

Mama Johnnie's always opened at 10:00 A.M. The proprietress herself, Johnnie Mae Dupres, an attractive, heavyset woman of seventy who didn't look a day over forty, was the first one to enter the establishment each morning at 8:30 A.M. to supervise a cleanup detail and begin preparing the food that would be on that day's menu.

Johnetta Dupres had been born in the Leeward Islands, but educated in the United States. She had received a bachelor's degree in world history from Roosevelt University in Chicago before returning to the islands and opening her successful restaurant in the early fifties. She was extremely knowledgeable concerning Saint Martin's history and traditions on both the French and Dutch sides of the island. She possessed a seemingly limitless amount of gossip about island residents. Also, she loved to talk and could hold forth for hours. Some of the more savvy residents and even a few tourists avoided her; others found her tales fascinating.

Penelope "Penny" Gibbs was a plump, round-shouldered tourist who wore thick tortoiseshell glasses. She had bad skin, but good teeth. She had arrived on the island in late February for a two-week vacation. She was staying at the Oyster Bay Beach Resort, which meant that the little lady had money. She was from Chicago, and when Mama Johnnie Mae Dupres discovered this, she took the homely tourist under her motherly wing.

Penny Gibbs had lunch at the popular restaurant every day during her stay on Saint Martin. On more than one occasion she had remained at Mama Johnnie's until closing. The one thing that Johnnie remarked about this fat child from the Windy City was that she sure could hold her liquor. None of the potent, fruit-flavored rum drinks that could put a bo'sun's mate off a China-bound freighter on his back seemed to faze her. Once Penny had even helped Mama Johnnie into a taxi after the proprietor had had one too many of her own concoctions.

Needless to say, Mama Johnnie spent a lot of time talking to Penny, who was a very good listener. The only thing that the American tourist had ever asked the Saint Martin native to go into greater detail about was one of the more legendary residents of the island. That resident was Julianna Saint, who was known in the world of international crime as *L'Ombre du Diable*—the Devil's Shadow.

Christophe La Croix was lying on the nude beach beside a young woman visiting the Virgin Islands from Portugal. Since he had accompanied Julianna Saint from Paris in early January, the Frenchman had developed a deep tan and his dark brown hair had been bleached blond by the sun. Hubert Metayer was still in France, but would soon be joining them. They had another job to do in the United States. A very big job, according to the little that Julianna had told him. She was up at her villa making plans, and he had been ordered not to disturb her. So he was on the beach in the altogether with this comely Portuguese wench. He had experienced carnal knowledge of this young woman in the extreme and was actually growing tired of her. Beneath his deep tan, Christophe smiled. Such was the way of the great lover.

"I'm thirsty," he said with a yawn.

Getting up on one elbow, she lowered one of her breasts over his face. "Would you like some of this?"

Shoving her away, he got to his feet. "Maybe later." He pulled on a pair of denim shorts. "Right now I want something cold and slightly alcoholic in a tall glass."

Pouting, she began putting on a bikini and a pair of sandals. Their skimpy dress was acceptable on the streets of Marigot, although nude bathing was only permitted on this beach.

They trudged across the sand into the town. A few minutes

later, they walked into the shady coolness of Mama Johnnie's. The proprietor was standing at the end of the bar with a woman who might as well have been invisible for all of the interest she generated in the oversexed Frenchman.

"*Bonjour*, Madamemoiselle Johnnie," he called.

"*Bonjour*, Christophe," she called back. "Rum punch?"

Christophe held up two fingers, indicating drinks for him and his scantily clad companion. They took seats on a couple of stools down the bar. Johnnie made the drinks, set them in front of the new arrivals, and returned to the woman she had been talking to.

The Portuguese tourist placed her hand on the Frenchman's knee. He shook it off.

"What's the matter, Christophe? You act like you don't love me anymore."

He laughed. "Who ever said anything about love?"

Abruptly she stood up and stormed from the bar. Christophe watched her go before picking up her untouched drink and draining off half its contents. Her absence would help him cut this afternoon's bar tab in half.

He had just started on the second rum punch when he caught part of the conversation in English that Johnnie Dupres was having with the other patron.

"Then Julianna . . . ," she whispered. ". . . Hubert was the one . . ."

The Frenchman stiffened. Concentrating, he focused on what they were saying.

The woman at the bar asked, "But how could she get into the museum without tripping the alarms?"

Johnnie noticed that Christophe was eavesdropping. She knew that he was an associate of Julianna Saint, and despite the bar owner's gossipy nature, she did not want to court trouble. She deftly changed the subject and began discussing cruise vessels.

Christophe made a show of swirling the ice cubes around in his drink, taking a pull, and getting up to go to the men's room at the rear of the bar. A few minutes later he returned. Johnnie was back in the kitchen, but the woman she had been talking to was still seated at the bar. He returned to his stool and took a closer look at her.

Mon Dieu, elle est laide, he thought. (God, she is ugly.)

On cue she turned to look directly at him and smiled.

Her teeth were pretty good, but he wouldn't screw this chick if she were the last woman on Earth. But that bigmouthed Johnnie Dupres had been talking to her about Julianna and Hubert. The woman was obviously not a native of the island and she didn't look like a cop. But she had displayed an interest in the Devil's Shadow, which could be dangerous.

Johnnie came back into the bar and motioned to Christophe for a refill. Shaking his head, he dropped money on the top of the bar and walked out. There was a combination newsstand, bookshop, and candy store up the street from Mama Johnnie's. Christophe knew that there was a telephone there. He dialed Julianna's villa.

"Allo," a servant answered.

"Je veux parler à Julianna."

"Qui est à l'appareil?"

"Christophe."

A moment later she came to the telephone.

"We could have a problem with a woman in Marigot," he said.

30

Larry Cole stood at the foot of the mountain. A path ran from the base and wound its way toward the top. It was a steep ascent and at times hazardous, but the Chicago cop had made this run every day since he arrived on the island a week ago. Now, clad in shorts and a tank top, he did a series of stretching exercises before beginning to jog. After only a short distance the exertion and the tropical heat had him sweating profusely. He sucked in air and felt his muscles respond to the challenge. The mountain rising above the blue waters surrounding Saint Martin became Cole's adversary, one he would either defeat or be defeated by.

The actual distance the man running along the winding mountain path would cover was two and a quarter miles. However, because of the angle of elevation and the altitude, he would expend the same amount of energy if he were to run ten miles on a flat surface. As always, when Larry Cole exercised in this manner he mentally examined the current case he was working on. That case began with the homicide of Greg Ennis.

From the moment that Cole and Blackie saw the mystery writer's body plunging to the unyielding Michigan Avenue sidewalk, the investigation had taken a number of bizarre and unusual turns. From the discovery that the Metropolitan Bank on Michigan Avenue had been broken into with nothing taken, to the psychic revelations of Dr. Silvernail Smith, the case had finally led him to this island overlooking Friar's Bay in the Caribbean.

First Cole tallied up what he knew. Greg Ennis had been killed by a pair of Mafia hit men in the employ of Jake Romano. Then the hit men ended up conveniently dead. Romano and Ennis had been cell-mates at Joliet, but there was no evidence that they had much contact after their release. But Cole was certain that Romano had ordered the mystery writer's death. And everything was connected to the burglary of the Metropolitan Bank, where Ennis had a bank account and a safety-deposit box. A safety-deposit box that had been found empty after the bank was mysteriously broken into.

The path widened as Cole approached a luxury residential area. There were villas built into the side of the mountain above and below the running man. From what he could see, each was equipped with a swimming pool, cabana, and guesthouse. The estates were owned by millionaires. One of those millionaires was Julianna Saint, who had been born poor on this very island, but was now one of its wealthiest residents. It was she whom Cole was interested in.

Clues from the real world and the realm of the psychic one had led him here. Silvernail had seen a female thief in his vision, who was responsible for Greg Ennis's death. Whoever had burglarized the Metropolitan Bank was a master thief. A computer search through Interpol had turned up a list of seven possibles—all female and each exceptionally skilled. There were files on them, but seldom had any of them been arrested. There were two Americans—one of whom had been operating since the 1950s and was not believed to still be active—an Englishwoman, a Russian, two Spaniards, a Japanese, and a French national. Julianna Saint was the French national, whose principal residence was on Saint Martin in the Virgin Islands.

Cole approached the top of the hill, where one of the most expensive structures on the island was located. As the villa came into view, the runner increased his pace. This was the toughest part of the self-imposed obstacle course. Here the ground sloped upward at a thirty-degree angle. With each step, Cole's leg muscles screamed from the exertion. His breathing came in sharp rasps, but he didn't slow down.

The files on the known or suspected female thieves were not as extensive as those on terrorists or other types of violent international criminals. In fact, most of the information contained in the individual dossiers could not have been compiled in the United States. This was because of First Amendment prohibitions against spying on citizens by police agencies without probable cause.

Julianna Saint's date of birth was unknown. Her age was estimated as being anywhere from her early thirties to mid-forties. She was in excellent physical shape, was exceptionally strong, fast, and agile, and had been educated in France, earning advanced degrees in mathematics. In the mid-seventies she was suspected of being involved in a burglary aboard the cruise ship *La Belle Liberté*, which had dropped anchor in Oyster Bay. Although she and a suspected accomplice, who had been employed on the cruise ship as a steward, were briefly questioned by the authorities, no charges were ever brought against either of them. The cruise ship employee was fired and vanished. There the storied odyssey of the woman known as *L'Ombre du Diable* began.

Cole reached the top of the mountain. Placing his hands on top of his head in order to fill his lungs with more oxygen, he jogged in place for a moment. He was on a rise overlooking the bay far below. The view was unbelievably beautiful. Behind him was the entrance to Julianna Saint's villa. The property was surrounded by a seven-foot-tall, white, sandblasted wall. From where he stood, Cole could not detect any movement inside the house, but his instincts told him that he was being watched. This had happened each time he had ascended the mountain. There was a large plate-glass window on the top floor of the villa. He suspected that his observer was concealed somewhere on the other side of that glass.

Removing a plastic water bottle from the Sokool holder strapped to his waist, Cole took a long drink before beginning the descent back down the mountain. For this trip to the Virgin Islands to be successful, Cole needed to get inside the white mountaintop structure he had just left. Complicating this task was the need for him to be invited inside. The cop from the Windy City knew that this would not be easy, but then nothing ever was.

Cole had been right about someone inside Julianna Saint's villa observing him. In fact, it had been the Devil's Shadow herself behind the upper-level plate-glass window. Clad only in a white bikini, which accentuated her ebony skin and voluptuous figure, she had been working in her library. When she was at home, she wore few clothes, which was a way of asserting her independence from the outside world. There was always a staff of servants on duty in the villa, but she had trained them so well that they never came in contact with her unless she called for them or something out of the ordinary occurred. The "help" were all native islanders and addressed the mistress of the house respectfully as "Madam Julianna."

She continued to watch the narrow-waisted black man jog back down the mountain. She had watched him perform this same maneuver every day for a week. To hike up from the beach was arduous enough; to run it, as the muscular man had just done, was quite impressive.

As the jogger vanished amidst the foliage below, Julianna turned from the window. Her library contained a very extensive collection of rare books and first editions. Book collecting was an all-consuming hobby of the famous international thief, and she had read everything contained on these bookshelves. When she did manage to get home to Saint Martin, she could spend hours reading while lying out by the pool.

A thought stopped her and she looked back through the plate-glass window overlooking the bay far below. The only people she had come into close contact with in the last eighteen months had been Ian Jellicoe, Hubert Metayer, Christophe La Croix, her domestics, and her clients. Somehow, without her having made a conscious effort to accomplish it, her work had become her life. Even now she was planning a job. She examined the model lying on a table at the center of the room. Unknown to the Devil's Shadow, a more extensive version of this model was set up in the recreation room of Jake Romano's Lake Shore Drive brownstone in Chicago. But Julianna had made modifications to this model, which she would duplicate on the actual edifice in the Windy City. She was about to go back to her labors when a member of her domestic staff knocked on the locked library door to announce that Christophe La Croix was on the telephone.

31

MARCH 2, 2005
3:35 P.M.

Christophe La Croix had donned a white cotton shirt, which was open to the navel, and a pair of leather sandals. Sunglasses and the same floppy hat he'd worn to shadow Ian Jellicoe on the transatlantic flight from Chicago to London completed the outfit.

He lounged against the wall of the shop from which he had called
Julianna Saint and waited for the homely tourist visiting Mama
Johnnie's bar to leave. Then, on the orders of the Devil's Shadow,
he was to find out where she was staying. Julianna had further
instructed him to take no action against the tourist without a direct
order from her. This last part had made Christophe frown, because
it was unnecessary. After all, he was not Hubert Metayer.

The afternoon was becoming increasingly hot and muggy.
Christophe's shirt was plastered to his back and sweat ran from
beneath the band of his hat down across his cheeks. Had he remained down on the beach with the Portuguese girl, he would never
have come across the bigmouthed bar owner and her equally big-
eared patron. But now he had no choice. He had a job to do for
Julianna, which he would carry out conscientiously and thoroughly.
Shrugging off the discomfort, he continued to wait.

Finally the frumpy-looking woman stepped out the front door
of Mama Johnnie's and walked off down the street. Christophe un-
wound his wiry body from his position against the wall and followed.

The woman walked slowly through the streets of Marigot, stop-
ping occasionally to glance at goods in shops or on display by a
curbside vendor. There were a lot of tourists in town, due to the
four cruise ships lying at anchor offshore, and Christophe managed
to blend in without difficulty. He noticed that his quarry moved
with a flat-footed clumsiness and was unusually awkward even for
someone with her excessive girth. She was also unsteady, which
Christophe surmised was due to the potent rum drinks she had consumed back at Mama Johnnie's. He only hoped that she would
remain ambulatory long enough to lead him to her hotel. There, for
a few dollars in the right employee's pocket, the assistant of the
Devil's Shadow would find out the woman's name and where she
was from.

Christophe maintained a twenty-foot distance between him and
the fat woman. Often he was forced to stop or he would have ended
up close enough to touch her. Not once did she ever turn around,

but he was skilled in the art of surveillance. He was aware that she could have a confederate tailing her in order to detect his presence. So he was as much aware of what and who was around and behind him as he was of the woman he was following.

He stopped at a fruit stand and deftly pilfered an orange without the vendor seeing him. He began peeling the fruit and was about to continue the surveillance when the woman disappeared.

Initially Christophe was not alarmed. The streets were still crowded and he figured that she had simply entered one of the shops or, possibly, stepped into an alley to rid herself of a rum-induced illness. He stopped under the awning of a souvenir shop and sucked on his orange, while casually scanning the street. A few minutes passed and she failed to appear. Gradually panic began setting in.

Dropping the remains of the stolen fruit to the ground, Christophe stepped out from beneath the awning and began searching for her. He looked inside each of the stores she could have entered, but she was not in any of them. He checked intersecting alleys and the nearest side street leading off the main drag. She was nowhere to be found.

Finally Christophe stopped in the middle of the main commercial strip of Marigot and snatched off his hat in frustration. He couldn't believe that the overweight woman had intentionally eluded him. Losing her had simply been a fluke. The skilled sneak thief had been looking one way while she had simply gone in an unexpected direction. After all, she was probably intoxicated, and drunks were notoriously unpredictable. Of course, Julianna would not be very happy over his failure, but perhaps he could still find out what he needed to know.

He turned around and headed back to Mama Johnnie's. He planned to pump the gossipy bar owner for information about the fat tourist. As he made his way through the streets of Marigot, Christophe La Croix was unaware that he was now the one being followed.

The woman, whom Johnnie Dupres would reveal to Christophe as being named Penny Gibbs from Chicago, Illinois, had vanished.

The trappings that had created her—wig, nose, thin coating of latex to simulate acne, and body padding—were now in the bottom of an oversized straw bag. Now the dark-haired, slender, rather pretty Sergeant Judy Daniels, known as the Chicago Police Department's Mistress of Disguise/High Priestess of Mayhem, tailed Christophe La Croix back to Mama Johnnie's bar.

Larry Cole cooled down from his marathon run up the mountain by taking a slow walk along the Oyster Bay Beach. Although it was not a nude beach, as was the one that Christophe La Croix had sunbathed on earlier, there were a number of topless females dotting the stretch of sand on the South Atlantic shore. As the tall, broad-shouldered American strolled by, quite a few admiring eyes followed him.

Since Cole had arrived on Saint Martin, the strenuous exercise, fresh air, and relaxing atmosphere had put him in the best shape of his life. The hot sun had kissed his skin a deep copper brown, and a regimen of push-ups, sit-ups, and squats had turned his body into a mass of rock-hard, rippling muscle.

He was staying at the Oyster Bay Beach Resort in an air-conditioned, two-room suite equipped with all the necessary vacation accoutrements, including cable television and a fully stocked mini refrigerator. The room was furnished in white wicker accented with French pastel fabrics. The balcony of his bedroom faced the mountain he had just climbed. With the naked eye he had a partial view of Julianna Saint's villa. Using the pair of Zeiss binoculars he had brought with him from Chicago, he could examine the white structure closely.

Crossing the hotel lobby, Cole climbed two flights of steps and entered his suite. Removing a bottle of Evian water from the refrigerator, he took a long pull before heading for the shower. A few minutes later, clad in a baby blue Oyster Bay Beach Resort bathrobe, he stood on the balcony admiring the view.

Larry Cole had seldom taken a real vacation during his career with the department. He had traveled extensively to locations as far distant as Europe and Asia; however, on each trip he had included some type of law enforcement activity on the itinerary. Criminal justice and forensics seminars or visits to local police forces had a tendency to eclipse the recreational activities. In fact, despite being in one of the most idyllic vacation spots in the world, what he was doing now was really not a vacation. He was not even registered at the Oyster Bay Beach Resort under his own name.

Cole smiled. He was technically on a spy mission in a foreign country. Lifting the bottle of Evian water, he toasted himself and said, "My name is Bond. James Bond."

The top detective on the Chicago Police Department was using the alias of Michael Holt. There was a background persona that went along with this name, because there was a real Mike Holt, who was a writer living in Albuquerque, New Mexico. Holt was a novelist who had written a number of books covering a wide range of subjects, including legal thrillers, mysteries, and a couple of well-received biographies. He was what was known in the publishing field as a "midlist" author, with respectable, if not blockbuster, sales. Larry Cole had read all of Mike Holt's books, which had been recommended to him by Jamal Garth. The policeman found the majority of them to be pretty good and at times particularly poignant. This was because the author wrote from the point of view of an African-American male.

A number of additional factors had entered into Cole's decision to adopt the Mike Holt identity on this sojourn to the Leeward Islands. One was that Cole knew enough about Holt to enable him to discuss the author's work with a fair degree of authority. Another factor was that the real Mike Holt not only shunned publicity, but would not even allow his photo to appear on the dust jackets of any of his books. The final factor was that Holt had personally given Cole permission to use his name to engage in this impersonation in the Leeward Islands, with one reservation. The New Mexico author was to receive a detailed report, with all applicable exhibits attached, at the conclusion of the mission. Despite his reclusiveness, Mike Holt had a loyal readership and was something of an international celebrity. Cole hoped to exploit this status while he was on Saint Martin.

Walking back into the suite, Cole was about to get dressed when he noticed the message light blinking on the bedside telephone. He crossed to the instrument and picked it up.

A computerized message recited, "The following message was left for you today at two-fifteen P.M."

There was a pause and then: "Mr. Holt, this is Cal Ferris. Thanks a bunch for the autographed book. I'm a big fan of yours, man. A big fan. I read all your stuff. I'm really looking forward to meeting you. Look, brother—that is, I hope that you are a brother, because I've never seen any pictures of you—instead of us getting together for a taste down at your hotel, why don't you come up to my villa tonight? I'm having a little barbecue and there will be some locals there along with a celebrity or two. I'm sure you'll enjoy yourself. Just tell the desk people at your hotel to have a car bring you up to Cal Ferris's place. It's built right into the side of the mountain near the summit. Stay cool and ciao, baby."

With a smile, Cole erased the message and hung up the telephone. Cal Ferris was a popular African-American comedian, who made frequent television appearances and had appeared in a few movies. When the undercover cop had begun planning this trip to Saint Martin, he had been aware that Cal Ferris owned a villa on the island. Cole had also been aware that on the evening of March 2 the comedian was throwing one of his famous parties. A party that Julianna Saint would almost certainly attend.

32

The jeweler was named Claude LeBreton and he was one of the most skilled in his trade in the world. Although he did not operate out of a jewelry store in a traditional sense, he was headquartered in Monaco, which was one of the safest and most security-conscious countries in the world. With a clientele who were counted among the most famous idle-rich jet-setters in the world, this particular jeweler made house calls.

A short, bald, rotund man, LeBreton always traveled by chauffeured limousine to wherever his current patron was located, as long as it was in the principality of Monaco. As a rule, he carried a fortune in gems and expensive timepieces in a custom-made black attaché case. He had never been robbed and harbored no concerns about his safety or that of the pricey merchandise in his possession. As long as he remained within the borders of Monaco, LeBreton had no security concerns.

In Monaco an atmosphere of safety was taken to the extreme. It was estimated that there was one policeman for every one hundred residents, which was the best cop/citizen ratio in the world, and the police force was one of the most modern and efficient in Europe. A system of constantly monitored, twenty-four-hour video surveillance cameras spanned the entire principality and all of its public areas. As Claude LeBreton saw it, the reigning prince had decreed that Monaco's residents and guests were to exist in a state of total security, so who was he, a humble but extremely wealthy tradesman, to worry?

On this windy but warm evening, LeBreton was on his way to the Prince Louis Hotel near the palatial Monte Carlo Casino. He was going there to show a potential client a selection of diamonds and emeralds, which would be set into a platinum setting to fashion a necklace. The gems themselves had an uncut value of over two million francs. After being properly set, with the price of his skilled workmanship thrown in and the proper profit margin calculated, the cost of the necklace would probably be somewhere in the vicinity of five to seven million francs. Perhaps the client would like a ring or a bracelet to match the necklace. LeBreton did not pause to estimate the cost of these additional items. If they were commissioned, so be it. If not, the necklace itself would be a profitable way to occupy his time.

The shiny black Mercedes pulled up in front of the Prince Louis Hotel and a doorman, wearing a white and red uniform, rushed forward to open the back door for the little man. He stepped out onto the carpeted runner leading up to the hotel's ornate entrance. A fringed red canopy for the protection of hotel visitors covered the single flight of steps.

"Good evening, Monsieur LeBreton. Again welcome to the Prince Louis," the doorman said.

"Thank you," LeBreton replied, walking past the doorman with precise, mincing steps to enter the marble-columned lobby.

Claude LeBreton's client was staying at the Prince Louis. She had called his secretary with a request for his services. The client had given her name as Countess Maria Teresa Grimaldi of Italy. Before returning her call, LeBreton had checked to see if there was such a person as this Countess Grimaldi, and found to his satisfaction that she was not only bona fide, but was rumored to be one of the richest women in Europe. After being informed of the specifications of the piece of jewelry she wanted made, the jeweler had prepared the appropriate sketches and assembled the gems and precious metal in pressed-block form to show the countess. Now he approached the concierge's desk in the lobby of the Prince Louis Hotel and asked to see his client.

The concierge was British, but he spoke excellent French, as well as Italian, German, and Japanese. He was neatly tailored and possessed a regal bearing, which he had learned to skillfully conceal when it became necessary. With LeBreton it was not *necessary*, as the Prince Louis Hotel's concierge considered the fat little jeweler to be no more than just another common tradesman.

"The countess is in Suite 641," the concierge said in French. "She is expecting you." With that he turned to attend to more pressing and, in his estimation, important duties.

LeBreton didn't dwell on the slight. He didn't like the British. Too many of them came on with the same snottiness as the concierge, whom the jeweler knew that he could buy and sell out of his pocket change. Without another word, LeBreton ambled off toward the elevator.

As he boarded a car for the ride, a frown crossed the jeweler's chubby features. The Prince Louis, like all of the hotels in Monaco, was expensive. In some cases, exorbitantly so. But there was expensive and then there was extravagant. For the guest of means, a mere suite could run three to four thousand francs a day. And from his prior visits to the Prince Louis Hotel, LeBreton knew that suites on the sixth floor were not the most expensive deluxe accommodations in Monaco. The jeweler did have to admit to himself that Suite 641 would be more than adequate by any standard; however, it would not be what a woman of Countess Grimaldi's reputed wealth and status would ordinarily find acceptable.

Claude LeBreton knew about such things, because he had been catering to the whims of the rich and famous for most of his life. However, a wary tingling sensation started at the base of his spine. He would make sure to get a sizeable deposit before he would do any actual work for this Countess Grimaldi.

Every step that the jeweler had taken since exiting his limousine in the front driveway of the Prince Louis Hotel in Monaco had been monitored by the security services of the principality. His journey across the lobby, his brief exchange with the concierge, the elevator ride, and now his trek down the corridor to Suite 641 had been studied and recorded. All appeared well. Suite 641 had been secured by an adequate draft drawn on a Swiss bank; the vivacious Countess Maria Teresa Grimaldi and her dark-complexioned male companion appeared bona fide; and the jeweler's visit was not unusual, as LeBreton had done business before with Prince Louis Hotel guests. But when the jeweler knocked on the suite door and was permitted access, he was no longer being watched by the principality's security forces. This was because, although Monaco was unusually safe, it was not a police state and the monied guests visiting the famous resort did demand a certain degree of privacy. After all, anyone would be a fool to commit a crime in Monaco.

But, as Julianna Saint had often remarked, Hubert Metayer was indeed a fool, and one of the worst variety, because he was a dangerous fool.

Suite 641 of the Prince Louis Hotel was, as expected, luxurious. It consisted of a spacious sitting room, a bedroom with a king-sized bed, and a bathroom equipped with gold fixtures. All of the rooms had French windows from which a partial view of the Mediterranean was visible. Every piece of furniture, art object, and miscellaneous item in the suite had been selected with care. It was a classy place, and was about to become the scene of a murder.

Hubert Metayer had worked for Julianna Saint for three years. Her reputation within the French underworld was spectacular, to say the least, and at the time Hubert had approached her, his criminal career was leading him nowhere except to a long stretch in prison. His objective in joining *L'Ombre du Diable*'s team was to upgrade his skills. It hadn't been easy becoming a prótegé of the infamous thief, but he had managed to persuade her to take him on as an associate. That is, as long as he curbed his violent tendencies and did only than what he was told. This had worked out, more or less, and he had learned a great deal. But as time wore on he found it increasingly difficult to take orders from a woman. Even one as brilliant as Julianna Saint.

Since he had been with her, Hubert Metayer had discovered that, prior to entering her employ, he had been no more than a lowlife petty crook compared to the sophisticated level at which Julianna operated. After the bank burglary in the United States,

Hubert decided that it was time for him to use the expertise he had gleaned from her to pull a job on his own. As he saw it, Julianna approached each assignment by conducting an unnecessarily exhaustive study of the target. She refused to employ violence and, as a rule, would utilize nothing more potent than various forms of sedatives, such as those that had been used on the bank guards in Chicago. But the thing that impressed Hubert Metayer most of all was Julianna's execution. Every move and possible contingency was carefully calculated and planned for. So, eschewing her exhaustive research, Hubert had selected a familiar target and set out to commit a robbery.

The Devil's Shadow was bold, which was part of her legendary persona. Hubert decided to become equally bold in the selection of his target. He didn't do any research because he didn't feel that he had to. He was not being foolhardy in this regard; he simply felt that he knew the area he would be operating in and also the movements of his target well enough that he didn't have to waste a lot of time on the setup. And Hubert was being particularly audacious, because he was going to commit this crime in Monaco, which was considered off limits to any European criminal with a brain in his head. However, he no longer had to labor under the same restrictions as his former fellow crooks, because he was now an international criminal mastermind in his own right.

Hubert knew the arrogant little Claude LeBreton's habits, because the criminal organization he had formally belonged to in Paris had once been hired to bodyguard the jeweler when he had ventured beyond the borders of Monaco. He also was aware that when LeBreton was in the principality, he traveled with an unarmed chauffeur and displayed little regard for his own safety. That was due to the French police being there to protect him. The thief had decided that this would not be the case today.

In Hubert Metayer's estimation, his plan to rob Claude LeBreton was as brilliant as anything ever conceived by the mind of the infamous Devil's Shadow. He had hired a German woman, who specialized in short con games and spoke fluent Italian, to pass herself off as this Countess Maria Teresa Grimaldi. He had opened an account, secured with cash, at a Swiss bank under a phony name and placed sufficient funds in it to cover the cost of the suite at the Prince Louis Hotel. Then he had his imposter call LeBreton and set up an appointment.

Hubert had made sure that she specified that she wanted to commission a diamond and emerald necklace in a platinum setting, which was just the type of garishly expensive item the fat little jeweler specialized in. Then all Hubert had to do was wait.

When LeBreton entered the suite, Hubert was waiting for him. And he did not have the compunctions about engaging in violence that Julianna Saint did. The phony countess, dressed in a sheer negligee, was seated by the window with the Mediterranean view behind her. The jeweler's attention was totally focused on the woman and he was unaware that Hubert had been standing behind the door. He silently followed LeBreton across the room. Pulling a garotte from his pocket and tightening the razor-sharp wire between clenched fists, he came up behind his victim. It was over quickly.

Upon witnessing the unexpected death, the phony countess became violently ill and barely made it to the ornate washroom. She was still retching into the toilet bowl when Hubert appeared at the door. He waited until she washed her face and rinsed out her mouth before he walked toward her, garotte extended.

Before leaving Suite 641, the thief opened LeBreton's attaché case. He shook his head and grinned when he discovered that the case wasn't even locked. The jewels, twelve large diamonds and fifteen brilliant emeralds, were contained in two leather pouches. The platinum ingot was wrapped in a soft cloth. Hubert was satisfied. Now it was time for him to make his escape.

From the single valise he had carried when he checked into the Prince Louis Hotel with the late Countess Grimaldi, Hubert removed a pair of dark glasses and a fake goatee. After putting them on and checking his appearance in the sitting room mirror, he realized that his disguise was not world-class, but with a snap brim hat included, he could walk right past the surveillance cameras and out the front door of the hotel. All the *flics* would have would be a grainy picture of a black man with a goatee, who was wearing dark glasses and a hat. He had been careful not to leave any fingerprints behind. There would be no connection to him, and by the time they started looking in earnest, Hubert would be on a flight to Paris. Connecting flights would transport him to New York and then on to his final destination in Chicago where he would rendezvous with Julianna and Christophe in a few days.

Exiting the suite, he placed a "Do Not Disturb" sign on the outer doorknob. Then he paused, looked right into the nearest surveillance camera, and waved. On his way out of the Prince Louis, he mused that the United States was the perfect place for him to fence his loot. Maybe he wasn't in Julianna Saint's league yet, but he was certainly on his way.

It took twelve hours for the bodies in Suite 641 to be discovered. The response from the French police was quite pronounced. The principality of Monaco came under the jurisdiction of the Sûreté, and the highest-ranking member of this contingent was Chief Inspector Jacques Benoit.

Benoit was a tall, gaunt man, who wore thick glasses and dressed in clothing that never seemed to fit right. He had gone bald while he was still in his twenties—he was now sixty—and was always looking for a way to regrow hair on the top of his head. Rogaine and Propecia had not worked for him, so he had gone to one of the most exclusive toupee designers in Paris and had a hairpiece made. And it was perfect. Perhaps too perfect, because instead of adding to the prefect's appearance, it made him look ridiculous.

But no one ever laughed at Jacques Benoit. At least not after they'd had any contact with him, because he was not only one of the most brilliant cops in Europe, but was ranked by his peers as among the best in the world.

Benoit could have had a more prestigious assignment within

the Sûreté, but he had used the political influence that had been bestowed upon him after he had solved a number of headline cases to get the job of top cop in Monaco. At his age he felt that he deserved a respite from the harsh labors of French law enforcement. So far, in the eighteen months that he had been the prefect here, there had been little major crime and no murders at all. That is, until today.

The forensics technicians had finished processing the suite, and Benoit's subordinates were waiting for the prefect to indicate the direction in which he wanted this investigation to proceed.

Benoit walked slowly around the suite from room to room. Periodically he would nod his head, which was adorned as always with the expensive hairpiece. He said nothing. Finally he turned to the detectives—two males and a female—who had accompanied him to the Prince Louis Hotel.

"Start with the videotape of the man who left this suite and waved at the surveillance camera in the corridor. Ascertain every possible physical characteristic that he possessed and run it through the computer files of known criminals. All you will get at this point are similarities in appearance, resulting in a long list of possible suspects. We can reduce the number as the investigation progresses."

He paused. "I want to know the real identity of the woman who passed herself off as Countess Maria Teresa Grimaldi. Also, see if we can get any additional tapes of her companion while they were staying here. He will probably appear the same as he did when he left, but it will give us more to go on." Another pause. "There is one more thing. Our killer and the woman spent two nights and an entire day in this suite. The housekeeper said they slept in the same bed. Have the woman's corpse checked for the presence of semen. If you find it, run a DNA check."

The prefect of the Monaco police contingent concluded with, "Our man thinks he's quite the criminal genius, but we'll nail him. We'll most certainly nail him."

33

Cole was driven from the Oyster Bay Beach Resort to Cal Ferris's villa in a twelve-seat GMC van. The driver was a middle-aged, dark-complexioned woman with a missing front tooth. He was her only passenger and she had been given instructions for the trip in French by the hotel concierge. She didn't speak English, but she fussed over her passenger as if he were royalty.

For this trip up the mountain, Cole had donned formal wear, complemented by a single-breasted white dinner jacket. Before leaving the room, he examined his appearance in the full-length bathroom mirror. The thought that he'd had earlier about Ian Fleming's fictional secret agent James Bond came back to him. However, tonight Larry Cole would not be armed.

He was delivered to the front entrance of the villa. While the hotel van was still some distance away, the lights and sounds of a party in full tilt carried to them down the mountainside.

Unlike Julianna Saint's villa, Cal Ferris's place was surrounded by a six-foot wrought-iron fence. There were a couple of muscular types with shaved heads standing outside the gate. When Cole got out of the van, they stepped forward to confront him.

"We help you, brother?" said the one whose thick neck seemed to disappear into his shoulders.

"I'm a guest of Mr. Ferris," he replied with a smile.

"Mr. Ferris has a lot of guests tonight, my man," snarled the second man, who had a toothpick stuck in the corner of his mouth. If Cole wasn't mistaken, this guy had been a fullback for the Seattle Seahawks a few years ago.

Their tone irritated the cop and an icy fury surged through him. Maintaining his composure, he said, "You boys need to mind your manners or somebody could come along who might not be as tolerant of your ignorance as I am."

They stiffened and Cole prepared for an attack. Then the one with no neck laughed and his partner's face split in a wide grin. "Take it easy, Mr. Holt. We know who you are. We're fans of yours. Cal wanted us to be on the lookout for you."

Cole remained guarded. "How did you recognize me?"

The two men exchanged puzzled looks. The former fullback said, "We're Cal's regular bodyguards. He turned us on to some of your books. We're big fans, brother. Real big fans."

The cop thawed a bit. "I appreciate that, fellas. It's always nice to run into people like you. Now, if you don't mind?" He pointed to the villa entrance.

"Oh, sure, Mr. Holt," No Neck said.

"Go right in, sir," the fullback chimed in.

The two behemoths parted and the man in the white dinner jacket walked between them. The driver of the hotel van had witnessed the exchange between the bodyguards and her handsome passenger. Although she could not understand what was said, when she noticed the big men go from being defiant to deferential, she laughed out loud, displaying her missing tooth, and drove off back down the mountain.

Cal Ferris's broad-shouldered companions were really not so much bodyguards as they were part of the comedian's ever-present entourage. Usually their presence alone was enough to ward off any potential problems that Ferris might encounter during his extensive travels. They were known to be a bit surly, to which their manner of greeting the recent arrival attested, but they were indeed fans of Michael Holt.

After Cole entered the villa, No Neck said to the fullback, "He sure didn't look like no author that I've ever seen."

"Yeah. He reminded me more of a cop."

The party was in full swing throughout the entire villa complex when Cole entered. A disc jockey manned a synthesizer connected to a pair of huge speakers, which were set up in a corner of the large flagstone-floored patio. The three-story, stucco main house, a kidney-shaped swimming pool, and a guesthouse surrounded the patio. The front door of the main house stood open, and a bar, manned by two bartenders, efficiently dispensed drinks. There was a long table laden with food and a smoking, drum-style barbecue grill beside the pool. Three attendants, clad in white aprons, ladled ribs, steak, chicken, and barbecue shrimp with all the accoutrements onto plates.

Then there were the guests. Between seventy-five and one hundred people circulated between the bar, the house, and the pool area. Some were dancing to the disc jockey's music, some sat at tables around the pool, and others were simply standing in small groups.

Cole stood a short distance inside the entrance and took in the spectacle of his first celebrity party. He recognized a Los Angeles Lakers basketball player, two pro golfers, and a smattering of movie stars. He didn't know any of the others, but they were all tanned, well-dressed, and reeked of money. Then there was the host, renowned comedian Calvin Ferris.

The celebrity host of this party in the Leeward Islands had been born in Lexington, Kentucky, as Calvin Harlan Ferris III. His father and grandfather before him had been successful veterinarians specializing in the care and treatment of horses. Early on in his life it was made quite clear to Little Calvin that he was expected to follow in the family tradition. That might have been all right, but at an early age he was kicked by a horse, which resulted in his developing a pathological fear of the large animals. As he grew up, Calvin Harlan Ferris III couldn't stand even to be around horses, much less learn to doctor them. On top of this, much to the disappointment of his very proper and professional father and grandfather, Calvin III became the class cutup in school. What his family never managed to understand was that Cal began clowning in school to hide his deep-seated fears and insecurities. And the more he was punished and criticized for his antics, the harder he worked to become even more audacious. But what no one, including the class clown himself, understood was that a comic genius was developing. A comic genius who would become known worldwide and make a fortune.

Cole saw his host standing by the swimming pool talking animatedly to a group of guests. Cal Ferris was a short, slender man who was almost slight in stature. He had a head that seemed a shade big for his body, and thickly pomaded, reddish brown hair, which he parted on the left. He was a consummate entertainer who was not only a brilliant stand-up comic, but also an excellent tap dancer, a good singer, and a natural-born dramatic actor. He made a great deal of money and he spent it liberally. Under different circumstances, Larry Cole would have been honored simply to meet Cal Ferris, but now the job came first.

The cop, posing as author Michael Holt, was about to cross the patio and introduce himself to his host when he detected a familiar scent. It was Clinique perfume, which Cole recognized because it had been one of his ex-wife's favorites. Turning around, Larry Cole came face-to-face with Julianna Saint.

Cal Ferris was at the top of his game tonight. He would remain at his villa on Saint Martin until early April. Then he would start a six-week engagement at the Luxor Hotel in Las Vegas. In late June he would begin filming a western in Los Angeles, and in the fall fly to New York to tape his own network television special. His time in the Caribbean would be profitably spent, as besides lying around the pool with the bevy of young things who gravitated to him wherever he went, he would also work on the new comedy routine he would stage in Las Vegas.

Ferris had been regaling his guests with one of his comedic anecdotes when he saw the tall black man in the white dinner jacket enter the courtyard. This had to be Mike Holt, and Ferris was forced to admit that the author was an impressive-looking dude. The comedian was about to disengage himself from his other guests to go over and welcome the author when Julianna Saint came in.

As always, Cal's neighbor from the top of the mountain looked like she'd just stepped off the cover of a slick fashion magazine. She was wearing a low-cut, full-length, off-white gown that adhered to every curve of her spectacular body like a second skin. Her black hair was worn up on top of her head, and the diamonds adorning her ears, throat, wrists, and hands sparkled brilliantly in the patio lights. Her simple act of walking into the courtyard imbued his party with an added dimension of charm and class.

Cal was on his way over to greet the author and his neighbor when Holt turned around to face Julianna. The two people stood less than a foot apart, and the comedian detected something quite dramatic taking place between them. The only way that Ferris could characterize what was happening was that a bolt of emotional electricity had passed between them. They seemed frozen in place until Cal reached them and said, "Good evening, folks, and welcome to the party."

Neither of his guests acknowledged him or moved for almost thirty seconds. Then Julianna smiled and extended her hand to the man in the white tuxedo. "Good evening, sir. My name is Julianna Saint."

The man bowed at the waist and gently kissed the back of her hand. Straightening up, he said, "How do you do, Ms. Saint? My name is Michael Holt."

"The famous author?"

"I don't know about famous, but I am an author."

"I have all your books. If you'll be staying on the island for a few days, it would be a great favor to me if you would autograph them."

"It would be my pleasure, Julianna."

Cal Ferris decided that it was time to interrupt this budding mutual admiration society. "Welcome to my party, Julianna. Mike, we spoke on the phone earlier. I'm Cal Ferris."

The introductions out of the way, Ferris decided to play Cupid. "Julianna, you're no stranger to my house. Why don't you show Mike around?"

Without hesitation she stepped forward and took Holt's arm.

The comedian watched his guests stroll off across the patio. Ferris admitted to himself that they looked good together.

They were inside the house at the trophy case. Behind the glass were the numerous awards Ferris had received, including two Emmys.

"It must be a very interesting profession," Julianna said. "That is, to be able to sit down and write novels."

"I enjoy it," Holt said, as he bent down to read the inscription on the Man of the Year Award Ferris had received from the NAACP.

When he didn't elaborate, she said, "Tell me, where do you get your ideas?"

He stood up and turned to face her. He was a head taller than Julianna, forcing her to look up at him. She had always been attracted to tall men.

"Ideas are everywhere," he said. "I could even incorporate this trip to Saint Martin into one of my books. Perhaps make it a romance novel."

"I didn't know you wrote romance novels, Mike."

He looked directly into her eyes. "There's a first time for everything, Julianna."

He got them drinks from the bar. She had champagne; he ordered a bourbon and water. They took seats at a table beside the pool. Resting her chin on her cupped hands, she leaned toward him. Her low-cut gown provided him with an inviting view of her cleavage.

"So what are you working on now?" she asked.

"A writer I know died mysteriously in Chicago a few months ago. I've been doing research into the events surrounding his death, and I think I will be able to uncover enough information to make an interesting, revealing book."

"What was the dead writer's name?"

"Ennis. Greg Ennis. But enough of this talk about me and my work. Why don't you tell me about yourself?"

Seemingly totally unaffected by the mention of Greg Ennis, she

said, "I'm in the import/export business, but that's so boring compared to what you do."

"No," he protested. "I'd really like to hear about it."

Grabbing his hand, she stood up and said, "And I would rather
dance."

Cal Ferris entertained his guests with his new comedy routine. To
accommodate everyone, cushioned deck chairs and a few benches
were set up on the patio. As the comedian picked up the microphone
to begin, he noticed that Julianna and the author were seated side
by side.

Ferris was aware that there had been other men in Julianna's
life, but she hadn't been seeing anyone on a regular basis in a long
time. In fact, the comedian had considered making a move on her
once himself, but she was a lot more woman than he could ever
handle. On top of that, by reputation she was rumored to be dangerous.

As Ferris began telling his first joke, he wondered if the
formidable-looking Mike Holt could handle her.

The author walked her up the road to her villa when the party was
over. He mentioned how steep the incline was.

She laughed. "But I see you running up the mountain every
day, Mike. And you seem to do it with ease."

"So you noticed me?"

She punched him gently in the shoulder. "A man like you is
hard to miss. I've watched you. In fact, I was even considering
joining you."

They reached the entrance to her villa. "What about tomorrow
afternoon?"

"I'll make you a deal," she said, opening the gate. "I'll run the
mountain with you and afterwards we'll have a refreshing swim in
my pool and then lunch."

"You've got a deal," he responded.

For a moment they remained in the same positions. Then Julianna stepped forward and kissed him on the cheek.

"Good night, Mike," she said, before going inside.

"Good night, Julianna." Then he turned and walked back down the road to Cal Ferris's villa. There the hotel van was waiting.

Julianna's villa was laid out in a similar fashion to Cal Ferris's, only hers was larger. There were night-lights illuminating the patio, which was of asphalt, while the comedian's was constructed of flagstones. Her pool was Olympic-sized, and like Cal, Julianna had constructed a guesthouse. Christophe La Croix was currently staying there.

All of Julianna's pool furniture was handmade of varnished wood. When she entered the courtyard, the Frenchman was lounging in a deck chair with a bottle of cognac on a table beside him.

"How was the party?" he asked, refilling his glass and pouring one for her.

"Very nice," she said, taking the drink.

"Why, Julianna, you are absolutely glowing. You've met a man."

She took a sip from the glass, but did not say anything else about her evening. "What did you find out about the tourist Mama Johnnie was talking to in Marigot?"

Christophe shrugged. "She gave me the slip, but I went back to Johnnie's and questioned her about the tourist. She told me that her name is Penny Gibbs from Chicago, Illinois, and that she is staying at the Oyster Bay Beach Resort. So I went over there and talked to a guy I know who tends bar inside the hotel. He checked the guest roster for me and discovered that there is no guest named Penelope Gibbs registered there. He checked all the way back to the first of the year and came up with nothing on anyone named Gibbs." He paused to take a swallow of his drink.

Julianna's eyes never left him as she waited.

Quickly he continued. "I had my guy check the guest list for anyone from the Chicago area and came up with a couple who are currently staying there. Their name is O'Hara and they are both over eighty. I was able to take a look at them down by the swimming pool and they didn't look anything like the woman I saw at Mama Johnnie's."

The Devil's Shadow turned her back on him and walked to the edge of the pool. Looking down into the water, she said, "What did you do then?"

She could feel his noncommittal shrug. No panic, no worry, simply going with the flow. At times such nonchalance enraged her. He responded, "What else could I do, Julianna? But if she's on this island, I'll find her."

She spun around and her eyes flared angrily. "Did it occur to you, Christophe, that the woman you so easily lost was not a fat, acne-scarred tourist, but possibly a skilled law enforcement operative?! That she was able to give you the slip because she was smart enough to detect your clubfooted surveillance techniques!"

Sheepishly Christophe lowered his head. He was particularly sensitive to criticism from her. For her part, she was sorry that she had used such a harsh tone with him, but losing that woman could be dangerous. Especially dangerous as their next assignment was in Chicago, where the woman posing as this Penelope Gibbs claimed to come from. There were also other complications that Julianna could not ignore, such as a handsome stranger in a white dinner jacket.

Regaining her composure, she said, "Now, listen to me, Christophe. Tomorrow you are to go back to the Oyster Bay Beach Resort and talk to each and every one of your contacts. You will give them a description of this Gibbs woman, and if you get even the most remote lead, you are to follow it up."

"But suppose I can't find her, Julianna?"

"I'm actually expecting that you won't."

"Pardon?"

She didn't answer him. Placing her still full glass down on the table, she turned and walked rapidly across the patio. Before she entered the house, she called over her shoulder to him, "Good night, Christophe, and I suggest that you get some sleep, because you have a busy day tomorrow."

The Frenchman picked up the cognac bottle and was about to refill his glass. Then *L'Ombre du Diable*'s words sank in. He re-corked the bottle, stood up, and walked into the guesthouse. Within minutes he was sound asleep.

Cole let himself in to his hotel room. Switching on the light, he went to the in-room safe and, after working the combination, removed a palm-sized portable radio. He switched it on and depressed a key. A couple of seconds went by and then Judy Daniels's voice came over the speaker. "How did it go, boss?"

The small radios they were using were special, closed-frequency models equipped with scramblers. They were effective over distances up to two miles and operated on a band that was difficult to find.

"I made contact, Judy. I'm meeting her tomorrow. How did things go on your end?"

"I'm going to have to drop my Penelope-Gibbs-from-the-Windy-City persona. That leaves me with four."

Cole smiled. *That's my Judy,* he thought.

"Okay, start at the beginning and tell me what happened."

34

Rome, Italy
MARCH 3, 2005
9:15 A.M.

B ishop Martin Simon Pierre De Coutreaux was addressing a group of fifty foreign priests visiting the Vatican. They were assembled in the chapel of Saint Andrew the Martyr. The pious prelate stood before them and held forth on a subject that he deeply believed in.

"The Lord Jesus Christ, after being in the desert for forty days and forty nights, was tempted by the Dark Angel, Satan. Using the power of evil, the Devil transported the Lord God Himself to the top of a mountain and displayed all of the kingdoms of the world to Him."

De Coutreaux emphasized his words with sweeping gestures, and his voice reverberated throughout the ornate chapel.

"And what did the Evil One ask in return for this gift of limitless power and riches?"

He paused to take in the engrossed stares of his audience. A couple of the younger priests were so fascinated that their mouths hung open as they absorbed every word. The bishop allowed a sardonic smile to play at the corners of his mouth. His voice dropped a couple of decibels and he nearly whispered, "All that the Evil One asked from our Lord in return was that He bow down and pay homage. That the Prince of Peace, the Son of God, the Lamb, should subordinate himself to the father of lies, deceit, and sin. And the Dark Angel was as real a physical being as was our Lord Jesus Christ. A physical being with the power of a supernatural entity. A being which can assume physical proportions, is ageless, and who is with us on this earth right now."

He pointed his index finger to take in the entire assembly. "He is with us now, walking the streets we walk, coming into contact with us, invading our institutions, and always looking for a way to lead us from the path of the righteous and into the fires of damnation. Be ever vigilant, my brothers in Christ, or you will fall prey to the Evil One and his minions. Now, let us pray."

Later the bishop took a solitary walk around Saint Peter's Square. He knew he had held the visiting priests spellbound; however, he didn't feel that he had gotten his message across. This was not a criticism of his fellow priests. It was simply that adherence to faith in the Almighty did not always extend to a belief in Satan. Too many of his fellow clerics, including his peers and superiors here in Rome, saw mankind as the most powerful cause for evil in the world. They failed to see the machinations of Satan in the wars, maimings, and other mayhem perpetrated by the species Homo sapiens on earth. Neither would they give a great deal of credence to De Coutreaux's ramblings about the devil and his followers existing in human form. The bishop had never personally come face-to-face with the Dark Angel, but he believed in his existence with the same certainty as his belief in the Almighty God. And somewhere deep down inside Martin Simon Pierre De Coutreaux, he spent more time dwelling on the existence of the devil than he did contemplating the presence of God. Now De Coutreaux was on the brink of being able to prove the physical existence of the devil or, at the very least, one of his followers.

The bishop stopped in front of the entrance to Saint Peter's Basilica. An elderly tourist walked past him and said, "Good morning, Your Eminence."

"Good morning," De Coutreaux responded.

Suddenly he became very much aware of who, what, and where he was. Bishop Martin Simon Pierre De Coutreaux was a high-ranking man of the cloth with a future that was virtually limitless in his calling. However, he had not begun life that way. In fact, where he had started and where he was now were as opposite in nature as the manifestation of demonic evil and that of angelic good.

Miami, Florida
JANUARY 16, 1975
2:05 P.M.

The cruise ship *La Belle Liberté* was docked at the Caribbean Island luxury cruise ship dock. The sixteen-hundred-passenger vessel was preparing for a seven-day cruise to the Virgin Islands. The ship would make stops at Saint Martin, Saint Thomas, and Freeport in the Grand Bahamas. The director of passenger services on *La Belle Liberté*, as was his habit at the beginning of each cruise, assembled the employees who would be servicing the ship's guests.

A white-haired, portly Swede, the director of passenger services adopted an outwardly congenial manner, which could vanish in the blink of an eye and turn hard as granite. Now, his Swedish accent evident, he laid down the law to his people.

"Each of you is a representative of this vessel and the Caribbean Island cruise line. As such, you will conduct yourselves in an orderly, professional, efficient, and unassuming manner." As he talked, he paced up and down in front of the precisely arranged ranks of employees like a general reviewing troops, which, in a manner of speaking, he was. "Our mission on this cruise, as it is on every voyage that we undertake for our employer, is to ensure that our guests are catered to and enjoy one of the most memorable vacation experiences of their lives. They must feel at all times that they are in a secure, relaxed environment. Whatever a passenger requests, if it is humanly possible to grant, you will do so quickly and always with a smile."

The employees were arranged by shipboard rank in the main dining room of the cruise ship. The section managers, clad in tuxedos, came first. Then the maître d's, bartenders, cabin stewards, waiters, and, finally, the busboys. Each one wore a distinctive uniform adorned with a Caribbean Island cruise line crest above their names. Only first names for service personnel were ever used aboard ship. Each employee was carefully screened before hire and most of them had previously worked for this or another cruise line. They were a competent staff of whom the Swedish-born director of passenger services was quite proud. It was because of them that *La Belle Liberté* was one of the most popular cruise vessels on the Miami-to-Caribbean run.

Before dismissing the service staff, the director of passenger services inspected them with the thoroughness one might have seen on a West Point parade ground.

As he started down the line of cabin stewards, he stopped.

"So you signed on once again, Charlie," the Swede said with a smile.

"Yes, sir," the steward in the burgundy waist-length jacket said, stiffening to attention.

"What is this, your sixth year with us?"

"Actually," the twenty-six-year-old man said, "it is my eighth. I started at quite a young age with Caribbean Island."

The director of passenger services raised his voice so that it would carry to the others assembled in the main dining room. "If everyone here did their jobs as well as Charlie does his, we would have to turn passengers back at the gangplank."

When the director of passenger services moved on, the steward beamed with pride over the compliment. Yes, he did do a good job. In fact, he did an exceptional job, but he was becoming increasingly aware that he had been doing this same job of steward for the Caribbean Island cruise line for a very long time.

One of the new bartenders aboard *La Belle Liberté* was an Irishman who had come over to the Caribbean run after serving on transatlantic passenger ships. Since boarding the vessel, he had become friendly with another bartender, who was from South Africa.

After the inspection, they went to their stations in preparation for passenger boarding at five o'clock. The Irishman and the Afrikaner were checking their liquor stores.

"The Swede seems a decent enough sort," the Irishman said. "It was nice of him to compliment that steward named Charlie."

The Afrikaner, a big, blond, square-jawed type, sneered, "He's too partial to darkies if you ask me. Constantly telling them what a good job they did at this or what a good job they did at that. Got them really suckered, because they're always looking for ways to shine up to him."

The Irishman didn't understand what the Afrikaner meant when he referred to the steward as a "darky." Although the majority of service personnel on *La Belle Liberté* were either black or Asian, the thin man whom the Swede had addressed in ranks possessed blond hair, hazel eyes, and a complexion as fair as the Irishman's own. He stated this to the Afrikaner.

"That's the problem with America," he responded. "The whites interbreed with the colored until you've got niggers like Charlie Martin running around all over the place."

The Irishman was stunned. He didn't say anything else to the Afrikaner about the steward; however, he began viewing Charlie Martin in a completely different light. Needless to say, the Irish bartender stayed as far away from the black steward as he could.

Charlie Martin was from Detroit, Michigan, by way of Haiti. His mother was a domestic who had immigrated to the United States at the age of sixteen. She had spent twenty-five years employed by members of the Ford automobile industry family in and around Detroit. His father, who was twenty years his mother's senior, had worked as a Pullman porter, but lost his job over some indiscretion that was never made completely clear to Charlie. From what he had been able to find out from overheard whispered conversations between his mother and some of her relatives living in the Detroit area, his father's dismissal from the railroad had something to do with a combination of his drinking and some missing money.

Both of Charlie Martin's parents were light-complexioned blacks. In the color-conscious atmosphere of Detroit in the post–World War II, pre-civil-rights era, his mother had quickly risen to a prominent position in the households she worked in. His father, who possessed more noticeable African features than his wife, went to work at the Church of Saint Simon Peter as a caretaker. Although the old man had a reputation for taking a drink from time to time, and always carried a half-pint bottle of Canadian Club whiskey somewhere on his person, he made sure that his family went to church every Sunday and on all holy days of obligation. However, the real head of the household was Charlie's mother, who carefully supervised her brood of four children—Charlie being the youngest and only boy, along with three girls.

The Martin children attended Catholic schools in Detroit, were taught by their mother to speak fluent French with the same facility that they spoke English, and, due to the expensive hand-me-downs from their mother's employers, dressed better than the other children. Charlie's mother was a truly exceptional woman, who taught her children as much about the world at home as they learned in school. And like their father, she was extremely religious. Only her religion extended beyond the boundaries of traditional Christianity into the realm of voodoo. She was not a practitioner of the dark arts, but she definitely imbued her children with respect for such practices, as well as fear and loathing of that special enemy of the human race, the Dark Angel Satan.

Charlie Martin graduated from high school in Detroit and received an academic scholarship to attend the University of Michigan. The year he spent in college was not a very good one for him. Although he had experienced racial discrimination in the past, when he got to college he was exposed to a systematic form of prejudice of a more intense variety. Charlie became so disillusioned that he left school, much to his mother's disappointment, to learn something about the world. This led to him signing on with the Caribbean Island cruise line.

The passengers began boarding *La Belle Liberté* promptly at 5:00 P.M. Charlie Martin was assigned to be one of the stewards on the Sun Deck, which was where the most expensive cabins were located. Each cabin on the Sun Deck consisted of a bathroom, two sleeping rooms, and a sitting room. The sitting rooms and bedrooms were equipped with plate-glass windows, which provided a panoramic view of the ocean when the cruise vessel was at sea.

Charlie checked each of his cabins prior to the passengers' arrival. Their luggage had already been delivered and would remain in the cabin untouched until the steward was summoned to unpack, if the passenger desired such a service. He entered Sun Deck Suite Three, which bore the brass identification "SD3" on the cabin door. The luggage was neatly stacked on the rack inside the door. Charlie was surprised to see that there were only two bags. Usually guests aboard *La Belle Liberté* traveled with a great deal more. But it was not the steward's job to determine how much or how little the passengers brought aboard.

He checked the cabin for cleanliness and to make sure the complimentary bottle of mineral water and box of chocolates were in place. As an added touch, Charlie Martin also left a single red rose with a card, bearing his name, welcoming the passenger on board in each cabin. Satisfied that all was in order, he was turning to leave when the door from the companionway opened. The steward turned and came face-to-face with the ugliest human being he had ever seen.

Rome, Italy
MARCH 3, 2005
NOON

Standing outside Saint Peter's Basilica in Vatican City thirty years later, Bishop Martin Simon Pierre De Coutreaux recalled the name of the passenger on *La Belle Liberté*. It was Viscount Maurice Phillipe Stephan De Coutreaux. And for the French Catholic bishop who had been born a Negro in Haiti named Charlie Martin, that was where it all began.

The cleric's meditation on his humble beginnings was interrupted by a young priest sprinting across Saint Peter's Square toward him.

"Your Eminence," he said, breathlessly, "the cardinal chamberlain has just passed away and the Holy Father wants to see you right away."

Bishop De Coutreaux lowered his head, made the sign of the cross, prayed in silence for a moment, and then turned to proceed to the pope's private quarters.

35

C ole slept late, ate a light breakfast consisting of coffee, orange juice, fresh fruit, and buttered croissants, and lounged around his room reading Mike Holt's latest novel. The book was a police procedural set in wintertime Denver. Some of the scenes, described against the backdrop of an urban snowscape, reminded Cole of Chicago. The fact that Holt's story revolved around a crew of bank robbers was particularly interesting to the cop, because of the crimes that had occurred in Chicago last year. But those were cases that he would deal with upon his return to the Windy City.

At 1:00 P.M. he closed the book, put on his running shoes, shorts, and a tank top. After filling his water bottle, he left the hotel and walked down Oyster Bay Beach to the foot of the mountain. It was a hot, muggy day with the temperature hovering at ninety-five degrees. There was a slight offshore breeze blowing, but it would be of little comfort on the run to the top of the mountain.

He had been waiting a few minutes when a white Jeep Cherokee, driven by one of the servants, pulled to a stop a short distance away and Julianna got out.

Julianna Saint was clad in a pink halter top with matching shorts, shoes, and socks. Her thick black hair was tied back in a ponytail, and a pink sweatband encircled her head. She had a water bottle in an insulated container clipped to her belt.

Even in this exercise outfit, the Devil's Shadow was exceptionally beautiful. "You're right on time," Cole said.

She smiled and replied, "In fact, I'm early. I believe that punctuality is a virtue that should be cultivated."

"Shall we stretch a bit before getting started?"

"I usually wait to stretch until the end of the run, but if you need to, go ahead."

He took that as a challenge. "No. I'll try it your way. Shall we get started?"

"I'll lead." With that she took off at a dead run, heading for the mountain trail.

At a slower pace, Cole followed. Within less than a minute, she had opened up a sizeable gap between them. Cole did not increase his pace at all. The run up the side of the Virgin Islands' mountain had become a race.

Christophe La Croix spent the morning nosing around the Oyster Bay Beach Resort. He was looking for any sign of the woman who had identified herself at Mama Johnnie's Bar as Penelope Gibbs of Chicago, Illinois.

Clad in casual attire, including an open cotton shirt, sandals, and sunglasses, the handsome Frenchman made discreet inquiries about the resort hotel's guests. He was known around the island and he was also quite generous in providing the appropriate recompense for the requested information. He came up empty.

As noon approached, Christophe became hungry and went to the Oyster Pearl Restaurant just off the lobby. He selected a table that provided him with a strategic view of the comings and goings at the Caribbean resort. He ordered a papaya-juice-and-rum cocktail and shrimp salad. As he consumed his lunch, he went back over the events of the previous day when he had lost the woman on the streets of Marigot.

When Christophe had given his ego sufficient time to heal, he was able to admit to himself that he had been given the slip by a skilled professional. He could console himself with the fact that he hadn't been on a real job, so to speak, but had simply been gathering information in what could be considered his own backyard. And who could expect the fat little tourist, who appeared drunk, to ever be capable of eluding someone as skilled as he?

Mentally he tallied up what he had. Penelope Gibbs was an

overweight, white female of medium height with bad skin and lank brown hair. Or at least that was the way she had appeared yesterday. Christophe did not employ disguises, but he was quite adept at changing his appearance. And even though he didn't use artificial methods to alter himself physically, he understood how such things were employed to create a false persona. So Penelope Gibbs's weight, acne-scarred skin, and lank hair could have been fake. Then he considered the most stunning possibility of all. The impersonator of this Penelope Gibbs might not be a woman, which meant he had been barking up the wrong tree for a full day.

Christophe La Croix finished his lunch, paid the bill, and left the restaurant. Slowly he strolled around the resort grounds. There were hundreds of guests in evidence and the woman or man he was looking for could be anyone. And if he couldn't locate her, there would be no way for him to find out if the questions she'd been asking at Mama Johnnie's bar were simple inquisitiveness or something that would later prove to be dangerous to the operations of the Devil's Shadow.

The old woman was wearing a long-sleeved, white leisure suit, which was buttoned up to the neck, despite the heat. She had snow white hair and liver-spotted skin, and wore black-framed sunglasses and a sombrero-style straw hat as protection against the hot sun. She sat at a table covered by a beach umbrella some distance from the ornate, oyster-shaped beach resort swimming pool.

She had been watching the man who was searching for Penelope Gibbs for most of the morning. Now, unbeknownst to him, Christophe La Croix passed within a few feet of the woman he was looking for. Behind her elderly-dowager disguise, Judy Daniels noticed that the Frenchman didn't pay her the slightest attention when he passed, although he eyed every shapely female in sight lying around the pool.

And while Christophe La Croix had been in search of Penelope Gibbs, Judy Daniels, the Mistress of Disguise/High Priestess of

Mayhem, had been gathering more and more information about him and his mysterious boss, Julianna Saint.

Picking up a glass dripping with condensation from the table in front her, she took a sip of iced tea. This might not be the best vacation that she'd ever had, but it sure was the most exciting.

36

MARCH 3, 2005
2:30 P.M.

Julianna Saint kept up the same fast pace that she had begun the run with as the mountain path became more steep. Her breathing deepened from a combination of the exertion and the elevation above sea level. But she was far from reaching the point of exhaustion. It was a requirement of her profession that she maintain herself in excellent physical condition. Also, as a child, she had played on this mountain and knew every nook and cranny from base to apex.

She glanced back to see if she could see her running mate. She knew that he was in good condition, but nowhere near in the shape that she was in. That was why she was shocked to find the man she knew as author Mike Holt about twenty-five yards behind her and slowly but steadily closing the distance between them.

Julianna turned her attention back to the run. She wasn't about to let him catch up to her. Exercising, like everything else she did in her life, was approached not only as a challenge, but with the absolute resolve that she had to excel. That meant outrunning the man behind her.

She quickened her stride and again glanced back. He was still there, maintaining the same pace. It didn't appear that he was exerting himself at all. Now her breathing had become a trifle ragged and sweat ran freely from her body. She smiled. She was having fun. It was almost as if she had returned to her childhood and was playing a game up here on the mountain. A game that she planned to win.

The footing became precarious, forcing her to slow down to negotiate the trail. Now he began gaining on her. She didn't look back, but she was aware of him so close behind her that she could almost feel his breath on the back of her neck. Julianna found the experience sexually stimulating. In her mind she could envision herself in a sexual embrace with her running companion. The erotic images spurred her on to make a greater effort.

The trail widened and then intersected with the paved road that ran in front of Cal Ferris's villa. It was there that Mike Holt caught up with her. He didn't try to pass her, but simply kept pace. She attempted to go faster, but her body refused to respond. She was rapidly running out of gas and in danger of hitting the proverbial athlete's "wall." The only thing keeping her going at this point was pride.

They climbed the final incline to the top of the mountain, where her villa was located. Her breathing came in sharp rasps and her leg muscles began tightening up, but she managed to finish the run. When they stopped, she leaned over, placed her hands on her knees, and fought to keep the contents of her stomach down. Placing his hands on top of his head, he walked around slowly.

"Now are you ready to stretch?" he asked.

She looked up at him. "You are really in good shape," she managed between gasps.

"Writing is such a sedentary occupation, I have to get out and exercise or I'll end up with love handles, a gut, and high blood pressure."

She stood upright. "C'mon. We can stretch inside."

They entered the gate. The patio was deserted, but there was an ice bucket containing bottles of water and lemonade on a deck table. He walked over and helped himself to a bottle of water. After taking a long pull, he was about to begin stretching when he noticed that his hostess was no longer with him. He looked around to find her walking toward the swimming pool on the other side of the patio. His eyes widened when she stripped off her jogging outfit and shoes before diving nude into the pool.

"Shouldn't you cool off and stretch a bit before jumping in cold water?"

"The water's warm enough," she called back to him. "Aren't you going to join me?"

"I don't have a swimsuit."

"You don't need one."

He hesitated a moment before shrugging, stripping off his clothes, and heading for the water.

José was a short, pockmarked Cuban, who was in charge of the domestic staff at the Oyster Bay Beach Resort. Primarily it was his job to ensure that all the rooms were cleaned and properly maintained. He earned a modest salary and no tips, which made him particularly susceptible to ways of making an extra buck by whatever means necessary.

Yesterday he had been approached by Christophe La Croix about locating some dumpy American woman whom he was looking for. José knew that the Frenchman paid well for information and was a protégé of the beautiful Julianna Saint, who lived on top of the mountain. Christophe was a notorious womanizer, but the female he was looking for was decidedly unattractive. So there was some other reason than amour that the Frenchman wanted her. Perhaps, the Cuban mused, she had money. To José it really didn't matter as long as Christophe paid.

So José had kept an eye peeled for this Penelope Gibbs from the United States, but had come up with nothing. Earlier today Christophe had returned to the Oyster Bay Resort for an update, but José had nothing to tell him. This time the Frenchman had instructed the Cuban to be on the lookout for anything out of the ordinary involving a woman at the island resort. José had kept his eyes open, but it was his ears that gave him the lead Christophe La Croix was looking for.

José was checking the maids in at the end of their shift when he overheard an exchange in Spanish. One of the maids, who worked the east wing, was telling another maid about a guest room in which three women were staying with only one bed. Being an employee of a hotel on a resort island had exposed José to many exotic and unusual lifestyles. But something about what the maid said began nagging him.

He decided to question her about this "three women in one room."

Most of the maids who worked for José were afraid of him, making it necessary for him to first convince her that she was not in trouble before he could get her to tell him the story.

When the maid finished, José went in search of Christophe.

The Frenchman met José at the waterfall that drained from the underground river into the bay. After an exchange of money, José said, "I heard reports that there were three women in Room 224 of the hotel. The reason the maid thought that there were three of them was because she saw three different women either coming out of or going into the room. So I took a look myself and discovered clothes in different styles and sizes."

Christophe began showing signs of impatience, forcing the Cuban to speed up his tale.

"There's only one woman staying in that room and I'll bet you that she uses those clothes to disguise herself. In the back of the closet there's a locked black case that probably contains makeup and other cosmetic devices. Now, get this. The maid described a woman fitting the description of your Penelope Gibbs coming out of the room a few days ago and then an elderly woman in a white leisure suit coming out this morning."

Christophe had taken it all in. Now he asked, "What is this woman's name?"

"She's registered as Judy Daniels."

37

Larry Cole was an experienced lover, but Julianna Saint had taken sex to the level of an art form. The nude dip in the swimming pool to cool down from their run up the mountain had been the opening move in an erotic ballet. Revealing her body to him in this manner had initially shocked his Christian-oriented, American-culture sense of morality. The undercover policeman did not consider himself either prudish or straitlaced about sex. But Julianna approached sex from the perspective of a liberated European woman. Needless to say, she taught Cole a thing or two about making love.

The first time between them had been at poolside after their swim. Julianna had been the aggressor and was forced to be quite insistent with the American, who was obviously self-conscious about them being outdoors. There were also servants inside the villa, who she assured him would never dare spy on her or her guests. When she had had him sufficiently placated to at least recline on one of her wood-framed, cushioned deck couches, she had done the rest.

When they were finished, she had provided him with a pair of brand-new, snug-fitting swimming trunks and a towel. Julianna had put on a bikini bottom, which was more of a G-string than an item of apparel. A cordless telephone rested on a table beside the sofa where they had made love. Punching in a one-digit number, she said a few words in French. A couple of minutes later a pair of servants carrying trays came out to the pool area. Julianna and her guest consumed a lunch of salad, broiled lobster, baked potatoes, and freshly baked bread. A chilled French white wine was served with the meal, and an apple tart with whipped cream for dessert.

They idled around the pool for a time after lunch, and then she got up, saying, "Let me show you my home."

He followed her inside the villa and found the interior to be quite impressive. Each room was artfully designed for both function and style. Cole commented that her home could have been featured in a decorating magazine.

Julianna turned to him, smiled, and said, "It was."

There were fifteen rooms on three levels and a wine cellar, which the cop accurately guessed could rival the best in the world. Throughout the tour, his hostess wore nothing but the skimpy bikini bottom. He also noticed that not once, as they moved from room to room, did they encounter any of the servants. But the servants were definitely there, and Cole was certain that they could be summoned to appear instantly by Julianna.

They entered her library on the top floor of the villa. Here the plate-glass window was located that provided the Devil's Shadow with a view down the mountainside to the harbor below. There were books lining the walls, a sophisticated computer hookup, a barren felt-topped table, an antique rolltop desk with matching desk chair, and a black leather sofa. On a table beside the sofa was a stack of hardcover novels. Each had been authored by Michael Holt.

Julianna went to the desk and removed a Mont Blanc Alexandre Dumas model fountain pen, which she extended to her guest. "Would you autograph my books for me, Mike?"

Taking the pen and unscrewing the cap, he said, "I'd be honored."

Judy Daniels had foreseen a problem like this developing for Larry Cole in his disguise as Mike Holt. So he had asked the real author to provide a sample of his handwriting and queried him on how he usually autographed books. Prior to leaving Chicago for the Leeward Islands, Cole had practiced the signature until he could scribble it with ease.

Sitting down on the couch, he picked up the first novel, opened it to the title page, and inscribed:

March 3, 2005

To *Julianna,*
       An extraordinary woman and
    a gracious hostess.

Best wishes,
Mike Holt

He was starting on the second inscription when he became aware of her doing something a few feet away. Glancing up, he saw that she had removed the skimpy bikini bottom and had reclined on the shag rug at the center of the room. Cole thought that he'd gotten used to her nudity, but now it was as if he were seeing her body for the first time.

"I want you to write something special for me in *A Space in Time,* Mike," she said in a soft, husky voice.

His pulse rate accelerated and he had difficulty concentrating on the forging of Mike Holt's signature. He said, "Each autograph will be a special one for you, Julianna."

He opened *A Space in Time* and was attempting to come up with a tastefully erotic inscription. He looked off across the room, seeking inspiration, when he noticed that her computer was on. The image on the screen was so familiar to Cole that it took him a moment to recognize what it was. Observing his scrutiny, Julianna got gracefully to her feet, went over, and switched the computer off. Then she returned to her place on the floor.

After completing the autograph, he recapped the pen and looked down at her.

"Now I have something special for you," she said. "Take those trunks off and come down here with me."

As they began to make love once more, the image he had seen on the computer screen remained with him.

They had a late afternoon snack of caviar, champagne, and sliced melon on a veranda leading off from her bedroom. A warm breeze blew off the Atlantic and they watched oceangoing cruise ships and smaller private vessels entering and leaving the harbor far below.

"How much longer will you be on the island?" she asked. Julianna was now wearing a white terry cloth robe that covered her to midthigh.

"I'll be leaving at the end of the week."

"Are you going back to New Mexico?"

He took a sip of champagne. "I have business in Chicago first."

"When will you be there?"

Cole noticed that something about Julianna had changed. Since that last time they had made love in her study, she had become more guarded. Even now she looked at him with a barely concealed wariness.

In response to her question, he said, "Probably early next week. Will you be in the States soon?"

She smiled and looked out across the harbor. "I don't think so, Mike. But then you never can tell."

"Will I be able to see you again before I leave the island?"

She turned to look at him. "You haven't even left my house yet. We can make plans later."

She stood up, shed her robe, and led him into the villa. This time they made love in a bed.

She gave him a tour of the island in her pastel gray BMW roadster. She told him a few things about Saint Martin's history.

"The island was originally settled by the Arawak Indians, who were conquered by the Caribs, which was a warlike tribe from South America. The Caribs executed the Arawak men, then ate them and raped their women."

"That's taking things to an extreme," her passenger said.

"I agree. Christopher Columbus arrived on November eleventh, 1493, which was the feast day of Saint Martin of Tours. Thus Columbus named the island for Saint Martin. The Spanish conquered the Indians and introduced slavery to the island. Besides Africans, Chinese and East Indians were imported to work the sugar plantations. This has resulted in the current island population having a mixture of Indian, African, Asian, and European blood. One of my ancestors was born a slave, but was freed when Saint Martin abolished slavery on April twenty-seventh, 1848."

"That was nearly twenty years before the Emancipation Proclamation in America," Cole said.

"Here in the islands we might not have the financial or industrial might of the United States, but we have managed to learn to live together without the scourge of racism."

"Touché," he said.

Julianna was a very good driver. She handled the roadster with an ease that was definitely impressive. She piloted the car around pedestrians and slower-moving vehicles and never once had to use her horn. And as they drove along, a number of people on the road waved and called out her name. Smiling, she returned each greeting.

"Does everyone on the island know you?" he asked.

Laughing, she responded, "Not everyone, but as I was born here, I am acquainted with quite a few of the natives."

It was late afternoon when she dropped him at the hotel. Getting out of the convertible, he said, "Will you have dinner with me tonight?"

"What time?"

"Eight o'clock, if that's not too late."

"I love late suppers and I know just the right restaurant. I'll pick you up here at seven-thirty."

He waited in the driveway until she had driven away. Then he headed for his room. Larry Cole, aka author Michael Holt, was whistling.

Christophe La Croix was waiting for Julianna when she arrived back at the villa. He noticed the smile on her face and could tell, due to his extensive experience as a lover, just how she had spent her afternoon. But he had urgent information for her about the mysterious woman he had been searching for. A mysterious woman whom Christophe had found.

He had used the computer in her villa to access the Internet to search the public records of the Chicago Police Department and a number of local Windy City periodicals dating back ten years. He was looking for any reference to the name Judy Daniels. Christophe came up with so many hits that he printed out over twenty-eight pages of information.

They conferred in her library with the doors closed. As Julianna paged through the data, Christophe gave her the gist of what was there.

"This Judy Daniels is currently a sergeant on the Chicago Police Department. She has something of a reputation as an undercover operative. They call her the Mistress of Disguise/High Priestess of Mayhem. She has been known to change her appearance with such frequency and thoroughness that not even some of her fellow officers recognize her.

"She began her career in the Narcotics Unit. But about a decade ago she transferred to the Detective Division, where she has remained on the personal staff of Chief of Detectives Larry Cole."

There were a number of photographs accompanying the computerized dossier. Julianna noticed a picture of a thin-faced, dark-haired young woman in a police uniform. The caption below the image read, "24 January 1990—Recruit Class 90-2." There were several other photos, and as Julianna glanced through them, Christophe became aware of her manner changing noticeably. From the at-ease, sexually satiated woman she had been when she came in, she had suddenly become *L'Ombre du Diable* at her most fierce.

Suddenly she leaped to her feet, throwing the remaining pages of the Judy Daniels dossier to the floor, and stormed over to the window overlooking the bay below. The sun was setting, contributing to a spectacularly beautiful scene. However, from her taut posture, Christophe could tell that his boss was not enjoying the view at all.

Christophe knew better than to ask her what was wrong. She would tell him if she thought it necessary for him to know. He began gathering up the discarded pages. He came across a reproduction from *The Chicago Times-Herald* newspaper for June 23, 1996. The headline read, "Policeman's Son Saved from the Clutches of Serial Killer Margo DeWitt." The picture below the headline was of a man, two women, and a child. Beneath the photo was a listing of the names of the people depicted. It read, "Detective Judy Daniels, Mrs. Lisa Cole, Larry 'Butch' Cole Jr., and Deputy Chief of Detectives Larry Cole."

Christophe was fairly certain that Julianna had been looking at this photo when her abrupt mood change occurred. But he was unable to fathom why she had—

"Christophe!" Her sharp tone interrupted his thoughts. "Make preparations immediately for us to leave the island for the United States."

"Are we going to Chicago?" He knew this was the location of their next job.

"Yes." She did not turn around.

Christophe La Croix did not question her orders. Originally they were not scheduled to leave the island until March 10. But if she wanted to go earlier, then so be it. After all, she was the boss.

Leaving the computer pages on the table beside Mike Holt's books, he left to do her bidding.

When he was gone, she turned from the window and walked over to the end table and looked down at the recently autographed books.

"You lied to me, Mr. Cole," she said, quietly. "For that, I will never forgive you."

38

MARCH 4, 2005
1:30 P.M.

When Julianna failed to show up at the hotel for their dinner date, Cole called the villa. The male servant he talked to spoke very little English, and the American's French had been learned from tourist phrase books and late night TV. Finally they were able to piece together enough of their native languages for the servant to communicate to Cole that Julianna Saint not only was not at home, but had left the island.

Puzzled, Cole hung up the phone. Just a few hours ago everything had been fine between them. Perhaps some type of personal emergency had occurred. Going to the wall safe in his room, he removed the walkie-talkie and contacted Judy.

"I think we have a problem, boss."

"What is it?"

"Someone was in my room while I was keeping an eye on the Frenchman. Whoever was in here was neat about it, but I arranged my clothing in a certain way and sprinkled a light coating of talcum powder on my makeup kit handle. When I came back, the powder was gone."

Cole didn't like the way this was starting to shape up. "I want you to go to Plan B, Judy."

They had formulated contingency plans, because of the possible dangers that could arise from them working undercover in a foreign land. Plan B for Judy meant that she was to check out of the hotel as soon as possible and return to the States.

"You're not going to stay here alone, Chief?" she protested.

"I'll only be here one more day. My Mike Holt disguise should hold up for that long."

"Suppose it doesn't."

"It will. Now, do what I told you, Judy. I'll see you back in Chicago in a day or so."

"Yes, sir," she acquiesced, sounding far from happy.

On the afternoon of March 4, Judy's plane took off from Saint Martin en route to Miami, where she would catch a connecting flight to Chicago. Now Cole was alone on the Caribbean island.

Cole decided against calling Julianna's villa again and instead decided to make his afternoon run to the top of the mountain. When he reached her villa, he would knock on the front gate and make his inquiries face-to-face.

The run was as arduous as ever, but he was becoming increasingly accustomed to it. This would be one of the things he would miss about Saint Martin. However, the most important thing that had happened to him on this island was meeting Julianna Saint.

The investigation he had conceived back in Chicago had not gone very well here in the Caribbean. The failure of this effort was totally his, because he had permitted himself to become romantically involved with the woman he was investigating. An involvement that was threatening to consume him with the intensity of an obsession.

If Julianna Saint was the professional thief who had broken into the Metropolitan Bank of Chicago, resulting in the death of Greg Ennis, Cole had not obtained one single shred of evidence to make a case against her. The Mistress of Disguise/High Priestess of Mayhem had uncovered some extensive background information about this so-called Devil's Shadow. But most of it consisted of rumor or gossip, such as the things that the owner of Mama Johnnie's bar had told Judy. So the Chicago Police Department's chief of detectives had gotten himself and a subordinate involved in an unauthorized investigation on foreign soil. On top of that, the trip had been at Cole's own expense.

He reached the blacktop road that ran in front of Cal Ferris's villa. As Cole jogged past the comedian's place, he noticed that the front gate stood partially open. A thought occurred to him. If he didn't find Julianna at home, he would come back here and ask Ferris if he knew what had happened to her.

At the closed mountaintop villa gate, Cole pounded for a full five minutes without getting any answer at all. He considered scaling the fence, but that would be an unauthorized entry, which the Saint Martin police might not view too favorably. That would result in his Mike Holt impersonation unraveling completely. Although Cole and Judy had been technically undercover while on the island, they had traveled on their own American passports. Cole had no way of knowing at this time that Judy being registered under her own name at the Oyster Bay Beach Resort had caused the destruction of the Mike Holt disguise. However, he was about to find this out.

Cole turned to head for Cal Ferris's villa to question him about Julianna when he saw the comedian's bodyguards standing a few feet away. One glance at their faces transmitted quite clearly to the American cop that they were looking for trouble.

Clad in tank tops, sweatpants, and gym shoes, the two men flexed their muscles, giving Cole an impressive display of their strength.

"You looking for something, Mr. Holt?" the former pro football player asked.

Staying loose, Cole responded, "As a matter of fact, I was. I had a date with Ms. Saint last night. When she didn't show up, I became concerned. I was just about to come over and ask Cal if he knew what had happened to her."

"Would you have a personal or a professional interest in her whereabouts, Mr. Holt?" No Neck said, before snapping his fingers and adding, "Or is the name Cole, as in Larry Cole of the Chicago Police Department?"

The cop smiled. "You guys always seem to be confusing me with someone else. Are you sure you haven't got it wrong again?"

"We're sure," the football player said, beginning to circle to Cole's right.

Cole realized that he was unarmed and outmuscled. But these guys were nothing but a pair of bodyguards who were basically employed to keep harmless nuts and overzealous fans away from their celebrity boss. They probably spent hours at the gym pumping their muscles into the truly awesome size they had on display for him right now. And they were undoubtedly strong and could easily crush the life out of him. That is, if they could get their hands on him.

Larry Cole had come off the tough streets of Chicago. He had been an all-city football player at Mount Carmel High School, which had fielded some of the best teams in the history of the State of Illinois. He had even gotten a scholarship to the University of Iowa. He had been a street cop for most of his life, which in a town as rough as the Windy City was quite an accomplishment. In order to survive, he had to be tough and know how to take care of himself. As such, he was skilled at engaging in hand-to-hand combat, Chicago style. That meant there were no rules.

No Neck had folded his arms across his massive chest and was waiting for his muscle-bound pal to do some serious damage to the cop who had impersonated Mike Holt. This Cole had a lot of nerve, No Neck thought, and for his trouble Cal wanted them to bust him up a bit. Maybe rearrange those matinee-idol features and break a bone or two. Nothing serious enough to have him laid up in a hospital for more than a week or so.

Then their prey did the unexpected. He attacked No Neck. With an unbelievable swiftness, the cop lunged at him, and before he could unwrap his beefy arms to defend himself, No Neck was struck in the throat and kneed so hard in the groin that he was certain that his scrotum had been rammed up into his chest. The pain that took over his body was so intense that all he could do was grasp the injured area with both hands and collapse into a writhing heap of muscle on the ground.

* * *

During his playing career, the ex–Seattle Seahawks football player had been a blocking back who had seldom carried the ball. His chief skill was getting out in front of the running back and blasting anyone in an opposition jersey who got in his way. He had been rather effective at this maneuver, which had led to him having a successful eight-year playing career. A career that had ended during one of his infrequent ball-carrying plays when he'd had the ligaments of his left knee torn up by an Oakland Raiders linebacker. The injury still bothered him when the weather was damp or cold, and he walked with a slight limp, which the man he intended to hospitalize had noticed.

Now he planned to propel his 250-pound, shaved-headed bulk at the author-impersonating cop. Then he would knock him to the ground, sit on his chest, and pound his face until it resembled a spilled cherry pie.

When the pretty boy disabled his No Neck partner, the ex–football player became enraged. Such emotion would have served him well in a contact sports contest in which brute force was the primary requirement. However, he was not on a football field, but in a street fight.

With a roar, he charged the smaller man. He was planning to "pancake" him, which meant that he would literally run Cole over, knocking him flat on his back. His charge brought him within a yard of the cop, when Cole deftly sidestepped him. Then the one-time amateur-level defensive back braced himself on one foot and kicked out with the other to strike the charging man in his surgically repaired knee. The muscular man's fierce roar became a terrible scream of pain. He landed in a writhing heap beside his No Neck partner, whose injured testicles were swelling rapidly.

Cole stood over his attackers for a moment, feeling no triumph or elation over what he had just done. In fact, he was experiencing a rising guilt. If he had stayed back in Chicago where he belonged, he would not have been forced to hurt these men. Then something occurred to him. They had known his true identity. He wondered how they had come by this information.

Stepping over the damaged bodyguards, he went in search of their boss, Calvin Harlan Ferris III.

39

Saint Thomas
MARCH 4, 2005
6:00 P.M.

Julianna had business to conduct on the Island of Saint Thomas, which was a United States territory. She had entered the island on her own French passport. Passing through U.S. Customs with Christophe, she declared nothing and stated that she was visiting the United States on business. The Customs official, who had seen this stunning black woman before, did not inquire as to what her business was. In the past she had told him that she imported French goods into America and exported American goods to Europe and the Caribbean.

There was a hired car waiting for her and Christophe outside the airport. The late-model Ford whisked them across the island to a warehouse near a harbor, which was somewhat off the beaten path. The driver waited while they entered the wood-framed building.

The man they had come to see was fat, unshaven, and unwashed. He wore a filthy pair of coveralls and had the stub of an unfiltered cigarette stuck in the corner of his mouth. His hands were dirty and scarred. And when he looked at Julianna, his expression left little to the imagination as to what he was thinking. However, he knew enough about her not to take his intention beyond a lusty gaze.

They did not use names. In the type of business they were in, it was unnecessary.

"I want the most compact, powerful industrial laser available," said Julianna, who was dressed in a red two-piece suit and white wide-brimmed hat, with white shoes and accessories. "It must be capable of cutting through four to six inches of steel as easily as a hot knife passes through butter."

The filthy man, whom Christophe made it a point to stand downwind of, spit the wet vestiges of tobacco and paper from his cigarette onto the floor. "You need a JFS3 industrial laser. They're used by the United States Air Force. I can get one for you"—he looked up at the ceiling and scratched the stubble of his chin—"in a couple of weeks."

"I need it in two days," she said, flatly. "And I want it delivered to an address that I will give you in Chicago."

"We are in a hurry, aren't we?" he said, fishing a bent cigarette out of a ragged package of Pall Malls. Breaking the butt in two, he stuffed half of it back into the pack and stuck the other half in his mouth. Lighting the cigarette with a kitchen match he ignited with his thumbnail, he added, "What are you going to do, slice open a bank vault?"

Neither Julianna nor Christophe responded. After a moment of protracted silence, the man picked up a scratch pad from the cluttered desk behind him and scribbled a figure on the paper with a pencil. He handed it over to the Devil's Shadow.

She examined it momentarily before handing it to Christophe, saying, "Pay the man."

The young Frenchman's eyes widened when he saw the price the disgusting man had quoted, but if Julianna wanted him to pay it, then he would do so.

When they returned to the hired car, Christophe said, "Wasn't that a bit expensive?"

She waited for him to open the car door for her. As she got in the backseat, she said, "It doesn't really matter. We'll simply pass the cost on to our client."

The hired car took them to the airport, where they boarded an eight-o'clock Air France jet, which would fly them directly to O'Hare International Airport in Chicago.

When the plane was airborne, they settled back in their first-class seats for the six-hour journey. Christophe had been keeping a close eye on the Devil's Shadow. Since they'd left Saint Martin, she had not been herself. He didn't know what had occurred with the man she'd met, but it was obvious to the Frenchman that things between them had not concluded well. He would have encouraged her to confide in him, but was certain that such an offer would be rejected. Christophe had known and worked for Julianna Saint for five years. During that time he'd never witnessed her express her private thoughts to anyone. So all he could do was be there in case she needed him and hope for the best.

In seat 1A of the first-class section of the Air France jet bound for Chicago, Julianna stared out into the darkness over the South Atlantic. The man whom she now knew to be Chief of Detectives Larry Cole of the Chicago Police Department had seldom been out of her thoughts since the moment she'd set eyes on him. Now she wished that she had never met him.

Tears filled her eyes and she kept her face turned to the window so that Christophe would not see her cry.

Julianna Saint considered herself to be a very fortunate woman. She was rich, beautiful, and talented. She had enough money to do whatever she wanted. But she realized one important thing about her existence on this earth, and that was that true happiness had managed to elude her. Maybe, she considered, it was something in her emotional makeup. Or perhaps she was cursed. As the Air France jet winged its way on through the night, she remembered.

Saint Martin
JANUARY 19, 1975
5:00 P.M.

Julianna Saint had been raised by her mother's brother, Walter Saint. Her mother had died when she was still an infant, and as she grew up to become a stunningly beautiful woman, three men came forward claiming to be her father. However, this was not until she became one of the wealthiest women on the island and developed a reputation as the infamous Devil's Shadow.

Walter Saint was a part-time fisherman and full-time thief. He was a short, fat black man with gray eyes and a light complexion. He sported a scraggly, unkempt beard and favored oversized Bermuda shorts and loud Hawaiian shirts year-round. In the Islands, from Saint Martin to Saint Thomas, he was known as a procurer. He did not deal in human flesh or any form of vice, but if a patron had the ability to pay, Walter Saint could obtain any item the person desired. This was as long as the item was located within the boundaries of the Leeward Islands, Bermuda, or Cuba, to which island the procurer would occasionally venture.

Walter's sixty-foot fishing boat was called *The Devil's Due* and, despite a shabby exterior, housed a pair of powerful diesel engines belowdecks that could be rigged to run in virtual silence. But the boat was merely a conveyance. The skipper of *The Devil's Due* made his living by his wits.

From the time that she could walk, Walter had trained Julianna to be a thief. By the age of seven she could easily remove a wallet from the pocket or purse of any tourist visiting the island. By the age of ten, she could deftly unsnap the clasp of a gold bracelet or necklace, using only the thumb and forefinger of one hand, and remove the item without the wearer being aware of what she was doing. Before her twelfth birthday, she was able to enter any residence on any island in the Caribbean without being detected.

Then, exactly one month into her thirteenth year, two things happened that changed her life. First was the realization that her uncle Walter was nothing more than a rum-swilling crook, who would eventually end up either dead or in jail as a result of the careless, drunken, devil-may-care manner in which he approached the commission of crimes. The other event was the steward off of the cruise ship *La Belle Liberté* coming to visit her uncle and offering him a strange proposition.

* * *

Walter Saint was fifty-six years old in January of 1975. His various endeavors throughout the Caribbean, both legal and illegal, had netted him a small fortune over the years. A fortune that he had squandered on booze and women. Now, as he slipped rapidly toward old age, a heavy depression began settling on him more and more. This led to him drinking himself into oblivion aboard *The Devil's Due* almost every night. In rum-induced dreams he kept envisioning a big score that would set him up for life. Make him enough money to enable him to buy a villa built into the side of a mountain on either Saint Martin or Saint Thomas. And even though his skills were rapidly deserting him, he still had Julianna, who was becoming more and more of a skilled thief with each passing year.

As the day wore on toward evening, Walter was sprawled under an awning on the deck of *The Devil's Due*. He had sat alone in the belowdecks cabin and consumed a fifth of 150-proof rum the night before. He didn't remember finishing the rum. When he woke up, feeling and smelling like he'd been smashed in a trash compactor, the empty bottle was rolling around the cabin floor as *The Devil's Due* bobbed up and down in its slip at the Marigot dock. And even though he had been drinking quite heavily of late and had developed a tolerance for alcohol, Walter Saint's body was not prepared for the abuse he had inflicted on it the previous night. His head ached, his stomach was in an uproar, and his pulse raced furiously.

Throughout the day he was aware of Julianna working around the boat. At one point, when she dropped something on the deck that drove him out of a sound sleep, he cursed her. But then he realized that if it hadn't been for her care, *The Devil's Due* would probably be sitting at the bottom of the harbor, with him still aboard.

Julianna had forced him to down a bowl of gumbo doused with Tabasco sauce, which caused him to sweat rivers. As the day wore on, he began feeling a bit more human, but was totally incapable of functioning as a human being. Then Charlie Martin, the steward from *La Belle Liberté*, appeared at the foot of *The Devil's Due*'s gangplank.

Walter Saint had no way of knowing how much trouble this particular visitor was going to cause him.

Julianna noticed Charlie Martin when he was still some distance from the slip where *The Devil's Due* was berthed. Her uncle Walter had taught her a great deal about being a thief, but even at her preteen age, she was aware that in order to survive in her hazardous, illegal, inherited profession, she would have to be very careful.

She was always on the alert for undercover cops or security officers from the cruise ships when she was picking pockets or lifting jewelry in Marigot. She'd also learned to be wary of certain types of "marks." Heavyset men with bulges under their shirts and black oxford shoes could spell off-duty cops from the States. Nervous people who clutched their purses or bags in both hands could spell disaster, because they were on the run themselves and had something to hide. Tourists visiting the island for the first time could also be extremely anxious and shun contact with the natives, which would make a thief's job more difficult, if not impossible, to do.

All of these things the young girl who would grow up to become the Devil's Shadow learned to recognize when she was twelve years old. That was why she was able to recognize Charlie Martin's fear while he was still some distance from *The Devil's Due*.

She sized him up physically as he approached the slip. His clothing was of fair quality, but had been purchased off the rack. The shoes were those of a worker who spent a great deal of time on his feet. The only jewelry he wore was a wristwatch, which appeared fairly new but didn't cost over a hundred dollars, and there was a gold Saint Jude medal around his neck. The medal had potential; however, the gold chain it was attached to was cheap. Any cash he was carrying was in his front pockets, because there was no visible bulge in either of his rear pockets. She was just about to reject him as a mark altogether when he came up to the slip and said in French, "Good afternoon, mademoiselle. I am looking for Monsieur Walter Saint."

Now Julianna could detect that this man was deeply frightened.

But it was a type of fear she had never seen before. Later she would be able to characterize it as a spiritual as opposed to a physical fear. She didn't know how true the old saying was as it applied to Charlie Martin at the time, but it was as if *le diable le chassait*—the devil was chasing him.

"Who's looking for Walter Saint?" she asked.

Julianna noticed that his French was very good, but spoken with an odd, almost undetectable accent. She could also tell that he had African blood, but only a small amount, and could easily pass himself off as a Caucasian.

His fear, the accent, and his neat workman's appearance intrigued the larcenous, precocious child. After he told her his name, she gave him permission to come aboard and led him to her uncle.

Walter Saint told Julianna to go below and fetch a bottle of liquor and a couple of glasses for him and his guest. The skipper of *The Devil's Due* ignored his guest's statement that he didn't drink. Julianna knew that he was driven not by hospitality, but rather his need to have a drink himself.

She found a half-empty bottle of bourbon in the galley, retrieved a couple of clean glasses, and filled a pitcher with cold water before returning to the deck. Walter and their guest were seated on a bench outside the wheelhouse. As she set the tray down between them, she noticed that her uncle appeared bloodless because of his heavy drinking, and Charlie Martin looked almost as bad, because he was thoroughly terrified.

She took a seat on the ship's railing adjacent to them. This action alarmed Charlie Martin.

"I was hoping that we could keep our discussion private," he said to Walter.

Pouring a shot of bourbon with trembling hands, he rasped, "Julianna's my partner. Any business that you have with me, you can discuss in front of her."

Their guest studied the young girl for a moment before finally agreeing. Then he began.

He spoke barely above a whisper and his eyes darted continuously around the deck of *The Devil's Due* to make sure there was no one eavesdropping on them.

"There is a passenger on board *La Belle Liberté*. His name is Viscount Maurice Phillipe Stephan De Coutreaux of France. He is eighty-six years old and in poor health, which is understandable. He is traveling alone and has a large amount of cash and some expensive jewelry in his cabin. One piece is a gold antique pocket watch, which is a hundred years old and encrusted with jewels. I would say, offhand, that there is maybe two or three hundred thousand francs in cash and other easily disposable items available to be taken."

Walter took a swig of bourbon, grimaced, and said, "Cruise ships have been known to have pretty good security, Charlie."

"I can get you on board without too much difficulty. The director of passenger services has authorized me to recruit and hire replacements for the ship's service staff on the island. You'll have official credentials."

Walter Saint thought about this for a moment. "So we get on board. What will this Viscount De Coutreaux be doing while we're robbing his cabin?"

"He takes a sedative every night at nine," he answered. "I know that it places him in a deep sleep, because I'm the one who gives it to him."

Walter emptied his bourbon glass and refilled it. "Two or three hundred thousand francs is hardly worth my and Julianna's trouble, Charlie. Maybe we get aboard and hit six or seven cabins on the deluxe accommodations deck, then—"

"No!" Charlie shouted, obviously startled by his own outburst. "I don't want any of the other passengers involved in this. Only Viscount De Coutreaux."

Walter began shaking his head when Julianna spoke up.

"What's in this for you, Charlie?"

The cabin steward looked off across the harbor and said, softly, "De Coutreaux has something that I want you to steal for me."

"And what is that?" Julianna demanded.

In the same quiet tone of voice he had used initially, he said, "A book."

"A book!" Walter Saint laughed. "What kind of book?"

Charlie Martin looked from the alcoholic thief to his young niece. Then he said, "A very special book called *Le Livre du Diable—The Book of the Devil.*"

For a moment neither Julianna nor Walter said anything. Then the old pirate began laughing. He laughed for a long time; however, he failed to notice that neither Charlie Martin or his niece even cracked a smile.

Over the Atlantic
MARCH 4, 2005
9:45 P.M.

Far below the Air France jet, the lights of Miami became visible. Julianna's memories were interrupted by the sound of Christophe's snoring. She turned from the window and stared at him for a moment. She was very fond of the young man sitting next to her. He was like the little brother that she never had. Her only relative had been Walter Saint, who had been dead for years. Suddenly the image of the man she had made such intense love to back on Saint Martin flashed before her with such force that she gasped. The sound awoke Christophe.

"What is it, Julianna?"

"Nothing, Christophe," she said. "Go back to sleep."

Like an obedient child, he turned slightly on his side and in a moment was once more sound asleep.

Before returning to her memories, she came to a decision. Actually, it was two decisions. When she got to Chicago she planned to settle with both the man who had lied to her and the man who had caused her grief earlier in her life. Chief of Detectives Larry Cole and Bishop Martin Simon Pierre De Coutreaux would soon feel the full wrath of the Devil's Shadow.

*   *   *

United Airlines flight 210 was two hours behind the Air France jet bearing Julianna Saint and Christophe La Croix. Seated in a window seat in the coach section, Larry Cole was in a solemn, contemplative mood. Cal Ferris, who had been surprised to see the policeman was unhurt after the confrontation with his bullet-headed bodyguards, had gladly volunteered to Cole that Julianna Saint had uncovered the Michael Holt deception. How she had done this, the comedian didn't know, but Cole suspected that it had something to do with Judy Daniels's Oyster Bay Beach Resort room being searched. So the entire operation was blown; however, Cole was certain that he would be seeing Julianna Saint again very soon. And when he did, it would be on his own turf in Chicago.

PART 3

"Someday we will meet again, Larry Cole."
Julianna Saint

40

Chicago, Illinois
MARCH 14, 2005
9:57 A.M.

Ian Jellicoe was registered in Suite 4402 at the DeWitt Plaza Hotel. The accommodations consisted of seven rooms and two baths, which was a bit much for even the very particular Englishman's tastes. However, since his return to the Windy City in early March, he had developed a relationship with a male exotic dancer at a Rush Street club. The dancer enjoyed the plush ambiance of the luxury hotel, so he had temporarily moved in. Jellicoe kept his guest restricted to three rooms in the suite. This enabled the Englishman to use the rest of the space to maintain the security of the assignments in which he was engaged.

The dancer was still asleep when Jellicoe left the suite to go on his daily five-mile run. When he returned, he ate breakfast alone, looked in on his guest, who had not stirred, and then left the suite. Downstairs he took a taxi to the corner of Randolph and Dearborn in the Chicago Loop. Within a space of a few blocks, the municipal, county, and state governments had their headquarters. At the center of this complex was the multistoried Richard J. Daley Center. This housed a number of governmental operations, including civil courts and miscellaneous administrative offices.

The Daley Center was surrounded by a spacious plaza, which was dominated by an iron sculpture by artist Pablo Picasso. The rust-colored work of art was a surrealist interpretation of a bird and stood fifty feet tall. It weighed over 162 tons, and when it had been unveiled in the early 1960s, it was labeled a "hideous monstrosity." Over the years the structure became as representative of Chicago as the Statue of Liberty was of New York and the Golden Gate Bridge was of San Francisco.

Carrying a computerized Graphix camera, which could take digitalized video as well as still photos, Jellicoe walked around the sculpture, photographing it from a number of angles. The visual record included the glass-and-steel Daley Center behind the statue, the Cook County Building across the street, and each of the intersecting streets. With his camera still on, he strolled completely around the Daley Center Plaza, covering Randolph, Clark, Washington, and Dearborn streets. Then he proceeded to walk north on Dearborn up to Wacker Drive, which bordered the south bank of the Chicago River. He walked west on Wacker to Clark Street and then southbound to Washington Street before proceeding east to Dearborn. By noon he had covered all of the access and egress routes around the statue, except from the air. Jellicoe did not think that this would be a problem, as aircraft—both helicopters and fixed-wing—were prohibited from flying over this densely populated area of the city.

Jellicoe's research completed, he hailed another taxi and gave the driver the address of the Field Museum of Natural History. Then he sat back to enjoy the view.

The Englishman had to admit that Chicago was an exceptionally beautiful city. From the research that he had done so far, he was aware that the city seal bore the phrase in Latin *Urbs In Horto,* which translates to "City in a Garden." Jellicoe was forced to agree that this was an apt description, as the entire town was plush with greenery and trees. He realized that had his former employer, Baron Alain Marcus Casimir von Rianocek, succeeded in destroying Chicago with a Russian-made tactical nuclear weapon planted in a subterranean area beneath the gigantic Sears Tower, Jellicoe would not be here now. The plot had been foiled by Larry Cole. Jellicoe, who hated the cop, was glad that Cole had indeed defeated Rianocek's plot because now the Windy City was going to make the Englishman a great deal of money.

It was an incredible day, with the sun shining out of a cloudless sky and the temperature hovering at an unseasonably warm mid-sixties to low seventies. There were city workmen wrapping green and gold bunting around light fixtures in the Loop area in preparation for the annual Saint Patrick's Day parade and celebration on March 17. Jellicoe's eyes actually glistened in anticipation. All of his labors would be accomplished before midnight on the eighteenth. Then not only would he have made a fortune from his separate clients, Mafia boss Jake Romano and Vatican bishop Martin Simon Pierre De Coutreaux, but he would also exact a fitting revenge on Julianna Saint and her two lowlife henchmen, Christophe La Croix and Hubert Metayer.

The cab dropped Jellicoe off at the rear entrance to the museum. He doffed the cashmere coat he had worn downtown as he entered the museum. Dressed in a custom-tailored charcoal gray pin-striped suit, he cut a stunningly stylish figure. He strolled across the rotunda with the camera draped around his neck. He had turned the camera off in the taxi, but as he walked down the steps to the lower level, he switched it back on. With a sensitivity that made flash attachments unnecessary, the camera recorded everything in front of Jellicoe. He found the door marked "Private," which was located between two display cases containing Native American artifacts of the nineteenth century. Jellicoe didn't even glance at the contents of the display cases. He had no interest in Native Americans of the nineteenth century or, for that matter, any other century. In fact, he had little use for anything contained in this house of fossils and ancient artifacts. There was actually only one part of history that Jellicoe was interested in, and that was the museum's resident historian, Dr. Silvernail Smith.

The Englishman spied a wooden bench against the far wall of an intersecting corridor. Taking a seat on this bench provided him with a personal, as well as an electronic, view of the gallery where the historian's office was located. Removing a copy of *Gentleman's Quarterly* magazine from his coat pocket, he settled in to wait.

Blackie Silvestri had to admit that Larry Cole had never looked better. The chief had returned from the Islands tanned and extremely fit. The only problem was that Cole's mood did not mirror his "back from a fun vacation" look. It wasn't so much that he was in a bad mood as that he had been remote and quiet. Blackie had asked his old partner if there was anything wrong, but Cole had simply replied that everything was fine. Yet the lieutenant caught him occasionally staring off into space. Yes, there was definitely something amiss, but until Cole decided to come clean, there was nothing that Blackie could do about it, so they went back to work.

"What's the status of our DeWitt Plaza bank robbers?" Cole asked.

The woman who had worn the ranch mink coat, her chauffeur, and the driver of the delivery van, whom Cole had wounded, had been going through the Cook County criminal justice system since December.

"The grand jury indictments came down in January and they're scheduled for trial in April," Blackie explained. "The bond has been set at a million dollars each, which they haven't been able to raise. Their attorney of record is none other than our old pal Sol Engstrom."

Cole leaned back in his desk chair. Blackie could easily see that he had lost two inches off his waistline while he was on vacation. Whenever the lieutenant went on furlough he always gained weight. The chief said, "So I assume they haven't made any statement?"

"Not a word," Blackie responded. "But we've got enough to put them away for a very long time. Those guns were the most sophisticated weapons our crime lab has ever seen. Custom-made jobs with no serial numbers."

Again Cole stared vacantly off into space as if his mind was somewhere quite far away from his body. Blackie waited him out.

"Maybe we need to consult a weapons expert on this," Cole finally said.

"You want to go over and see Silvernail?"

Cole nodded. "I haven't talked to him since I got back in town. Sign out one of the assault rifles and we'll take it over to the museum."

"Sure thing, boss," Blackie said, getting up and leaving the office.

Dr. Silvernail Smith had gotten back into his daily routine, more or less. He worked on museum exhibits, did any necessary research in his office, and attended curator Nora Livingston's weekly staff meetings. Outwardly he was fine, but internally was a different matter.

The historian had surrendered himself to his fate. During the months since he'd heard his dead brother's voice, he had fought with all of his psychic might against what he considered to be the inevitable. Such efforts had been in vain, because the woman was coming. In fact, with each passing day she was getting closer.

The historian had been examining a dagger that had been discovered at an archaeological dig in South America. It was either a workman's implement or had been used as a weapon by a person of meager resources. The knife was believed to be from the Mayan civilization, but Silvernail did not believe that it was that old. He put his magnifying glass down and was about to turn on his computer to consult the historical reference program when he experienced a bone-chilling shudder. Clutching his arms around himself, he ground his teeth together and shut his eyes tight until it passed. When he managed to straighten up, he found that his body was drenched in an icy sweat. Some would consider such symptoms the first stage of a violent bout with the flu. However, Silvernail knew better. What was affecting him was far more deadly than any influenza virus, no matter how virulent.

Silvernail managed to make it to the small washroom in his office, where he stripped off his flannel shirt and washed himself at the sink. He had just dried off and put on a clean shirt when there was a knock at his office door. Straightening his spine and forging his face into the most relaxed expression that he could muster, he went to admit his guests.

"This is a Steyr-Mannlicher military assault weapon," Silvernail said, examining the Bullpup that Cole and Blackie had brought with them in a Chicago Police Department vinyl evidence bag. "It was outlawed in the United States and it's my understanding that the current Geneva Accords conference has involved some arguments in favor of banning it internationally. That would be a pity."

Cole and Blackie expressed surprise at the historian's comment.

Silvernail smiled. "This is one of the most efficient firearms ever made. It is compact, lightweight, powerful, and accurate. A perfect soldier's weapon."

"That gun was used by a gang of bank robbers, Doc," Blackie said with a disapproving frown.

"So I understand, Blackie, and they have been used to rob two banks, right?"

"Yeah," the lieutenant responded.

Cole could see where this was going. He interjected, "The robbers had the police outgunned with the Bullpup, Silvernail. If we're going to find out the best way to combat these weapons on city streets, we need to discover as much as we can about them."

Silvernail reached into the evidence bag and removed a box of cartridges. "Now, these are extremely deadly," he said, examining one. "I've never seen anything like this before. Obviously, like the rifle, the cartridges are custom-made."

"Do you have any idea who could have put something like this together?" Cole asked.

The historian continued to study the bullet. "There are maybe five or six gunsmiths in the world who are capable of this level of craftsmanship."

"Could you make us a list of the gunsmiths?" said Cole.

"Maybe I won't have to, Larry. There's a gentleman named Massad Ayoob, who is the director of the Lethal Force Institute in

New Hampshire. He is a master weapons specialist, who trains expert shooters from all over the world. If you can leave this ammunition with me for a day or so, I'll contact him and find out what I can and maybe be able to come up with who made it."

"Sure thing," Cole said, as Blackie began repacking the rifle for its return to the crime lab. When the lieutenant was finished, Cole said, "Could you give us a moment alone?"

Blackie nodded and left the office.

"Are you okay, Silvernail?" Cole asked with concern.

Appearing exhausted, the historian replied, "At one time or another, we all must face challenges in our lives. You have confronted a number of your own and survived. Now I must once more face mine."

Cole started to add something, paused, thought better of it, and said, "Okay. Take care of yourself and I'll give you a call tomorrow about the rifle cartridges."

Out in the exhibit gallery, Cole looked around for Blackie. Then he heard the lieutenant whisper, "Hey, boss, I'm over here."

Cole spied his partner crouched down behind a display case. Puzzled, Cole walked over to him and asked, also in a whisper, "What are you doing?"

Blackie grabbed Cole's arm and pulled him out of the corridor into shadow. "Take a gander down there at the dressed-up dude sitting on that bench."

Cole followed Blackie's line of sight. The chief of detectives immediately recognized the blond man in the elegant charcoal gray, pin-striped suit, but it took him a moment to recall his name. It was Jellicoe. Ian Jellicoe.

Jellicoe finished the article he'd been reading in *GQ*. He had become particularly engrossed in a piece about a new style of blazer that he planned to have made as soon as he returned to England. Closing the magazine, he looked down at the viewer of his camera and saw a man walking down the museum gallery toward him. He had seen two men enter Silvernail Smith's office a short time before, but he hadn't paid them much attention. He was only interested in the scruffy-looking historian whom Bishop De Coutreaux was so fascinated with. Then he recognized the man approaching him. It was Larry Cole.

The Englishman kept his head down as Cole's image began expanding in the viewfinder. Jellicoe didn't know if the cop was after him, which wasn't necessarily alarming, as he hadn't done anything to warrant official scrutiny. However, he was cunning enough to realize that under the circumstances—with him working for Jake Romano and Bishop De Coutreaux on less than legitimate enterprises in Chicago—it would be best to avoid any contact with the police.

Acting as casual as he could, while keeping his face averted, Jellicoe stood up and turned to head for the south stairs. He didn't look in the approaching policeman's direction, and after he'd proceeded a short distance, he thought he would make good his escape, when someone stepped in front of him. The Englishman stopped and looked up into the face of Lieutenant Blackie Silvestri.

"Excuse me, sir," Blackie said with a forced cordiality, flashing his badge in Jellicoe's face. "We're investigating a complaint of a man exposing himself in this area. Our suspect has blond hair and also wears tailored suits just like yours. Would you mind assuming the position?" He pointed at a nearby wall.

"I beg your pardon?" Jellicoe responded, exhibiting glacial annoyance.

"I'm sorry. I guess we have a kind of communication problem here, pal," Blackie sneered. "Something about two cultures separated by a common language, or some such. So I guess I'm going to have to walk you through it."

With that the lieutenant grabbed Jellicoe by his immaculately pressed suit jacket collar and hurled him against the corridor wall.

"This is police brutality!" Jellicoe shouted. "I'm a British national! You can't do this to me!"

The museum visitors in evidence stopped to gape and a security guard trotted down the corridor toward the disturbance. Cole, who had been slowly tailing Jellicoe, halted the guard, flashed his badge, and ordered him to keep the spectators back. Then Cole joined Blackie, who was roughly but efficiently frisking the Englishman. In the process, the suspect's clothing was becoming quite disheveled, much to his chagrin.

Finished with the search, Blackie stepped back and said, "He's clean, boss. The only thing he's carrying is this camera." The lieutenant had removed it from around Jellicoe's neck.

Standing spread-eagle with his hands against the wall, Jellicoe said an outraged, "That is private property. You have no right to examine it without a warrant."

Cole moved over to stand beside the suspect. The chief leaned his back against the wall and folded his arms across his chest. They were standing less than six inches apart, but Jellicoe refused to look at the cop.

"As you are a guest of the United States government," Cole said, "we would greatly appreciate your cooperation in this matter, Ian. It is Ian Fitzwalter Jellicoe, isn't it?"

"You know bloody well who I am, Cole. I met you and this thug of yours when I came to this country to claim Baron Alain Marcus Casimir von Rianocek's body after the two of you killed him."

"Well, Ian," Cole continued, "as Lieutenant Silvestri has already informed you, we're investigating a complaint about a man fitting your description who has been exposing himself in the vicinity of this museum."

"Can I take my hands off the bloody wall?" Jellicoe said, his voice hoarse with rage.

"I don't know," Cole said. "What do you think, Blackie? Will Ian behave if we let him turn around?"

Grinning, Blackie replied, "Sure he will, boss. I bet he's just bubbling over with enthusiasm to assist us."

"You can turn around," Cole said to the suspect.

Jellicoe's jacket was open and one of the buttons was now

loose. His shirt had been pulled out and his tie was askew. Other than that, he was undamaged. As he began straightening his clothing, he said, "You're going to hear from my barrister about this outrage. I plan to sue both of you and your department for quite a large sum of money." Jellicoe's clothing once more intact, his outrage began swelling. "That cock-and-bull story you made up about me resembling an exhibitionist won't—"

"You can save all of that, Jellicoe." Cole's voice had now become as harsh as Blackie's. "We didn't make up the suspected sex offender. He's very real and has been plaguing the lakefront area for the last few months, which we can document. Now, we'd be perfectly within our rights as American law enforcement officers to take you in for further investigation. Maybe put you in a lineup and have our molester's victims take a look at you. Of course, we'll contact the British consulate, if you wish."

A bit of the color drained from the Englishman's face. "Will that be absolutely necessary?"

Cole smiled. "Not if you cooperate with us, it won't."

"And what type of cooperation do you require?"

"That's the ticket, Ian," Blackie said.

Then, much to Jellicoe's frustration, Cole and Blackie watched his recently made videotape.

41

MARCH 14, 2005
1:57 P.M.

Sergeant Judy Daniels sat in her cubicle at Chicago police Detective Division headquarters. Today she was dressed in a masculinely cut black business suit and thick-framed glasses with windowpane lenses, and wore her hair combed to hang down to her shoulders. She sat rigidly at her computer with her back ramrod-straight. Her eyes were glued to the monitor screen in front of her. She was coordinating all of the information she had obtained on Saint Martin about Julianna Saint, the woman suspected of being the Devil's Shadow.

Judy had found it interesting that everyone on the island had been so willing to talk candidly about the woman who was reputedly an international criminal. In fact, it was almost as if the residents of the island were very proud of this *L'Ombre du Diable*. Some of the accounts of her exploits were no more than fanciful tales possessing dubious credibility. When Judy was disguised as Penny Gibbs, Johnetta Dupres, the owner of Mama Johnnie's bar in Marigot, had regaled the Mistress of Disguise/High Priestess of Mayhem for hours about Julianna Saint. The tavern owner had portrayed the thief as part Robin Hood, part Joan of Arc, and all Wonder Woman. And reportedly there was nothing on earth, no matter what it was or how well it was guarded, that the Devil's Shadow could not steal. Yet this woman had no police record to speak of, with the exception of a temporary detention by the police on Saint Martin in 1975. But the crimes that Julianna Saint was rumored to have committed had indeed occurred. Of this, Judy had found documentary proof.

Scouring the Criminal Events Information System, she had come up with the details of each crime. And what Judy had discovered was genuinely awesome by any standard.

On February 9, 1982, Van Damm's jewelry store in Zurich had been broken into by a burglar who tripped the alarm system and carried out the crime within a span of two minutes and thirteen seconds. By the time the police arrived, the thief was gone with over half a million dollars in jewelry. The case remained open, but there were no suspects and no leads.

On April 11, 1984, two priceless paintings by the French impressionist Mantegny were stolen from the Guggenheim Museum in New York. This time the alarms, although working perfectly according to the detectives investigating the crime, were not triggered. The paintings were given a cash value of fifteen million dollars by the museum's insurance company. Again there were no leads or suspects; however, this was the first time that rumors began circulating in the underworld about a very skilled black female thief.

Then the evidence room of the Boston Police Department was broken into on Christmas Day 1990 and the legend of the Devil's Shadow was born.

Judy recalled the incident. At the time she was a rookie police officer working out of the Twelfth District on the West Side of Chicago. The shock waves of what had occurred in Boston reverberated throughout the entire American law enforcement community.

On that holiday the Boston Police Department had a skeleton staff on duty in their headquarters building. The proceeds from a recently cracked burglary ring were stored in a locked vault in the basement of the facility. The burglars had been seized with three million dollars in cash and jewelry, which was contained in locked evidence bags and stored in the vault. The vault itself was secured with a combination that only the facility watch commander on duty possessed. This combination was changed on a monthly basis. Access to the vault was limited to authorized Boston Police Department personnel only, who had to present proper identification and be escorted to the vault by the watch commander or his designee. Despite all of these precautions, the burglary proceeds were stolen from the vault.

Initially it was believed that the theft was committed by a member of the department. However, an exhaustive investigation by the Internal Affairs Division absolved any of the officers of criminal culpability. However, the on-duty watch commander was suspended from duty for negligence. Then rumors began circulating about who had broken into the Boston Police Department evidence vault.

Supposedly it was a lone female burglar who had entered police headquarters at 1:00 A.M. on that Christmas morning, when most of the officers were otherwise occupied. She had made it to the vault without being detected, disabled the locking mechanism, and removed the evidence bags. Then she had managed to escape without being seen.

The Boston police officials investigating the theft gave the rumors little credence, but then stories began appearing in the gossip columns of international tabloids about this same female thief. A woman who was responsible for a number of crimes of stealth worldwide. And as the nineties passed into the twenty-first century, the reputation of this elusive thief increased to mammoth proportions.

Judy couldn't find any direct reference as to where the Devil's Shadow moniker came from, but it was believed that Inspector Jacques Benoit of the Sûreté had given it to her after a series of jewel thefts in Paris. This led to the Interpol reference submitted by Benoit in June 2001, which was based solely on circumstance, coincidence, and innuendo. A French national named Julianna Saint had been reported in the area of a number of the crimes committed by this Devil's Shadow. The Interpol information was confidential and had no evidentiary value in the United States whatsoever. Sitting at her computer console, Judy relaxed her rigid posture, removed her windowpane glasses, and exhaled a heavy sigh.

"What the heck," she mumbled, "I still can't prove anything."

Manny Sherlock was walking past her cubicle and overheard her comment. "What can't you prove?"

She looked up at him. "That this Julianna Saint is really the Devil's Shadow."

He took a seat in a chair next to her desk. "Isn't this Devil's Shadow supposed to be a myth? Kind of like the Pink Panther?"

Judy rolled her eyes. "So I guess that makes me Inspector Clouseau."

"I didn't say it, you did."

She looked back at her computer screen. "All I've got is a report from Chief Inspector Jacques Benoit of the Sûreté placing her in the same cities where some of the burglaries have occurred."

Manny's eyebrows shot up. "Did you say the Sûreté Inspector was named Benoit?"

"Yes. Jacques Benoit."

"We received a lookout message from him while you and the boss were gone. Switch over to the Crime Message program."

It took her a moment to get the new program on-line. Then she located the wanted message from Jacques Benoit, the prefect of police in the Principality of Monaco.

"Hello!" Judy said.

"You have something?"

She pointed at the screen. "Benoit is looking for a professional French criminal named Hubert Metayer, who is wanted for a double homicide in Monaco. This Metayer is believed to be in the United States, but there is no reference to anyone by that name entering through U.S. Customs."

"I don't see how that will help you with this Devil's Shadow," Manny said.

"It might not, but according to some of the people I talked to on Saint Martin, Julianna Saint has two companions or, more appropriately, assistants. One of them is a tall, broad-shouldered, lover-boy type named Christophe La Croix, who I ran into on the island. The other one is this Hubert Metayer."

The Mistress of Disguise/High Priestess of Mayhem began entering additional instructions into her computer. "Let's see what we can find out about this Hubert Metayer."

The abandoned Amalgamated Copper Works complex was located just outside of Michigan City, Indiana, sixty minutes from Chicago. The complex consisted of five buildings, which had been in a continuously deteriorating state of disrepair since the industrial-metal-producing business had been absorbed by a Pennsylvania-based conglomerate in the late 1990s. The owners of the property had been shopping around for a buyer, but the complex location and the asking price had made prospects for a sale doubtful.

The property was managed by the Chicago law firm of Peck, Goolsby, Engstrom and DeLacey. The owners of the land the factory buildings rested on lived in California and relied on the law firm to take care of the required upkeep and other problems connected with the property. However, the owners were unaware that the factory was currently being used without them being compensated and without their authorization. Had any of the owners of the land located on ten acres of Indiana countryside happened to drop by, he would have immediately noticed the armed sentries patrolling the ten-foot-tall Cyclone fence encircling the property and the uniformed security guard at the front gate, who was not only big, mean, and surly, but also discouraged inquiries at the point of a gun. Had one of the property's rightful owners decided against his better judgment to inquire further as to what was going on inside the abandoned complex, his life would have been in definite danger. But thankfully for all parties concerned, none of the owners did show up, and the few travelers passing the formerly vacant complex gave no thought at all to what was going on inside.

With the silent acquiesence of attorney Sol Engstrom, the Chicago Mob had taken over the complex and, after securing the perimeter, turned the former Amalgamated Copper Works into a training area.

The trainees had been carefully selected from the ranks of organized crime families nationwide. Present were expert shooters, wheel men, and hard-core criminals who were not only very good at what they did, but possessed the important attribute of being able to keep their mouths shut.

The training they were undergoing was extensive, consisting of an arduous physical exercise routine, weapons training in the main building of the complex, which had been soundproofed, and strategy classes. The strategy classes were held in the main foundry, and all eight of the trainees were required to attend three sessions daily. The course of study was very concentrated, and discipline harsh. However, not one of the trainees had ever gotten out of line either at the complex or in the inexpensive motels in and around Michigan City in which they stayed. This was due to two reasons: First, they were each being paid one million dollars apiece, and second, if they screwed up in even the slightest way or failed to do exactly what they were told when they were told to do it, then they would be immediately killed.

Besides the classroom training, there was a full-sized model constructed in a former factory storage area, which had once been used to store gigantic spools of copper cable. The model was an exact duplicate of the original, right down to such mundane items as trash receptacles, doorknobs, and windowpanes. The training model was a replica of the security loading platform of Union Station in Chicago, complete with a full-sized armored car.

There were three instructors for the eight trainees. Each was a former career member of the United States military. The retired army Special Forces lieutenant colonel, retired army ordnance sergeant major, and the retired Marine Corps first sergeant had extensive experience in both the academic and practical aspects in the art of war. They drilled their charges unmercifully, and the six men and two women had responded exceptionally well. Despite only one of them having any prior military training, the trainees reacted instinctively to the discipline, numerous drills, and classes on tactics. In small-arms training, one of the women—a slightly built blonde— was so good that, in the estimation of the Marine noncom, she could have qualified for the USA Olympic pistol team.

Now the trainees were being put through their final drills prior to going operational in seventy-two hours. Dressed in combat fatigues without headgear, they approached the mock-up of the Union Station security area. The retired colonel, clad in camouflage fatigues and a green beret without insignia, was about to signal the start of the exercise by blowing a metal whistle when the former sergeant major called to him from the warehouse entrance. Delaying the exercise, the colonel waited for the sergeant to trot over to him. The former military men conferred briefly in whispers and a few minutes later a black Lincoln Town car pulled up at the warehouse entrance. The trainers and the trainees had seen this car before, but no one had ever gotten out of it. They figured that this was the boss of the operation, who had so far remained anonymous. However, to the people assembled in this warehouse, who they were working for didn't matter. The money they would be paid and the extent of the planning going into this event made such an introduction unnecessary.

The luxury car remained at the entrance as the colonel snapped to attention and saluted the Lincoln. Then he executed a smart about-face and gave the command for the exercise to commence.

As the trainees went into action, the black car remained in place, its engine idling softly. The entire exercise took ten minutes and eighteen seconds, which was nearly a full minute below the projected time frame. When they were finished, the colonel had the trainees stand down before he again turned to face the Town Car. No acknowledgment came from the black car and it remained only a moment longer before slowly pulling away.

Jake Romano was seated in the backseat of the black car. He was concealed behind tinted windows, which shielded him from the outside world. The car itself had been leased and the license plates were registered to a Mob-owned dealership in Oak Lawn, Illinois.

The Mob boss had watched the training exercise with concentrated interest. His two ever-present bodyguards were in the front seat and had witnessed the training operation. The most ambitious crime in history would be taking place on Saint Patrick's Day. As the Lincoln pulled onto the highway and sped back to Chicago, Romano picked up a book from the leather seat beside him. He was three-quarters of the way through *The History of Train Robberies in America*, by Sir Harlan Nash, a history professor at the University of Chicago. Before Romano resumed reading, he thought about the cop who had foiled his last robbery plan at the DeWitt National Bank. The Mob boss was certain that Larry Cole would not get in the way this time, because the famed cop would be occupied with other matters. Other matters of a very serious nature.

Before they arrived back in the city, Romano had finished the book.

42

The flatbed truck drove down Clark Street past the Cook County Building and made a left on Washington. At Dearborn Street the driver executed another left and traveled a half block north. The rush hour was still in progress and there was a great deal of traffic in the Loop area. Snapping on his turn signal, which caused a warning alarm to begin beeping in synchronization with the light, he inched over the curb onto the sidewalk. The pedestrian traffic on the west side of Dearborn parted grudgingly for the heavy vehicle. A scowling, middle-aged woman screamed, "Don't you know you're supposed to yield the right of way to pedestrians, ya damned fool?!"

The driver ignored her and kept going until he reached the Picasso statue. Then he and the cab passenger got out.

A pair of guards stationed in the lobby of the Richard J. Daley Center and a traffic cop in the Washington and Dearborn intersection witnessed the truck's manuever with disbelief. As this trio of law enforcement officials converged on the offending vehicle, the driver and his companion began unloading a large canvas tarpaulin from the truck bed.

The traffic cop reached them first. A thirty-year veteran of the department, he cocked his police cap with the blue-and-white checkerboard band back off his forehead, pulled a traffic citation book from his pocket, and said, "I think you gentlemen have a problem."

The two men stopped working and turned to face the officer as the two Daley Center guards approached them from the rear. For a moment the policeman thought that the black man who had been the truck passenger was going to cause trouble. However, the young white driver grinned and said with a foreign accent, "I hope there will be no difficulty, Officer. We are authorized to be here."

A belligerent tone slipped into the cop's voice. "And who gave you this so-called authorization?"

The driver raised his hands and said, "May I retrieve a letter from my inside pocket?"

The guards flanked the two workmen and waited to see how the traffic cop was going to handle this.

"Go ahead," the policeman said.

Carefully the young man reached into his dark blue jumpsuit, which his companion wore a duplicate of, and removed a folded sheet of paper. He handed it to the cop.

It was a reproduction of a letter from the mayor of the City of Chicago, addressed "To Whom It May Concern." The gist of the communication that the traffic cop read was that the Belmont Metal Works Company, which the two men in the blue jumpsuits worked for, was authorized to refurbish the Picasso statue in the Daley Center Plaza. Said work was to commence on March 15 and conclude no later than March 18.

Handing the letter back, the traffic cop said, "I guess you guys are legit, but the next time you drive into the plaza, let me know beforehand and I'll clear the traffic for you."

The black man glared at the policeman, but the younger guy said a contrite, "Yes, sir, Officer. We'll be certain to provide you with a timely notification the next time we are here. But tonight we'll have to leave the truck where it is."

The cop shrugged. "You've got the mayor's okay for this, so that won't be a problem. I'll let the patrol cars in the area and the sector sergeants know. You won't be hassled." He turned to look up at the giant sculpture. "You're going to give the old bird a real face-lift, huh?"

For the first time since this confrontation had begun, the black man spoke. The cop noticed that he had an accent almost as pronounced as the truck driver's. The thought crossed the cop's mind, *Foreigners are taking over everything.* But this was quickly erased by the black man's snarled words.

"When we get through with your Picasso, you won't even recognize it."

The cop started to question him as to what he meant, but the truck driver quickly added, "We're going to make it look brand-new, Officer."

"I bet," the cop said, skeptically. "But I've lived in this town all my life, and as far back as I can remember, this ugly old sculpture has looked exactly the same. I don't think that you two are going to be able to do much to change it." With that the traffic cop tipped his cap and returned to the intersection.

Seeing that the policeman was satisfied with the truck being parked in the plaza, the guards returned to their Daley Center lobby post. On the center's computer they entered a message about the crew cleaning the Picasso, which read:

Workmen have parked a truck in the plaza for the purpose of refurbishing the Picasso. Authorization checked by the CPD at 1822 hours—14 March 2005.

Out in the Daley Center Plaza, Christophe La Croix breathed a sigh of relief. Again Hubert Metayer had almost blown Julianna's plans. The Devil's Shadow had carefully put together the front of this Belmont Metal Works Company. The letter from the Windy City's chief executive was a forgery, but Julianna had done a masterful job of hacking into the City of Chicago computer system. Messages had been planted with the Department of Buildings, the police department, and the fire department, authorizing the renovation. With her usual brilliance, Julianna was using the complicated municipal bureaucracy against itself. By the time any curious cops or nosy city officials cut through the red tape to find out what was going on, the deed would be done.

Utilizing a hoist in the back of the truck, they raised the tarpaulin up to the top of the sculpture and proceeded to drop the canvas to conceal the entire structure. It took them an hour to complete the task and they attracted a substantial number of onlookers; however, no one questioned what they were doing. Again, this was as Julianna had anticipated. No one would ever suspect that anyone would try to steal this statue. Now, their initial task completed, the assistants of *L'Ombre du Diable* walked away, leaving the truck behind.

The vehicle and the covered Picasso would be observed by any number of people over the next forty-eight hours, but no one would question what was happening or why. Although what was going to take place in the Richard J. Daley Center Plaza would not qualify as the crime of the century, it would certainly equal other horrific events in the history of the Windy City. An event that would rank with the Great Chicago Fire of 1871 and Baron Alain Marcus Casimir von Rianocek's attempt to destroy the city with an atomic bomb back in 2002.

Ian Jellicoe and the Rush Street male exotic dancer who had been staying with the Englishman in the DeWitt Plaza suite prepared to go out for dinner. It was their practice to dine at a different Near North restaurant each night. Since returning to the hotel after his ordeal at the hands of Larry Cole and Blackie Silvestri, Jellicoe had managed to regain his composure, after consuming a couple of glasses of wine from a bottle he had opened personally. He had learned his lesson after the incident on the transatlantic flight during which Julianna Saint had had him drugged. Now he poured all of his own drinks.

Surrounded by a rosy halo of inebriation, the immaculately dressed Englishman left the suite of rooms on the forty-fourth floor of the DeWitt Plaza Hotel. At his side was the exotic dancer, clad in a brown leather pants suit with a noticeable coating of foundation makeup and rouge on his face.

The elevator transported them to the twenty-fifth-floor hotel lobby, where they were required to change cars for the ride down to the main floor. Feeling the effects of the wine and absorbed with his companion, Jellicoe failed to notice Julianna Saint sitting on a sofa at the far end of the lobby. After they had boarded the elevator, the Devil's Shadow rose from her seat.

She was dressed in a black dress she had purchased in Paris, a black hooded cape, and black high-heeled shoes. She was noticed by a number of guests and hotel personnel, but they only thought of her as an exceptionally beautiful woman. No one questioned where she was going or why. This was a requirement of her trade and she had been practicing this precept for a long time.

On the forty-fourth floor, she went to the door of Jellicoe's suite. As she traversed the corridor, she was outwardly casual, but acutely sensitive for any signs of danger. The door to the suite was secured by a computerized card-accessing system, which operated on a magnetic principle. Inserting the hotel-issued key card into the lock reversed the polarity of the electrical field securing the door. Such a security system was not only state-of-the-art, but also supposedly impossible to defeat.

Julianna removed a small, square device of her own design from the pocket of her cape and held it in front of the lock. She switched it on momentarily, which produced the same effect as that of a legitimate guest inserting a card. The only problem with her device was that it was extremely powerful and could easily short out the locking mechanism completely if she was not careful with its application. This would be an undesirable development, because Jellicoe would be alerted to her presence.

Less than five seconds after she turned the device on, the locking mechanism disengaged. Pushing the suite door open, she detected the faint aroma of combustion. Stepping inside, she examined the exterior door panel for signs of scorching. It appeared undamaged, but the internal workings were a different matter. She only hoped that this security system would hold up until the Englishman vacated the suite.

When she shut the door, the locking mechanism engaged. She had come to find out what Ian Jellicoe was up to. She planned to carry out her assignments for Romano and De Coutreaux, but Jellicoe had been less than forthright with her in the past, so what she was engaging in now was a form of life insurance policy.

Wearing a pair of thin black gloves and slipping out of her heels, which she placed in one of the pockets sewn into the lining of her cape, she began to systematically search the suite. The living room, dining area, bedroom, and connecting bathroom that Jellicoe and his guest were using yielded nothing unexpected. Then she came to a locked door leading off the main corridor, which bisected the suite. She permitted a smile to curl the corners of her mouth. There was a piece of dark thread tied loosely around the doorknob. This was Jellicoe's crude attempt at detecting an unauthorized entry. Julianna removed the thread and placed it in a small cloth drawstring bag tied to her waist. She would remember to replace the string in the exact same position that she found it in when she left. Then Julianna Saint picked the lock and entered Ian Jellicoe's secret room.

The basic decor of the small office had been selected more for style than function. There was a lot of overstuffed wooden furniture, a computer terminal, which she knew Jellicoe would never touch, and a telephone console. Each of the electronic devices bore the DeWitt Plaza Hotel logo. Then there were the items lying in plain view on top of the highly varnished mahogany desk—Ian Jellicoe's black leather portfolio and a compact video camera.

She noticed that Jellicoe had replaced the lock on the portfolio. Julianna shook her head. This one was no more secure than its predecessor. She had it unlocked in less than five seconds.

Ian Jellicoe was an intelligent man, but he wasn't very smart when it came to protecting himself. His portfolio contained a number of items, including a copy of the videotape Julianna had stolen from Greg Ennis's safety-deposit box. There was a leather-bound pocket notebook, which contained a number of entries in the Englishman's precise block print. She read notes dealing with her new job for Jake Romano and the task for Bishop De Coutreaux. There was a name scrawled on the bottom of the page for the fourteenth of March 2005. It was in Jellicoe's hand, but nowhere near as neat as the other entries. It took her a moment to decipher the two words. When she did, Julianna tensed and took in a sharp breath. The name Jellicoe had written was Larry Cole.

She had no time to dwell on why Jellicoe had written down the policeman's name. Filing this information away for future reference, she continued the search.

The next item of interest she turned to was the video camera. A cassette was still in it, so she noted the elapsed playing time of one hour and forty-three minutes, rewound the tape, and began viewing it from the beginning.

The Devil's Shadow watched the downtown Chicago street scenes and decided to fast-forward the tape. She had an idea as to what Jellicoe was doing, but she had to question the reason why. Julianna had never asked for the Englishman's help, nor would she have accepted it had such aid been offered. And she didn't like this at all. Jellicoe was casing her job.

The views on the video camera screen were well known to her, as she had been examining these same streets since January. She continued to keep the fast-forward mode on and images whizzed by on the screen until the tape shifted from exterior street scenes to the interior of a building. She slowed the tape, but for long moments the images broadcast remained static. Julianna also knew this area. It was the lower level of the Field Museum of Natural History, not far from the office of Dr. Silvernail Smith. She didn't like this either, but she was glad that she had decided to take a look at what Jellicoe was up to.

Then there was movement and a man's image appeared, expanding rapidly at the center of the screen. Even with the tape continuing to move quickly, she instantly recognized him. She had just slowed the tape to normal speed when she heard a noise. Someone was attempting to enter the suite. Julianna Saint froze.

43

For the most ambitious criminal undertaking of his life, Jake Romano was taking no chances. With less than seventy-two hours to go, he was checking out every possible contingency that could have an effect on his plan. As such, the Mob boss and his ever-present pair of bodyguards were at DeWitt Plaza to check out Ian Fitzwalter Jellicoe.

The Englishman had set everything up as he had been instructed to do by Romano. The diversion would go off as planned, which would absorb the complete attention of the entire city. This would allow his organization to walk away with two hundred million dollars. Jellicoe knew nothing about the planned robbery, but he did have a connection to Romano and the diversion, which would take place during the Saint Patrick's Day Parade. However, after the deed was done, the Mafia boss planned to get rid of not only Jellicoe, but also the French thief and her crew.

But first things first. Romano wanted to know what Jellicoe had up his sleeve. The Mob boss had his people keeping an eye on the Englishman while he was in Chicago. Romano was aware of the romantic liaison with the Rush Street male exotic dancer. The relationship was not a problem for the Mob, but with so much at stake, it would be wise to take a look around Jellicoe's DeWitt Plaza Hotel suite.

The hotel concierge ran a high-priced call-girl operation, which was Mob-protected, so it was a simple matter to obtain a pass card. They had been admitted by the concierge personally through a rear delivery door and transported to Jellicoe's floor by way of a service elevator. The concierge, a nervous little man who sweated profusely, was ordered to take the elevator out of service and wait while Romano and his men checked out the suite.

The corridor was empty as the three men, who were all dressed in dark clothing, approached the door to Suite 4402. Romano stood back as one of the bodyguards swiped the pass key through the access port. On the first try nothing happened. He repeated the procedure and this time the lock emitted a grinding noise before the door snapped open. The three mobsters entered, closing the door behind them.

Inside the entrance, Romano stopped and held up his hand, signaling his men to not only halt, but also remain silent. The bodyguards stared quizzically at their boss. They had it on good authority that the Englishman and his boyfriend were having dinner at Orly's Restaurant on Wells Street. The suite was supposed to be empty.

They stood in silence for a few moments. Finally Romano whispered, "I heard something. Spread out and check everything."

The bodyguards pulled silenced 9-mm Berettas from beneath their jackets and began advancing into the suite. Anything that moved was going to get shot. Romano, who was unarmed and seldom carried a gun, remained by the door. If there was anyone in here, he was confident that his men would find him.

Julianna Saint slipped out of Jellicoe's secured room and moved silently into the shadows at the rear of the suite. The rooms were arranged in a circular configuration, and two of the three men who had entered were advancing on her location from separate directions. There was a service exit off the kitchen area, but it was adjacent to the corridor entrance. One of them was standing at that entrance, which effectively eliminated that escape route. So her only option was to remain in the suite and elude detection. Now she would have to live up to the name that she'd been given by Chief Inspector Jacques Benoit of the Sûreté and become the embodiment of the Devil's Shadow.

Romano's bodyguards were not security experts, but instead cold-blooded killers. This was one of the attributes that the Mob boss had considered as among the most important for them to possess when he had selected them. The two broad-shouldered, brutal-featured men possessed no reservations about killing, and on the orders of Jake Romano, they would kill anyone at any time. Motivation for committing murder didn't matter to them and they didn't possess anything even remotely resembling a conscience. Romano had also chosen them because they were antisocial psychopaths who would, at a single word from him, kill each other.

However, everything that made them valuable to the Chicago Mob boss made it easier for Julianna to elude them.

As they came on with guns raised, they were looking for any movement, which would, in turn, draw an immediate, violent reaction. Like cops searching for an armed suspect, they swung their pistols in 180-degree arcs covering all possible angles of attack—as long as the target was a normal-sized standing adult. They did not consider the possibility of someone being below or above them.

There was a dining room table with chairs for eight in an alcove six feet from Jellicoe's locked room. Julianna slipped silently beneath this table, covered herself completely with her cape, and lay motionless. She left a space between the cloth covering her and the carpeted floor, so she could see the searchers. The Devil's Shadow had been in place for less than ten seconds when a pair of thick-soled black shoes came into view. The wearer's feet were long, wide, and thick, which would indicate a big man. A big, dangerous man.

The black shoes stopped moving and she heard him trying the door to the locked room. He called out, "I've got a locked door here, boss!"

There was the sound of two equally large men converging on the area. Now Julianna could see three pairs of shoes arranged in a straight line: black oxford, black oxford, custom-made loafer, custom-made loafer, black oxford . . .

* * *

Jake Romano shook the doorknob. Then he stepped back and studied the frame and locking mechanism. A look of rage contracted
the mobster's face and he lashed out a kick aimed at the center
of the door. The door didn't budge, but the force exerted shot back
through his body and knocked him to the floor. He landed with a
resounding crash against the far wall in a sitting position. Had he
looked slightly to the right, he would have seen the irregular shape
lying in shadow beneath the dining area table. But the frustration
of his failed attempt to get into the locked room, as well as the pain
shooting from his ankle to the base of his spine, prevented him
from seeing anything other than the locked door.

The bodyguards helped him to his feet.

Romano was unable to straighten up as he snarled, "There's
somebody hiding in there. Go get the pimp."

The bodyguards knew that he was talking about the concierge,
who was waiting for them at the service elevator. As one of the
bodyguards left the suite to do his bidding, Romano glared at the
locked door.

Less than a minute later, the concierge, still sweating, rushed
in.

"Open this door," the Mob boss ordered.

"Certainly, sir," he said, hurrying forward and removing an
access card from a holder hanging from a chain around his neck.
He inserted it into the port and waited for the green light to signal
that the door was unlocked. Nothing happened.

"I don't understand what could be the trouble," the concierge
said, frantically.

Now in a full-blown rage, Romano snatched one of the bodyguards' guns, slapped the concierge on the side of the head with it,
and aimed at the door. It took four shots from the Beretta to destroy
the locking mechanism. Then the bodyguards rushed in, followed
by their limping boss.

The concierge, his head beginning to bleed, stumbled over to
the dining area table, pulled back a chair, and sat down. His foot
struck something, but the pain forced everything else that was oc-

curring around him to recede to the point of trivia. Cradling his head in his hands, he closed his eyes and took deep breaths.

When the DeWitt Plaza Hotel concierge sat down at the dining area table, his foot struck the leg of a chair that Julianna had moved when she vacated her hiding place. She moved rapidly and silently away from the dining area into the far corridor leading to the bedrooms. From there she could easily make it to the front door of the suite and make good her escape. The sounds of Romano and his men searching the study carried to her. With the exit door in sight, the Devil's Shadow stopped.

Why is Romano here? she asked herself.

Romano leaned against the wall while his bodyguards went through the room. They broke into Jellicoe's portfolio and dumped the contents on top of the desk. Then they began ransacking the room, pulling out drawers and overturning furniture.

"Stop it!" Romano shouted. "What in the hell are you guys searching for?"

The bodyguards stopped and turned to look sheepishly back at their boss.

"Pick that stuff up," he said, pointing at the contents of the portfolio, "and put it back inside the case. We'll take it with us. What are those?"

They looked down at the videocassettes, which were on the floor. When they had entered, these cassettes had been stacked neatly on the desk next to the now-destroyed computer terminal. A bodyguard picked them up. One of the cassettes was marked "Copy—Metro Bank—December 2004." The other two bore no markings at all; however, these were equipped with a video camera adapter. Romano instantly realized the significance of the date on the marked cassette. Then he said, "Where's the video camera?"

The bodyguards began looking around, but finally were forced to raise their hands in frustration.

"Okay, let's get out of here," Romano said.

They picked up the portfolio and the tape cassettes and followed the Mob boss out of the room.

"Boss," said the bodyguard who usually drove Romano's Lincoln, "what are we going to do about him?" He nodded at the concierge, still seated in the dining area with his bleeding head cradled in his hands.

Romano looked from the bullet-riddled door to the man who had provided them with clandestine access to this suite. "Give me your gun," he said to the bodyguard whose Beretta had not been fired.

The silenced pistol was handed over and Romano limped to within arm's reach of the concierge. The little man did not look up as Romano fired three bullets into the back of his head.

"This just became a burglary/homicide," he said, handing the weapon back. "I want those guns at the bottom of Lake Michigan before dawn. Let's get out of here. I need to call my doctor." Romano grimaced in pain as he led them to the suite door. He waited until one of the bodyguards checked the outside corridor and then they were gone, leaving the suite door ajar.

When she had been alone for a full five minutes, the Devil's Shadow emerged from her hiding place behind a thick curtain in the luxury suite's living room. She had not only witnessed the murder that Jake Romano had committed, but she had also recorded, for the second time, the Mob boss performing the deed on tape.

When she had heard them entering the suite, Julianna was holding Jellicoe's camera in her hand and staring at the image of Larry Cole. Unconsciously she had held on to the camera when she slipped out of the room and secreted herself beneath the dining area table. Deciding to remain in the suite to see if she could find out what Romano was up to, she had activated the "record" function on the camera. From her place of concealment, she had taped Romano murdering the concierge. She didn't know what she was going to do with the "Romano Murder" tapes, as she now dubbed them, but they gave her a tremendous bargaining chip to use against the Chicago mobster.

With a parting glance at the brutally slain concierge, Julianna Saint left the suite.

44

MARCH 14, 2005
8:52 P.M.

Larry Cole parked his unmarked police car on Michigan Avenue and entered DeWitt Plaza. The shootout that he had been involved in last December came back to him as he rode up in an elevator to the hotel lobby. After changing cars, he got off on the forty-fourth floor, which was teeming with police personnel investigating the homicide of the DeWitt Plaza concierge in Suite 4402.

All of the officers present knew the chief of detectives, who made it a practice of showing up at murder investigations. At the door to the suite he spoke to the uniformed officer on duty there to protect the crime scene from the unauthorized and the curious. "Has the crime lab finished processing the scene?"

"Yes, sir," said the fresh-faced young officer, whose uniform looked brand-new. "They went through the entire place. Lieutenant Silvestri is inside talking to the Area Three detectives."

"Thanks," Cole said, entering the suite. The instant he crossed the threshold he knew why Blackie had called him. Seated on a couch in the living room area at the front of the suite were Ian Jellicoe and a garishly dressed, elaborately made-up young man.

Blackie walked toward Cole from the rear of the suite. The lieutenant stepped up close to his boss and said in hushed tones, "This is none other than our old friend Ian Jellicoe's suite. Him and the guy sitting next to him said that they went out to dinner at a restaurant on Wells." Blackie checked his pocket notebook. "It was Orly's, an Italian joint with pretty good food. The detectives assigned to the case verified that they were there between six-twenty and seven-thirty. They took taxis there and back to the hotel, which we're checking out. Jellicoe's buddy is a dancer at the Club Exotica on Rush. His show starts at ten. They came back here to cool out for a couple of hours, found the door open and the concierge dead in the dining area back there." Blackie cocked his thumb over his shoulder at the rear of the suite. "Now, on the surface," the lieutenant continued, "it looks like the killers forced the concierge to let them in so that they could burglarize the place and then killed him so that he wouldn't talk."

"But you don't buy that," Cole said.

"Whatever went down here was a lot heavier than any burglary gone wrong. For one thing, the front-door locking mechanism has been damaged by some type of sophisticated electronic lock-opening device. The concierge carried a pass key, so why did our offender need to use a burglar's tool?"

Cole played devil's advocate. "Suppose the offender entered the suite and was surprised in the act by the concierge?"

Blackie shrugged. "That can't be ruled out, boss, but the concierge's station is at a desk in the lobby, and the hotel people we talked to said that the dead guy seldom left it. He also has a record as a procurer of ladies of the evening. Very high-priced ladies of the evening. He hasn't been busted in a while, but the Vice Control Division has been keeping an eye on him for the last couple of months. Obviously our boy Jellicoe isn't into female companionship, so there's no reason for our late DeWitt Plaza Hotel concierge to be up here. And there's one more thing."

Cole waited.

"The victim was supposedly real nervous when he came on duty at five o'clock. According to the night manager, he was preoccupied and was sweating like he'd been in a sauna. At about six he left the lobby and wasn't seen or heard from again until Jellicoe and friend found him with his skull ventilated."

"There's a lot of Mob influence in these North Shore call operations," Cole said. "Our dead concierge could have been connected. What was taken in the burglary?"

"I was just about to ask Ian the same thing," Blackie responded. "I guess this is his lucky day."

Cole shot him a questioning look. "He finds a dead body in his hotel room after a burglary has been committed and you say it's his lucky day. Blackie, you're getting jaded."

"Oh, I wasn't talking about that, boss. I mean it's his lucky day because he's seen us twice."

All Cole could do was shake his head. Then they walked over to the Englishman and his houseguest.

"Where are we?" Christophe asked Hubert.

"Don't worry about it," the black Frenchman snapped. "We're not lost."

Hubert was driving the rented Pontiac down Western Avenue at Ninety-fifth Street on the far southwest side of the city. They were looking for a tavern called The Shaken Martini. When Hubert had asked Christophe to accompany him with the promise of a free dinner, he hadn't said where they were going to eat. They were staying at separate Loop hotels, which was the way they operated whenever they were on a job for Julianna. When Hubert picked him up at the SwissHotel on Wacker Drive, Christophe thought they were going to a Loop restaurant. But Hubert drove over to Lake Shore Drive and sped south. A half hour later they pulled up in front of a dimly lighted bar.

"Is this where we're going to eat?" Christophe asked, incredulously.

"No," Hubert responded, shutting off the engine. "I've got to see someone. Then we'll eat. C'mon."

"Why do you need me?"

"Backup," Hubert said, reaching into the glove compartment and removing a .38-caliber snub-nosed revolver. He tossed the gun into Christophe's lap.

"Hubert, what's going on?" There was a pleading tone in the young Frenchman's voice.

"I need you to cover me while I talk to a guy. I'm selling some merchandise I picked up in Europe. If things go okay, I'll cut you in for a piece of the action."

Still Christophe hesitated. Finally, as he had never been able to refuse Hubert in the past, he got out of the car and followed him into The Shaken Martini.

The bar was dark, but pleasantly equipped in red leather and chrome. Subdued lighting reflected off a highly varnished mahogany-topped bar. There were four people, a woman and three men, seated at the bar, and three more patrons, two females seated together and a lone male, in the booths along the wall. A sixtyish potbellied man wearing a white apron tended bar. Hubert approached him.

"I'm looking for Mr. Tomasini."

The bartender looked warily at the two Frenchmen and then pointed at the lone man seated in the back booth. They turned to see a thick-featured man with curly, dark brown hair.

"Wait here," Hubert said to Christophe. "Have a drink. It's on me. Bartender, take care of my friend."

"Yeah, yeah," the bartender said with a pronounced lack of enthusiasm. As Christophe sat down, the bartender muttered, "This ain't no pawnshop."

Now Christophe was tense. Hubert was up to something, and the thing with the gun was in complete violation of the orders that Julianna had given them just the day before.

Christophe became aware of the bartender standing in front of him.

"So what'll it be?"

The Frenchman figured that this man had copied his surly manner from 1940s and 1950s American gangster movies. Christophe ordered a Perrier with a twist. The barkeep scornfully rolled his eyes. A short time later he slapped a bottle and a glass of ice on top of the bar. Then, with exaggerated slowness, he placed a slice of lemon on a napkin next to the glass.

"Anything else?"

"No, *mon ami*," Christophe said. "This will be quite adequate."

"What are you and that black guy anyway, French?"

Christophe nodded and made a show of filling his glass in order to discourage further conversation. Taking the hint, the bartender walked away.

Christophe took a long pull of his drink, because his mouth had gone dry. He took a look around at the other patrons. A couple looked like the same type of hollow-eyed heavy drinker found in any cheap bar in any city in the world. Then there were the two guys at the far end of the bar adjacent to the booth where Hubert and the curly-haired man were seated. The French thief's criminal instincts took over and, while not appearing to do so, he studied the men at the bar closely.

They were muscular types with mean faces, dressed in casual clothing. They were drinking beer, and when one of them lifted a bottle of Amstel Light to his mouth, Christophe took a careful look at his left hand. The lighting was indeed dim, but Christophe possessed exceptionally keen eyesight, which had served him well in the past. So he was able to see the gold-coin ring surrounded by jewels on the man's pinky finger and his recently manicured fingernails.

Christophe checked the other one. He was pretty much the same, although the Frenchman was unable to see his hands because he was wearing gloves.

Christophe drained off the rest of his Perrier and looked over at the booth where Hubert was still talking to the curly-haired man. Their heads were bent low over the table as they appeared to be examining something. Christophe again turned to study the men sitting a few stools away. He was able to put it together quickly enough.

Hubert was fencing stolen goods and the curly-haired guy was the buyer. The manicured man with the pinky ring and the one in gloves were standing by to rob Hubert. This placed Christophe right in the middle of a very dangerous situation.

Then angry voices echoed through the bar. Hubert and the curly-haired man were arguing.

"This is worth ten times that amount!" the black Frenchman shouted.

"Then take it to a legit jeweler and get face value for it, pal," Curly Hair said with a pronounced South Side of Chicago accent. "This junk is so hot it's burning my hands."

Hubert was getting to his feet when the men at the bar made their move. Both of them pulled guns—the one with the pinky ring, a .38 four-inch-barrel revolver; his gloved companion, a .25-caliber, silenced automatic. Christophe watched the entire thing unfold in a slow-motion, old-time nickelodeon tableau. It was as if his eyes were freeze-framing each move made by the actors in this violent play.

The man with the revolver began dropping into a bent-leg stance and raising his gun with both hands to point the barrel at Christophe. The other one was concentrating on Hubert, but having trouble handling the small weapon while wearing gloves. Then the first shot was fired. Christophe, the European lover, was surprised that this bullet came from his gun.

When the man with the gold-coin pinky ring had pointed his gun, Christophe had instinctively pulled the .38 that Hubert had given him. He made no conscious effort to either aim the weapon or pull the trigger, yet he managed to hit his adversary in the face dead center. As the man with the pinky ring fell to the floor, the other patrons scattered and the bartender dropped from sight behind the bar.

The man wearing gloves was firing the silenced .25 into the booth where Hubert had been arguing with the fence. Christophe took aim and fired at the shooter. He missed, shattering a Coors beer sign on the far wall. Christophe fired again and struck the jukebox. He was about to try it once more when Hubert opened fire from the booth, hitting the shooter four times and hurling his dead body back against the bar. Then Hubert placed the barrel of the automatic flush against the curly-haired man's forehead and pulled the trigger, blowing the top of his head off.

The interior of The Shaken Martini was thick with gun smoke and the stench of cordite. The bartender and the surviving patrons either hugged the floor or were crouched down in a booth. For a long moment no one moved. Then Hubert struggled to his feet and moved slowly toward Christophe. The black man carried a Glock 9-mm pistol in one hand and clutched a cloth bundle in the other. The entire right side of Hubert's body was covered with blood.

"You will have to drive," Hubert said, through clenched teeth. "I've got a couple of bullets in me." Then he walked out the door into the night.

Cursing the day he'd ever set eyes on this man, Christophe followed.

45

MARCH 14, 2005
9:59 P.M.

Julianna Saint was in her room at the Drake Hotel. She was sitting in a chair in front of a window that provided her with a view of North Lake Shore Drive. She had Ian Jellicoe's video camera on her lap and she had freeze-framed Larry Cole's image on the screen. She didn't know how long she'd been staring at it. Actually, her mind was back on Saint Martin and the time she had spent with the policeman. She had nothing but the memory of a one-night stand and the lie this man had told her. Yet he had seldom been out of her thoughts since the moment she had set eyes on him.

She pressed the "photocopy" button and a snapshot of the video image was ejected from a port on the side of the camera. Staring at the picture filled her with bitterness. Now she had a memento of their brief union. She was also aware that the reason Cole had impersonated author Michael Holt and been accompanied to Saint Martin by the disguise artist Judy Daniels was to investigate the Devil's Shadow. Julianna was forced to admire Cole's tenacity. No law enforcement official had ever gotten this close to her during her infamous career, and she vowed that he would get no closer.

Getting up from her chair, she walked over to the desk and picked up a book of matches. As if the act would purge her of Cole's memory, she burned the photo in an ashtray. Watching the flames die, leaving a residue of ash, she realized that the hollow emptiness still remained. But of one thing she was certain: The pain wouldn't last forever. At least she hoped not.

The telephone rang.

She crossed to the bedside table and picked up the receiver. "Hello."

It was Christophe.

The safe house was only to be used in case of an emergency. Wherever Julianna Saint operated, she always had a place to retreat to other than her principal residence. In Chicago she had rented a furnished house on the South-Side in a nondescript, predominantly black, middle-class neighborhood. The house was a brick tri-level in fairly good condition, which had been previously owned by a senior citizen who was wealthy enough to have a live-in maid. The furniture was dated but clean. Julianna had paid a security deposit and three months rent in advance. The place was equipped with food, extra clothing, a four-by-four vehicle with a full tank of gas in the garage, five thousand dollars in cash, and emergency medical supplies. There were no weapons.

Julianna met Christophe and Hubert at the house shortly after midnight. Before leaving the cars they had driven parked in the alley behind the garage, Julianna checked out the house and the surrounding area for anything that might prove threatening. Then she helped Christophe bring Hubert inside.

Hubert was barely conscious when they got him into an upstairs bedroom, and Julianna was alarmed over the amount of blood he had lost. But there was no way the wounded thief could be taken to a hospital. The Devil's Shadow would have to save his life by removing the two .25-caliber bullets from his body.

Julianna and Christophe undressed him. She noticed that Christophe was trembling uncontrollably, which would make him totally useless in assisting her.

"Go downstairs and take a single shot of brandy," she ordered. "Then sit down and compose yourself. As soon as you're ready, come back up here. We've got work to do."

Obediently, displaying gratitude, he turned to leave the room. Her voice stopped him before he could get out the door.

"Only one shot of brandy, Christophe."

He managed a weak smile. "I'll be lucky if I can keep even a swallow down, the way my stomach feels right now."

He returned less than fifteen minutes later. By that time Julianna had outfitted the room for a surgical procedure. It was as sterile as she could make it. Hubert had been sedated, and an IV started to keep him from getting too weak. She had cleaned up her patient, injected him with a dose of antibiotics, and examined his bullet wounds. There was one in his left shoulder and another in his chest. She was worried about the chest wound; however, she was fairly certain that the small-caliber bullet had not penetrated the rib cage, but was lodged deep in his pectoral muscle.

As soon as Chistophe was ready, Julianna went to work. She had learned her medical skills years before from her uncle Walter Saint, who had practiced his own form of emergency medicine in a far less sanitary manner aboard *The Devil's Due*. His patients were Caribbean criminals who could not seek legitimate medical attention for fear of coming to the attention of the police. And when Walter was sober enough to wield a scapel, he was a fairly good surgeon, whom Julianna had watched remove bullets, sew up knife wounds, and even amputate a foot. He had lost more patients than he saved, but then that was the nature of his illegal medical practice. Julianna had built on what she had learned from her uncle to the point that Hubert Metayer had a better than average chance of surviving these wounds.

It took her an hour and a half to remove the bullets. Ordinarily it would not have taken so long, but the bullet in Hubert's chest had broken in two on impact. This made it necessary for Julianna to probe the wound for both fragments. Then she stitched up the incisions, gave Hubert another dose of antibiotics, and checked his temperature. It would be hours before he would regain consciousness, then she would have a better idea as to his condition. But in her estimation, Hubert Metayer would live. In one regard, the wounded man was lucky, because had she been a different type of person, Hubert would have died under the knife.

Julianna and Christophe removed the sterile surgical garb they had worn during the operation. Then they both went down to the kitchen.

While he heated canned soup in a saucepan on the stove and put bread, cheese, and fruit on the table, Julianna sipped from a glass of Napoleon brandy. She stared off vacantly into space for a time and then got up and went into the living room. There she had left the bloodstained cloth bundle Hubert had refused to let go of all the way from The Shaken Martini to the safe house. When she returned to the kitchen with it, Christophe remained at the stove, keeping his back to her as he stirred the soup.

She spread open the uncut gems and the platinum ingot on the kitchen table. They were now encrusted with Hubert's blood.

"Did you know about this?" she asked Christophe.

"No," he replied without turning around. "I swear it, Julianna. I thought we were going to dinner. Then he took me into this bar and a few minutes later the shooting started."

She forced Christophe to tell her everything. Then she once more examined Hubert's loot. Everything here was worth, at best, a few thousand francs. Hubert had finally reverted back to what he really was, a cheap crook. The great Devil's Shadow had finally been burned, because she had attempted to make a silk purse out of a sow's ear.

Julianna and Christophe consumed their meal in silence. Then she told him to take one of the other bedrooms of the safe house and get some rest. She checked on Hubert, did a perimeter check of the property to make sure that the sanctity of their hiding place was not threatened, and returned to her patient's room. He was still unconscious.

Julianna removed her shoes, took a wool blanket from the closet, and curled up in an armchair next to the bed. Dawn was breaking, and as she looked out at the quiet street, she realized how tired she was. But she couldn't sleep. At least not just yet. Her top priority was to get Hubert ambulatory. He didn't have to be completely well, just capable of walking onto a plane bound for Europe. Once rid of him, she would have nothing to do with him ever again. What he had done was irresponsible and dangerous.

Julianna looked from the window to her unmoving patient. She had been in a situation very much like this before. She turned to look back out the window and the memory returned.

Saint Martin
JANUARY 20, 1975
3:00 P.M.

The cruise ship *La Belle Liberté* was preparing to weigh anchor and sail to Saint Thomas. The ship's staff had been brought up to full strength and the passengers were having a great time. As the vessel put out to sea, cabin steward Charlie Martin checked on a new hire in the housekeeping department.

The head of housekeeping was a slightly built, hardworking, American-born black woman, who was considered a better worker than she was a supervisor. This made her susceptible to suggestions on how to run her section from more senior ship's personnel.

Charlie Martin had cultivated her as a friend long before Viscount Maurice De Coutreaux came into his life.

"That girl Julianna shows promise, Charlie," the head housekeeper said. "She is a hard worker and listens carefully to instructions, which not a lot of young people do nowadays."

Internally the steward breathed a sigh of relief. Everything was working out. Now if he could just get Julianna assigned to the Sun Deck. He made the suggestion to the head housekeeper and she instantly agreed.

Charlie went to his post on the Sun Deck. He checked each of his cabins to make sure the maids had cleaned them properly and the appropriate amenities had been left, such as champagne for the drinkers and mineral water for the nondrinkers. Then he went to check on Viscount Maurice Phillipe Stephan De Coutreaux.

Charlie Martin knocked, as always, before letting himself in to Cabin SD3. The instant he stepped across the threshold, the smell hit him. It didn't matter how thoroughly the cabin was cleaned or how many flowers Charlie placed inside, the odor remained. It was nothing overpowering, but still noticeable. The young steward initially had had difficulty identifying what the smell was. On the outbound journey from Miami to Saint Martin, it had come to him. What was infesting Viscount Maurice De Coutreaux's cabin on *La Belle Liberté* was the stench of impending death.

The occupant of Cabin SD3 was seated at a desk in front of a plate-glass window, which provided a view of the ocean from the starboard side of *La Belle Liberté*. When he heard the steward enter, he turned and said, "You're late, Charlie."

It was always the same when Charlie Martin set eyes on Viscount De Coutreaux. He had to initially steel himself against the man's spectacular ugliness. De Coutreaux possessed the face of a living gargoyle. His eyes were reptilian slits with irises of an oddly mixed gray-green color, his nose more resembled a beak than a human feature, and his lips were full, resembling thick sausages over a chin that disappeared into a slack-skinned neck. He still had a head of thick hair that was completely white and worn long to hang to his shoulders. Arthritis had withered his joints and curled him into a stoop-shouldered skeleton who walked with a slow shuffle. However, his mind was sharp and he possessed a vast amount of knowledge accumulated over his eight-plus decades of life. And Viscount Maurice Phillipe Stephan De Coutreaux knew things that would alter the course of the young cabin steward's life.

"Come in and sit down, Charlie." De Coutreaux's voice was weak, coming out in a slightly breathless croak. "I have a great deal more to tell you about the Dark Angel and his minions."

Charlie Martin was terrified of this ugly old man, but he found that he was drawn to De Coutreaux with the same destructive fascination that a moth has for an open flame. As he crossed the cabin and sat down, Charlie recalled how the relationship had gone from passenger/steward to teacher/pupil. A relationship that had led to Charlie Martin, from Haiti by way of Detroit, Michigan, contacting Walter and Julianna Saint to plot the commission of a shipboard theft.

It had been their first day at sea out of Miami. Charlie was on duty when the service button rang for Cabin SD3. He had responded reluctantly, because of the aging passenger's ugliness and the bad smell in his cabin. But Charlie Martin was a dedicated employee of the Caribbean Island cruise line, and duty came first.

The passenger was at the desk in the same position he would be in whenever Charlie came to the cabin. He even slept in this chair, which Charlie would witness him do each night after he took his nightly medication, which the steward administered.

"Are you a Christian, Charlie?" De Coutreaux asked.

"Yes, sir. I was raised a Catholic in Detroit. My parents were devout churchgoers."

"Then you believe in the presence of evil as well as good?"

All those lectures his mother had given him about the Dark Angel—Satan—came rushing back to him. But he didn't know how much of his childhood teachings he should reveal to this passenger. He answered De Coutreaux simply, "Yes, sir. I believe that there is evil in the world."

It was at this time that De Coutreaux placed his age-withered hand on the ancient, hand-tooled, leather-bound book lying on the desk. Charlie Martin was introduced to *The Book of the Devil*.

Over the next two days at sea, the young steward was exposed to De Coutreaux's terrifying tales and beliefs about Satan.

"Look back through history, particularly at the warmongers— Alexander the Great, Julius Caesar, Genghis Khan, Napoleon, Hitler. Each was reputedly a military genius, which is no more than a way of legitimizing mass murder. But were these men actually gifted or were they guided by the influence of the physical embodiment of Satan on earth? A physical embodiment who stood in the shadows, remaining virtually anonymous, while guiding these so-called military geniuses on the path of plunging the known world into war.

"At any one time on this earth there are six of these satanic beings operating. They are extremely difficult to locate and identify, but there is one certain way to detect them."

On each occasion, before Charlie could obtain some critical piece of information from De Coutreaux, the viscount would end the session. But everything was written down in the book. A tome that had been compiled by hand in Greek, Latin, and French over a period of centuries by the enemies of Satan, who followed the Word of God.

Once Charlie had asked De Coutreaux if he could read the book. At least the part written in French. The viscount had refused, explaining simply that the cabin steward was not ready for the dangerous knowledge that it contained. Charlie was obsessed with finding out what was inside that ornate leather binding, but De Coutreaux carefully locked the book in the cabin safe each night before he took the medication that placed him into a deep sleep.

For the first time in his career as a steward for the Caribbean

Island cruise line, Charlie's work suffered. On the journey to Saint Martin, he had drawn a complaint from a passenger for poor service and was late reporting for duty. Both incidents were due to him being unable to sleep.

The night before they were to drop anchor off of Marigot, De Coutreaux summoned Charlie to his cabin. When he arrived, the passenger said, "Would you like to see one of the devil's minions?"

Charlie's mouth went dry and he was unable to respond.

"Get a wheelchair and pick me up at seven," De Coutreaux instructed. "Tonight we are going to the Promenade Room."

What Charlie Martin had seen that night in the Promenade Room of *La Belle Liberté* convinced him that there was indeed an embodiment of Satan walking the earth. He had also come to the decision that he had to possess *The Book of the Devil,* which Viscount De Coutreaux refused to let him read.

Now they were sailing to their next port of call on the Island of Saint Thomas and Julianna Saint was on board. They planned to rendezvous with Walter Saint on *The Devil's Due* to make their getaway. Charlie didn't know what he would do after he got the book away from the ugly old man. But with it in his possession, the cabin steward would be a great deal more powerful than he had been before. He also realized that he would be in a great deal of danger.

In Cabin SD3 the viscount was saying, "Tonight my fellow passenger Mr. Raymond Lavery will once more go dancing in the Promenade Room. When he does so, if all goes well, we will have proof of his satanic connection."

Stunned, Charlie Martin said, "May I ask what such proof will be?"

De Coutreaux held up his hand. "No, Charlie, but let me tell you how I know Lavery's true identity." Again he opened the book. "Satan's followers possess certain identifiable traits. Among them are the manifestation of tremendous talents in a number of complex fields of endeavor and long, youthful life spans. Here—" he pointed to a page on which Charlie was only able to see a smattering of handwritten words on yellowing paper—"I have documented records of this Raymond Lavery having lived for over two hundred years."

The steward did not bother to ask De Coutreaux to give him a look inside the book itself, because Charlie knew that such a request would be denied. But after tonight he would no longer have to ask.

"When you come for me tonight," De Coutreaux began, "we will—"

"I cannot attend you tonight, sir."

The reptilian slits that were De Coutreaux's eyelids widened. "Why not?"

"I have been neglecting my duties since you came aboard," Charlie responded, honestly. Then he told a lie. "I have to work on another deck this evening to make up for this dereliction."

"But this is important, Charlie," De Coutreaux argued.

"Don't worry," the steward said. "I will have someone accompany you to the Promenade Room this evening and I'll look in on you during my break."

De Coutreaux seemed far from pleased at this development, but he had no choice. However, before Charlie left the cabin, he handed the steward an envelope and instructed, "Make sure that this is slipped under Mr. Raymond Lavery's cabin door."

The steward had opted out of accompanying Maurice De Coutreaux on the final night that he would be in the employ of the Caribbean Island cruise line because he wanted to study the child thief Julianna under pressure. Charlie knew his way around *La Belle Liberté* well enough to be able to keep De Coutreaux and the girl under surveillance without them knowing that he was there. When they returned from the Promenade Room to Cabin SD3 at about midnight, Julianna was supposed to steal the book from the Frenchman's safe. Then Charlie Martin's new life would begin.

* * *

When Julianna Saint first set eyes on Maurice Phillipe Stephan De Coutreaux, she was amused as opposed to being frightened or revolted. All he was, in her estimation, was an ugly, smelly old man. In fact, she had seen scarier cartoon faces on television.

"So your name is Julianna," he said, squinting to read the name tag pinned to her uniform.

In her Caribbean Island burgundy jumper and white blouse, Julianna curtsied. "I was named after my mother, sir."

"And you speak such good French, my child. Where were you educated?"

"On Saint Martin, sir." She positioned the wheelchair so he could climb into it. As he did so, she reconnoitered the cabin. The safe was in a corner beside the desk. To her it was a simple enough device, which Walter had taught her how to break into without too much difficulty. Then she checked his jewelry. On his left hand was a large, jewel-encrusted gold ring with the engraved letter *D* in a ruby stone. It would probably fetch a decent price. Then there was the twenty-four-karat gold watch chain. According to Charlie Martin, the watch it was connected to was expensive. However, this Viscount De Coutreaux would have to be carrying a great deal of cash in that safe in order to make this worth Julianna and Walter's trouble. If not, then she planned to hit as many cabins on this deck as she could before they docked in Saint Thomas Harbor at dawn.

With De Coutreaux comfortably seated in the wheelchair, the thirteen-year-old Julianna Saint wheeled him out of the cabin.

Maurice De Coutreaux sat in his wheelchair at a table in the Promenade Room and watched a man in a tuxedo whirl around the dance floor. Raymond Lavery was a dark-haired, sharp-faced American with broad shoulders and a narrow waist. He moved with the practiced care of a professional dancer, and each night since the cruise had begun, he had squired a half dozen beautiful dance partners onto the floor and deftly led them through a number of ballroom and popular dances without missing a step.

De Coutreaux knew a great deal about Raymond Lavery. He

was a millionaire who had made his fortune within the short period of two years on the New York Stock Exchange. Prior to that he had worked as a high-ranking official for the U.S. State Department and taught Advanced Political Theory at Princeton. He had Ph.D. degrees from the University of Toronto in European history and Stanford University in chemistry. Lavery was an accomplished pianist, an eight-under-par golfer, and, quite obviously, a talented ballroom dancer. Everything that he attempted, he succeeded at, but De Coutreaux knew that his success did not come naturally. He was on board *La Belle Liberté* to expose Lavery.

The dance ended and Lavery escorted his exquisite redheaded partner to a table on the opposite side of the dance floor from De Coutreaux's table. Lavery poured a glass of champagne from a bottle in an ice bucket and whispered something in his companion's ear. Then he stood up and walked across the dance floor toward De Coutreaux. As he approached the ugly old man in the wheelchair, there was a decidedly demonic look of anger on his face.

Raymond Lavery towered over Maurice De Coutreaux. For a long moment the bigger man did not speak. Then he removed a folded sheet of paper from his inside jacket pocket and tossed it on the table. "Do you mind telling me the meaning of this note?"

De Coutreaux remained composed. "I am an educated man, Monsieur Lavery. Perhaps I have not achieved your level of proficiency in the field of academia, but I am capable of communicating quite effectively in your native tongue. So I do believe that my message is self-explanatory."

Agitated, the American pulled out a chair and sat down. He placed a large, hairy hand facedown on the tablecloth. "Your note said that you believe I am a devil worshipper."

"Oh no, my dear Monsieur Lavery. Not a devil worshipper, but a demonic entity. A possessor of an unholy power, which you utilize to accomplish evil."

Lavery stared at De Coutreaux. "You must be insane."

"Possibly," the Frenchman said. Then, while Julianna, who was attending De Coutreaux, sat a short distance away looking on, the old man pulled a thin, razor-sharp knife, which had been concealed up his sleeve, and stabbed Raymond Lavery in the back of the hand.

The incident in the Promenade Room became a major topic of conversation on *La Belle Liberté* the night before they docked on Saint Thomas. Viscount Maurice Phillipe Stephan De Coutreaux was taken into custody by the ship's first officer and confined in a makeshift brig belowdecks. Raymond Lavery was treated in the dispensary. The ship's surgeon cleaned the wound, which bled heavily, applied two stitches, bandaged the hand, and gave his patient a tetanus shot. However, Lavery did not take the doctor's advice to go to his cabin to rest, but instead returned to the Promenade Room. There he laughed off the incident, proclaimed his knife wound the work of a demented, extremely ugly lunatic, and proceeded to dance into the wee small hours of the morning. In all of the confusion, he failed to notice that he was no longer in possession of his cabin key.

Charlie Martin was waiting for Julianna when she returned to Cabin SD3. He immediately noticed the blood on her blouse.

"What happened?" he demanded.

She laughed. "That old man sure is crazy. He went and stabbed this guy right in the back of his hand. Then your Viscount De Coutreaux grabs this napkin, wipes up the blood, gives me the napkin, and tells me to hide it for him. One of the ship's officers arrested him and took him to the brig."

"Where is the napkin?"

She reached into a pocket of her uniform and removed the white cloth stained with Raymond Lavery's blood. Charlie snatched it from her.

Julianna glared at the steward. "You know, you're getting to be almost as crazy as that old man."

"Don't worry about me," he snapped. "You've still got a job to do."

After a moment's hesitation, she turned to the cabin safe. It took her seven minutes to get it open.

Inside was some American currency and a few gold coins along with the handwritten *Book of the Devil*. She handed the book to Charlie and began counting the money. As if in a trance, he carried the book over to the desk and sat down in De Coutreaux's chair. Slowly and with great reverence, he opened it and began scanning the pages.

The young girl who would one day be known as the Devil's Shadow snorted. "There's maybe four thousand dollars here tops, and the old man's still got the jewelry you promised us."

Charlie never looked up from the book. Pocketing the money, Julianna glanced around the cabin. There was nothing else here worth stealing; however, she realized that there were other pickings available on the luxury liner. Silently she let herself out of the cabin without the steward being aware that she was gone.

Charlie Martin was still reading some hours later when the cabin door opened and Viscount Maurice Phillipe Stephan De Coutreaux was ushered in by a uniformed ship's officer bearing the shoulder-board rank insignia of a full lieutenant of the cruise line. Upon seeing the officer, the steward jumped to his feet.

The lieutenant was about to admonish Charlie Martin for lounging in a passenger's cabin when De Coutreaux spoke. "I asked this young man to wait for me, sir. I'm sure that he got bored after I was detained in your jail for most of the night."

The lieutenant appeared flustered, but he masked his displeasure and stated, officiously, "You are still confined to your cabin, Monsieur De Coutreaux, until we dock in Saint Thomas momentarily."

"As you wish," the Frenchman said, crossing the cabin and taking his usual seat behind the desk. "You may leave us, Lieutenant."

When they were alone, De Coutreaux said to the steward, "So, what did you think of my *Book of the Devil*?"

Charlie was surprised that the old man was not angry about the book having been removed from the safe without his permission. In response to De Coutreaux's question, he said, "It is the most fascinating thing that I've ever read. At least the part that I could understand." Charlie paused a moment and then produced the blood-stained napkin from his uniform jacket pocket. "Julianna left this for you."

The ugly old man's face lit up. "Now we can prove what Mr. Raymond Lavery really is! Where is Julianna?"

The deck lurched slightly as *La Belle Liberté* dropped anchor in Saint Thomas Harbor. Charlie answered, "I don't know. I haven't seen her for hours."

Chicago, Illinois
MARCH 15, 2005
8:03 A.M.

In the recliner in the bedroom of the safe house, Julianna Saint caught herself dozing and snapped awake. It took her a moment to recognize her surroundings. Then, when she saw Hubert lying on the bed with an IV dripping into his arm and his chest bandaged, it all came back to her. But her memories of that night aboard *La Belle Liberté* so many years ago were still with her.

Shoving the memories out of her mind, she stood up and checked her patient. He seemed to be doing as well as could be expected under the circumstances, which took care of one of the Devil's Shadow's more immediate problems. She had two days to take care of the others.

Folding up the blanket she had wrapped around her, she went to wake Christophe.

46

It had been a busy morning for Chief of Detectives Larry Cole. Besides dealing with a desk full of paperwork and the ordinary crimes and mayhem that had taken place in the Windy City overnight, he was wrestling with a couple of unusual cases. One was the murder of the concierge in Ian Jellicoe's suite at the DeWitt Plaza Hotel, and the other was the shooting that had left three men dead in a South Side bar the previous night.

What personally intrigued Cole about the triple bar homicide was that the shooters had been attempting to sell stolen merchandise to a Mob-connected fence named Nick Tomasini. The fence and a couple of strong-arm types with lengthy police records named Burke and Conroy were all dead. According to the supervising officer at the scene of the shooting—Sergeant Patrice Russell—the shooters were described as a muscular, hard-featured black man and a slender, handsome white man, both of whom spoke with French accents. From what Cole and Judy had uncovered on Saint Martin, the chief of detectives was fairly certain that the shooters were Hubert Metayer, who was also wanted for murder in Monaco, and Christophe La Croix. That meant that Julianna Saint was here in Chicago, which Cole had expected. However, the anticipation and the reality were proving to be very different experiences for the veteran cop.

Cole was aware that since his return from the Leeward Islands, he had not been functioning at an optimum level. He was extremely fit and had never looked better, which everyone in the headquarters complex, including the superintendent, had been telling him. But something inside of Cole was wrong. There was a hollowness present, accompanied by a sense of deep regret. What had started out to be the investigation of the murder of mystery writer Greg Ennis had become a major episode in Cole's personal life.

He turned his desk chair around so that he could see the far wall of his private office. There all of his awards and citations were arranged. Larry Cole had received every honor for valor and bravery issued by the Chicago Police Department. He had also been commended by the FBI, Scotland Yard, Interpol, and the New York Police Department. He was known throughout the law enforcement profession as a terrific cop. Now he wondered what his esteemed colleagues would say if they knew he'd fallen in love with a professional thief.

There was a knock on his office door, followed by Blackie, Manny, and Judy entering. Blackie said, "Are you ready to go to the airport?"

Cole nodded. "Butch's plane from Detroit arrives at noon. I've got plenty of time to get to Midway." Cole's son was coming to live with him in Chicago so that he could attend Northwestern University. It had taken some persistent persuading on Butch's part to get his mother, Lisa, to allow him to move back to Chicago. But like his father, when the younger Cole wanted something badly enough, he kept at it until the objective was achieved.

"We were going to go with you," Judy said.

"Yeah," Manny added. "We thought you'd need some help with his motorcycle, so I drove Lauren's van."

"So who's going to run the store while we're out goldbricking at the airport?" Cole asked, jokingly.

"I've got Rob Pet and Gene Warling from Homicide sitting in," Blackie said. "We won't be gone all day. Barbara, Jamal, and Angela are also coming."

"What is this, a welcoming committee?" Cole laughed. "The kid's going to get spoiled after receiving all of this attention. And, Manny, the motorcycle is coming by rail the day after tomorrow. You and Judy can go with Butch to pick it up at Union Station."

With that they filed out of the office and headed for Midway Airport.

* * *

Dr. Rodney Gunn was the orthopedic surgeon Jake Romano's personal physician referred him to. After a physical examination and X-rays, the doctor met with the mobster and his wife, Alicia, in his private office. Romano could not stand up straight and was in obvious pain.

"You have a ruptured disc," Dr. Gunn said. "I'm not going to recommend surgery at this time, but in order for you to begin recovering, you'll need to follow my instructions to the letter."

With his wife's help, Romano limped out to the Lincoln in the medical center parking lot. The bodyguards who had accompanied him to the DeWitt Plaza Hotel the previous night jumped out of the car to lend assistance. Romano waved them away. With some difficulty he climbed into the backseat. Emitting a loud groan, he managed to get himself adjusted.

When they were rolling, Alicia began. "Dr. Gunn says you can't be on your feet for more than fifteen minutes a day, Jake, so I'll have a bed moved into your study so you won't get terribly bored and can get some work done. Now, this prescription is very potent, so you will have to . . ."

Jake Romano felt like someone had stabbed him in the small of his back with a red-hot poker. He was totally incapable of any motion without experiencing near paralyzing pain. If it were physically possible for him to do so, he would have kicked himself for losing his temper; however, he understood why it had happened. The Mob boss had been under a great deal of stress lately, and when he had discovered that locked door he had lost his temper. The death of the hotel concierge was also something that he regretted, but it did not overly concern him. This morning's newspapers had reported the murder at DeWitt Plaza as a burglary gone bad. But now Romano was handicapped at a very crucial time. Perhaps the most critical of his life. The Mob boss had never been forced to live with pain before. At least not for any prolonged period of time. Now he planned to find out how tough he really was.

His wife was lecturing him. "I know it's going to be hard to remain immobile, like Dr. Gunn ordered, but it's for your own good, dear. How you could have crushed a disc is beyond me. You've been working much too hard lately. You're going to have to take it easy for a while."

Alicia was irritating him, but he didn't show it. This was not the time to complicate matters further with domestic problems. He would go along with the doctor's orders for a day or so. But on the seventeenth, when the Score of the Century went down, Jake Romano—Chicago Mob boss—was sure as hell going to be there.

Jamal Garth found a parking place for his silver Lexus in the parking lot across from the main entrance to Chicago's Midway Airport. Angela DuBois and the disguised Vivian Mattioli got out of the car. The woman wearing the frizzy orange wig stopped and stared with frightened eyes at the main terminal.

"C'mon, Vi," Angela said. "We're already late."

Vivian began moving slowly, while the author and his companion waited for her. The former Mafia don's daughter now noticed a strange inflexibility about the people who had become her only friends in the world since Greg Ennis's death. She'd also been aware of an underlying tension between them and her when they were in the Presidential Towers condominium apartment, where Vivian had been hiding since December. The frightened woman would have remained there indefinitely; however, of late Garth and Angela had begun forcing Vivian to accompany them on lengthy excursions away from the apartment building. Ventures that she was certain placed her in peril.

Initially Vivian had managed to overcome her fear, since on those first few trips they'd done no more than eaten at local restaurants and gone to the movies. But now they were dragging her to a busy airport to meet someone. When she had asked who it was, Angela had become oddly evasive.

"It's the son of an old friend, Vi, but that shouldn't matter. You can't stay holed up in the apartment forever. You've got to get out and learn to be with people again."

But to Vivian Mattioli, every moment spent away from her place of sanctuary was inherently dangerous.

Putting her head down, she followed them into the terminal.

Butch Cole sat in window seat 6A of Southwest Airlines flight 219 from Detroit as it taxied to the Midway Airport terminal. The flight had taken less than an hour, which was in fact only ten minutes more than the drive from his stepfather's house in Southfield, Michigan, to the airport. The decision to move to Chicago had not been a hasty one for Larry Cole Jr. It had actually been coming for a long time.

His mother, Lisa, had divorced his father eight years ago. Since that time, except for holidays and summer vacations, he had lived with her. For most of that period, they had lived alone. Then in Butch's freshman year of high school, the former Lisa Cole met Detroit attorney James Perry. After a two-year courtship, his mother became Mrs. Lisa Perry.

Butch did not dislike his stepfather, but he wasn't crazy about him either. They had maintained a cordial relationship, more or less, as long as they went their separate ways. In the four years that Butch had lived with his mother and the man he referred to simply as "Perry," the two males had never gone anywhere without Lisa accompanying them. Perhaps the problem was that James Perry was an unspectacular individual who was of below average height, four inches shorter than Butch at age sixteen, and, according to Lisa, was a fairly good tax lawyer.

Perry was a Detroit Tigers baseball team fan; Butch rooted for the Chicago White Sox. Perry was a basketball devotee whose Detroit Pistons lost more games to the Chicago Bulls than they won. Butch, like his father, was a football fan who rooted for Notre Dame and the Chicago Bears. Perhaps the two men could have gotten around their divergent sporting-venture points of view, but there was one thing that they couldn't get around. That was Butch's father, Larry Cole Sr.

The Detroit tax attorney managed to barely conceal a fierce

resentment for the Windy City cop, whom he had actually never met face-to-face. But just about once a year on average, the elder Cole received national media attention for cracking one mammoth criminal case or another. For James Perry, who spent his days in Michigan tax courts and IRS offices, this was a major cause of strife in his personal life. Luckily, Perry was a patient man, because it all worked out in the end. Larry Cole Jr. was moving to Chicago to live with the great Chicago Police Department chief of detectives, leaving him and his wife in peace.

The passengers began to deplane in Chicago, and Butch, carrying a canvas carryall, was in the middle of the pack stepping into the Midway Airport terminal. He was surprised to see the reception committee waiting for him. The young man was indeed flattered. He almost felt like a celebrity.

"Hi, Butch," the silver-haired Barbara Zorin said, as she stepped forward to embrace the tall, broad-shouldered teenager. Butch silently remarked that Barbara hadn't changed since the moment they'd met when he was a child. He noticed the same thing about Jamal Garth. The young man wondered if it had anything to do with their mystery-writing profession.

Then there was Blackie, Manny, Judy, Angela DuBois, and his father. More than anyone else in the world, with the exception of his mother, these people were his family. He checked out the Mistress of Disguise/High Priestess of Mayhem, who was wearing her "vamp" look with black hair combed into a helmetlike Cleopatra style, long false lashes, and heavy crimson lipstick. She might have been able to fool the average observer with this disguise, but not him. Actually, she had only been able to fool him once, and on that occasion she had not played fair. Then Butch saw the woman standing behind Jamal Garth. There was no doubt in his mind that she was wearing a disguise.

Butch rode in the front seat of his father's police car on their way to the Lake Shore Drive condo, which would be his new permanent address. His father drove, and Blackie and Judy were in the backseat. The others followed: Garth, Angela, and the woman in the disguise in the silver Lexus; Manny and Barbara Zorin in an unmarked Ford police car.

The elder Cole surprised his friends when they arrived at his condominium to find that he'd had a caterer bring in cold cuts, soft drinks, and even a chocolate sheet cake to welcome his son back to Chicago. He further surprised Blackie, Manny, and Judy when he informed them that they'd been given the afternoon off to attend the festivities. Everyone was eager to participate, with the exception of one attendee—the quiet woman in the red wig who had been introduced to Butch Cole and the cops as Jamal and Angela's live-in maid, Lucy.

Judy and Manny were putting out paper plates for the cold cuts in the dining room while the guests mingled together in the living room. The redheaded "Lucy" was standing behind Jamal Garth and Angela DuBois.

Manny whispered, "Isn't that taking being a wallflower a bit too far?"

Without changing expression, she responded, "That fake nose will fall off if she sneezes, and she needs to either shampoo that wig or buy a new one. But I guess I'd be antisocial and keep my head down if the Mafia was after me."

"Are you telling me that she's . . . ?"

"Put a sock in it, Manny," she cautioned. "We'll wait to see how the boss wants to handle this."

They had cut the cake and everyone was sitting in the living room when Jamal Garth said, "Could I see that book you picked up on Saint Martin, Larry?"

"It's in my study," Cole said, getting to his feet. "I'll get it for you."

"I'll go with you," Garth said, rising as well. "I want to take a look at your new computer."

*　*　*

As the two men walked to the rear of the apartment, the woman in the red wig, who was on the couch, slid closer to Angela DuBois.

Although she had felt relatively safe during the months she had been hiding at the Presidential Towers apartment, Vivian Mattioli had undergone a deep personality change. She was still the frightened, introverted woman who had begged Jamal and Angela to hide her back in December. However, since that time she had become a great deal more suspicious and infinitely more cunning. This last quality she had developed as a result of her hosts' tutelage.

Vivian was forced to admit that these were nice people, once she had gotten over her initial terror. But they were still cops, and if Larry Cole discovered who she really was, Vivian was certain that Jake Romano would find out. Then she would end up just as dead as her father and Greg Ennis.

She had been too nervous to eat much, but she had consumed three cans of soda. When Jamal left the room with Cole, she waited a minute or two before nudging Angela.

"I have to go to the bathroom."

Angela had been talking to Barbara Zorin and the woman who looked like Cleopatra. Angela was irritated by the interruption, but she managed to say to Butch, "Lucy needs to use the ladies' room. Could you show her where it is?"

"Sure," the young man said, leading her to the back of the apartment past the closed door to his father's study.

In the washroom, Vivian relieved herself, washed her hands, and then examined her reflection in the mirror above the sink. Her eyes were weary with fear and she looked ridiculous in the frizzy wig and fake nose.

"You've got to get out of here, Lucy," she said with the squeaky voice she had learned to use in public.

Larry Cole refused to allow anything to darken his spirits on this day. His son was once more going to live with him, which meant that he had a bona fide family once again. For too many years he had lived alone, with police work the primary focal point of his existence. Cole realized that the department would still remain important to him; however, now his son would come first. And Cole vowed to always make this so.

When Jamal told him that their strange-acting maid was really Vivian Mattioli, a material witness in not only her father's murder, but also her lover's, Cole had refused to get angry. He did say, "Why did you wait so long to tell me, Jamal?"

The mystery writer shrugged. "If you recall, Larry, I was once a fugitive from justice myself. It's hard to understand that point of view unless you've been there yourself. Greg Ennis was also my friend, and Vivian asked me to keep her secret. So I did."

Cole didn't feel that this was the time to start an argument. They would have to get some protection for the Mattioli woman right away. He opened the study door and called out, "Blackie?"

The lieutenant came lumbering down the hall with a can of Miller Draft beer in his hand. Cole told him about Vivian Mattioli.

"You mean Lucy is Vic Mattioli's kid?" Blackie said, incredulously.

Cole nodded. "And we need to get some protection for her. Jamal, I want you and Angela with me when I talk to her."

Looking far from happy, Garth followed them back into the living room. Everyone was present with the exception of the woman in the frizzy red wig, who had answered to the name Lucy.

"Where is she?" Garth asked Angela.

His companion looked around in confusion. "She was just here a moment ago."

"The last time I saw her she was in the kitchen," Barbara Zorin said.

Cole crossed the dining room and entered the kitchen. The back door was standing open and Vivian Mattioli was gone.

47

B ishop Martin Simon Pierre De Coutreaux was in his Vatican office working on the manuscript for his new book when a telegram was delivered by a young priest. The bishop didn't open it immediately, as he was engrossed with the writing of one of the final chapters on the martyrdom of Jacques de Molay, the grand master of the Knights Templar. Finally, before he transferred the handwritten words into typed text, he noticed the sealed goldenrod envelope lying on his desk.

Initially the bishop believed it to be a communication from one of the fans of his historical works. After all, there was no one else in the world who would communicate with the Vatican prelate in this fashion. He was slitting the envelope with a letter opener when a thought made him pause. At least he no longer had anyone with a personal connection to him who would send him a telegram.

When the bishop, who was now the acting cardinal chamberlain of the Holy Roman Catholic Church, read the telegram, he felt a chill pass through him that froze the blood in his veins. His hands began to tremble, and to keep from dropping the sheet of paper on which the message was written, he spread it out on the desk blotter in front of him and read it once more:

March 16, 2005

Bishop Martin S. P. De Coutreaux
Vatican City, Italy
Your Eminence,

Your presence is requested in Chicago, Illinois, USA, to receive requested material concerning historian S. Smith— Field Museum of Natural History. Requested material must be delivered to you personally at the Field Museum of Natural History in Chicago at 7:30 p.m. on March 17, 2005.

J. Saint

The bishop leaned back in his chair and exhaled a long sigh. Then, in an uncharacteristic display, he slammed his fist onto the desk with such force that the telegram flew off the surface and landed on the other side of the office.

Chicago, Illinois
MARCH 16, 2005
6:08 A.M.

Wearing pajamas, a bathrobe, and slippers, Jake Romano used a cane to make his way slowly down the stairs of his Lake Shore Drive brownstone. His wife was still asleep when he got out of bed. His brain was fuzzy from the narcotic-based prescription the orthopedic surgeon had written him, but he didn't plan to take another dose until he was forced to. The Mob boss was determined to keep his mind sharp for tomorrow.

The domestic staff was already stirring in the kitchen, and one of his bodyguards, who was still half-asleep, sat at the dining room table hunched over a doughnut and cup of coffee. He became a bit more alert when Romano limped in.

"Morning, boss," the bodyguard said, running a thick-fingered hand across his unshaven face.

Ignoring the greeting, the mobster barked, "Have the cook fix me a bacon-and-fried-egg sandwich on whole wheat toast and a pot of coffee. Then I want you to bring it to me in the study."

"Right away, boss."

By the time Romano got himself situated in the recliner that Alicia had moved into the study, the bodyguard was knocking and coming in with the bacon-and-egg sandwich and a pot of coffee on a tray. The Mob boss grinned, despite his pain, at the image of the burly, unshaven man carrying the tray up at shoulder level like a waiter in a restaurant.

"Where do you want it, boss?" the bodyguard asked.

Romano indicated the end table next to his chair. He then ordered him to retrieve the laptop computer from the desk on the other side of the room. On the wall behind this desk was a painting of the Chicago skyline. Behind this painting was the mobster's private safe, which still contained the .44 magnum that he had used to execute Victor Mattioli. The safe also held the copies of two videotapes of him killing the former Mafia don. Both of these copies he had obtained at one time or another from Ian Jellicoe. Romano planned to eventually dispose of the Englishman, but now he had more important business to take care of.

After the bodyguard left, the Mob boss moved with a stiff-legged, slow gait to lock the study door. Returning to the recliner, he consumed his sandwich and two cups of strong black coffee. While he ate, Romano was very much aware of the continuous ache emanating from the small of his back. He would ignore it, because tomorrow the job went down, and he planned to be alert to go over every detail of the operation. There could be no slip-ups, like what had occurred at the DeWitt National Bank on December 18.

Turning on the laptop, Jake Romano entered his password to access the private program. That password was "ELOCL." This held a particular significance for the mobster, because it was "L. Cole" spelled backwards. The plan Romano had been so painstakingly putting together appeared on the computer screen.

What Mafia don Jacob Romano was planning was a train robbery. At one time in American history such crimes had been commonplace. The first such robbery had been committed in 1834. The take, one thousand dollars. One of the most spectacular had been committed by Butch Cassidy's "Hole in the Wall" gang in 1900. The proceeds of this crime amounted to twenty thousand dollars. Cassidy's gang dynamited the car; however, the application of too much explosive completely obliterated the train car, spewing cash across the countryside. Then there was the British Great Train Robbery of 1963 in which £2.5 million was stolen. A bold, ingenuous crime carried out by a bunch of amateur English crooks, who were all caught or later identified. In America, the railroads, with governmental assistance, cracked down on train robberies. For the average criminal, it wasn't worth the effort, no matter how great the return, with the full wrath of the United States government bearing down on them. But Jake Romano was not an average criminal.

$200 million scores do not come along every day. In fact, they seldom occur during an entire criminal career. Actually, what Romano had done was gone looking for the place where he could steal an extraordinarily large sum of money. At the outset of the operation, the Mob boss decided to use whatever force was required to gain his objective, even if it meant going up against the United States government.

So he had initially looked at banking institutions, such as the Chatham Savings and Loan Bank and the DeWitt National Bank. And the takes from these financial institutions were respectable, but hardly adequate for the mobster's needs. Jake Romano needed a great deal more, so he began making inquiries.

He had discovered that on the seventeenth of each month, between noon and 2:00 P.M., a train carrying a large amount of cash for Chicago area and northern Indiana banks arrived at Union Station. An armored train car, which was loaded at the Philadelphia Mint, would bring in new bills of various denominations. On March 17, 2005, the money train would be carrying $200 million in cash.

One of the problems faced by the train robbers of the past was the weight of large sums of money, and $200 million was a *hefty* sum in every sense of the word. But the problem of bulk was one that the federal government had also faced and solved, much to the Chicago Mob boss's satisfaction.

All of the bills being shipped by armored train car on March 17 would be in the one-hundred-dollar denomination. The bills were new and stacked in eighteen-inch-tall vertical "bricks." The bricks were fitted between wooden plates and wrapped in cellophane, then packed into a thirty-six–by–forty-six-inch red metal box called a "tanker." Each tanker contained twenty-five bricks and had a value of $100 million. The shipment coming in on March 17 consisted of two tankers.

It had taken a great deal of research for Romano to discover the date, time, destination, and amount of the shipment. By way of bribery, intimidation, and the occasional threat, Romano had discovered every detail connected with the March 17 shipment. The most formidable obstacle his robbery crew would face was gaining access to the armored train car. One of a number of cars connected to a powerful, fast-moving locomotive, the armored car was virtually impregnable. It could be derailed, but entering it by force was impossible. Also, there were enough guards inside armed with automatic weapons to hold off a formidable assault force until help could be summoned. So in order to get at the money, the robbery team would have to wait for the train to arrive and the guards to open the door. Then the Mob boss planned to hit them hard and fast with an assault force that would have awed the notorious Butch Cassidy.

And it would all go down tomorrow during the annual Chicago Saint Patrick's Day Parade.

Jake Romano's back was starting to give him fits. No matter how he attempted to arrange himself in the recliner, it was impossible for him to ease the pain. It was horse-pill time.

As he reached for the medicine vial in his pocket and fumbled a painkiller into his palm, Romano came to the decision that all was in readiness. He dry-swallowed the pill and chased it with coffee. Tomorrow the heist of the century was going down, and there was nothing that Larry Cole and his police department could do to stop it.

The canvas-covered Picasso statue in the Richard J. Daley Center Plaza attracted mild attention from the thousands of people in the downtown area of the city on the day before Saint Patrick's Day. One of the city work crews, without looking beneath the canvas, had placed a cardboard green derby atop the structure and plastered the exterior of the canvas with four-leaf clovers made out of green and gold paper. A banner reading, "Happy St. Patrick's Day" completed the decorations.

Julianna Saint exited an elevator into the tenth-floor corridor of the Daley Center, where the Cook County probate courtrooms were located. The corridor windows outside the courtrooms provided a view of the plaza below. Lifting a pair of binoculars to her eyes, she studied the comings and goings around the shrouded statue.

The throngs of pedestrians and the bumper-to-bumper vehicles traveling the streets of the Loop moved in a steady stream without paying any overt attention to the covered landmark. It was as the skilled thief had anticipated. This sculpture did not directly affect their lives, so what happened to it actually didn't matter. At least as long as it remained where it was. By this time tomorrow Julianna expected there to be a far different reaction from the people of Chicago in regards to their prized Picasso.

As the Devil's Shadow continued to study the scene below, a truck pulled up on the east side of the plaza and a group of men clad in workmen's clothing got out. They had been hired by her, and Christophe, acting as foreman, was with them. This was the next move in the commission of this audacious theft. The workmen were going to construct a metal skeleton beneath the canvas that would enable her and Christophe to scale the structure. Then, utlizing the powerful laser she had purchased on Saint Thomas, Julianna was going to dismantle the statue.

She returned to the main floor of the Daley Center and walked across the plaza to sit down on a stone bench near one of the ornate water fountains. Donning a pair of sunglasses against the brilliance of the sun shining out of a cloudless sky, she watched the workmen. They had been hired from a local construction company, and after the scaffold was erected, they would be dismissed. Then the rest of it would be up to her and Christophe.

There was no way that the Devil's Shadow and her lone assistant could remove the entire 162-ton structure from this place. However, they could steal the head, which would deface the artwork and make its return of sufficient importance to demand a substantial ransom.

Julianna got up and strolled slowly around the plaza. This job had been contracted through Ian Jellicoe by Jake Romano, who was a cold-blooded, sadistic killer. She couldn't see the theft of the Picasso as a moneymaking Mob scheme. It wasn't much of a stretch for her to arrive at the conclusion that what she had been hired to do was a diversion to direct attention from another operation that would be taking place simultaneously. That meant that she and Christophe would be expendable as far as Romano was concerned. Then she could anticipate the Mob boss doing one of two things: sacrificing them to the police or killing them. Of course, Julianna would never permit either eventuality to occur. After all, she was the Devil's Shadow.

She stopped a short distance from the work site and watched the scaffold taking shape. She had a busy day tomorrow. She was going to put Hubert on a plane bound for Paris and steal the head of the Daley Center Picasso. Then there was the task for Bishop Martin Simon Pierre De Coutreaux. Julianna was actually looking forward to the reunion with her old friend.

48

MARCH 17, 2005
MIDNIGHT

A high-pressure system formed over the Pacific Ocean and swept eastward with hurricane force. Above the Rockies a storm gathered momentum and began to pull warm air from the South to mix with cold Canadian air. The system produced tornadoes over Kansas, Missouri, Nebraska, and Iowa. Violent thunderstorms were reported in the central United States from the Canadian border to the Gulf of Mexico. Light rain began falling in the Chicago area late in the evening of the sixteenth of March. In the early morning hours of the seventeenth, the sky west of Chicago lit up from horizon to horizon with lightning bolts. A clap of thunder accompanying one of those electrical discharges from the heavens drove Hubert Metayer awake.

The French thief had been conscious periodically over the past twenty-four hours, but each time he had slipped back into the dark void created by the drugs Julianna Saint had given him. Now he remained awake, feeling a dull pain emanating from his right arm and a sharp, burning sensation encompassing the entire right side of his chest. He was thirsty, hungry, and extremely weak, but he was glad to be alive. He tried to rise from the bed, but found himself unable to do so. He suspected that he was in one of the Devil's Shadow's innumerable safe houses. On cue, as he had that thought, she stepped up beside the bed.

She lifted his head and held a cup of cold water to his lips. "Sip it slowly, Hubert." He noticed that her tone was harsh. However, he didn't care. He deserved it. He should have been more alert and seen the threat posed by the two men in the bar. Hubert wondered what had become of his merchandise.

Julianna remained standing over him. "Your wounds are not severe, but you will be in pain for a few days. I have hired a nurse to accompany you on a Concorde flight to Paris in the morning."

"I can't return to France on my passport," he managed in a hoarse voice. "The *flics* are after me."

The Devil's Shadow assumed a glacial pose. "That is your problem, Hubert. But you're getting on that plane or I'll turn you in to the police on this side of the Atlantic myself."

"You need me for the job," he argued.

"You no longer work for me, Hubert. In fact, I want nothing more to do with you." She pointed at the cloth bundle on the floor next to the bed. "That's yours. Take it with you when the nurse comes in the morning."

She turned and walked away. At the door, she stopped. Over her shoulder, she called back to him, "Don't try to get clever on me, Hubert, and consider making a call to the police or some such other foolishness. I'm way ahead of you on every count, so simply go back to Europe and take your chances with Inspector Benoit of the Sûreté."

Julianna Saint left the safe house.

Hubert stared up at the ceiling for a long time after she was gone. Then he began to test his strength. He might not be at the top of his game physically, but he was far from the point where he would permit Julianna Saint or anyone else to simply discard him like so much trash. And her threats didn't faze him either. After all, despite his bullet wounds, he was now a master criminal in his own right.

The freight barge sailed out of Michigan City, Indiana, bound for Chicago. The skipper had forty-five years experience on Great Lakes waterways and deftly negotiated his flat-bottomed craft along the western shore of Lake Michigan and then up the Chicago River. The brunt of the gale-force winds battering the boat was deflected by the skyscrapers of the Chicago Loop rising up on each side of the riverbank. The skipper eased into a wharf below Wacker Drive and Clark Street. As his deckhands tied up the boat, he cut the engines and settled in to wait. It was 3:00 A.M.

The rain and high winds continued to roar across the Chicago area as the night progressed toward morning. The storm had wreaked havoc on the Saint Patrick's Day ornaments decorating the downtown area. Much of the kelly green and gold bunting had been ripped from the trees, lampposts, and facades of buildings and was now deposited on the sidewalks and streets and in gutters. In some places the decorations clogged sewer drains, causing water to accumulate into small lakes that would slow rush-hour traffic to a near standstill.

The gigantic green derby hat and "Happy St. Patrick's Day" banner that had adorned the canvas tarpaulin over the Picasso had been destroyed along with the other decorations. The statue's covering had been battered and soaked with rain by the storm, but was still intact. The truck that Christophe had parked in the plaza two days before was still there. Now, as dawn broke on Saint Patrick's Day, a black panel truck drove north on Dearborn from Washington Street and bumped over the curb into the plaza. The silver writing on the sides of the truck read, "Belmont Metal Works."

A security guard stationed in the Daley Center lobby peered through the plate-glass windows at the new arrival. The heavy rain and dim natural and artificial lighting available at this early morning hour made it impossible for him to see anything more than the silhouettes of the panel truck and the two dark-clad figures who got out of it. By rights the guard should have left his nice, warm, secure, dry lobby post and gone outside to personally check out whoever had just arrived. But he got off duty at 6:00 A.M. and didn't feel like getting wet for nothing. He didn't even follow procedure by logging the panel truck's license number into the security computer system. After all, he rationalized, the refurbishment of the landmark statue had already been authorized.

Julianna and Christophe were dressed in midnight blue coveralls and ball caps. Above the visor of each cap were goggles with specially treated lenses. Christophe began unloading equipment from the rear of the panel truck while Julianna slipped beneath the canvas covering. A series of lights powered by a portable generator, which had been secured in a locked metal box, was attached to the scaffolding. Julianna switched on the generator and the lights flashed on, illuminating the 162-ton structure. Christophe entered carrying two heavy boxes, which he placed at the base of the statue. Opening them, he removed an electronically powered magnet attached to a heavy metal cable and the JFS3 industrial laser. When all was in readiness, the Devil's Shadow and her assistant began climbing up the scaffolding constructed around the Picasso statue. Outside the canvas covering, the storm continued to howl as the gray, overcast sky began brightening over the city.

49

I don't think we're going out there today, Butch," Larry Cole said, staring out the living room windows of his condominium at what they could see of Grant Park and Lake Shore Drive below. They had been planning to go for their usual four-mile morning run along the lakefront. The rain continued to fall heavily, and low clouds and poor visibility forced the cars traveling below to turn their headlights on.

Butch sighed. "My first day back in Chicago in three months and it would have to rain."

"There will be other days," Cole said, squeezing his son's shoulder. "Tell you what, after you pick up your motorcycle from the train station and drop it off in the garage downstairs, have Manny and Judy bring you back to headquarters and we'll have a workout in the new police gym."

"Cool."

An hour later, Cole walked into his office and found a message waiting for him. It was written on an interdepartmental routing slip from the office of the superintendent to the chief of detectives and had been left with the Detective Division night duty officer at nine o'clock the previous evening.

It read:

OFFICE OF THE SUPERINTENDENT 16 MARCH 2005

TO: Larry Cole
              Chief of the Detective Division

FROM: Malcolm J. Towne
                   Executive Assistant
                   Office of the Superintendent of Police
SUBJECT: Annual St. Patrick's Day Parade and
                   Mayoral Reception

The Mayor of the City of Chicago requests your presence on the reviewing stand, which will be located on the west curb of State Street north of Madison Street, for the annual St. Patrick's Day Parade, which will step off at 11:00 A.M. on 17 March 2005 from Lake and State Streets and proceed south to Congress Parkway. Following the parade you are also invited to attend a reception at City Hall.

The Superintendent has assured me that you will be available.

                              Malcolm J. Towne
                              Executive Assistant

Cole glanced out his office window at the heavy rain continuing to fall on the city. He laughed. The parade was going to be a disaster in this weather. However, Cole was ready for it, because on a visit to England a few years ago he'd picked up a heavy raincoat and matching hat of the type worn by North Sea fishermen. Wearing this rain gear would keep the chief of detectives not only warm, but also dry. Cole wondered if Towne and the rest of the mayor's guests would be as well protected.

The four assault teams left the former metalworks factory outside of Michigan City, Indiana. They would travel to Chicago in three vehicles—a two-ton truck, which contained their equipment and would also be used to transport the proceeds of the robbery, a late-model GMC van, and a well-preserved 1991 Pontiac. Each member of the team carried a lightweight assault rifle with one hundred rounds of ammunition and a .50-caliber semiautomatic pistol with three extra bullet clips. They also wore body armor.

The three former military men who had trained the assault teams watched the vehicles drive through the gate and speed off toward Chicago. All of the assault team members had scored high in every phase of the training. This morning, prior to the operation commencing, the cadre had noticed no signs of tension in any of them. They would do well today. Very well.

After seeing their charges off, the trainers were heading back across the training area to their private quarters to pack when the gate guard came up behind them. The burly, brutal-featured man, who had been carefully watching the comings and goings in and around the former metalworks complex for Jake Romano, pointed a Steyr-Mannlicher assault rifle at the backs of the former military men and opened fire. The custom-made, high-powered rounds tore them to pieces.

Using a remote-control device, the guard shut all of the doors leading into the buildings. Then he drove a late-model white Cadillac out the front gate and parked on the shoulder of the highway in front of the complex. After securely locking the gate behind him, he got back into the Caddie and drove a quarter of a mile down the road to a spot where he could still maintain visual contact with the complex. The remote-control device was lying on the front seat beside him. Picking it up, he pushed the red button on its face, which started the process. He did not wait around to see the result.

The signal from the remote set off an incendiary device in the main building, which was connected to a high-yield explosive. The process took a quarter of an hour to run its course. Then an explosion with the force of ten tons of TNT rocked the countryside. The resulting fire burned for twelve hours and smoke clouds from the conflagration could be seen as far away as Gary, Indiana.

Sister Mary Louise Stallings was assigned to Our Lady of Peace Catholic Church in the Washington Park Boulevard neighborhood of Chicago. On this stormy morning she was down at the chancery of the Archdiocese of Chicago to pick up a check for her pastor, Father Phil Cisco, to cover the cost of redecorating the interior of the church. The nun, a pretty woman with blond hair and a flawless complexion, was clad in the traditional habit of her order. She was seated outside the comptroller's office in the main hall when the black stretch limousine pulled up in front of the building at 155 West Superior.

As Sister Mary Louise looked on, a uniformed chauffeur got out and came around to open the passenger-side back door. The severe-looking Bishop Martin Simon Pierre De Coutreaux, in full clerical garb, stepped out. The chauffeur held an umbrella over the bishop's head as he crossed the sidewalk to the front door. In the lobby a short distance from where Sister Mary Louise was seated, a portly, white-haired monsignor rushed forward to greet the new arrival.

"This is a great honor, Your Eminence," the monsignor gushed. "Having the acting cardinal chamberlain with us here in Chicago is unprecedented."

Maintaining a glacially superior manner, the bishop said with a noticeable French accent, "You are most kind, Monsignor . . . ?"

"O'Brien."

"Monsignor O'Brien." The bishop pronounced the name with a condescending tone. "I will only be in Chicago for twenty-four hours. After I pay my respects to your cardinal, I have business to take care of in the city. I will need a car and someone to provide me with directions."

"Of course, Your Eminence," the monsignor said, wilting under the bishop's sharp tone. "I will find someone to help you."

De Coutreaux fixed Monsignor O'Brien with a gaze that could cut through stone. "You cannot assist me?"

"Alas, no, Your Eminence. I am from Toronto and have only been in this archdiocese for a short time."

The bishop emitted a sound between a hiss and a snort. It was then that Sister Mary Louise, who had lived in Chicago since she had joined the convent, spoke up. "Perhaps I can be of some assistance to Your Eminence."

De Coutreaux turned to look at the nun. She noticed that his stare went right through her, as if she were invisible or not even there at all. But Louise was not the type of woman who could be cowed by anyone.

"Where would you like to go?" she asked.

After a moment's hesitation, he said, "The Field Museum of Natural History."

The nun smiled, "It is located in Museum Park on the lakefront. Of course, this is Saint Patrick's Day and traffic in the Loop and on Lake Shore Drive will be quite heavy."

"I won't be going there until this evening," the bishop said.

Sister Mary Louise started to question why he would be going to the museum at night, but that was none of her business. Removing a small notebook and gold mechanical pencil from her pocket, she said, "I'll write the directions down for you."

The bishop fixed her with his piercing gaze and replied, "That will be most kind of you, Sister."

Vivian Mattioli had managed to make good her escape from Larry Cole's apartment; however, she was not at large for long. Anticipating that the woman would try to make a run for it when her identity was discovered, Judy Daniels had called for a tactical team from the First Police District to stand by in front of the chief of detectives' apartment building. It had been a simple matter for them to pick up the former Mafia princess in the frizzy red wig when she exited the building. After a brief struggle, she had surrendered.

She had been placed in protective custody and held under guard in a Michigan Avenue hotel. She refused to talk to Cole or any of the other cops. Mixed with the fear that had drained all of her color was a furious anger at the betrayal of Jamal Garth and Angela DuBois. People who she had thought were her friends. Now she felt very much alone in the world.

Three policewomen were stationed in the drab but comfortable hotel room with her. One of them was present at all times and none of them displayed the slightest relaxation in their vigilance while they were on duty. Food was delivered to the room every eight hours by another officer, and when she was first brought here, Vivian had refused to eat. But hunger finally overcame her and at about midnight she had consumed a cold steak sandwich, a bag of potato chips, and a carton of milk. Breakfast had consisted of sweet rolls and coffee, which Vivian had attacked with an unexpected appetite. As the gray, stormy morning wore on toward afternoon, she found herself looking forward to lunch. She had said little to the officers guarding her and spent the majority of her time watching cable television channels. Vivian was starting to become resigned to her fate when Lieutenant Blackie Silvestri arrived.

When Vivian set eyes on the heavyset policeman, her cheeks colored and she looked away. He reminded her of one of her father's Mafia soldiers, whom she had never felt comfortable around to begin with. Under her current circumstances, Silvestri's appearance terrified her. She focused her attention on the television set and attempted to block out the rest of the world.

Vivian heard him saying something to the on-duty female police officer and then he was standing over her. "I wonder if I could talk to you, Ms. Mattioli."

Without looking up, she mumbled, "I don't have anything to say to you."

For a long time he didn't move. Then he pulled out the desk chair and sat down next to her. She continued to stare sightlessly at the TV.

"I knew your father when I was a kid. We came from the same West Side neighborhood. It's generally just called the Taylor Street area. You ever been there?"

She didn't respond.

"Your father was a few years older then me, but everybody knew Vic the Stick."

This struck a nerve with the frightened woman. Once, when she was a child, Vivian had overhead her mother jokingly refer to her father as "the Stick." When she'd asked for an explanation as to what the nickname meant, her mother had merely smiled and said, "Your father doesn't like to be called that anymore, Vivian. He's respectable now."

Although she was intrigued by what Silvestri had just said, she refused to show it.

Blackie continued. "Yeah, before he became a made wise guy, Vic used to hustle pool at Angelo's Billiard Parlor on South Ashland Avenue. Your old man could play a dynamite game of eight ball. Once I saw him run the table six consecutive times. Not many pros could do that. Did you ever see your father shoot pool?"

In spite of herself she said, "No. We didn't even have a pool table in the house. Are you saying that my father was a pool shark?" She found that she was warming to the cop.

"One of the best. Why, there was this one time, some years ago, when Paul 'the Rabbit' Arcadio, the Chicago Mob boss at the time, challenged the head of the Gambino family of New York to an Outfit-sponsored pool tournament. Supposedly, millions of dollars were put up over which town had the best pool shooters, the Windy City or the Big Apple." Blackie chuckled. "The New Yorkers sent four guys from the East Coast to meet the challenge. The Rabbit only had one shooter. Your father. And you know what, Vivian? You don't mind if I call you Vivian, do you?"

She was completely enthralled now and said, "Sure," before adding an awed, "What happened?"

"Vic the Stick beat the New York pool shooters hands down." Now Blackie laughed. "This one time, during the Mob pool tournament, the Stick set up a four-cushion bank shot on the eight ball. No one, including me, thought he could make it, but . . ."

Procedure required that the female officer remain in the hotel room while the male lieutenant talked to the Mattioli woman. The policewoman was a twelve-year veteran of the CPD, an eight-year veteran of the Detective Division, and no stranger to interrogation techniques. But she was aware that she was witnessing a master at work and made a mental note of everything Lieutenant Silvestri did, from his tone of voice, to the casual manner in which he sat slouched in the chair, to the ease with which he got Vivian Mattioli to open up to him. Open up to him and finally tell him that murdered mystery writer Greg Ennis had possessed a videotape of current Mob boss Jake Romano brutally executing her father.

"You are not supposed to be out of bed, Jake," Alicia Holland Romano railed at her husband.

She followed him to the front door of the brownstone. Romano, while continuing to ignore her, leaned heavily on a cane and walked with slow, painful steps. One of the ever-present bodyguards accompanied him. The other bodyguard was behind the wheel of the black Lincoln, which sat idling at the curb.

The Mob boss's face was set in hard lines, indicating the agony that he was in. However, he had refused to take his medication that morning. Stepping out onto the stoop, he turned to his wife and said, "This can't be helped, dear. After today I'll follow the doctor's orders to the letter."

The bodyguard opened an umbrella and held it over Romano's head as they descended the stone steps in the rain. Alicia remained standing in the doorway. For the first time since she had been married to this man who was reputedly a mobster, she was frightened.

50

MARCH 17, 2005
11:00 A.M.

The luck of the Irish held. The rain stopped and the wind died down half an hour before the Saint Patrick's Day Parade was scheduled to step off. As the color guard and the University of Illinois marching band took their positions to lead the parade down State Street from Lake, the sun came out and the temperature began to rise from the mid-forties to reach a high in the low sixties by midafternoon.

On the reviewing stand, feeling slightly ridiculous in the heavy raincoat he had donned, Larry Cole was seated with a number of other dignitaries. Half of the seats were currently empty, as the politicians were assembled behind the marching band leading the parade. This was a Chicago tradition. The mayor was at the center of the first rank, and usually the governor marched beside him. The rest of the pecking order was determined by a combination of political prominence, guile, and, occasionally, brute force. When they reached the reviewing stand, the politicians would file into their seats to watch the rest of the parade.

It was considered an honor to be invited to sit on the reviewing stand. That is, if you were running for public office or had political aspirations. Larry Cole was not a politician. In fact, he did everything that he could to avoid political involvements. However, in a town like Chicago, which operated on a unique style of machine politics, this was not always possible for a high-ranking police officer. So he was forced to sit here on a busy workday and make nice with the politicians.

The color guard and marching band were passing the reviewing stand when Malcolm Towne arrived. It was obvious that the executive assistant had been drinking. He plunked himself down on the bleacher seat next to Cole and said, "Fine day for a parade, huh, Cole?"

Even out of doors, the smell of booze was detectable on Towne's breath. Cole turned his head and slid over to give his inebriated nemesis more room. It was going to be a long parade.

The flatbed truck that had been parked in the Daley Center Plaza next to the Picasso statue began to move. The traffic was heavy due to the parade taking place a block away, and a uniformed security guard stationed in the Daley Center lobby had been asked to assist the driver onto Dearborn Street. Ordinarily the guard would have told the refurbishment crew to call the city cops and get their help. But the woman who had requested the guard's assistance was the prettiest construction worker that he had ever seen.

The truck, with Christophe at the wheel and Julianna beside him, drove north on Dearborn to cross Randolph Street. They were headed toward the Chicago River.

A man in a black leather coat and dark glasses was standing on the northeast corner of Dearborn and Randolph. As the truck drove past, he removed a cellular phone from his coat pocket and punched in a number.

Jake Romano answered on the other end, "Yes."

"They're rolling, boss, and the baby should be on board."

"Follow them. When they reach the barge, call me back and I'll arrange a reception committee."

"You got it," the man in the black coat said, disconnecting and waving for a late-model GMC van, which had been double-parked on Dearborn across from the Daley Center, to pick him up. The van was forced to stop for a red light before crossing the intersection. By the time the man in black was inside, the truck was no longer in sight.

The tailing vehicle was forced to halt for another light at Lake Street and the traffic became more dense, due to the parade, as they approached Wacker Drive. By the time they reached the Chicago River, the truck had vanished. The man in black jumped out of the GMC van and checked the berth where the industrial barge had been tied up. It was also gone.

Frustrated, he once more activated the cell phone to inform Jake Romano that they had lost the Devil's Shadow.

A half mile west of the parade route was the majestic Union Station. Despite the festivities at the east end of the downtown area, traffic in and around the glass-and-chrome, block-square structure was quite hectic. The majority of the people entering and leaving the station were either catching, meeting, or arriving on the numerous passenger trains pulling into Chicago, which had been the hub of transcontinental rail traffic since before the Civil War. Besides passengers, a large amount of freight arrived by rail daily in the Windy City. Some of it was livestock for the meat-packing and food-processing plants, and some of it was merchandise for the retail markets of the Midwest. Then there were the bulk personal items, like the red Honda motorcycle belonging to Butch Cole. There was also a large quantity of newly printed one-hundred-dollar bills with a value of $200 million.

Manny Sherlock drove his wife's Chevy Blazer north on Canal Street and pulled into the "Merchandise and Baggage" pickup/delivery entrance on the east side of the station. Butch and Judy Daniels were with him.

"Why didn't you just ride the motorcycle from Detroit to Chicago, Butch?" Judy was saying. "It's only about a four-hour trip."

Today the Mistress of Disguise/High Priestess of Mayhem was clad in her teenager disguise. Her hair was pulled back in a ponytail, she had on a pair of wire-frame glasses with dark blue, oval lenses, had a smattering of false freckles dotting her nose and cheeks, and wore a two-sizes-too-large Chicago Cubs T-shirt, faded blue jeans, and white canvas shoes with black anklet socks. She looked no older than Butch.

Butch laughed at her question. "Are you kidding, Judy? My mother and father would have had a fit if I even proposed such a thing. They still treat me like a kid."

"You are a kid," Manny said, as he braked to a stop behind a truck that was waiting in line to enter the loading dock area. "Do you have your shipping documents?"

"You've asked him that three times since we left the apartment building, Manny," Judy scolded. "What's with you today?"

"Blackie told me to make sure that we pick up the motorcycle and get Butch back to the chief's place without any mishaps."

"I never have mishaps, Manny," Butch said. "Only an occasional adventure or two."

Manny frowned as if he had developed a severe case of indigestion. "That was probably what Blackie was talking about."

*   *   *

The four robbery teams approached their objective from different directions. Four of the men and the two women parked their cars in the public lot across the street from the main entrance to the station and proceeded to the lower-level merchandise-pickup area on foot. Their weapons were concealed in luggage or in parcels they carried, as opposed to being directly on their persons. Despite the rain and wind earlier in the day, they did not wear long outer garments. This would be counterproductive to them moving fast to carry out the Robbery of the Century. Also, they collectively figured that it would be hot enough when the action started.

The truck contained the two biggest and strongest male members of the robbery crew. It was stopped directly in front of Lauren Sherlock's Blazer on the ramp leading down to the loading dock. In the rear of this truck was a forklift, which would be driven directly onto the armored train car to remove the two tankers containing the money. But before they could do this, they and their accomplices would first have to take control of the train car.

The excitement of the moment forced the pain of Jake Romano's ruptured disc to recede; however, it was still with him. This was the moment he had been working for since the day he joined the Chicago Mob. He felt powerful and more alive than at any time before in his life, and he wasn't going to let anything stand in his way.

His Lincoln, with his bodyguards in the front seat and him in the rear alone, was parked on State Street south of Congress Parkway. A short distance away, the Saint Patrick's Day Parade terminated. There was a small army of cops assigned to traffic and crowd control in the area, but none of them were paying any attention to the black car. That was due to the "City of Chicago—Official Parade Vehicle" sticker affixed to the windshield. Romano had procured the identification in case his car needed to cross the parade route.

Romano knew that the operation at Union Station was commencing. That event drew the major portion of his attention; however, he could not completely ignore the French thief's sideshow operation. For the diversion he had set up to work effectively, he needed to bring the Chicago Police Department into play. Romano knew that at this very moment Larry Cole was on the parade reviewing stand at State and Madison. The mobster had obtained this knowledge because he now controlled Malcolm Towne. The executive assistant had been caught in a drunken escapade with a scantily clad woman who was not his wife. The whole thing had been filmed from behind a two-way mirror in a cheap, Mob-owned hotel room. Towne had been blackmailed into keeping tabs on Cole.

The Devil's Shadow having given his people the slip didn't faze Romano. Actually, it would make things more interesting from this point on. Now it was time for the Black Knight of the Windy City to do his thing.

Romano used his computer to tap into the Office of Emergency Communications system. The message appeared on the computer screen of the OEC's chief supervisor. Then things started to happen very fast.

"I know we haven't always seen eye to eye, Cole," Towne was saying, as the Saint Patrick's Day festivities raged around them. "But I think you're one helluva cop."

Larry Cole was a basically tolerant person, but Towne was really pressing him. Next, Cole expected this drunken southern lawyer to claim that some of his best friends were black. The chief of detectives was saved by his portable telephone.

"Excuse me," he said to Towne, getting up and making his way off the reviewing stand. Cole noticed that quite a few of those present were intoxicated. He hoped that whoever was calling him would provide a valid excuse for an early exit.

In the doorway of an office building, he activated the phone. It was Blackie.

Cole listened to the lieutenant's report concerning Vivian Mattioli's admission that Greg Ennis possessed a videotape of Jake Romano executing Victor Mattioli. But without the tape itself and the gun used to commit the crime, they didn't have much of a case against the current Mob boss.

"For the time being we're going to continue to keep her in protective custody, Blackie," Cole said. "To be on the safe side, contact the state's attorney's office and have a formal statement taken from her. But we need to find that tape and the gun Romano used."

"After all this time, I wouldn't know where to begin looking for it, Larry," Blackie said.

"We'll just have to give it our best shot. I'll see you back at headquarters. I'm leaving the parade right now."

Cole had left his car in the Grant Park underground garage. He had made it to Wabash and Madison when his telephone rang again. Standing on a busy Loop street beneath the elevated tracks, he silently cursed this age of instant communications.

"Chief Cole, this is Sergeant Davenport from the superintendent's office. The boss wants you to meet him in the plaza of the Daley Center as soon as you can get there. Apparently a serious problem has developed with the Picasso statue."

At that instant, as he stood at the intersection of Wabash and Madison in the Chicago Loop, Larry Cole recalled the familiar image he had seen on Julianna Saint's computer screen down in the Leeward Islands. It was the Picasso statue. As the chief of detectives began making his way back across the Chicago Loop, he was certain that the Devil's Shadow had struck again.

51

MARCH 17, 2005
11:59 A.M.

The security plan for the cash delivery via rail at Union Station had been set up by the FBI and was infallible. At least it was supposed to be, as long as all of the security personnel did their jobs correctly and there were no malfunctions with the equipment.

The plan, the personnel, and the hardware had been put in place ten years ago, and at the time, among law enforcement and security specialists, the entire system was considered a state-of-the-art marvel. In fact, a few of the more practical-minded considered the system elaborate overkill.

The "money car" was fashioned with walls made of six-inch titanium and was virtually indestructible. The car was internally self-sufficient, possessing independent heating, oxygen, and drinking-water facilities. It was pulled over the rails by a locomotive, but could independently disconnect itself from the other cars and operate by way of a self-contained motor for up to one hundred miles.

The train car's communication system was also state-of-the-art. At least it had been in 1995. The security officers inside the car could contact the outside world by two-way radio, computer hookup, or cellular telephone. Each communications system was equipped with a backup, and if all communications failed or were disabled, there was an emergency button connected to a satellite uplink that would initiate a pronounced law enforcement response.

According to the FBI-authored security plan, a supervisor and six federal security officers were required to be on board the train car during a cash transport. Each federal security officer had received extensive training in procedure, was an expert marksman, and was capable of performing multiple tasks under emergency conditions. They were also required to go through periodic training at the FBI Academy at Quantico, Virginia, as well as qualify on the firearms range annually.

Once the armored car arrived at its destination, the guards were required to signal by radio and computer to officials outside the car that they had arrived. In turn, the security personnel outside were to signal back a coded "all clear." Then, in concert, the two entities were to simultaneously unlock the train car's inner and outer doors.

The system was impressive and had never been challenged, with the exception of a drill in 2001. On that occasion the FBI had staged a mock assault on the money car, which had resulted in the internal security team receiving a 72 percent efficiency grade. This was far from acceptable; however, additional training and a retest were never scheduled. After all, from fiscal and functional perspectives, 72 percent was a passing grade.

Never, in all of the years that the current procedures had been in place, was any attempt ever made to rob the car or otherwise interfere with its operation. This had led to the adoption of certain unofficial, substandard security practices.

Due to manpower shortages, the daily complement of officers was reduced from seven to three, with no supervisors present. Generally, due to the deadly dull routine, only the newest or least competent were assigned to the money-train run. Of the primary communication systems, only one—the two-way radio hookup—was functional, and all of the backups had failed completely due to a lack of proper maintenance.

The signal to open the exterior doors had begun malfunctioning eighteen months ago and had never been repaired. Now, when the train arrived at the station, an override button inside the car was used to open both the inner and outer doors. This occurred as soon as the train stopped moving without an all clear being obtained.

When the doors opened, another set of guards, usually two to three in number, were waiting to take charge of the money and transport it to the Federal Reserve Bank on LaSalle Street. Then the bored security officers who had accompanied the money from Philadelphia would gratefully turn over the cash tankers and go off duty until the train was due for the return run.

This routine had not varied in ten years, and no unusual or severe problems had ever been reported. That is, until the delivery of $200 million at noon on March 17, 2005.

"What is wrong with this guy?!" Manny yelled, leaning on the horn. The sound reverberated against the stone walls of the subterranean driveway of Union Station. However, the offending two-ton truck didn't move.

Exasperated, Judy said, "Look, Manny, why don't you let me and Butch out here and we'll walk over to the delivery area? After we pick up the bike we'll ride it back to the chief's place."

"But Blackie . . . ," the sergeant began, but Judy and Butch were already getting out. Then, as they walked past the offending truck and up onto the loading dock in front of the bulk-merchandise pickup area, the truck moved, clearing a path for the Blazer. "I don't believe this," Manny said in frustration.

The truck drove slowly past the delivery area. Driving around the truck, Manny could see Judy and Butch walking along the loading dock. He was about to again sound his horn as a protest at the offending truck when he caught himself. *What is wrong with you today, Sergeant Sherlock?* Yes, Blackie had told him to make sure Butch didn't go chasing after any more stickup men. But the lieutenant had said it more as a joke than an order. After all, Butch was with Judy and there were no armed robbers at Union Station. Nevertheless, Manny decided to stick around and wait for them outside.

The clerk who took Butch's shipping documents was the most muscular female that either he or Judy had ever seen. While they waited for her to come over to the counter, she stacked a couple of heavy crates that had the warning stenciled on the sides, "Metal Parts— Extremely Heavy—Use Caution When Lifting." However, the clerk hefted them with an impressive ease. She wore her hair in a long ponytail, had on light makeup, and wore a uniform that was stretched to the bursting point across her shoulders and thighs. With a dazzling smile, she came over to Butch and Judy and said a cheerful, "May I help you?"

Butch presented his shipping documents and the clerk punched in the invoice number on a computer. As she worked the keys, the muscles of her forearm rippled. "A red Honda motorcycle with Michigan tags," she said.

"That's it." Butch beamed.

"Your machine?" the clerk said, giving the teenager a once-over.

"Yes, ma'am."

"What do you bench-press?" she asked.

"My best was three hundred pounds."

"I bet you could get up to five hundred easy." She reached across the counter and squeezed his shoulder and biceps muscles. "You've got the right bone structure and—"

"Excuse me," Judy interrupted, "but we do need to get going."

The clerk again flashed her dazzling smile. "Sure thing." She looked back at her computer screen. "The motorcycle hasn't been unloaded yet. But if you'd like, I can give you a pass to go down to the platform where the freight car is located." She began writing on a pad of green paper. "Give this to the guard at the security checkpoint and he'll let you through. See Al on track five. He's my training partner and will get your bike off for you. Me and Al work out at Connie's Gym in Calumet City, Larry," she said, reading his name off the invoice. "You should—"

Judy took the pass from the clerk's hand and, pushing Butch ahead of her, said, "Thank you very much. I think we can handle it from here."

"Nice body," Butch said, as they walked from the loading dock down the ramp leading to the platform. "And did you see her biceps, deltoids, and that waistline?"

"She's not your type," Judy said. "You'd go in more for intellectuals."

"Oh, I don't know about that, Judy. I think strong women are sexy."

"Young man, we really need to talk."

They reached the bottom of the ramp, where the security checkpoint was located. An iron-mesh grating with a double door at its center stretched across the corridor. At the side of this entrance was a sign: "Authorized Personnel Only." The gate was unmanned.

Butch was about to go through the gate when Judy stopped him. "There should be a guard here."

"Maybe he's taking a break."

"Then he should have locked the gate before he left."

"You want to wait for him?" Butch asked.

Judy shrugged and said, "We do have written authorization from your muscle-bound friend, so I guess it's okay. Let's go."

Butch Cole and Judy Daniels walked through the gate, headed for track five. The train bearing the money delivery car was sitting on track six.

For security purposes, the freight-delivery platforms had been isolated from the passenger areas, but procedures were antiquated and seldom followed. Jake Romano was counting on it.

Four of the men and the two women of Romano's assault team proceeded to the security checkpoint on foot. The guard stationed there was a fifteen-year veteran of the private security firm servicing the train station and was conscientious in the performance of his duties. Ninety seconds prior to the assault team's arrival, the guard had passed a trio of bank guards through the checkpoint. They were en route to pick up the cash arriving in the money car. One of the bank guards was riding a motorized cart to transport the money from the platform to the armored truck, which was parked in the loading dock area.

The train station security checkpoint guard saw the six members of Romano's assault team approaching, but he did not become alarmed until one of them, a petite blond woman who reminded the guard of a younger version of a former Chicago mayor, pulled a compact automatic weapon from a canvas bag and pointed the barrel at his head. He surrendered immediately.

Then the elaborate plan that Romano had so meticulously put together hit its first snag. Each of the members of the initial assault team wave had a specific task to perform. The blond woman was to take and maintain control of the security checkpoint guard; four other members were to proceed with her and the guard to platform six and do whatever was necessary to take control of the money car; and the sixth and last member was assigned to secure the security checkpoint gate until the team members from the truck arrived with the forklift. Then he was to padlock the gate and follow the forklift operators onto the platform to retrieve the money.

This sixth assault team member had trained for weeks to perform this task and had done well in simulations. However, in the words of a famous American football coach, "He left his game on the practice field." With adrenaline flooding into his system, which caused his heart to beat at a furious pace, he charged through the gate behind the others. He had completely forgotten about his assignment. He was a criminal engaged in an armed robbery, and as long as he had a gun in his hands, his brain refused to function.

Forcing the checkpoint guard in front of them, the robbers proceeded down the platform. The area was virtually deserted with the exception of the occasional railroad worker or baggage handler. The assault team corralled these stragglers and forced them to follow the guard. By the time they came within sight of the money car, the doors were already open and one of the two money tankers had been loaded onto the motorized cart for delivery to the armored car. The three money car guards were standing on the platform with their weapons holstered. Two of the three bank guards had their weapons unholstered and pointed at the ground. But by the time they realized that anything was amiss, they were surrounded by six well-armed, extremely dangerous people.

Then someone decided to become a hero.

The armored car guard driving the cart reached for his weapon, a thirty-year-old .357 magnum that had been maintained in fairly good condition. It had remained in its holster because he needed both hands to operate the cart. In a fairly impressive maneuver, he dropped his right hand to grasp the handle of the weapon and managed to pull it free of the leather. He didn't have a chance to take aim at any of the members of the assault team, but he got off one shot. The bullet went over the heads of the robbers and struck a light fixture hanging from the ceiling twenty yards away. Before he could get off a second shot, the robbers cut him to pieces, their specially equipped weapons coughing silent death. This became the second hitch in Romano's plan.

*   *   *

Judy Daniels and Butch Cole had proceeded a short distance onto platform five when the shot rang out from platform six. Instinctively Judy reached out and grabbed Butch by the arm and pulled him down with her into a kneeling position. She removed a compact Beretta pistol from beneath her sweatshirt and flipped off the safety.

"What's going on, Judy?" he said with confusion and fear.

"I don't know, but that shot came from up ahead on the adjacent platform." She looked around. There was an empty freight train berthed at platform six opposite the money car. "Stay close to me," she said, slipping off the platform and crossing the tracks. Butch was right behind her as she climbed into a vacant freight car. She carefully peered out the door leading onto platform six and witnessed an armed robbery in progress.

*

The two men who had arrived in the truck drove the forklift up to the money car. The other robbers had taken control of the guards and remaining railroad personnel. The dead guard, bleeding from multiple gunshot wounds, was lying facedown on the platform. One of the men drove the forklift onto the train car while the other shoved the tankers into position for the lift bars to pick them up. The forklift was backed out onto the platform and proceeded toward the exit. The transport vehicle operator's partner, his assault rifle in a toolbox, walked beside the forklift. The rest of the robbers herded everyone into the money car and secured the door to lock their captives in. Then the robbers returned their assault rifles to the containers that had concealed them when they entered the train station and followed the forklift.

They proceeded at a good pace, but did not hurry. Then, as they were passing a freight car on the opposite track, the blond sharpshooter halted. A male walking beside her asked, "What's wrong?"

"Weren't the doors of these cars closed when we came in?"

"I don't remember," he said, continuing toward the exit. "What difference does that make now?"

She started to snatch the assault rifle from the canvas bag she was carrying and was going to take a look inside the car, but by then the others had left the platform. Hefting her bag, she followed.

Judy and Butch waited in the freight car until the robbers were gone. Then they carefully left their place of concealment.

"This robbery was just like the others," Judy said. "They even carried the same type of assault rifle."

"We've got to stop them," Butch said.

"We will." She removed a radio from a belt holster. "But it's going to take time for the Emergency Response teams to get into position. We've got to follow them."

"What about using my motorcycle?"

A series of images flashed through the mind of the Mistress of Disguise/High Priestess of Mayhem. She and Butch had been in danger together before and survived. Blackie had sent Manny with them today to keep Chief Cole's son out of trouble. And a very well-planned armed robbery with at least one civilian dead had just gone down. She came to a decision quickly.

"Go get your motorcycle," she said. "I'll let Manny know what happened here and get the ball rolling."

52

MARCH 17, 2005
12:17 P.M.

The impact of the desecrated statue in the Daley Center Plaza was devastating. All traffic in the area came to a complete halt and everyone gawked at the headless landmark. There was also another element present at the scene. An eerie silence enveloped the heart of one of the largest, most densely populated cities in the world. At the center of this macabre tableau stood a group of police officers led by the superintendent of police, Chief of Detectives Larry Cole, and Lieutenant Blackie Silvestri.

"I can't believe that this is happening," the superintendent said with dismay. "In my thirty-three years on this job I've never seen a crime like this."

Cole was studying the area of the statue where the laser beam had cut cleanly through the metal. The scaffolding was still in place, but Cole didn't go near it. The crime lab was on the way to collect what available evidence there was. However, Cole was fairly certain that the Devil's Shadow would have covered her tracks with the same thoroughness that she had employed to plan and execute this audacious theft.

"Do you have any ideas on this, Larry?" the superintendent asked. "The head of this statue has got to be extremely heavy, making it difficult to transport."

"She probably figured all of that out beforehand, but I don't believe she'll take it too far."

The superintendent frowned. "You said 'she.' How do you know the thief is a woman?"

"Right now it's just an educated guess, boss, but before the day is over we'll know for sure."

Ian Jellicoe checked out of the DeWitt Plaza Hotel. After paying his bill, he took an elevator to the main floor and exited into the passenger loading area at the south end of the hotel. The two trunks he carried around on his global jaunts had been loaded into a DeWitt Plaza courtesy Cadillac limousine for transport to O'Hare International Airport. The Englishman was booked on a British Airways flight to London, which was scheduled to leave at 4:00 P.M. Jellicoe was eager to get out of Chicago and he never planned to do business with the likes of Jake Romano again. He was fairly certain that the Mafia boss was responsible for the burglary of his hotel suite and the death of the concierge. In Jellicoe's estimation, such actions were barbaric. Despite their illegal pursuits, professional criminals had to operate on some type of code of honor. Without it, they would not only descend into a state of chaos, but would become extremely vulnerable to law enforcement officials like the meddling Larry Cole and his thug sidekick Blackie Silvestri.

Jellicoe climbed into the rear of the limousine and settled in, being careful to adjust the creases of the trousers of his navy blue suit to prevent wrinkles. He was the lone passenger, but there was another man in the front seat with the driver. Jellicoe didn't give them a second thought, as he was more concerned about his luggage being properly stored in the boot.

The limo pulled away from DeWitt Plaza and proceeded south on Michigan Avenue. Jellicoe became lost in thought as the sights of the Windy City flowed past him. He wondered how Julianna's operation was going. He was fairly certain that Romano would be setting a trap for her after she carried out the theft. And as far as Jellicoe was concerned, it would serve her right after what she had done to him. He had been paid for the job, and with the money Romano had paid him for the Greg Ennis material and this current task, Jellicoe could afford to take some time off. It was a good time of year to visit Brazil. He was making plans for the journey after he settled some affairs in Great Britain when he noticed that they were crossing the Chicago River, going in the opposite direction from the airport.

"Excuse me," he said to the driver, "but are you sure you know where you're going?"

The front-seat passenger—a wiry, hard-faced little man— turned around and pointed a .45 nickle-plated automatic at Jellicoe. "We know exactly where we're going, Ian, so sit back, shut up, and enjoy the ride."

The Saint Patrick's Day Parade was concluding and the participants, disbanding at Congress Parkway and State Street on the south end of the Loop, were creating a massive traffic jam. Ensnared in the throng of marching bands and ornate floats was Mob boss Jake Romano's black Lincoln. Despite the confusion raging around him and fierce pain caused by his ruptured disc, Romano was completely focused on the robbery taking place at Union Station.

On his laptop computer screen a digitally enhanced image of the station and the surrounding streets was projected. Two patterns were displayed: one in blue, the other in red. The blue pattern was a computer-generated progression of the routes the four robbery teams were taking to enter the station, commit the robbery, and then leave the station. The program's running time was eleven minutes and eighteen seconds. The red pattern displayed the real-time events taking place in carrying out the crime. The man riding shotgun in the truck was keeping Romano posted on their progress via cellular telephone. These notifications were made at the beginning of the operation, at the five-minute-forty-eight-second mark, and at the conclusion after they had taken the money and were leaving the building. The red pattern was running a full minute ahead of the blue one, which was quite gratifying to the Mob boss. He had always been a firm believer in the superiority of man over machine.

Jake Romano had a bank of cell phones in the rear seat of the Lincoln. Now, as he entered the final instructions to alter the red progression on the computer program, one of the other units rang.

"Yeah?" he said. It was a trusted Mob underboss calling.

"A black guy who talks with a French accent showed up at Tony Amato's fencing operation over on Taylor Street a little while ago, looking to unload some hot merchandise. When Tony wouldn't play ball with him, he tried to get tough and Tony cracked him with a blackjack. Tony was going to dump him out in the alley, but one of his guys heard that you were looking for some French-speaking types and called me."

"Where is the Frenchman now?" The robbery crew's line began ringing again, making Romano impatient to terminate this conversation.

"We took him to the abandoned storefront where Constantine's candy store used to be. The windows are blacked over and the building's being rehabbed and is vacant right now. The Frenchman's got a couple of bullet holes in him, boss."

The robbery connection line rang a second time. "I haven't got time to go into this right now. Hold the Frenchman until I get back to you. I think he's got some information I want."

Romano snatched up the other phone. "Talk to me."

"We're clear of the train station and proceeding on the designated route out of town. We should reach I-94 in less than five minutes. Everything is proceeding as planned."

"Excellent," Romano said. "Make sure you're not being tailed and call me back when you reach the city limits."

"Yes, sir."

In the truck containing $200 million in stolen cash, the robber riding in the passenger seat returned the phone to his pocket and checked the exterior rearview mirror. They were traveling southbound on Canal Street approaching Roosevelt Road. Then they would travel west to the Dan Ryan Expressway, which would take them out of Chicago into northern Indiana.

The street behind them held a fair amount of traffic, but all of the vehicles were moving at a good pace. There were no signs of a tail, but the stickup men were looking for cop cars and not a red Honda motorcycle with a couple of kids riding it.

53

MARCH 17, 2005
1:03 P.M.

What in the hell would anyone want with the head of the Picasso?" Blackie asked, as he drove Cole from the Daley Center Plaza to the Grant Park underground garage to pick up his car.

The chief of detectives was staring sightlessly out the window. It took him a moment to break out of his trance and respond to the lieutenant's question. Cole's tone was subdued. "Maybe to hold it for ransom. There's always the possibility that there is something going down in connection with the theft that we're not aware of at this point."

"One thing is for certain. We'd better get it back, and fast."

"We will, Blackie," Cole said.

The police radio came to life. "Car Fifty Adam." It was Blackie's call number.

Grabbing the dash-mounted microphone, Blackie responded, "This is Fifty Adam."

"Be advised that two Emergency Special Weapons Response Plan Level Ones have been implemented by Cars Fifty Boy and Fifty Charlie. The ESWR units are responding to the Dan Ryan Expressway at Roosevelt Road and Thirty-fifth Street and Lake Shore Drive. They have been instructed by Fifty Boy and Fifty Charlie to intercept three vehicles containing heavily armed robbery suspects from Union Station. Be advised, Fifty Adam, that a homicide has been reported in connection with this robbery."

"I copy that," Blackie said into the microphone. "Be advised that I am en route to Thirty-fifth and Lake Shore Drive with Car Fifty. What are the descriptions of the suspect vehicles?"

As the dispatcher gave them the information, Cole scribbled it in his pocket notebook. He was aware that his hand trembled slightly. Fifty Boy was Manny Sherlock's call number, and Fifty Charlie was Judy Daniels's. They had both accompanied Butch to pick up his motorcycle at Union Station, where the armed robbery with the fatality had occurred. The danger gene that Blackie had talked about some weeks ago was at work once more.

Returning the microphone to the dashboard mount, Blackie turned on the police car's emergency headlights and electronic siren and said, "Here we go again."

In the wake of the December bank robberies in Chicago, the Emergency Special Weapons Response Plans had been drawn up by Larry Cole. There were four stages to this plan, starting with Level

Four and escalating to Level One. Each stage called for a specially trained group of officers in full body armor and armed with high-powered, fully automatic weapons to respond to incidents in which heavily armed perpetrators committed crimes in the city. To ensure an immediate and pronounced police presence at such incidents, two on-duty officers in each of Chicago's twenty-five districts had received special training and carried the weapons and body armor at all times in the trunks of their police cars. Area detectives also responded, depending on how serious the situation became.

A Level One Response called for eight officers and two sergeants. The targeted areas on this late winter afternoon were Roosevelt Road at the Dan Ryan Expressway and Thirty-fifth Street at Lake Shore Drive. Guided by the information provided by Sergeant Judy Daniels, riding on the back of Butch Cole's motorcycle, and Sergeant Manny Sherlock in his wife's Blazer, the response units were waiting for the suspect vehicles to arrive. Judy had alerted Manny to what had gone down inside the station, and the sergeant had followed the robbers when they entered their cars in the parking lot. He was grateful that the GMC van and the 1991 Pontiac stayed together as they crossed the Loop and drove south on the Lake Shore Drive from Monroe Street. As the suspect vehicles approached, the Emergency Response units converged on them.

The truck carrying the proceeds from the Union Station robbery crossed the Roosevelt Road overpass and made a left turn to travel onto the Dan Ryan Expressway. The red motorcycle was still behind them. The truck's occupants were maintaining their vigilance, but the more distance they put between themselves and the train station, the more relaxed they became. Then, in the seeming blink of an eye, all four tires of the truck were shot out and five police cars blocked their path. Before they could consider any resistance, the cops from the ESWR unit had them surrounded and covered with large-bore automatic rifles.

Using the loudspeaker mounted on the roof of a police car, a sergeant broadcast the order, "You are under arrest! Get out of the truck immediately with your hands on top of your head!"

With no other options available, the two burly stickup men surrendered. A short distance away, Judy and Butch, still astride the motorcycle, watched the operation conclude.

"I'd better let your father know that you're okay, Butch. By now he knows what we've been up to."

"Do you think he'll be angry?"

"Probably," Judy said. "Then he's going to give us both medals."

The ESWR units that intercepted the vehicles on Lake Shore Drive did not have it as easy. To minimize the risk to innocent motorists traveling on the scenic lakeside highway, additional police personnel were employed to reroute traffic from I-55 and impose traffic cutoffs for vehicles on the Drive. This was done very carefully; however, the professional criminals being tracked were exceptionally cunning. In fact, before they left the downtown area they were aware that they were being tailed.

The blond female sharpshooter had wanted to do something immediately about Sergeant Manny Sherlock in the Chevy Blazer. But the man wearing workmen's clothing who was driving the Pontiac had told her to hold off on any shooting. "There are too many people down here, and if he is a cop, he'll be in touch with a bunch of other cops, who should start showing up real soon."

"Then it's going to be harder to get away," she protested.

He laughed. "Don't worry, sweetheart. I've done this kind of thing before." He had driven the tractor trailer containing the armored car taken from the Chatham Savings and Loan Bank, as well as the taxi cab that the lone DeWitt National Bank robber had escaped in. He was confident that they could outgun any Chicago cops dispatched to apprehend them. This time he was wrong.

When Judy called to tell him about the robbery that had just gone down inside Union Station, Manny was certain that the Mistress of Disguise/High Priestess of Mayhem was pulling his leg. He figured that this was her way of getting back at him for being uptight with Butch.

"I'm not kidding, Manny!" she shouted. "Now, there are two women and four men about to walk out of the station. I need you to identify their vehicles so we can broadcast an 'all call.' I'm going to give you their descriptions, so you'd better start writing."

His wife had a pad of paper stuck to the dashboard with a suction cup. As Judy began giving him the details, he scribbled them down. "White middle-aged female, blond hair worn short, medium height and weight, wearing a plaid two-piece suit and medium-heel black shoes. Number two is a tall black male, shaved head, muscular build, medium complexion . . ."

Manny no longer had to continue writing, because two people who were carrying bags that could accommodate compact automatic weapons walked out of the main entrance of the station. They not only fit the descriptions Judy had so far given him, but were accompanied by four others carrying the same type of luggage. They crossed to the parking lot and got into two vehicles. They left the lot together with Manny following.

Coordinating everything with Judy, he initiated the Emergency Special Weapons Response unit activation. The only bad moment he had was when Judy told him that they were going to follow the truck carrying the robbery proceeds on Butch's motorcycle. He remembered Blackie's admonishment about keeping the kid out of trouble. Manny shrugged and mumbled to himself, "So much for that."

Midday traffic on Lake Shore Drive was fairly heavy, but Manny had never been very good at shadowing suspects, and despite staying six car lengths back, he was sure that they had made him. He was absolutely right. Now all he could do was hold on and hope that they wouldn't make any unexpected moves until they reached the ESWR contact point.

The bank robber behind the wheel of the Pontiac became aware of the sudden change in the traffic pattern on Lake Shore Drive. Within a matter of a few blocks, they went from fairly dense traffic behind them to a thoroughfare virtually devoid of any other vehicles except their own and the tailing Blazer. He decided that now was the time to make a stand.

The robbery teams had practiced this maneuver back at the training facility outside of Michigan City. Using their vehicles, they were to form a two-sided barricade. From the protection of this barricade they were to repel any law enforcement response to the Robbery of the Century. They did not know that their comrades in the truck were being taken into custody at that very moment. And despite them having to shoot the bank guard back at the train station, they were itching for some action. Especially since they assumed they had their adversaries seriously outgunned.

The Pontiac had been the lead vehicle since they left the station. Now the driver activated the four-way flashers and slowed his speed. The GMC van also slowed and activated its warning lights. In concert the two vehicles skidded sideways on the expressway, leaving a five-foot space between them. The six robbers exited the vehicles into this space with their automatic rifles at the ready. Their first target was the Chevy Blazer being driven by Sergeant Manfred Wolfgang Sherlock.

The ESWR units had taken up positions on the Thirty-first Street overpass and on both sides of the southbound Lake Shore Drive parkway when the robbers opened fire on Sergeant Sherlock. In turn, the officers returned fire from eight different locations. A fierce firefight ensued. Its duration was approximately ninety seconds. When it was over, five of the criminals were dead, and the sixth, the man in work clothing who had driven the 1991 Pontiac, had sustained seven bullet wounds. He did not regain consciousness and would die en route to the hospital. The first real test under field conditions for the Emergency Special Weapons Response units was a success.

* * *

Cole and Blackie arrived on the scene a few minutes later to find the ESWR personnel mopping things up and Manny Sherlock examining what was left of his wife's car. After checking out the dead robbers and the efforts under way to clear Lake Shore Drive, they walked over to the sergeant.

Before Manny had executed a controlled 180-degree skid and made it out of the line of fire beneath the Thirty-first Street overpass, the Blazer had been riddled with bullets. The rear and side windows had been pulverized, the back tires and the front driver's-side tire had been shot out, and the left side of the black car was pockmarked with bullet holes. Manny, who had been sprayed with bullet fragments and flying glass, had a few minor cuts on his face and the backs of his hands, but was otherwise unhurt.

"You're lucky to be alive, kid," Blackie said, walking around the Blazer to better assess the damage. "Not too many people would be able to walk away from something like this."

Dejectedly Manny said, "When Lauren sees her car, she's going to make me wish that I *was* dead."

Cole slapped the sergeant on the back. "Don't sweat it, Manny. You, Judy, and Butch just saved the United States government two hundred million dollars and bagged some very bad people in the bargain. I'm quite sure that the superintendent will consider this a line-of-duty incident and the city will gladly pay for the damages."

This brightened the sergeant's spirits considerably; however, before he could get too carried away, Cole added, "Let the paramedics look at those cuts, Manny. Blackie, call a tow truck to pick up the Blazer. Both of you meet me back at headquarters as soon as you can. We've still got a lot of work to do today."

54

The rains came again; however, not as heavily as they had fallen before the Saint Patrick's Day Parade. A steady downfall doused the city from midafternoon onward and there was no forecast for any letup for the next thirty-six hours. In fact, if the temperatures continued to plummet, there was a strong possibility of snow before midnight.

This day had been a total disaster for Mob boss Jake Romano. The carefully planned robbery that he had masterminded with such meticulous care was a failure. The only positive aspect about the Union Station train robbery was that most of his robbery crew members were dead. That lessened the chance of anyone deciding to make a deal with the cops. But there were two of them in custody. They were soldiers borrowed from the Cleveland Mob. The Mafia don in Cleveland would demand not only compensation for his loss of personnel, but also that Romano obtain legal representation for them as well as provide any necessary amenities and protections while they were in prison. The others being dead reduced Romano's responsibilities to the families he had borrowed them from. However, he would still be required to provide some form of service or compensation for their loss as well. The Chicago Mob boss was getting deeper and deeper into debt with each passing minute and frantically looking for a way to pull out of this financial tailspin.

With pains shooting from the small of his back down both legs, Romano was in a bad way physically, but he forced himself to concentrate. Through his computer hookup and by way of his cellular telephones, he had pieced together what had happened to his plan and the $200 million he had designated to build his "Star of the Great Lakes" casino. Despite a minor problem or two at the outset of the operation, from the robbery itself all the way through the last minute of the planned exit from the train station, everything had gone well. Then a combination of bad luck and the intervention of a few cops who worked for Chief of Detectives Larry Cole had made it all go bad.

Romano brooded for a time and then, as his chauffeured Lincoln cruised the downtown streets aimlessly while his bodyguards waited for him to give them the word, he finally ordered, "Drive over to the old neighborhood. Pull the car into the alley behind the vacant candy store. I need to talk to a Frenchman."

During the short trip to the Near West Side, Romano came up with a plan to cut his losses. But first he would have to locate the Devil's Shadow.

Hubert Metayer was alive, but he had been in better shape. He was tied to a chair in the basement of a building. A pair of Mob types wearing garishly expensive clothing without any sense of style stood guard over him. He had not been treated roughly, except when the Mob fence refused to even look at his stolen merchandise. Had Hubert not been weak from bullet wounds and the loss of blood, he could have stopped the oily-haired mobster from knocking him unconscious with a blackjack. Hubert figured that they'd rob him of his loot and then exercise one of two options: They would kill him or let him go. But here he was, tied to this chair with these two goons watching him. They were waiting for someone, and when whoever it was arrived, Hubert would learn about his future.

There were the sounds of footsteps overhead and then a door at the top of the wooden staircase opened. Three men descended slowly into the basement. Two of them Hubert had never seen before. The third, who walked with a cane, he recognized. It was Jake Romano, the head of the Chicago Mob.

Romano conferred in whispers with one of the men who had been standing guard. Then the Mob boss crossed to stand over Hubert.

"Do you know who I am?"

Hubert nodded.

"Are you aware that right now I hold your fate in my hands?"
Again Hubert nodded.

"Now, I am in need of some information, and you, *mon ami,*
to use your own language, are going to give it to me, sooner"—
Romano turned to look over his shoulder at the four men standing
menacingly on the other side of the basement—"or later."

Hubert Metayer understood the threat quite clearly. "What is it
that you wish to know, Monsieur Romano?"

"Where is Julianna Saint and the head of the Picasso statue?"

Ian Jellicoe was in the exact same situation as Hubert Metayer;
however, the Englishman was tied to a chair in a vacant warehouse
on the South Side of the city. The two men who had kidnapped him
from DeWitt Plaza stood guard, and Jellicoe was terrified over his
prospects. In fact, he was surprised that he was not already dead.
But as the hours wore on, he began to have some hope that he
might get out of this. They wanted something from him that he
couldn't fathom at this point. But he vowed that he would give
them anything as long as it kept him alive.

The two mobsters sat at a small wooden table a short distance
away. There was a pocket-sized chessboard set up on the table surface. They had played a series of games since they'd brought Jellicoe here. The Englishman was close enough to see their moves,
and it was obvious that the larger man was the better player. Of the
five games they had played, he had won three and lost one; there
had been one draw. Jellicoe was something of a chess aficionado in
his own right, and he had to give his captors credit; they played a
decent game. But Jellicoe didn't offer any advice on moves. So far
they had not harmed him, and he didn't want to give them any
excuse to alter that pattern.

The bigger man was about to place his smaller companion in
check when a telephone rang. The hard-faced little man pulled the
device from an inside jacket pocket and said into it, "Yeah."

He listened for a time and then questioned the caller, "Are you
sure that's where he wants us to bring him?"

A pause to listen.

Then, "Okay, we're on the way."

After breaking the connection, he said to his partner, "The boss wants us to bring Ian here to meet him in Museum Park over on the lakefront."

Without a word, the big man stood up and walked toward Ian Jellicoe. As he approached, he pulled a knife from his pocket to cut the ropes binding the Englishman to the chair.

55

MARCH 17, 2005
6:35 P.M.

The Chicago Police Department headquarters complex at Thirty-fifth Street and Michigan Avenue was enveloped in a media/law enforcement vortex. Another armed robbery in the Windy City had been thwarted by the police. But this crime involved the federal government, as the money train was operated under the auspices of the United States Postal Service. This brought in not only the postal inspectors but also the FBI. The new police complex was alive with cops from the federal and local levels, as well as electronic and print media types.

The press conference was held in the headquarters auditorium at 6:30 P.M., or 1830 hours military time. Representatives from the federal law enforcement agencies flanked the U.S. attorney, the Cook County state's attorney, Chief Larry Cole, Lieutenant Blackie Silvestri, Sergeant Manny Sherlock, Sergeant Judy Daniels, who had changed into a dark blue business suit and black medium-heel shoes, Butch Cole, and the superintendent of police. The mood was decidedly upbeat and stopped just short of being downright festive. For a governmental agency that was generally on the receiving end of criticism from the press and the public, the CPD now had the opportunity to show what a good job they were doing. In addition to this, there was a new star to be recognized, who was not a police officer, but instead a civilian. This was Larry "Butch" Cole Jr.

To start the press conference, the superintendent read a prepared statement. Then the Q and A session began. The initial questions were directed at the superintendent and Chief Cole, Blackie, Manny, and Judy in regards to the recovery of the money and the Lake Shore Drive shootout with the deceased robbers. Finally a reporter from *The Chicago Times-Herald* was acknowledged and addressed a question to Butch.

"Young Mr. Cole," began the reporter, a rather pretty brunette, "isn't this the second time that you have recently been involved with armed-robbery suspects?"

Cole directed his son to the podium microphone to give his response. Hesitantly Butch stepped forward and squinted into the glare from the lights of the many cameras trained on him. In a muffled voice he said, "I followed some—"

Cole stepped forward and adjusted the microphone for his son. He whispered, "Talk directly into the mouthpiece, Butch."

He began again. "I followed some men in a car, who killed a couple of security guards after a bank robbery last December at DeWitt Plaza."

"Didn't they shoot at you?" the reporter asked.

"Yes, ma'am," Butch said, obviously uncomfortable at being the focus of so much attention.

"But you weren't hurt?" she pressed.

Butch shrugged and with a boyishly shy grin said, "They missed."

The auditorium erupted with laughter. A new media star had been born in Chicago. The rest of the press conference was devoted to the theft of the Picasso from Daley Center Plaza.

After the press conference, Cole, Butch, Blackie, Manny, and Judy returned to the Detective Division offices.

"So how do you feel, kid?" Blackie said, draping a thick, hairy forearm over the young man's shoulders. "I mean becoming an overnight law enforcement hero like me and your dad?"

"I guess it's okay, Uncle Blackie, but I didn't like all of those lights on me."

"Wait until he sees himself on television," Cole said. "Then those lights won't seem so bad."

The duty sergeant handed Cole a message. It was from Dr. Nora Livingston, the curator at the Field Museum of Natural History.

"See if you can keep our new 'star' out of trouble while I make a phone call," Cole said, entering his private office as they began kidding Butch about his TV appearance.

He dialed the curator's number, and after only one ring she answered, "Hello?"

"Good evening, Nora. It's Larry Cole returning your call."

"Hi, Larry. I know that you're busy with police business, but I wanted to remind you about the Museum Founders Saint Patrick's Day affair tonight. You already bought a table. I also wanted you to talk to Silvernail."

In all of the excitement of this day, Cole had indeed forgotten about the party. He had purchased the fifty-dollar-a-plate table and had invited Barbara Zorin, her son Brian, Jamal Garth, and Angela DuBois to be his guests. With Blackie, Judy, Butch, and himself, the table would be nearly full. Placing guests in the remaining seats, he had left to the curator's discretion.

"We'll be there, Nora," Cole said.

56

MARCH 17, 2005
7:15 P.M.

Due to her concern for Silvernail, curator Nora Livingston had neglected her duties, despite the party taking place in the museum. There were a number of tasks she could put off until tomorrow, but there were some things that she had to take care of tonight.

She glanced out the windows of her office at the traffic on south-bound Lake Shore Drive, and saw that darkness had fallen on the city.

Carrying a clipboard, she left her office on the upper level of the museum and descended to the basement. She could check on the party later. She was en route to the delivery area beneath the southwest wing of the building. A delivery of artifacts for a new exhibit on the history of transportation had arrived this afternoon. It was usually Silvernail's job to check in such items, as well as authenticate them. But the historian hadn't been himself lately, so she would have to perform this task herself.

Nora was passing the lower level of the Egyptian tomb when a figure stepped from the shadows to stand in front of her. The movement was so sudden and silent that it frightened her badly. She came very close to screaming, but caught herself when she recognized Silvernail.

"I'm sorry if I startled you, Nora," he said. "I didn't think you had stayed so late."

"There is a private Saint Patrick's Day party in the east wing, so the museum will remain open until ten P.M. The party is sponsored by the Museum Founders Club, so I decided to stick around until the heavy hitters call it a night," she said. "I thought you were up in the Native American exhibit."

The historian straightened his spine and actually appeared to grow right before her eyes. "I have been neglecting my duties for much too long, Nora. I have been praying for guidance and it was given to me. Now I know exactly what to do."

She stepped forward and touched his arm. "Can you tell me about it?"

"Certainly. But I see that you are carrying the invoices for the new exhibit pieces. It is my job to check them in. If you'd like, you can accompany me to the delivery area and I will explain."

She smiled. "That sounds like a cheap enough date to me."

As they began walking slowly through the bowels of the museum, he began explaining what he had been going through since

Larry Cole had come to see him last December. Silvernail folded his arms across his midsection and grasped his elbows to assume a traditional Native American posture. "I have had a very unusual life, Nora. I have been places and seen things which are not only impossible to explain, but which would appear to be supernatural. But the realm of the occult has merely been a sideline for me. An avocation forced upon me, because I was born with the talent to see beyond our physical existence. In a bygone era, such an ability would be considered a manifestation of evil. Something dispensed by the devil to confound and defile the souls of the faithful. But I am here to tell you that all such gifts come from God."

They entered the corridor leading to the delivery area. At the end of this corridor was a locked door to which both the historian and the curator possessed keys.

"When Larry Cole came to me in December to inquire about the death of the mystery writer Greg Ennis, I began probing into the spirit world and I touched a woman. A woman who is at once a thief and at the same time the person who was responsible for the writer's death, although she didn't kill him."

"I don't understand," Nora said with confusion.

"It is not a simple thing for me to grasp either," he said. "I do know that this woman is dangerous, but is not a murderer. And that is what placed me firmly on the horns of a dilemma, which I have wrestled with over these past three months. You see, Nora, in that initial vision I had of this thief for Larry Cole, I saw her killing me."

Enthralled with his story, Nora removed a key ring from her pocket, selected the appropriate key, and unlocked the delivery area door. Together they walked into a combination storage area and loading dock. Silvernail flicked a switch on the wall inside the entrance and an overhead bank of fluorescent lights blinked on. However, there were two banks of lights and one remained out, leaving a great deal of the huge area in darkness.

He turned the light switch off and then back on, but the result was the same.

"I guess we'll have to do our work in the dark," he said.

"I can go back to my office and get a flashlight," she volunteered.

"I don't think that will be necessary. There should be enough illumination for me to see if everything has arrived that is supposed to go into the exhibit. I'll authenticate the items in the morning."

They advanced into the dimly lighted area. The artifacts they had come in search of were stacked in crates along the far wall. Still clutching his folded arms across his midsection, Silvernail gave the shipment a quick scan. He noticed the discrepancy instantly. There were more items than there should have been. He began an examination of their markings.

The exhibit the artifacts would be displayed in was to be a depiction of every form of transportation from the invention of the wheel in prehistoric times to the Wright Brothers' first flight, which ushered in the era of aviation. The items had been purchased from museums all over the world and had high price tags. Some of them, such as an original Model T Ford, had not been bought outright, but only loaned to the Field Museum by the Smithsonian Institution in Washington, D.C. It would have to be returned in five years. Each of the packing cases was labeled by lot number, point of origin, and final destination. The number of crates coincided with the information on the shipping invoice on the curator's clipboard. But there was an additonal item with this shipment. It was at least twenty feet tall and covered with a canvas tarpaulin. The Museum of Natural History contained millions of very old, extremely valuable items. This made it necessary for everything to not only be strictly accounted for, but also kept in its proper place. Whatever this canvas-covered object was, it was not where it was supposed to be.

Silvernail unfolded his arms and let them hang down at his sides. He bent his knees to go into a slight crouch. Nora noticed the tension emanating from him and it alarmed her.

"What is it, Silvernail?"

"There is someone in here with us, and that"—he pointed at the tarpaulin—"does not belong."

"Maybe we should leave and come back after Larry Cole arrives."

Without taking his eyes away from the shadows in front of him, he said, "What was that you said about Cole?"

"Larry is attending the Saint Patrick's Day affair tonight. He should be here soon."

"We don't have time to wait for him now," Silvernail said, advancing farther into the darkness.

"Silvernail, wait," she called to him, noticing the terrified tone in her voice. She made no move to follow and he didn't stop.

He came up to the canvas and paused to examine it. A thick hemp rope encircled it from top to bottom and side to side. Reaching down, he removed a bone-handled, razor-sharp hunting knife from a sheath strapped to his ankle. He cut the rope away and pulled off the canvas. Despite her standing some distance away, he heard Nora's startled gasp. What he had uncovered was the severed head of the Picasso statue.

Then Nora Livingston screamed.

Knife still in hand, Silvernail spun around to see that the curator had been grabbed from behind by a tall man in dark clothing. The historian was about to rush to her aid when a woman wearing a dark-colored jumpsuit stepped from behind one of the packing crates. With more stunned fascination than terror, Silvernail watched her raise a CO_2 pistol to aim at him. Before he could make any move to defend himself, she fired.

The dart struck him in the neck and punctured his jugular vein with a thin, hollow needle. The projectile discharged thirty milligrams of the clear liquid drug ketamine into his system. The drug took affect immediately.

He was only capable of remaining on his feet for a few seconds. He managed to drop to one knee before rolling over on his back.

His breathing became labored and his vision blurred. He began to sweat profusely as the paralysis set in. Then the hallucinations began.

Nora struggled in vain against the man who was holding her. She was forced to watch in horror what the woman did next. After firing the dart, she walked over to kneel down on the concrete floor next to the historian's prone form. From a cloth bag strapped to her waist, she removed a plastic package containing surgical instruments. Ripping the package open, she put on a pair of surgical gloves. Then she removed a rubber bladder attached to a long tube, which was tipped with a four-inch long, sheathed needle.

"What are you doing to him?!" Nora screamed, as the woman ripped Silvernail's shirt open and positioned the needle directly above his heart. With one quick movement, she plunged it downward through the ribs and directly into the heart itself. As blood began rushing into the bladder, curator Nora Livingston fainted.

57

MARCH 17, 2005
8:00 P.M.

Bishop Martin Simon Pierre De Coutreaux followed the directions that Sister Mary Louise Stallings had given him to locate the Field Museum of Natural History on the lakefront. He hadn't quite known what to expect when he arrived there, but the front of the building was illuminated and it was obviously open for business at this late hour. He was driving a Ford that the monsignor loaned him back at the chancery. Now he turned in to the parking lot and was stopped by two uniformed men. One was obviously a security guard, who was armed, and the other was a museum guide dressed in a dark blue raincoat, adorned with the museum crest, and gray trousers. Against the rain he held an umbrella over his head.

De Coutreaux rolled his window down. He had left his religious garb back in the hotel room he had taken near the chancery. Now he wore a black suit and dark gray crew-neck sweater.

The guide said, "May I have your name, sir?"

De Coutreaux stiffened with a mixture of outrage and alarm. "Why do you need my name?"

The men standing in the rain exchanged puzzled glances. "The party inside the museum tonight is invitation only, sir," the guide said.

In her telegram Julianna had stated that she wanted him here at the museum tonight, but she hadn't mentioned anything about a party.

"I am Martin De Coutreaux," he said, keeping his gray eyes cast sightlessly forward.

The guide scanned a list and said, "Bishop Martin Simon Pierre De Coutreaux of the Vatican?"

Had he been a less pious prelate, he would have audibly cursed Julianna Saint at this moment. "The same," he responded, icily.

"You may leave the car here, Bishop," the guide said. "We'll have someone park it for you. When you are ready to leave, an attendant will retrieve it from the lot."

De Coutreaux got out of the car and headed for the canopy leading up to the museum entrance a short distance away. He had also borrowed an umbrella from the chancery, which he held over his head against the falling rain. As he entered the museum he encountered no one other than museum employees.

Inside the main rotunda, at the top of a short marble staircase, was a table manned by a couple of toothpaste-ad female greeters wearing cocktail dresses. He was once more forced to give them his name. One of them, a redhead whose hair color obviously came out of a bottle, searched through the plastic-encased name tags. When she came up with the one with his name on it, she said, "That's odd. There are two tags inside this case."

He watched her remove the square of white cardboard behind

the one on which "Bishop Martin S. P. De Coutreaux" was written. She said, "I guess this Charlie Martin's got mixed up with yours, Your Eminence."

De Coutreaux felt his face redden. Now he couldn't help himself. His thoughts screamed, *Damn you, Julianna Saint!*

He was escorted to table thirty, where four people were already seated. With no other options available, he was forced to take one of the vacant chairs.

There was a black couple, consisting of a gray-haired man and an attractive dark-complexioned woman with short, curly hair, as well as a white woman of about sixty and a blond man in his thirties, whose resemblance to the woman was so pronounced that it made it obvious that they were closely related. The black man smiled when De Coutreaux sat down and, extending his hand, said, "Hello. I'm Jamal Garth." He then provided introductions for the others at the table, but De Coutreaux was too preoccupied with the extent of his exposure to recall their names. He introduced himself simply as "Martin." Then he made a show of picking up the program from the table in front of him and burying his nose in it.

As Saint Patrick's Day parties generally go, this one was sedate. The white-cloth-covered tables with the china settings and Field Museum–engraved silverware was set up in the Hall of Egypt exhibit. At one end of the gallery, which had been partitioned off from the rest of the museum by screens ornamented with Egyptian figures, a string quartet played softly. There were two cash bars set up, which were doing a fairly brisk business. Most of the attendees on this rainy evening were from the ranks of Chicago's social and business elite. The attire was basic "after five" and the guests mingled amiably in groups around the partitioned-off area.

De Coutreaux couldn't understand what Julianna was up to, but he didn't like this type of visibility. However, it was supremely important for him to expose this Silvernail Smith as a spawn of Satan. This would be accomplished when the Devil's Shadow gave him a sample of the historian's blood. As had been the case with Raymond Lavery aboard the cruise ship *La Belle Liberté* thirty years ago, such blood would not be the blood of a human being, but instead that of a wild beast—a wolf, a hyena, or a dog—signifying that the host was a member of a uniquely predatory species that preys upon human souls. An entity that Bishop De Coutreaux would risk everything to destroy.

This last thought interrupted the cleric's musings. At least he would risk *almost* everything. He would never give up his position in the Church. To do so would be to concede to the evil he had fought against so tirelessly for three decades.

More guests arrived at table thirty. De Coutreaux merely glanced up as the newcomers sat down, leaving only one remaining seat vacant. Again there were brief introductions, which the bishop paid little attention to. He realized that his silence and lack of interest in any of the others would be perceived as rudeness, but that could not be helped. For the most part, they ignored him, and as the waiter began serving the salad course, De Coutreaux even considered moving to a table with fewer guests. However, a glance around the dining area revealed that all of the other tables were filled. All that he could do was make the best of it until the infamous Devil's Shadow revealed what she was up to.

Beginning to eat, he picked up bits and pieces of the conversation between the other diners. Most of the comments were directed to a young black man. As was the case with the silver-haired woman and the young blond man, the black teenager bore a striking resemblance to the broad-shouldered man seated directly across the table from the bishop. From what De Coutreaux had been able to pick up, the young man, whom they called "Butch," had been involved in some type of police operation earlier today. This forced De Coutreaux to pay closer attention, which made him aware that a number of the people seated at table thirty were police officers.

Once more Bishop Martin Simon Pierre De Coutreaux cursed the Devil's Shadow. Then the final member of the party at table thirty arrived.

Julianna Saint, wearing a low-cut black evening gown and a diamond necklace that reflected light as if it had its own power source, sat down in the seat next to Bishop Martin Simon Pierre De Coutreaux.

58

March 17, 2005
8:03 p.m.

There were four cars in the caravan that turned off Lake Shore Drive in to the Field Museum of Natural History parking lot. The lead car was a dark van with tinted windows. It was flagged down by the museum greeter and the security guard. When the van driver's window was rolled down, the pair of museum employees found themselves looking down the barrel of a silenced pistol.

Two men in dark clothing leaped from the back of the van to disarm the guard and force him and the greeter across the parking lot. Along the way they collected all of the parking lot attendants. At gunpoint they forced their captives under the canopy leading up to the museum entrance. There they were joined by the occupants of the other vehicles from the caravan.

There were fifteen armed Mafia soldiers accompanying Jake Romano. The pressures of the day and the pain from his bad back had forced his face into a grim mask. He was pale and leaned on his cane in a stoop-shouldered shuffle that made him appear to have shrunk remarkably from his six-foot-five-inch height. But despite his ailments, Romano was still a very dangerous man. Accompanying the mobster's entourage were Hubert Metayer and Ian Jellicoe, both of whom were handcuffed. In Romano's estimation, they were highly expendable hostages.

The group proceeded to the reception table, where the two full-sized Barbie dolls were checking in guests and dispensing name tags. The women were forced to join the other museum employees who had been led inside.

"Get me the guest list," Romano rasped at one of his men.

The paper was snatched from the table and handed over. Romano scanned the list quickly and his pained expression eased a bit when he read the names of the guests at table thirty. Crushing the paper in his hand, he turned to his men. "Nobody goes in or out of the museum until I tell you different. We're going to crash the Saint Patrick's Day party."

Leaving four of his soldiers to cover the hostages, he led the others into the exhibit hall where the party was taking place.

The desert was hot and arid. Silvernail was still a child and was following an old man toward the mountains off in the distance. There the future historian would be subjected to the ancient Native American ritual that would transform him into "The Man Who Walks in Blood." The ritual would come close to killing him and he would never be the same again. Then would come the wars.

The man known as Field Museum historian Dr. Silvernail Smith had spent many years as a warrior fighting in conflicts on every continent on the planet. On the walls of his office were a number of photographs and drawings depicting events in his life. Some of them were historically accurate and others were mere fantasy. But they did tell the tale of a fascinating existence. Now Silvernail Smith relived that long life and was certain that it was now coming to a violent end.

He had foreseen what was happening to him at this instant in the visions that had begun months ago. Everything was the same in the agonizing reality, right down to the woman who had done the deed. Now he was preparing to see the Face of God.

"Silvernail!"

He heard his name called from a great distance. He was being summoned, but was this voice from the land of the living or that of the unknown beyond Death's door?

"Silvernail, wake up!"

The voice was now much closer and he recognized it. Nora Livingston was calling to him. At that instant he realized that he was not dying. He forced his eyes open to find himself lying on the stone floor of the delivery area. Nora was kneeling over him, and behind her loomed the massive head of the rust-colored Picasso statue.

For a long moment he was unable to move. Although its effects were receding, the drug still held him firmly in its grasp. Then there was the pain in his chest.

Silvernail Smith, among his many other accomplishments, was a medical school graduate, so it didn't take him long to piece together what had happened. And when he finally had it, despite his condition, he felt slightly ridiculous. The dark woman in his vision and in the agonizing reality in which he now found himself had no intention of killing him. She had merely wanted a sample of his blood. Why, he didn't know, but he planned to find out.

With a great effort he struggled into a sitting position. He felt as if a red-hot stake had been thrust into his chest. Convulsing with pain, he laughed at the thought that a stake had been driven into his heart, but it had not killed him.

"Where . . . did . . . she . . . ?" His voice was not working very well.

"I think they're in the museum," she responded. "After she stabbed you in the chest, I fainted."

"How . . . long . . . ?"

She looked at her watch. "Forty-five minutes. Maybe an hour. It's difficult to recall what time we came down here."

He tried to stand up and failed. Extending his hand to her, he said, "Help me, Nora."

It was a struggle, but she got him on his feet. Then, as Silvernail leaned heavily on the curator, they made their way back into the museum.

* * *

In the brief period of time that he was seated at table thirty before Julianna Saint appeared, Larry Cole had decided that he was going to relax and enjoy the evening with his friends and his son. As usual, there were unsolved cases to occupy a major portion of his waking hours, and he was determined to solve the most pressing of them. When he had gone off-duty earlier this evening, at the top of his list was getting to the bottom of the Greg Ennis murder, which has absorbed so much of his attention since December. Then he would find a way to bring charges against mobster Jake Romano for the murder of Victor Mattioli, and, of course, recover the head of the Picasso landmark. But for tonight he planned to put all of that on hold. The only mystery facing the chief of detectives right now was the odd man with the sharp features seated at the table with them. When they arrived, Cole had noticed that this man had been detached to the point of rudeness. Cole assumed that Nora Livingston had placed him here, but as the stranger wasn't volunteering any information about himself, Cole ignored him.

They were still talking about Butch's TV appearance. Barbara and her son Brian, who was a prominent East Coast artist and major novelist in his own right, had seen the newscast and complimented Butch on his performance. Jamal and Angela DuBois had missed the evening news, but they planned to see the late editions when they got home.

A waiter came to the table and took their cocktail order. After they were served, Blackie stood up and, lifting a glass of draft beer, intoned, "I would like to propose a toast."

The others lifted their glasses with the exception of the antisocial stranger, who kept his face buried in the event program.

"To all of us here at this table who have encountered the infamous Cole family danger gene and have survived to tell about it."

They all clinked glasses, because at one time or another all had found themselves in very dangerous situations due to their relationship with Larry Cole.

The toast concluded, Angela DuBois turned to Cole and asked, "How is Vivian doing?"

Cole had planned to tell her and Jamal what the Mattioli woman had revealed to Blackie about Jake Romano, but he was unable to do so with the stranger seated at their table. So for the time being, he was forced to reply, "She's fine. It's my understanding that she's going to provide us with some very valuable information about a recent crime."

Cole was seated between Angela and Blackie. To respond to her question about Vivian Mattioli, Cole had turned in his seat, which placed his back to the exhibit hall entrance. Angela and Jamal had been listening to what Cole was saying, but as he concluded his statement, he noticed Angela's eyes shift slightly to look in the direction of their quiet guest. Cole turned to follow her line of sight just as Julianna Saint walked up to the table.

"Good evening," the Devil's Shadow said, taking the last vacant seat between the stranger and Butch. She stared directly at Cole. "And how are you, Mr. Cole, or are you going by your Michael Holt alias tonight?"

It took Cole a moment to respond. "It's good to see you again, Julianna. You're looking well."

"Thank you. You also appear to be maintaining your high fitness level. But there are no mountains in Chicago. What do you do for intense aerobic training?"

He shrugged. "I find jogging along the lakefront sufficient."

She maintained eye contact with him. "Alone?"

"My son usually accompanies me. Allow me to introduce you. Larry Cole Junior, this is Mademoiselle Julianna Saint."

Impressed with the exotic woman's appearance, Butch said, "Hello, Ms. Saint."

She glanced around the table at the others. "Although I've never met the rest of you, I feel as if I've known each of you for a long time." She started with Jamal. "You, sir, are the internationally acclaimed author Jamal Garth. I've read your books in both French and English. Next to Michael Holt, at least the *real* Michael Holt, you are my favorite author. And you, madam," she said to Angela, "are Ms. DuBois, Mr. Garth's companion."

Angela nodded stonily at Julianna. Although Angela was also French, there was something about the elegantly dressed woman that she didn't like.

The Devil's Shadow turned her attention to Barbara Zorin. "You are also a famous novelist, whose work I have also read and enjoyed. Do I have the honor of addressing B. S. Zorin?"

"*Bonjour,* Mademoiselle Saint," Barbara said.

"*Bonjour,*" Julianna responded before turning her attention to Barbara's son. "On one of your mother's book jackets, her family was listed. Besides her husband, Anthony, there are two sons, Brian and Paul. And you are . . . ?"

"Brian," the young man said with a slight bow. "It is a pleasure to meet you, Ms. Saint."

Then came the remaining guests. "You, sir, are Lieutenant Blackie Silvestri."

Blackie didn't know what was going on, but he nodded a greeting.

"And last but not least," Julianna said with some animation, "the Mistress of Disguise/High Priestess of Mayhem. I'm sorry I missed you on your recent visit to the Leeward Islands. I would have certainly invited you to my villa for lunch."

"I was actually too busy watching your handsome friend Christophe La Croix running around the island in circles looking for me," Judy said, defiantly.

"As Larry once said to me," Julianna responded, "touché."

The man seated next to the Devil's Shadow had remained rigidly motionless during this verbal byplay. Now Julianna turned to him. "Let me introduce Bishop Martin Simon Pierre De Coutreaux, who is currently the acting cardinal chamberlain of the Holy Roman Catholic Church."

The silent guest's features contracted in anger and he was about to say something to Julianna when a woman's scream echoed through the exhibit hall.

59

Romano's soldiers were heavily armed and fanned out across the exhibit area to take control of the partygoers. Using the hostages as shields, they effectively prevented any interference. One of Romano's personal bodyguards grabbed the redheaded receptionist roughly by the back of the neck and forced her in front of him toward table thirty. She began struggling and he tightened his grip unmercifully, making her cry out. Everyone in the room heard her scream. Before they could react, it was too late.

At Romano's direction, four of his men, brandishing Uzi submachine guns, covered table thirty. The Mob boss moved over to stand behind Julianna Saint. Despite his obvious pain, he managed a cruel smile. "Now, isn't this a cozy gathering. My favorite people in all the world in the same place at the same time."

"What do you hope to accomplish with this charade, Romano?" Cole challenged.

The Mob boss's smile vanished. "I plan to accomplish a great deal, Mr. Cole, and along the way I will also settle a couple of old scores."

"I heard you look real good on television, Jake," Blackie said.

Romano glared at the lieutenant. "What are you talking about, Silvestri?"

"Oh, a certain videotape that's floating around. It captures you and your predecessor on the day he was killed."

"I heard that same rumor from one of these nice mystery writers' colleagues," Romano said. "Fellow named Greg Ennis. I heard he met with a bad accident."

"Ennis was killed, Romano," Cole said, "and somebody's going down for it."

Again the smile returned. "But not tonight, Chief Cole. Not tonight. Now, I have some business to conduct with Ms. Saint, which will require the presence of you and your guests. By the way . . ." Romano paused and looked down at Butch. "Isn't this the young man who has become the darling of the Chicago media?"

"Leave him alone, Romano!" Cole said, angrily.

"I wouldn't think of harming a hair on his head, Chief," Romano said. "At least not yet. Now, all of you, on your feet!"

"Excuse me," De Coutreaux said, "but I have nothing to do with these people."

"That's too bad, my friend," the Mob boss said, "but you seem to have been at the wrong place at the wrong time. You're coming with us."

With that, six soldiers forced them at gunpoint from the Egyptian exhibit hall into the main rotunda. The remaining soldiers stayed to cover the party guests.

Slowly Silvernail and Nora made their way from the delivery area in the bowels of the museum into the basement. An elevator whisked them to the main rotunda, which they entered from the southwest end of the immense building just as the Mafia soldiers herded Cole and his party from the Egyptian exhibit hall at the northeast end beneath the Tyrannosaurus rex skeleton. The historian was getting stronger, but was still forced to lean heavily on the curator for support. Luckily, they were still in the shadows of the upper balcony and were not seen by the mobsters. As soon as they spied the guns, they retreated into a darkened gallery. Seconds later, the group marched past, headed for the south upper-level stairwell.

"What's going on?" Nora whispered.

"Those people with the guns are obviously quite dangerous, and the woman who attacked me is with them."

"What are we going to do?"

"Help Larry and the others," Silvernail said with determination.

* * *

Julianna walked between Larry and Butch Cole.

"Do you know what this is all about?" Cole asked her.

"Mr. Romano wants something from me," she said.

"The head of the Picasso?"

She smiled. "Why don't we wait and see what develops, Larry?"

At the bottom of the south staircase leading to the upper galleries, they stopped.

Romano, who had been forced to move slowly behind them, finally caught up. He shuffled over to stand in front of Julianna and Cole. "There are two items that I need, Ms. Saint. I'm quite sure you know what they are."

The Devil's Shadow made no reply. She knew that he was talking not only about the Picasso, but also the videotapes she possessed.

"I must caution you that I have had an extremely bad day due to the interference of certain people in my affairs." He cast a glance in the direction of the cops and Butch Cole. "So you could say that I don't have a great deal of patience. Where is the statue?!"

She remained silent.

"Very well," Romano said, turning away. "To impress upon you that I am extremely serious, I have arranged a demonstration. I believe, Ms. Saint, that you are acquainted with Hubert Metayer and Ian Jellicoe." He looked up at the top of the staircase. The others followed his gaze to find a bizarre scene starting to unfold.

Two of Romano's soldiers were standing beside a six-foot-tall wooden barrel, which had been removed from a museum exhibit.

"I have a tremendous interest in history," the Mob boss was saying. "In fact, in my younger years I spent a great deal of my free time in this museum. I was particularly fascinated with the History of Ancient Rome exhibit, which is located on the upper level." His sadistic smile returned. "I guess that would be understandable with a name like Romano. But as I was saying, I studied the biographies of Julius Caesar, Augustus, Caligula, and even a long-forgotten general named Marcus Atilius Regulus. It was Regulus, or rather Regulus's death, that gave me the inspiration for what you are about to witness. Now, I will ask you one last time, Julianna. Where are the items I seek?"

Still standing next to Larry Cole, she refused to respond.

"Very well," Romano said, raising his left arm. "Release the barrel!"

When the Mob soldiers turned the barrel on its side, a muffled scream was heard coming from inside. They positioned the wooden structure on the top step and then kicked it over the edge. The group standing in the rotunda below watched it gain momentum the closer it came to the bottom. And as it did so, the horrible screams of two male voices increased to blend into a terrible howl of pain. Then, when the barrel struck the marble floor of the museum rotunda, it burst open, revealing its grisly contents. The spectators looked down on what was left of the bodies of Hubert Metayer and Ian Jellicoe.

Barbara Zorin, Jamal Garth, Angela DuBois, and Butch Cole averted their eyes. The cops, Brian Zorin, and Julianna Saint stared in horror at the remains. Bishop De Coutreaux made the sign of the cross, lowered his head, and began to pray silently. The Mafia soldiers standing guard over the hostages reacted in various ways. Some became ill, some appeared indifferent, and others looked to be enjoying the spectacle immensely. Jake Romano enjoyed it most of all.

"You see," the sadistic, well-read Mob boss explained, "the Carthaginians also placed the captured Roman general Regulus in a barrel over two thousand years ago, just like your friends here, Julianna. Then razor-sharp spikes were driven into the barrel from top to bottom." He swept his hand over the bloody debris on the floor. "And the barrel was rolled down a hill to—"

"Julianna." A weak voice was heard. They all searched for its origin amidst the bloody remains.

The bodies of the Frenchman and the Englishman had been ripped apart and it was impossible to detect one from the other. There was still movement present as nerves spasmed for the final time as the host body died. Blood began flowing from inside the smashed barrel across the museum floor like a dam draining into a river. The voice had come from the center of the carmine pool. It was that of Hubert Metayer.

"Julianna," was repeated in a strangled whisper.

The Devil's Shadow took a step forward, but could make out nothing on the floor in front of her that remotely resembled her former colleague.

"Hubert?" she said, softly.

It took another moment for the dying man to form the words. Then he managed, "Julianna . . . I am sorry. . . . I . . . tried to . . ." Then he was gone.

For a long time there was no sound in the rotunda. Then Jake Romano began banging the tip of his cane rhythmically on the blood-spattered floor. "Bravo!" he said. "To die well shows a certain sense of style. I hope that the rest of you live up to the high standard set by Monsieur Metayer, because I have many more historically horrible delights for you."

Julianna spun toward the Mob boss and would have certainly attacked him physically if Larry Cole had not restrained her. Standing securely in Cole's grasp, she glared at Romano and said, "It is you who will die tonight, Mr. Romano. That I swear on the graves of my parents." Then she took in a deep breath, shook off Cole's hands, and shouted, "Now, Christophe!"

All of the lights in the Field Museum rotunda were extinguished, plunging the area into pitch blackness.

Christophe La Croix was not within actual earshot of Julianna Saint when she gave him the order to cut off the electricity. The thief was in curator Nora Livingston's office on the upper level of the museum. In that office was a control board that possessed the capability of overriding all of the power controls in the museum, including the lights and temperature levels. There was also a computerized security board, which enabled the viewer to monitor any area of the museum via a closed-circuit TV hookup equipped with audio.

After the Devil's Shadow had extracted the blood from the historian, she had ordered Christophe to go to the curator's office. From that location he was instructed to monitor her movements in the museum in order to facilitate her escape from the party. Once at his post, he had watched her enter the Egyptian exhibit hall with amusement, due to the reaction she received from the men present. Actually, Christophe had also been quite impressed when she removed her dark-colored jumpsuit to reveal the black evening gown and diamond necklace. Applying a little makeup and a dab of perfume, Julianna was ready to attend a king's coronation. The only flaw was that she carried the plastic bottle containing the historian's blood in her purse.

When the Mafia had shown up, things had become tense for both those attending the Saint Patrick's Day party and Christophe. However, he had deftly manipulated the museum's monitoring controls to follow Julianna to the south end of the rotunda. His sweaty hand had remained on the master switch as the drama had unfolded below. When Christophe had learned that Hubert Metayer and Ian Jellicoe had been inside the barrel, he had emitted an audible sob, but did not reliquish his vigilance. When Julianna gave him the word, he obeyed instantly.

The rotunda was plunged into pitch blackness for thirty seconds. During that brief period no one moved. The lights going out at once confused and frightened everyone, both mobster and captive alike. Luckily, as there had been no order for them to do so from Romano, none of the soldiers opened fire. A few fingers did tighten on triggers. Then, as suddenly as they had gone out, the lights came back on, but at full power, as opposed to the half power of off-peak hours, The effect was like a flashbulb going off in their faces.

Fighting to clear his own vision along with the others, Larry Cole recognized the opportunity to take the upper hand on the mobsters. Before the lights had gone out, Cole had measured the distance between himself and the nearest Uzi-wielding mobster. When the lights came back on, the cop leaped toward this man, who was using his free hand to shield his eyes. The submachine gun hung impotently down at his side.

A hard blow to the stomach bent him double and Cole confiscated the weapon. Blackie and Judy saw the chief's move and they followed by attacking on their own. Blackie used a maneuver similar to Cole's to disarm a soldier with a .45, and Judy resorted to the most effective one-blow attack for a woman to utilize when fighting a man: a kick to the testicles.

The Mob soldiers at the top of the staircase, who had kicked the spike-studded barrel containing Hubert and Ian Jellicoe down the stairs, pulled their guns and were about to make a fight of it. They never got the chance. A twelve-inch steel arrow was fired from the opposite side of the rotunda, to strike first one of them and then the other in the chest. Dropping their weapons, they tumbled down the steps to land among the detritus of their earlier handiwork.

Within a matter of twenty seconds, the tables had been turned. The other Mob soldiers gave up when they discovered that fighting would be suicidal. Jake Romano was dying.

The hollow needle attached to the tube Julianna Saint had used to extract Silvernail Smith's blood protruded from the Mob boss's chest. Blood spurted into the air with each beat of his heart. As they all looked on in horror, Romano attempted to pull the needle out, but he only succeeded in shoving it in deeper. Finally, as the color drained rapidly from his face, he collapsed facedown on the rotunda floor.

The cops were too busy disarming the soldiers and herding them against the nearest wall to provide immediate assistance to the Mob boss. Then, when Silvernail and Nora rushed from the shadows, Cole walked over to Romano's prone figure. The historian, carrying a twelfth-century crossbow that had fired the steel arrows with deadly accuracy, joined him. The crossbow and arrows had been hastily snatched from an exhibit. By the time they got to the blood-soaked Mob boss, it was too late.

"What happened to him, Larry?" Silvernail asked. The pumping action of Romano's heart had been reduced to a trickle.

Cole looked around the brightly illuminated rotunda. Of the hostages whom Romano's soldiers had forced from the Saint Patrick's Day party in the Egyptian exhibit, two were missing. Julianna Saint and the man she had introduced as Bishop Martin Simon Pierre De Coutreaux. Cole didn't know how the churchman fitted into what had happened tonight, but he was a material witness. Larry Cole wanted Julianna Saint on a number of criminal charges. As he stood looking down at the dead body of Jake Romano, he realized that one of those charges against her would be murder.

He turned to tell Blackie to seal off the building and noticed Butch standing a short distance away. His son's face was flushed with excitement and fear.

"You okay, Butch?"

He nodded his head. Then he asked, "Who was that woman, Dad?"

Cole thought about it for a moment. "That's a long story, son. A very long story."

EPILOGUE

MAY 1, 2005

9:10 A.M.

Larry Cole was at his desk at police headquarters, wading through the normal heavy volume of morning paperwork. In the past few weeks there had been an intensity about the chief of detectives that had never been witnessed before. He was working like a man possessed; however, he had not become a tyrant. Actually, the only person he'd become hard on was himself.

His workday began at 8:00 A.M. after the morning jog with his son. The next ten hours were spent between his desk and the streets, where he had been known to arrive at the scene of fast-breaking cases even before the assigned detectives. At six o'clock each night, he would go home to have dinner and be with Butch. But often, perhaps too often in the opinion of his staff, he would return to the office after midnight and work into the wee small hours of the morning. Twice in the past month, Blackie had found Cole asleep at his desk. This wasn't good.

Despite this destructive lifestyle, he wasn't showing any obvious signs of stress except appearing tired occasionally. At all times there was a sad, distant air about him, even with his son, whom Cole was spending more time with than ever. However, it was difficult for any of those close to him to nail down what was actually wrong with Larry Cole.

He finished the paperwork and set everything aside for Blackie to pick up later. Then he sat silently for a moment, staring off into space. Belying his vacant expression, his mind was alive with feverish thought.

On that Saint Patrick's Day night, which seemed now to have occurred in another lifetime, Cole was certain that the responding CPD units he had summoned to the Field Museum would effectively seal off the building so that no one could get out. Then he had led a systematic search of the structure from top to bottom. A search that had turned up the head of the Picasso statue, which Silvernail had directed them to in the sublevel storage area. A search that had failed to apprehend Julianna Saint, her assistant Christophe La Croix, or the mysterious Bishop Martin Simon Pierre De Coutreaux.

After the assault he had suffered at the hands of the Devil's Shadow, Silvernail had been transported to University Hospital at the insistence of curator Nora Livingston. But before he had entered the Chicago Fire Department ambulance, the historian told Cole what Julianna Saint had done to him.

"But why would she want your blood?" Cole asked, as they walked through the falling rain to the ambulance parked in front of the museum.

Silvernail, clutching his chest where the needle had been inserted directly into his heart, said, "If I don't miss my bet, she, or someone who hired her, wants to find out if I'm human or not."

"That doesn't make sense," Cole argued. "I can look at you and tell that you're human."

Silvernail stopped. With the rain streaming down his face he said, "There are religious zealots in the world today, Larry, who believe that they can examine blood or even flesh and detect the presence of evil. Such arcane beliefs are based on pure superstition, but there are a great many who will go to any extreme to prove that an embodiment of Satan exists in this world."

As the historian climbed into the ambulance, Cole remembered the name of the man Julianna had introduced at the party in the museum. Bishop Martin Simon Pierre De Coutreaux.

*   *   *

In his police headquarters office on the first day of May, Cole unlocked his center desk drawer. Inside was a leather folder he used to keep personal papers in. Opening the folder, he removed a stack of neatly typed reports. This was his personal copy of everything that had been discovered about the Devil's Shadow. These papers also revealed the motive for the murder of mystery writer Greg Ennis, whose death had gotten Cole involved in this case five months ago.

The videotapes of Jake Romano in the act of assassinating Victor Mattioli and then murdering the concierge in Ian Jellicoe's suite at DeWitt Plaza had been delivered to Cole by a Loop messenger service on the eighteenth of March. Blackie and Judy had paid the service's main office a visit and interviewed the clerk who had taken the shipment order. The young black man remembered the beautiful woman with the exotic accent who had come into the Wabash Avenue office the day before Saint Patrick's Day. She had left a generous tip and was quite insistent that the delivery not be made before the morning of the eighteenth of March.

So Julianna had decided to expose Jake Romano before the confrontation at the museum ever took place. That, in light of the events that had occurred, didn't matter now. The fact that Julianna had killed Jake Romano did. Cole realized he would have a difficult time convicting her of the crime, because no one had actually seen her in the act of jabbing the needle into the Mob boss's heart. But Cole would indeed charge her if he could catch her.

The pages in Cole's file had been compiled by Judy Daniels and contained the most extensive dossier on the international criminal known as the Devil's Shadow, or *L'Ombre du Diable,* in existence. Cole had gone over this data many times, and during each review he'd found the contents compelling. It was not the subject matter that drew the absorbed attention of Chicago's highest-ranking detective, but instead the fact that he was in love with Julianna Saint.

He realized that what was happening to him was illogical to

the point of pure insanity, but in this relationship his brain could not control his heart. And he was not new to difficult or conflicting relationships. At times it seemed as if every intimate involvement he had ever had with a female ended up in disaster, including the marriage that had produced his son.

Julianna Saint was different. Different because she was a criminal and he was a cop, which doomed any type of relationship between them to failure. If he had his way, he would see the woman he loved go to prison. He wondered how this would affect him. At this moment the thought was too disturbing to contemplate, as he didn't even know where she was.

The file began in January 1975 with a report of the detention on Saint Thomas of two *La Belle Liberté* cruise vessel employees accused of committing a shipboard theft. One was an American cabin steward named Charles Martin, the other a thirteen-year-old French national named Julianna Saint. They were arrested after attempting to board a fishing trawler called *The Devil's Due,* which had dropped anchor in the harbor a short distance from the cruise vessel. The police on Saint Thomas were acting on the complaint of a cruise-ship passenger named Raymond Lavery, whose cabin had been burglarized. There was an interesting item related to the victim in this crime. He had also been stabbed the night before by a fellow passenger. Cole found it interesting that the offending passenger was named Maurice De Coutreaux. The policeman had obtained photographs from Saint Thomas of both Julianna and Charles Martin. He instantly recognized Bishop Martin Simon Pierre De Coutreaux as the former ship's steward. Reading further into the report, Cole discovered that it was Maurice De Coutreaux who had intervened on behalf of the cruise-ship employees and kept them from going to jail. How he had done this was a thirty-year-old mystery.

There was a third party taken into custody on Saint Thomas in 1975. That was the captain of *The Devil's Due,* whose name was Walter Saint. Cole guessed accurately that he was a relative of Julianna; however, he had no way of knowing that she was his last surviving kin. During the brief period that the trio were in custody,

Walter Saint had died of a heart attack. Julianna and Charles Martin were released, and a few years later the legend of the Devil's Shadow began.

Cole stopped reading. He wondered what had happened in Julianna's life before she turned to crime. He speculated that if he had met her before, he could have prevented her from taking that path. He shook his head. What he was engaging in now was pure fantasy. She was what she was, and he was irrevocably what he was.

His intercom buzzed. "Yes?"

"It's time to go to the ceremony, boss," Blackie said.

Closing the file and returning it to his desk, Cole replied, "I'm on the way."

The head of the Picasso had been reattached and the statue restored. The mayor had invited the superintendent, Cole, Butch, and all of the officers involved in the recovery to attend the rededication ceremony at 10:00 A.M. Leaving the office, Cole was struck by the thought that this visit to the Daley Center Plaza would do no more than remind him of Julianna Saint.

Rome, Italy
MAY 1, 2005
5:45 P.M.

Bishop Martin Simon Pierre De Coutreaux was safely back in his office in the Vatican. With the aid of Julianna Saint, he had made good his escape from the Field Museum of Natural History in Chicago. She had grabbed his hand and whispered urgently, "Come with me now!" He had been forced to blindly follow her through the dark after the lights went out. How she was able to see was a mystery, but when the lights came back on, they were standing beside a fire-exit door next to an exhibit depicting life in the Neanderthal Era. To say that he was terrified at this point would have been an understatement.

"This door will lead you back to the parking lot, Charlie," Julianna said.

He was too relieved at escaping from this dangerous situation to take issue with her for addressing him by that name. "Thank you, Julianna."

"And this is yours," she said, removing a brown paper parcel from her shoulder bag.

He hesitated before taking it.

"The historian's blood," she said. "You paid handsomely for it."

Quickly he snatched the package and went through the door. That was the last he had seen of Julianna Saint. Less than twenty-four hours later, he was back in Rome.

Bishop De Coutreaux had risked a great deal. If his former life had been discovered, he would be ruined. Yes, he was a remarkably talented man of the cloth, who had distinguished himself in many ways. But he was also a Negro from Detroit, who had once been involved in a cruise-ship theft. If he were exposed, his fall from grace would be swift and final. Then the false identity that he had constructed for himself with the aid of Viscount Maurice De Coutreaux would unravel and all would be lost.

Back on Saint Thomas thirty years before, Maurice De Coutreaux had enlisted the dismissed cabin steward Charlie Martin to continue the fight against the devil's followers the viscount had spent his life hunting. It was De Coutreaux who had arranged the fictional background identification leading to the creation of Martin Simon Pierre De Coutreaux. This enabled Charlie to enter a seminary outside Marseilles, France. With the help of the De Coutreaux fortune, Father Martin De Coutreaux had risen through the ranks of the Catholic Church. The false identity had held up for thirty years. A false identity that Julianna Saint could destroy.

However, De Coutreaux did not expect any problems from the Devil's Shadow. That policeman back in Chicago would be hunting her. For his part, the bishop never planned to return to the United States. Now the only dilemma facing him was that he had been wrong about the museum historian Silvernail Smith. A laboratory analysis of the blood had revealed that it was type O and of human origin, with no foreign or unusual properties present. This did not faze Bishop De Couteaux, because he planned to continue the work begun by Viscount Maurice De Coutreaux in ferreting out the devil's minions.

That the blood of Raymond Lavery had also proven to be completely human also did not disconcert De Coutreaux or his predecessor. They were firm believers in the dictates of *The Book of the Devil,* whose origins were shrouded in mystery. Bishop De Coutreaux would continue his mission against the forces of Satan.

Chicago, Illinois
MAY 1, 2005
10:13 A.M.

There were two helmeted riders aboard the red Honda motorcycle that roared east from Lake Shore Drive on Upper Wacker. At Clark Street the two-wheeler caught a left-turn arrow on the caution light and sped south. At Randolph Street the red bike bounded up over the curb, deftly avoided a few startled pedestrians, and skidded to a halt behind the Picasso statue, once again covered in canvas. A speaker's platform had been set up beside the monument and a number of Chicago police officers were stationed around it to provide security. Two patrolmen noticed the motorcycle being operated on the sidewalk and walked toward it.

The riders got off with the visors on their matching helmets down. The cycle's operator saw the cops advancing and reached into an inner pocket to remove a black leather case. He flashed a sergeant's badge at the cops, which caused them to shrug and return to their post. Then the riders took off the helmets.

"I should have tried that years ago, Butch," Manny said with unbridled enthusiasm. "That was great!"

Appearing a bit nervous, Butch said, "You were driving kind of fast, Manny. I mean, as my dad always says, this thing only has two wheels and no bumpers."

Manny considered this for a moment. "You've got a point. What is this, a Honda?"

Butch nodded.

"I'll have to have something bigger, like a Harley. A big Harley."

All Butch could say by way of reply was, "Whatever you say, Manny."

Manny and Butch slipped into their seats beside Larry Cole, Judy, and Blackie just as the superintendent of police got up to make some opening remarks before introducing the mayor. Blackie cast a disapproving look at the latecomers, but didn't say anything. Judy, dressed in her windowpane horn-rimmed glasses and a tan business suit, had a pretty good idea what had occurred, because Manny had told her he wanted to give Butch's motorcycle a spin. The Mistress of Disguise/High Priestess of Mayhem knew that Manny, when he was not under Cole's or Blackie's scrutiny, drove like a maniac.

A few rows of metal folding chairs had been set up on the floor of the plaza facing the speaker's platform. Members of the media and a smattering of aldermen, department heads, and assorted VIPs occupied these seats. A crowd of about two hundred others stood behind the section, making the less–than–earth-shattering municipal event fairly well attended.

A bright sun shone out of a blue sky dotted with sporadic white clouds, and a pleasant breeze blew across the plaza. It was a beautiful day, and as Larry Cole sat there feeling the sun beaming down on him, he began experiencing a level of relaxation and well-being he hadn't felt in months. It was at that moment that two things happened. He remembered with some degree of satisfaction that he had discovered why Greg Ennis had been killed, and the romantic hold that Julianna Saint held over him was beginning to recede.

When the mayor rose to rededicate the Picasso, Cole recalled the news he had received just as he left headquarters to come here. The Cook County state's attorney had decided to classify Jake Romano's death as "justifiable homicide." That meant that Julianna Saint was off the hook for murder. But she was still wanted for grand theft for stealing the head of the Picasso. Of course, Cole would have to catch her first, which no police officer in the world had yet been able to do.

The ceremony concluded and they filed off the reviewing stand. After paying their respects to the mayor, Cole and his crew were about to head back to headquarters when the chief turned to Sergeant Sherlock. "Would you drive my car back to the station for me, Manny?"

The sergeant had actually been looking forward to another devil-may-care ride on Butch's motorcycle, but under the circumstances he said a cheerful, "Sure thing, Chief."

After witnessing this exchange, Blackie asked Cole, "How are you going to get back?"

Cole nodded at Butch. "My son will give me a ride."

Then, as Blackie, Judy, and Manny looked on, the chief of detectives donned the bright red helmet, put the visor down, and climbed on the back of the Honda behind Butch. Carefully Butch rolled across the Daley Center Plaza to join the flow of traffic traveling south on Clark Street.

When they stopped at a red light, Butch said, "Thanks, Dad."

"Just get me back to the office in one piece."

"No problem."

On the ninth floor of the Richard J. Daley Center, Julianna Saint, dressed in a kelly green dress and a black wide-brimmed hat with matching purse and shoes, looked down at the red Honda motorcycle driving away from the plaza. She had watched the entire rededication ceremony from this window. The only item she had used to shield her identity from curious police officers was a pair of dark sunglasses. There was a somewhat crude composite sketch of her and Christophe La Croix being circulated. However, none of the male law enforcement officials she had encountered paid much attention to her face at all, and the females didn't look beyond her expensive apparel.

Christophe, dressed in a gray flannel suit and conservative shirt and tie, stepped up beside her. He also wore dark glasses and carried a briefcase, which made him blend in with the army of lawyers trying cases in this building.

"It is dangerous for us to remain here any longer, Julianna," he cautioned.

Without needing to be prompted further, she turned from the window and proceeded to the elevator with Christophe by her side. As they waited for a car to arrive, he heard her whisper in French, "Someday we will meet again, Larry Cole."